MAN'S FATE
(La Condition Humaine)

MAN'S FATE
(La Condition Humaine)

by André Malraux
Translated by Haakon M. Chevalier

VINTAGE BOOKS
A Division of Random House
New York

CONTENTS

Principal Characters

CH'EN TA ERH, a Chinese terrorist.

KYO GISORS, half French and half Japanese, one of the organizers of the Shanghai insurrection.

OLD GISORS, Kyo's father, one-time Professor of Sociology at the University of Peking.

MAY GISORS, Kyo's wife.

BARON DE CLAPPIQUE, a Frenchman, a dealer in antiques, opium and smuggled wares.

KATOV, a Russian, one of the organizers of the insurrection.

HEMMELRICH, a German, a phonograph-dealer.

LU YU HSÜAN, his partner.

KAMA, a Japanese painter, Old Gisors' brother-in-law.

FERRAL, President of the French Chamber of Commerce and head of the Franco-Asiatic Consortium.

VALÉRIE, Ferral's mistress.

MARTIAL, Chief of the Shanghai Police.

KÖNIG, Chief of Chiang Kai-shek's Police.

VOLOGIN } Communist officials at Hankow.
POSSOZ }

PEI } young Chinese terrorists.
SUAN }

MAN'S FATE

(La Condition Humaine)

Part One
March 21, 1927

Twelve-thirty midnight

SHOULD he try to raise the mosquito-netting? Or should he strike through it? Ch'en was torn by anguish: he was sure of himself, yet at the moment he could feel nothing but bewilderment—his eyes riveted to the mass of white gauze that hung from the ceiling over a body less visible than a shadow, and from which emerged only that foot half-turned in sleep, yet living—human flesh.

The only light came from the neighboring building—a great rectangle of wan electric light cut by window-bars, one of which streaked the bed just below the foot as if to stress its solidity and life.

Four or five klaxons screamed at once. Was he discovered?

Oh, what a relief to fight, to fight enemies who defend themselves, enemies who are awake!

The wave of uproar subsided: some traffic jam (there were still traffic jams out there in the world of men—). He found himself again facing the great soft smudge of gauze and the rectangle of light, both motionless in this night in which time no longer existed.

He repeated to himself that this man must die—stupidly, for he knew that he would kill him. Whether he was caught or not, executed or not, did not matter. Nothing existed but this foot, this man whom he must strike without letting him defend himself—for if he defended himself, he would cry out.

3

Ch'en was becoming aware, with a revulsion verging on nausea, that he stood here, not as a fighter, but as a sacrificial priest. He was serving the gods of his choice; but beneath his sacrifice to the Revolution lay a world of depths beside which this night of crushing anguish was bright as day. "To assassinate is not only to kill, alas. . . ." In his pockets, his fumbling right hand clutched a folded razor, his left a short dagger. He thrust them as deeply as possible, as though the night did not suffice to hide his actions. The razor was surer, but Ch'en felt that he could never use it; the dagger disgusted him less. He let go the razor, the back of which pressed against his clenched fingers; the dagger was naked in his pocket. As he passed it over to his right hand, his left hand dropped against the wool of his sweater and remained glued to it. He raised his right arm slightly, petrified by the continued silence that surrounded him, as though he expected some unseen thing to topple over. But no—nothing happened: it was still up to him to act.

That foot lived like a sleeping animal. Was it attached to a body? "Am I going mad?" He had to see that body—see it, see that head. In order to do that—enter the area of light, let his squat shadow fall upon the bed.

What was the resistance of flesh? Convulsively, Ch'en pressed the point of the dagger into his left arm. The pain (he was no longer aware that it was his own arm), the certainty of torture if the sleeper were to awaken, released him for an instant: torture was better than this atmosphere of madness. He drew close. Yes, this was the man he had seen, two hours before, in broad daylight. The foot, which nearly touched Ch'en's trousers, suddenly turned like a key, then turned back to its position in the silent night. Perhaps the sleeper felt his presence, but not enough to wake up. . . . Ch'en shuddered: an insect was running over his skin! No!—blood trickling down his arm. And still that seasick feeling.

One single motion, and the man would be dead. To kill him was nothing: touching him was the impossible. And it was imperative to stab with precision.

The sleeper, lying on his back in the European-style bed, was wearing only a pair of short drawers, but his ribs were not visible under the full flesh. Ch'en had to take the nipples as gauging points. He tried holding the dagger with the blade up. But the left breast was the one away from him: he would have to strike at arm's length through the mosquito-netting. He changed the position of the dagger: blade down. To touch this motionless body was as difficult as to stab a corpse, perhaps for the same reason. As if called forth by this notion of a corpse, a grating sound suddenly issued from the man's throat. Ch'en could no longer even draw back, for his legs and arms had gone completely limp. But the rattle became regular: the man was not dying, he was snoring. He again became living, vulnerable; and at the same time, Ch'en felt himself ridiculed. The body turned gently towards the right. Was he going to wake up now? With a blow that would have split a plank Ch'en struck through the gauze. Sensitive to the very tip of the blade, he felt the body rebound towards him, flung up by the springs of the bed. He stiffened his arm furiously to hold it down: like severed halves drawn to each other, the legs sprang together towards the chest; then they jerked out, straight and stiff. Ch'en should have struck again—but how was he to withdraw the dagger? The body, still on its side, was unstable, and instead of being reassured by the convulsion which had just shaken it, Ch'en had the impression of pinning it down to the bed with this short blade on which his whole weight rested.

5

Through the great gash in the mosquito-netting, he could see very clearly; the eyelids open—had he been able to wake up?—the eyeballs white. Around the dagger the blood was beginning to flow, black in that deceptive light. In its balanced weight the body still held life. Ch'en could not let go the handle. A current of unbearable anguish passed between the corpse and himself, through the dagger, his stiffened arm, his aching shoulder, to the very depth of his chest, to his convulsive heart—the only moving thing in the room. He was utterly motionless; the blood that continued to flow from his left arm seemed to be that of the man on the bed. Although outwardly nothing had happened, he was suddenly certain that this man was dead. Scarcely breathing, he held the corpse down—as firmly as ever—on its side—held it thus in the dim motionless light, in the solitude of the room.

Nothing bore witness to the struggle—not even the tear in the gauze, which seemed to have been divided into two strips—nothing but the silence and the overpowering intoxication into which he was sinking. Cut off from the world of the living, he clung to his dagger. His grip became increasingly tighter, but his arm-muscles relaxed and his entire arm began to tremble. It was not fear—it was a dread at once horrible and solemn, which he had not experienced since childhood: he was alone with death, alone in a place without men, limply crushed by horror and by the taste of blood.

He managed to open his hand. The body sagged gently, face down, pressing the handle sideways. A dark blot began to spread on the sheet, grew like a living thing. And beside it, growing too, appeared the shadow of two pointed ears.

The door was at a distance, the balcony was nearer; but it was from the balcony that the shadow loomed.

Although Ch'en did not believe in spirits, he was paralyzed, unable to turn round. He jumped: mewing! Half relieved, he dared to look: it was an alley-cat. Its eyes riveted on him, it stalked through the window on noiseless paws. As the shadow advanced, an uncontrollable rage shook Ch'en—not against the creature itself, but against its presence. Nothing living must venture into the wild region where he was thrown: whatever had seen him hold this dagger prevented him from returning to the world of men. He opened the razor, took a step forward: the creature fled by way of the balcony. Ch'en pursued it. . . . He found himself suddenly facing Shanghai.

In his anguish the night seemed to whirl like an enormous smoke-cloud shot with sparks; slowly it settled into immobility, as his breathing grew less violent in the cooler outside air. Between the tattered clouds, the stars resumed their endless course. A siren moaned, and then became lost in the poignant serenity. Below, far down, the midnight lights, reflected through a yellow mist by the wet macadam, by the pale streaks of rails, shimmered with the life of men who do not kill. Those were millions of lives, and all now rejected his; but what was their wretched condemnation beside death, which was withdrawing from him, which seemed to flow away from his body in long draughts, like the other's blood? All that expanse of darkness, now motionless, now quivering with sparks, was life, like the river, like the invisible sea in the distance—the sea. . . .

Breathing at last to the very depth of his lungs, he seemed to be returning to that life with infinite gratitude —ready to weep, as much upset as he had been a few moments before. "I must get away. . . ." He remained, watching the stir of the cars, of the passers-by running

7

beneath him in the lighted street, as a blind man who has recovered his sight looks, as a starved man eats. Avidly, with an unquenchable thirst for life, he would have liked to touch those bodies. A siren filled the whole horizon, beyond the river: the relief of the night workers, at the arsenal. Stupid workers, coming to manufacture the firearms destined to kill those who were fighting for them! Would this illuminated city remain possessed like a field of battle, its millions hired for death, like a herd of cattle, to the war-lords and to Western commerce? His act of murder was equal to incalculable hours of work in the arsenals of China. The insurrection which would give Shanghai over to the revolutionary troops was imminent. Yet the insurrectionists did not possess two hundred guns. Their first act was to be the disarming of the police for the purpose of arming their own troops. But if they obtained the guns (almost three hundred) which this go-between, the dead man, had negotiated to sell to the government, they doubled their chances of success. In the last ten minutes, however, Ch'en had not even given it a thought.

And he had not yet taken the paper for which he had killed this man. He went back into the room, as he would have returned to a prison. The clothes were hanging at the foot of the bed, under the mosquito-netting. He searched the pockets. A handkerchief, cigarettes . . . No wallet. The room remained the same: the mosquito-net, the blank walls, the clear rectangle of light; murder changes nothing. . . . He slipped his hand under the pillow, shutting his eyes. He felt the wallet, very small, like a purse. In shame or horror—for the light weight of the head through the pillow was even more disturbing—he opened his eyes: no blood on the bolster, and the man did not look at all dead. Would he have to kill him again

8

then? But already his glance, encountering the white eyes, the blood on the sheets, reassured him. To ransack the wallet he withdrew towards the light, which came from a restaurant filled with gamblers. He found the document, kept the wallet, crossed the room almost on the run, locked the door with a double turn, put the key in his pocket. At the end of the hotel corridor—he made an effort to slow his pace—no lift. Should he ring? He walked down. On the floor below, that of the dance-hall, the bar and the billiard-room, ten or more persons were waiting for the lift which was just stopping. He followed them in. "The dancing-girl in red is damned good-looking!" said the man next to him in English, a slightly drunk Burman or Siamese. Ch'en had the simultaneous impulse to hit him in the face to make him stop, and to hug him because he was alive. Instead of answering he mumbled incoherently; the other tapped him on the shoulder with a knowing air. "He thinks I'm drunk too. . . ." But the man started to open his mouth again. "I don't know any foreign languages," said Ch'en in Pekingese. The other kept silent and, intrigued, looked at this young man who had no collar, but who was wearing a sweater of fine wool. Ch'en was facing the mirror in the lift. The murder left no trace upon his face. . . . His features—more Mongolian than Chinese, sharp cheek-bones, a very flat nose but with a slight ridge, like a beak—had not changed, expressed nothing but fatigue; even to his solid shoulders, his thick good-natured lips, on which nothing unusual seemed to weigh; only his arm, sticky when he bent it, and hot. . . . The lift stopped. He went out with the group.

He bought a bottle of mineral water, and called a taxi, a closed car, in which he bathed his arm and bandaged

9

it with a handkerchief. The deserted rails and the puddles from the afternoon showers shone feebly. They reflected the glowing sky. Without knowing why, Ch'en looked up: how much nearer the sky had been a while back, when he had discovered the stars! He was getting farther away from it as his anguish subsided, as he returned to the world of men. . . . At the end of the street the machine-gun cars, almost as gray as the puddles, the bright streaks of bayonets carried by silent shadows: the post, the boundary of the French concession; the taxi went no farther. Ch'en showed his false passport identifying him as an electrician employed on the concession. The inspector looked at the paper casually ("What I have just done obviously doesn't show") and let him pass. Before him, at a right angle, the Avenue of the Two Republics, the limit of the Chinese city.

Isolation and silence. From here the rumbling waves carrying all the noises of the greatest city of China sounded infinitely remote, like sounds issuing from the bottom of a well—all the turmoil of war, and the last nervous agitations of a multitude that will not sleep. But it was far in the distance that men lived; here nothing remained of the world but night, to which Ch'en instinctively attuned himself as to a sudden friendship: this nocturnal, anxious world was not opposed to murder. A world from which men had disappeared, a world without end; would daylight ever return upon those crumbling tiles, upon all those narrow streets at the end of which a lantern lighted a windowless wall, a nest of telegraph wires? There was a world of murder, and it held him with a kind of warmth. No life, no presence, no nearby sound, not even the cry of the petty merchants, not even the stray dogs.

At last, a squalid shop: *Lu Yu Hsüan & Hemmelrich,*

Phonographs. Now to return among men. . . . He waited a few minutes without freeing himself entirely, knocked finally at a shutter. The door opened almost immediately: a shop full of records arranged with care, having vaguely the look of a poor library; the room back of the shop, large, bare, and four comrades in shirt-sleeves.

The shutting of the door caused the lamp to swing back and forth: the faces disappeared, reappeared: to the left, quite round, Lu Yu Hsüan; Hemmelrich, who looked like a boxer gone to seed, with his shaved head, broken nose, and protruding shoulders. In back, in the shadow, Katov. To the right, Kyo Gisors; in passing over his head the lamp accentuated the drooping corners of his mouth; as it swung away it displaced the shadows and his half-breed face appeared almost European. The oscillations of the lamp became shorter and shorter: Kyo's two faces reappeared by turns, less and less different from each other.

Gripped to their very stomachs by the need to question him, all looked at Ch'en with an idiotic intensity, but said nothing; he looked at the flagstones sprinkled with sunflower seeds. He could give these men the information they wanted, but he could never convey to them what he felt. The resistance of the body to the knife obsessed him—so much greater than that of his arm: but for the unexpected rebound, the weapon would not have penetrated it deeply. "I should never have thought it was so hard. . . ."

"It's done," he said.

In the room, before the body, once the spell of unconsciousness was over, he had not doubted: he had *felt* death.

He handed over the order for the delivery of the fire-arms. Its text was lengthy. Kyo was reading it:

"Yes, but . . ."

They were all waiting. Kyo was neither impatient nor irritated; he had not moved; his face was scarcely contracted. But all felt that he was dumbfounded by what he had just discovered. He spoke at last:

"The arms are not paid for. *Payment on delivery*."

Ch'en felt anger fall upon him, as if he had allowed himself stupidly to be robbed. He had assured himself that the paper was the one he wanted, but had not had time to read it. For that matter, he could have done nothing about it. He drew the wallet from his pocket, gave it to Kyo: photos, receipts; no other items.

"We can manage it with men of the combat-sections, I guess," said Kyo.

"Provided we can climb aboard," answered Katov, "it'll be all right."

Silence. Their presence tore Ch'en from his terrible solitude, gently, like a plant that one pulls from the earth to which its finest roots still hold it fast. And at the same time that he was getting nearer to them, little by little, it seemed as if he were discovering them—like his sister the first time he had come back from a brothel. There was the tension of gambling-halls at the end of the night.

"Did everything go all right?" asked Katov, at last putting down the record that he had been holding all this time and advancing into the light.

Without answering, Ch'en looked at the kindly face which suggested a Russian Pierrot—little mischievous eyes and an upturned nose which even this light could not make dramatic; yet he knew what death was. He got up; he went to look at the cricket asleep in its tiny cage;

Ch'en might have his reasons for keeping quiet. The latter watched the motion of the light, which enabled him to keep from thinking: the tremulous cry of the cricket awakened by Katov's approach mingled with the last vibrations of the shadow on the faces. Always that obsession of the hardness of flesh, that desire to press his arm violently against the nearest object. Words could do nothing but disturb the familiarity with death which had established itself in his being.

"At what time did you leave the hotel?" asked Kyo.

"Twenty minutes ago."

Kyo looked at his watch: ten minutes past one.

"Good. Let's get through here, and get out."

"I want to see your father, Kyo."

"You know that IT will undoubtedly be tomorrow."

"So much the better."

They all knew what IT was: the arrival of the revolutionary troops at the last railroad stations, which was to determine the insurrection.

"So much the better," repeated Ch'en. Like all intense sensations, those of murder and of danger, as they withdrew, left him empty; he longed to recover them.

"Just the same, I want to see him."

"Go there tonight; he never sleeps before dawn."

"I shall go there about four."

Instinctively, when he felt a need to communicate his innermost feelings, Ch'en turned to old Gisors. He knew that his attitude was painful to Kyo—all the more painful in that no vanity was involved—but he could not help it: Kyo was one of the organizers of the insurrection, the Central Committee had confidence in him; so did Ch'en; but Kyo would never kill, except in battle. Katov was nearer to him—Katov who had been condemned to five years of hard labor in 1905 when, as a medical student,

13

he had tried to blow up the gate of the Odessa prison. And yet . . . .

The Russian was eating little sugar candies, one by one, without taking his eyes off Ch'en who suddenly understood the meaning of gluttony. Now that he had killed, he had the right to crave anything he wished. The right. Even if it were childish. He held out his square hand. Katov thought he wanted to leave and shook it. Ch'en got up. It was perhaps just as well: he had nothing more to do here; Kyo was informed, it was up to him to act. As for himself, he knew what he wanted to do now. He reached the door, returned, however.

"Pass me some candy."

Katov gave him the bag. He wanted to divide the contents: no paper. He filled his cupped hand, took a mouthful, and went out.

"Can't've been so easy," said Katov.

He had been a refugee in Switzerland from 1905 to 1912, the date of his clandestine return to Russia, and he spoke French without the slightest Russian accent, but he slurred some of his vowels, as though he wanted to compensate for the necessity of articulating carefully when he spoke Chinese. As he now stood almost directly under the lamp, very little light fell on his face. Kyo preferred it so: the expression of ironic ingenuousness which the small eyes and especially the upturned nose (a sly sparrow, said Hemmelrich) gave to Katov's face, was all the more pronounced as it jarred with his essential character.

"Let's get through," said Kyo. "You have the records, Lu?"

Lu Yu Hsüan, all smiles and as if ready for a thousand little curtseys, placed the two records examined by

Katov on two phonographs. The two had to be put into motion at the same time.

"One, two, three," Kyo counted.

The hissing sound of the first record covered the second; suddenly stopped—one heard: *send*—then continued. Another word: *thirty*. More hissing. Then: *men*. Hissing.

"Perfect," said Kyo. He stopped the movement, and started the first record again, alone: hissing, silence, hissing. Stop. Good. Labeled "worn-out records."

On the second: *"Third lesson. Run, walk, go, come, send, receive, one, two, three, four, five, six, seven, eight, nine, ten, twenty, thirty, forty, fifty, sixty, hundred. I have seen ten men run. Twenty women are here. Thirty—"*

These false records for the teaching of languages were excellent; the label, perfectly imitated. Nevertheless Kyo was puzzled.

"Didn't my voice record well?"

"Very well, perfectly."

Lu expanded in a smile, Hemmelrich seemed indifferent. On the floor above, a child cried out in pain. Kyo was nonplused:

"Then why was the recording changed?"

"It wasn't changed," said Lu. "It's your own. One rarely recognizes one's own voice, you see, when one hears it for the first time."

"The phonograph distorts it?"

"It's not that, for no one has trouble recognizing the voices of others. But one doesn't have the habit, you see, of hearing oneself. . . ."

Lu was giving himself over to the Chinaman's delight in explaining—especially to a man of superior mind.

"It's the same in our language. . . ."

"Good. Are they still coming to fetch the records tonight?"

"The boats will leave tomorrow at daybreak for Hankow. . . ."

The hissing records were shipped by one boat, the records with the text by another. The latter were French or English, according to whether the mission of the region was Catholic or Protestant. The revolutionaries sometimes used real language-teaching records, sometimes records recorded by themselves.

"At daybreak," thought Kyo. "How many things before daybreak. . . ." He rose:

"We need volunteers, for the firearms. And a few Europeans, if possible."

Hemmelrich stepped up to him. The child, up there, cried out anew.

"The kid is answering you," said Hemmelrich. "Is that enough? What in hell would you do with the kid who's going to croak and the woman who is moaning up there —not too loud, so as not to disturb us? . . ."

The almost hateful voice was indeed that of the face with the broken nose, the deep-set eyes which the vertical light replaced by two black stains.

"Each one has his job," answered Kyo. "The records also are necessary. . . . Katov and I will do. Let's go and get some fellows (we'll find out on the way whether we attack tomorrow or not) and I . . ."

"They may discover the corpse at the hotel, you see," said Katov.

"Not before dawn. Ch'en locked the door. They don't make the rounds."

"P'rhaps he had made an engagement."

"At this hour? Not very likely. Whatever happens, the essential thing is to have the ship change its anchorage: so if they try to reach it, they will lose at least three hours before finding it. It's at the end of the port."

"Where do you want to have it moved?"

"Into the port itself. Not to a dock of course. There are hundreds of steamers. Three hours lost at least. At least."

"The capt'n will be suspicious. . . ."

Katov's face almost never expressed his feelings: the ironic gayety remained. At this moment, only the tone of his voice betrayed his anxiety—all the more markedly.

"I know a specialist in the business of firearms," said Kyo. "With him the captain will feel confident. We don't have much money, but we can pay a commission. . . . I think we're agreed: we'll use the paper to get on board, and we'll manage after that."

Katov shrugged his shoulders as if to signify that this was obvious. He slipped on his blouse, which he never buttoned at the neck, handed Kyo the sport-jacket hanging on a chair; both shook Hemmelrich's hand warmly. Pity would only have humiliated him more. They went out.

They left the avenue immediately, entered the Chinese city.

Low clouds heavily massed, torn in places, left the last stars visible now only in the depth of their rifts. The movement of the clouds animated the darkness, now lighter and now more intense, as if immense shadows had come, fitfully, to intensify the night. Katov and Kyo were wearing sport shoes with crêpe soles, and could hear their own steps only when they slipped in the mud; in the direction of the concessions—the enemy—a light outlined the roofs. Slowly filling with the long wail of a siren, the wind which brought the subdued rumble of the city in state of siege and the whistles of launches

17

returning to the warships, passed over the dismal electric bulbs at the ends of blind alleys and lanes; around them crumbling walls emerged from empty darkness, revealed with all their blemishes by that unflinching light from which a sordid eternity seemed to emanate. Hidden by those walls, half a million men: those of the spinning-mills, those who had worked sixteen hours a day since childhood, the people of ulcers, of scoliosis, of famine. The globes which protected the electric bulbs became misty, and in a few minutes the great rain of China, furious, headlong, took possession of the city.

"A good district," thought Kyo. Since he had started to prepare the insurrection, over a month ago, working from committee to committee, he had ceased to see the streets: he no longer walked in the mud, but on a map. The scratching of millions of small daily lives disappeared, crushed by another life. The concessions, the rich quarters, with their rain-washed gratings at the ends of the streets, existed now only as menaces, barriers, long prison walls without windows; these atrocious quarters, on the contrary—the ones in which the shock troops were the most numerous, were alive with the quivering of a multitude lying in wait. At the turn of a lane his eyes were suddenly flooded by the lights of a wide street; veiled by the beating rain it preserved nevertheless in his mind a horizontal perspective, for it would be necessary to attack it against rifles, machine guns that fire horizontally. After the failure of the February uprisings, the Central Committee of the Chinese Communist Party had intrusted Kyo with the coördination of the insurrectional forces. In each of these silent streets in which the outline of the houses disappeared under the downpour that carried a smell of smoke, the number of the militants had been doubled. Kyo had asked that it be increased from

2,000 to 5,000, and the military direction had succeeded within the month. But they did not possess two hundred rifles. (And there were three hundred rifles on the *Shantung* that slept with one eye out there on the choppy river.) Kyo had organized one hundred and ninety-two combat groups of about twenty-five men each, all provided with leaders; these leaders alone were armed. . . .

They passed in front of a public garage full of old trucks transformed into buses. All the garages were "marked." The military direction had constituted a staff, the assembly of the party had elected a central committee; from the moment the insurrection broke out, it would be necessary to keep them in contact with the shock groups. Kyo had created a first liaison detachment of a hundred and twenty cyclists; at the firing of the first shots, eight groups were to occupy the garages, take possession of the autos. The leaders of these groups had already visited the garages and would have no trouble finding them. Each of the other leaders, for the last ten days, had been studying the quarter where he was to fight. How many visitors, this very day, had entered the principal buildings, asked to see a friend who was unknown there, chatted, offered tea before leaving? How many workers, in spite of the beating downpour, were repairing roofs? All positions of any value for the street-fighting had been reconnoitered; the best firing-positions marked in red on the plans, in the headquarters of the shock groups. What Kyo knew of the underground life of the insurrection helped him to guess what he did not know; something which was infinitely beyond him was coming from the great slashed wings of Chapei and Pootung, covered with factories and wretchedness, to make the enormous ganglia of the center burst; an invisible horde animated the night.

19

"Tomorrow?" said Kyo.

Katov hesitated, stopped the swinging of his large hands. No, the question was not addressed to him. To no one.

They walked in silence. The shower, little by little, died down to a drizzle; the tattoo of the rain upon the roofs diminished, and the black street became filled with the bubbling of the streams in the gutters.

Their facial muscles relaxed; then discovering the street as it appeared to the eyes—long, black, indifferent—it struck Kyo as being an image of his past, so great was the obsession which urged him forward.

"Where do you think Ch'en went?" he asked. "He said he wouldn't go to see my father before four. To sleep?"

An incredulous admiration lurked in his question.

"Don't know. . . . To a whorehouse, perhaps. . . . He doesn't get drunk."

They reached a shop: *Shia, Lamp Dealer.* As everywhere, the shutters were fastened. The door was opened. A hideous little Chinaman stood before them, his figure cutting across the dim light from within: with the halo surrounding his head his slightest movement caused an effect of oily light to slip down over his thick nose studded with pimples. The globes of hundreds of storm-lanterns hanging in rows extending to the invisible back end of the shop, reflected the flames of two lighted lamps standing on the counter.

"Well?" said Kyo.

Shia looked at him, rubbing his hands unctuously. He turned round without speaking, made a few steps, rummaged in some hiding-place. The grating of his finger-nail on a piece of tin set Katov's teeth on edge; but already he was returning, his braces sliding off his shoulders. . . . He read the paper he was bringing, his head lighted from below, almost glued to one of the lamps. It was a report of the military organization which was working with the railroad-workers. The reënforcements which were defending Shanghai against the revolutionaries were coming from Nanking: the railroad-workers had declared a strike; the White Guards and the soldiers of the governmental army were forcing those whom they could seize to run the military trains under penalty of death.

"One of the workers arrested caused the train he was running to be derailed," read the Chinaman. "Dead. Three other military trains were derailed yesterday, the rails having been torn up."

"Have the sabotaging generalized and note on the same reports the manner in which repairs may be made with the least delay," said Kyo.

"For every act of sabotage the White Guards shoot. . . ."

"The Committee knows it. We'll shoot too. Something else: no trains with firearms?"

"No."

"Any news about when our troops will be in Ch'êng Ch'ou?"[1]

"I have no midnight news yet. The delegate of the Syndicate thinks it will be tonight or tomorrow. . . ."

The insurrection would therefore begin the next day or the day following. They would have to await the instructions of the Central Committee. Kyo was thirsty. They went out.

They were now near the spot where they were to separate. Another ship's siren called three times, in jerks, then once again in a long-drawn moan. Its cry seemed to

[1] The last station before Shanghai.

21

expand in the rain-saturated night; it died out at last, like a rocket. "Could they be getting anxious aboard the *Shantung?*" Absurd. The captain was not expecting his customers before eight o'clock. They resumed their walk, their thoughts magnetized by the ship with its cases of guns, anchored out there in the cold and greenish water. It was no longer raining.

"And now to find my man," said Kyo. "I'd feel more easy, just the same, if the *Shantung* would change anchorage."

Their ways were no longer the same; they fixed a meeting, and separated. Katov was going to get the men.

Kyo finally reached the grilled gate of the concessions. Two Annamite sharpshooters and a colonial sergeant came to examine his papers: he had his French passport. To tempt the post, a Chinese merchant had hung little cakes on the barbs of the wires. ("A good idea for poisoning a post, later on," thought Kyo.) The sergeant gave him back his passport. He soon found a taxi and gave the driver the address of the *Black Cat.*

The car, which the chauffeur drove at full speed, met a few patrols of European volunteers. "The troops of eight nations are on guard here," said the newspapers. This did not matter much: it did not enter into the plans of the Kuomintang to attack the concessions. Deserted boulevards, indistinct figures of petty merchants whose shops consisted of a pair of scales on their shoulders. . . . The car stopped at the entrance to a tiny garden lighted by the luminous sign of the *Black Cat.* In passing by the cloak-room, Kyo noticed the hour: two o'clock in the morning. "Fortunately one can wear what one pleases here." Under his dark-gray sport-jacket of rough material he was wearing a pull-over.

The jazz-orchestra had reached the point of exhaustion. For five hours it had kept up, not gayety, but a savage intoxication to which each couple anxiously clung. All at once it stopped, and the crowd broke up: at the end of the hall the clients, on the sides the professional dancers: Chinese girls in their sheaths of brocaded silk, Russian girls and half-breeds; a ticket per dance, or per conversation. An old man with the look of a bewildered clergyman remained in the middle of the floor making motions with his elbows like a duck. At the age of fifty-two he had spent the night out for the first time, and, in terror of his wife, had not dared to return home. For eight months he had been spending his nights in the night-clubs, innocent of laundry, changing his linen in the shops of the Chinese shirtmakers, behind a screen. Merchants on the verge of ruin, dancers and prostitutes, those who knew themselves menaced—almost all of them—kept their eyes on that phantom, as if he alone could hold them back on the brink of destruction. They would go to bed, exhausted, at dawn—when the rounds of the executioner would begin again in the Chinese city. At this hour there were only the severed heads in the cages, still black, their hair dripping with rain.

"Like monkeys, my dear girl! They'll be dressed up like monkeys!"

The buffoonish voice, that might have belonged to Punchinello, seemed to come from a column. With its nasal twang, set off by a note of bitterness, it evoked the spirit of the place with peculiar appropriateness, isolated in a silence full of the clinking of glasses above the bewildered clergyman. The man Kyo was looking for was present.

He circled the column, and discovered him in the crowd at the end of the hall, where there were several rows of tables not occupied by the dancing-girls. Above

23

a pell-mell of backs and bosoms in a mass of silky garments, a Punchinello, thin and humpless, but who resembled his voice, was making a buffoonish speech to a Russian girl and a half-breed Filipino girl seated at his table. Standing, his elbows glued to his sides and his hands gesticulating, he spoke with all the muscles of his razor-edged face, hampered by the square of black silk which covered his right eye, injured no doubt. No matter what he wore—this evening he had on a dinner-jacket—Baron de Clappique gave the impression of being in disguise. Kyo had decided not to accost him here, to wait until he went out.

"Absolutely, my dear girl, absolutely! Chiang Kai-shek will come in here with his revolutionaries and shout—in classic style, I tell you, clas-sic! as when he takes cities: 'Dress these merchants up like monkeys, these soldiers like leopards (as when they sit down on freshly painted benches)! Like the last prince of the Liang dynasty, absolutely, my dear, let's climb on board the imperial junks, let's contemplate our subjects dressed, for our distraction, each in the color of his profession, blue, red, green, with pigtails and top-knots; not a word, my dear girl, not a word I tell you!' "

Then becoming confidential:

"The only music permitted will be Chinese bells."

"And you, what will you do in all that?"

His voice became plaintive, sobbing.

"What, my dear girl, you can't guess? I shall be the court astrologer, I shall die trying to pluck the moon out of a pond, one night when I am drunk—tonight?"

Scientific:

". . . like the poet Tu Fu, whose works *certainly* enchant your idle days—not a word, I'm sure of it! Moreover . . ."

24

A ship's siren filled the hall. Immediately a deafening clash of cymbals swallowed it up, and the dance began again. The Baron had sat down. Making his way among the tables and couples, Kyo reached an unoccupied table a little behind his. The music had drowned all other noises; but now that he had got nearer to Clappique, he heard his voice once more. The Baron was pawing the Filipino girl, but he continued to talk to the slim-faced Russian girl, all eyes:

". . . the trouble, my dear girl, is that there is no more caprice in the world. From time to time"—pointing with his forefinger—"a European minister sends his wife a l-little parcel by post, she opens it—not a word . . ."

His forefinger to his lips:

". . . it's the head of her lover. They still talk about it three years later!"

Tearful:

"Lamentable, my dear girl, l-lamentable! Look at me. You see my face? That's what twenty years of hereditary whimsicality lead to. It resembles syphilis.—Not a word!"

Full of authority:

"Waiter! champagne for these two ladies. And for me . . ."

Once more confidential:

". . . a l-little Martini."

Severe:

"V-very dry."

(Assuming the worst, with the police, I have an hour before me, thought Kyo. Just the same, how long is this going to last?)

The Filipino girl laughed, or pretended to. The Russian girl, wide-eyed, was trying to understand. Clappique continued to gesticulate, his forefinger animated, rigid with authority, calling for attention to his confidences. But Kyo scarcely listened to him; the heat was making him sleepy and, with it, an anxiety which had been prowling in the back of his mind tonight as he walked was now slowly rising in the form of a confused weariness: that record, *his* voice which he had not recognized a while ago, at Hemmelrich's. He thought of it with the same complex uneasiness that he had felt when, as a child, he was shown his tonsils which the surgeon had just removed. But it was impossible for him to pursue his own thoughts.

". . . in short," barked the Baron, winking his free eyelid and turning toward the Russian girl, "he had a castle in Northern Hungary."

"You're Hungarian?"

"Not at all. I'm French. (For that matter, my dear girl, I don't give a good God damn!) But my mother was Hungarian.

"So, as I was saying, my grandfather lived in a castle over there, with vast halls—ver-ry vast—dead ancestors below; pine-trees all around; many p-pine-trees. A widower. He lived alone with a gi-gan-tic bugle hanging over the fireplace. A circus passes through. With a female equestrian performer. Pretty . . ."

Magisterially:

"I say: pretty."

Winking again:

"He carries her away—not difficult. Takes her into one of the great rooms. . . ."

Commanding attention, his hand raised:

"Not a word! . . . She lives there. Stays on. Gets bored. You would, too, little girl"—he caressed the Filipino girl—"but patience. . . . He didn't have such a good time, either, for that matter: he spent half the after-

26

noon having his finger-nails and toe-nails po...
barber (he still had a barber attached to the c...
while his secretary, the son of a filthy serf, read to him—
reread—aloud, the history of the family. Charming occupation, my dear girl, a perfect life! Besides, he was usually drunk— She . . ."

"She fell in love with the secretary?" asked the Russian girl.

"Magnificent, little girl, ma-gni-fi-cent! My dear
friend, you are magnificent. R-re-mar-ka-ble perspicacity!"

He kissed her hand.

"But she slept with the pedicure, not being endowed
with your esteem for things of the spirit. Noticed then
that grandfather beat her. Not a word, useless: they're
off.

"Absolutely furious, he paces his vast halls (still with
the ancestors below), declares himself ridiculed by the
two jokers who were splitting their sides over the affair,
in an inn *à la* Gogol in the county seat, with a broken
water-jug and carriages in the courtyard. He pulls down
the gi-gan-tic bugle, can't manage to blow into it and
sends his overseer forth to call his peasants to arms. (He
still had rights, in those days.) He arms them: five fowl-
ing-pieces, two pistols. But, my dear girl, there were too
many of them!

"Then, they strip the castle: and now, our peasants
are on the march—imagine, i-ma-gi-ne, I tell you!—armed
with foils, arquebuses, wheel-lock guns, and God knows
what else; rapiers and swords, grandfather in the lead,
towards the county seat: vengeance pursuing crime.
They are announced. Comes the game-keeper, with the
armed police. Ma-gni-fi-cent scene!"

"And then?"

27

away their arms. Grandfather
_____ same, but the guilty parties had
_____ post-haste in one of the dusty car-
_____ ed a peasant girl for the female eques-
_____ er pedicure, and got drunk with the sec-
_____ time to time he would work on one of his
l- _____ ments. . . ."

"_____ whom did he leave the money?"

"A matter of no moment, my dear girl. But, when he died," his eye popping wide open:

". . . they found out everything, everything he'd been hatching all that time, while he was having his feet scratched and chronicles read to him, gloriously drunk! They obeyed him: he was buried under the chapel, in an immense vault, upright on his horse that had been killed, like Attila. . . ."

The din of the jazz ceased. Clappique continued, much less of a Punchinello, as if his clownishness had been softened by the silence:

"When Attila died, he was propped up on his rearing horse, above the Danube; the setting sun made such a shadow across the plain that the horsemen beat it like dust, terrified. . . ."

He sat musing, seized by his dreams, the alcohol and the sudden calm. Kyo knew what proposals he was to make. But he was only slightly acquainted with him, though his father knew him well; and Clappique was even less familiar in his present rôle. Kyo was listening to him impatiently, but not without curiosity (as soon as there was a free table in front of the Baron he would move over to it and signal him to go out: he didn't want to accost him, nor to call him ostensibly). It was the Russian girl who was talking now, in a slow, rasping voice—drunk with insomnia perhaps:

"My great-grandfather also had fine lands. . . . We left because of the Communists, you see. So that we wouldn't have to live cooped up with everybody else, so that we would be respected; here there are two of us to a table, four to a room! Four to a room. . . . And we have to pay rent! . . . Respected. . . . If only alcohol didn't make me sick! . . ."

Clappique looked at her glass: she had scarcely drunk. The Filipino girl, on the other hand. . . . Perfectly placid—she was basking like a cat in the heat of semi-intoxication. Useless to keep track. He turned to the Russian girl:

"You have no money?"

She shrugged her shoulders. He called the waiter, paid with a hundred dollar bill. When the change was brought, he took ten dollars, gave the rest to the woman. She looked at it with a weary precision.

"Good."

She was getting up.

"No," he said.

He had the compassionate look of a friendly dog.

"No. Tonight it would bore you."

He was holding out his hand. She looked at him again:

"Thanks."

She hesitated:

"Just the same . . . If it would give you any pleasure . . ."

"It will give me more pleasure some day when I have no money. . . ."

Punchinello reappeared:

"That'll be before long. . . ."

He drew both her hands together, kissed them several times.

Kyo, who had already paid, joined him in the empty entrance-hall:

"Let's go out together, shall we?"

Clappique looked at him, recognized him:

"You here? 'T's unb'lievable! Why . . ."

This bleating was broken off by the raising of his fore-finger:

"You're going to the devil, young man!"

"That's all right."

They were already on their way out. Although the rain had ceased, water was as much in evidence as air. They took a few steps on the garden sand.

"There is a steamer in port," said Kyo, "with a load of firearms. . . ."

Clappique had stopped. Kyo, having taken an additional step, had to turn round: the Baron's face was scarcely visible; the large illuminated cat, the sign-board of the *Black Cat*, surrounded him like a halo:

"The *Shantung*," he said.

The darkness and his position—against the light—allowed him to express nothing; and he added nothing.

"There's a proposition," Kyo went on, "at thirty dollars per gun, from the government. There's no answer yet. I have a buyer at thirty-five dollars, plus a three-dollar commission. Immediate delivery, in the port. Wherever the captain wishes, but in the port. He can weigh anchor immediately. We'll take delivery tonight, with the money. His representative has agreed: here's the contract."

He handed him the paper, lighted his cigarette-lighter, protecting it with his hand.

"He wants to get ahead of the other buyer," thought Clappique while inspecting the contract . . . *unmounted pieces* . . . "and make five dollars per firearm. That's obvious. Well, what do I care: there is three dollars in it for me."

"All right," he said aloud. "You will leave me the contract, of course?"

"Yes. You know the captain?"

"Well—there are people I know better, but I know him, all right."

"He might be suspicious (especially down-stream, there). The government can have the firearms seized, instead of paying, no?"

"Indeed not!"

Punchinello again. But Kyo waited for what would follow: what did the captain have at his disposal, to prevent his men (and not those of the government) from seizing the arms? Clappique continued in a more muffled voice:

"Those goods are sent by a regular contractor. I know him."

Ironically:

"He's a traitor. . . ."

An odd voice in the dark, when there was no facial expression to back it up. It rose, as if he were ordering a cocktail:

"A regular traitor, ver-ry dry! For all this passes through the hands of a legation which . . . Not a word! I'll take care of this. But to begin with, it's going to cost me a pretty taxi bill: the ship is a long way off. . . . I've got left . . ."

He fumbled in his pocket, pulled out a single bill, turned round so that the light from the sign-board would fall upon it.

". . . Ten dollars, my dear! That won't do. I'll no doubt be buying some of your uncle Kama's paintings for Ferral before long, but in the meantime . . ."

31

"Fifty—will that do?"

"That's more than enough."

Kyo gave it to him.

"You'll let me know at my house as soon as it's done."

"Agreed."

"In an hour?"

"Later than that, I think. But as soon as I can."

And in the same tone as the Russian girl had said: "If only alcohol didn't make me sick . . ." almost in the same voice, as if all the creatures of this place had found themselves in the depth of an identical despair:

"All this is no joke. . . ."

He went off, head bowed, back stooped, hatless, his hands in the pockets of his dinner-jacket.

Kyo called a taxi and had himself driven to the boundary of the concessions, to the first side-street of the Chinese city, where he had arranged to meet Katov.

Ten minutes after having left Kyo, Katov had passed through several corridors, had got through gates, and had come to a white, bare room, well lighted by storm-lanterns. No window. Under the arm of the Chinaman who opened the door to him, five heads leaning over the table. Their eyes on him, on the tall figure known to all the shock groups: legs apart, arms dangling, his blouse unbuttoned at the neck, nose upturned, hair tousled. They were handling different models of grenades. It was a *ch'on*—one of the Communist combat organizations that Kyo and he had created in Shanghai.

"How many men enrolled?" he asked in Chinese.

"Hundred and thirty-eight," answered the youngest Chinaman, an adolescent with a small head, a very prominent Adam's apple, and drooping shoulders, dressed as a worker.

"I absolutely need twelve men for tonight."

"Absolutely" found its way into all the languages that Katov spoke.

"When?"

"Now."

"Here?"

"No: in front of the Yen T'ang gang-plank."

The Chinaman gave instructions: one of the men left.

"They'll be there within two hours," said the chief.

Judging by his hollow cheeks, his tall thin body, he seemed very weak; but the resoluteness of tone, the tenseness of the muscles of his face testified to a will-power wholly sustained by nerves.

"How is the teaching progressing?" asked Katov.

"With the grenades we're doing very well. All the comrades know our models now. With the revolvers— the Nagans and the Mausers, at least—we'll be all right too. I've made them work with empty cartridges. I've been offered the use of a cellar that's quite safe."

In each of the forty rooms in which the insurrection was being prepared the same problem presented itself.

"No powder. It'll come perhaps; for the moment let's not talk about it. And the rifles?"

"We're doing well with those too. It's the machine-guns that are worrying me, if we don't get a chance to try them out with the blanks."

His Adam's apple rose and fell under his skin each time he answered. He went on:

"And then is there no way to get more weapons? Seven rifles, thirteen revolvers, forty-two charged grenades! One man out of every two has no firearms."

"We're going to get them from those who have them. Perhaps we'll soon have some revolvers. If it's for tomorrow, how many men will not be able to use their firearms, in your section?"

The man reflected. Thought made him look absent-minded. An intellectual, thought Katov.

"When we've taken the rifles of the police?"

"Absolutely."

"More than half."

"And the grenades?"

"They'll all know how to use them; and very well. I have thirty men here who are relatives of those who were tortured to death in February. . . . If only . . ."

He hesitated, ended his phrase in an embarrassed gesture. A deformed hand, but slender.

"If only . . . ?"

"Those bastards don't use the tanks against us."

The six men looked at Katov.

"That doesn't matter," he answered. "You take your grenades, six of them tied together, and you throw them under the tank: at the count of four it'll blow up. If necessary you can dig ditches, at least some going in one direction. You have tools?"

"Very few. But I know where to get some."

"Get hold of some bicycles, too: as soon as it begins each section ought to have its contact agent, in addition to the central one."

"You're sure the tanks will blow up?"

"Absolutely! But don't worry about it: the tanks won't leave the front. If they leave it, I'll come with a special squad. That's my job."

"What if we're taken by surprise?"

"We'll see them coming: we have look-outs close by. Take a set of grenades yourself, and give one to each of three or four fellows you are sure of. . . ."

All the men of the section knew that Katov, condemned after the Odessa affair to detention in one of the less severe prisons, had voluntarily asked to accompany the wretches sent to the lead-mines, in order to instruct them. They had confidence in him, but they were still uneasy. They were afraid neither of rifles nor of machine-guns, but they were afraid of the tanks: they felt powerless against them. Even in this room to which only volunteers had come, almost all of them relatives of men who had died by torture, the tank inspired blind terror, like a supernatural monster.

"If the tanks come, don't worry, we'll be there," Katov went on.

How could he leave with such feebly reassuring words? In the afternoon he had inspected some fifteen sections, but he had not encountered fear. These men were not less brave than the others, merely more precise. He knew he would not be able to dispel their fear, that save for the specialists under his own command the revolutionary formations would run before the tanks. It was probable that the tanks would be unable to leave the front; but if they reached the city, it would be impossible to stop them all with ditches, in these quarters where there was such a criss-cross of small streets.

"The tanks will absolutely not leave the front," he said.

"How are we to attach the grenades?" asked the youngest Chinaman.

Katov showed him. The atmosphere became a little less heavy, as if this manipulation were a token of future action. Katov, very uneasy, took the opportunity to leave. Half the men would not know how to use their arms. At least he could count on those whom he had organized into combat groups charged with disarming the police. Tomorrow. But the day after tomorrow?

35

The army was advancing, was getting nearer every hour. Perhaps the last station was already taken. When Kyo returned they would no doubt be able to find out in one of the information-centers. The lamp-dealer had received no news since ten o'clock.

He waited some time in the narrow street, without ceasing to walk; at last Kyo arrived. Each told the other what he had done. They continued their walk in the mud, on their crêpe soles: Kyo small and supple as a Japanese cat, Katov swinging his shoulders, thinking of the troops who were advancing, guns gleaming in the rain, toward Shanghai glowing red in the heart of the night. . . . Kyo, too, wanted to know if this advance had not been stopped.

The street where they were walking was the first one in the Chinese city. Because of the proximity of the European quarter it was lined with pet-shops. They were all closed: not a creature outside, and not a cry disturbing the silence, between the siren-calls and the last drops that fell from the horned roofs into the puddles. The animals were asleep. After knocking, they entered one of the shops: that of a dealer in live fishes. The only light, a candle fixed in a holder, was feebly reflected in the phosphorescent bowls aligned like those of Ali-Baba, and in which the illustrious Chinese carps slept, invisible.

"Tomorrow?" asked Kyo.

"Tomorrow; at one o'clock."

At the back of the shop, behind a counter, an indistinct human being was asleep with his head in his elbows. He had scarcely looked up to reply. This shop was one of the eighty posts of the Kuomintang through which news was transmitted.

"Official?"

"Yes. The army is at Ch'êng Ch'ou. General strike at noon."

Although nothing in the shadow had changed, although the dealer drowsing in his cell had made no motion, the phosphorescent surface of all the bowls began to stir feebly: soft, black, concentric waves rose in silence. The sound of the voices was awakening the fishes. A siren, once again, became lost in the distance.

They went out, resumed their walk. The Avenue of the Two Republics again.

A taxi. The car set off at reckless speed. Katov, sitting at the left, leaned over, looked at the driver closely.

"He is *nguyen*.[1] Too bad. I'd abs'lutely like not to be killed before tomorrow night. Easy, old chap!"

"So Clappique is having the ship moved," said Kyo. "The comrades in the government outfitting-shop can supply us with cops' uniforms. . . ."

"No need. I have more than fifteen of them at the post."

"Let's take the launch with your twelve men."

"It would be better without you. . . ."

Kyo looked at him without speaking.

"It's not very dangerous, but it's not exactly child's play either, you know. It's more dangerous than this idiot of a driver who's starting to speed again. And it's not the moment to ask you to get out."

"Nor you either."

"It's not the same thing. *I* can be replaced, now, you see. . . . I'd rather you would take care of the truck which will be waiting, and the distribution."

He hesitated, embarrassed, his hand on his chest. "I have to give him a chance to think it over," he was thinking. Kyo said nothing. The car continued to speed

[1] In a state of craving (of opium addicts).

37

between streaks of light blurred by the mist. There was no doubt that he was more useful than Katov: the Central Committee knew the details of everything he had organized, but on index-cards, whereas for him the insurrection was a living thing; the city was in his skin, with its weak points like wounds. None of his comrades could react so quickly as he, so surely.

"All right," he said.

Lights more and more numerous. . . . Again, the armored trucks of the concessions, and then, once more, the dark.

The car stopped. Kyo got out.

"I'll go get the uniforms," said Katov: "I'll come and fetch you when everything is ready."

Kyo lived with his father in a single-story Chinese house; four wings surrounding a garden. He passed through the first one, then through the garden, and entered the hall: right and left, on the white walls, Sung paintings, Chardin-blue phœnixes; at the end a Buddha of the Wei dynasty, almost romanesque in style. Plain divans, an opium table. Behind Kyo, the windows, bare like those of a work-shop. His father, who had heard him, entered: for some years he had been suffering from insomnia, was able to sleep only a few hours toward dawn, and welcomed joyfully anything that would help to pass the night.

"Good evening, father. Ch'en is coming to see you."

"Good."

Kyo's features were not his father's, which were those of an ascetic abbot, accentuated tonight by a camel's hair dressing gown. His mother's Japanese blood appeared to have softened their lines to form Kyo's samurai face.

"Has anything happened to him?"

"Yes."

No further question. Both sat down. Kyo was not sleepy. He told him about the show Clappique had just put on for him—without mentioning the firearms. Not, indeed, that he mistrusted his father; but he needed too much to be solely responsible for his own life to confide to him more than the general nature of his actions. Although the old professor of sociology of the University of Peking, dismissed by Chang Tso Lin because of his teaching, had formed the best revolutionary cadres in Northern China, he did not participate in action. Whenever Kyo came into his presence, his own will to action was transformed into intelligence, which rather disturbed him: he became interested in individuals instead of being interested in forces. And, because he was speaking of Clappique to his father who knew him well, the Baron now appeared more mysterious than a while ago, when he was looking at him.

". . . he finally touched me for fifty dollars. . . ."

"He is disinterested, Kyo. . . ."

"But he had just spent a hundred dollars: I saw it. Mythomania is always a rather disturbing thing."

He wanted to know just how far he could continue to use Clappique. His father, as always, was trying to discover what was profound or singular in the man. But what is deepest in a man is rarely what one can use directly to make him act, and Kyo was thinking of his guns:

"If he needs to believe himself rich, why doesn't he try to get rich?"

"He used to be the foremost antiquarian in Peking. . . ."

39

"Why does he spend all his money in one night, then, if not to give himself the illusion of being rich?"

Gisors blinked, threw back his longish white hair; his old man's voice, in spite of its weakened tone, took on the sharpness of a line.

"His mythomania is a means of denying life, don't you see, of denying, and not of forgetting. Beware of logic in these matters. . . ."

He extended his hand uncertainly; his restrained gestures hardly ever went sideways but straight before him: his motions, when he resorted to them to round out a sentence, did not seem to push aside, but to seize something.

"Everything has happened as though he wanted to prove to himself this evening that, although he lived for two hours like a rich man, wealth does not exist. Because then *poverty does not exist either.* Which is essential. Nothing exists: all is dream. Don't forget the alcohol, which helps him. . . ."

Gisors smiled. The smile of his thin lips, drooping at the corners, expressed his idea with more complexity than his words. For twenty years he had used his intelligence to win the affections of men by justifying them, and they were grateful to him for a kindness which they did not suspect had its roots in opium. People attributed to him the patience of a Buddhist: it was the patience of an addict.

"No man lives by denying life," answered Kyo.

"One lives inadequately by it. . . . He feels a need to live inadequately."

"And he is forced to."

"He chooses a way of life that *makes* it necessary—his dealings in antiques, perhaps drugs, and the traffic of firearms. . . . In conjunction with the police whom he no doubt detests, but whom he coöperates with in such deals for a fair remuneration. . . ."

It didn't make much difference: the police knew the Communists didn't have enough money to buy firearms from the clandestine importers.

"Every man is like his affliction," said Kyo: "what does he suffer from?"

"His affliction, don't you see, has no more importance, no more sense, touches nothing deeper than his lies, or his pleasures; he really has no depth, and that is perhaps what describes him best, because it's rare. He does what he can to make up for it, but that requires certain gifts. . . . When you're not tied to a man, Kyo, you think of him in order to foresee his actions. Clappique's actions . . ."

He pointed to the aquarium in which the black carps, soft and lacy like streamers, rose and fell.

"There you have them, . . . He drinks, but he was made for opium: it's also possible to choose the wrong vice; many men never strike the one that might save them. Too bad, for he is far from being without worth. But his field doesn't interest you."

It was true. If Kyo was unable to think in terms of action this evening, neither could he become interested in ideas: he could think only of himself. The heat was penetrating him little by little, as at the *Black Cat* a while ago; and once more the obsession of the records went through him like the weariness tingling through his legs. He told of his astonishment at the records, but as though he were referring merely to one of the voice-recordings which had been made in the English shops. Gisors listened, caressing his angular chin with his left hand: his hands, with their slender fingers, were very beautiful. He had bent his head forward: his hair fell over his eyes, though his forehead was bald. He threw it back with a toss of the head, but his eyes had a far-away look:

"I've had the experience of finding myself unexpectedly before a mirror and not recognizing myself. . . ."

His thumb was gently rubbing the other fingers of his right hand, as though he were sprinkling a powder of memories. He was speaking for himself, pursuing a line of thought which excluded his son:

"It's undoubtedly a question of means: we hear the voices of others with our ears."

"And our own?"

"With our throats: for you can hear your own voice with your ears stopped. Opium is also a world we do not hear with our ears. . . ."

Kyo got up. His father scarcely saw him.

"I have to go out again soon."

"Can I be of any use to you with Clappique?"

"No. Thanks. Good night."

"Good night."

Kyo, lying down in an attempt to reduce his weariness, was waiting. He had not turned on the light; he did not move. It was not *he* who was thinking of the insurrection, it was the insurrection, living in so many brains like sleep in so many others, which weighed upon him to such a point that there was nothing left in him but anxiety and expectation. Less than four hundred guns in all. Victory—or the firing-squad, with some refinements. Tomorrow. No: by and by. A matter of speed: everywhere disarm the police and, with the five hundred Mausers, arm the combat groups before the soldiers of the governmental armored train entered into action. The masses were ready. Half the police, who were dying of starvation, would undoubtedly pass over to the insurgents. Which left the other half. But the insurrection was to begin at one o'clock—the general strike, therefore, at noon—and most of the combat groups had to be armed before five o'clock. "Soviet China," he thought. To conquer here the dignity of his people. And the U.S.S.R. increased to six hundred million men. Victory or defeat, the destiny of the world hovered here close by. Unless the Kuomintang, once Shanghai was taken, tried to crush its Communist allies. . . . He started: the garden door was being opened. Recollection buried anxiety: his wife? He listened: the door of the house shut. May entered. Her blue leather coat, of an almost military cut, accentuated what was virile in her gait and even in her face—a large mouth, a short nose, the prominent cheek-bones of the Germans of the North.

"It's really going to start very shortly, Kyo?"

"Yes."

She was a doctor in one of the Chinese hospitals, but she had just come from the section of revolutionary women whose clandestine hospital she directed:

"Always the same story, you know. I've just left a kid of eighteen who tried to commit suicide with a razor blade in her wedding palanquin. She was being forced to marry a respectable brute. . . . They brought her in her red wedding gown, all covered with blood. The mother behind, a little stunted shadow, that was sobbing, of course. . . . When I told her the kid wouldn't die, she said to me: 'Poor little thing! she would almost have been lucky to die. . . .' Lucky. . . . That tells more than all our speeches about the condition of women here. . . ."

German, but born in Shanghai, a doctor of Heidelberg and Paris—she spoke French without an accent. She threw her béret on the bed. Her wavy hair was drawn back, so that it would be easy to fix. He felt like stroking it. Her very broad forehead, also, had something masculine about it, but since she had stopped talking she was becoming more feminine—Kyo did not take his eyes off her—because the release of tension softened her features, because fatigue relaxed them, and because she had taken off her béret. It was her sensual mouth and her eyes that animated her face—her eyes, sufficiently bright to make the intensity of her glance seem to come, not from her pupils but from the shadow of her forehead over the wide orbits.

Attracted by the light, a white Pekingese came trotting in. She called it with a tired voice:

"Little woolly dog!"

She caught it in her left hand, raised it caressingly to her face:

"Rabbit," she said, smiling, "little rabbit. . . ."

"He looks like you," said Kyo.

"Doesn't he?"

She looked in the mirror at the white head glued against hers, above the little joined paws. The amusing resemblance was due to her high Germanic cheek-bones. Although she was barely pretty, he thought of Othello's phrase, adapting it: "O my dear warrior. . . ."

She put down the dog, got up. Her half-open coat now partly exposed her high breasts, which reminded one of her cheek-bones. Kyo told her the night's happenings.

"At the hospital this evening," she said, "some thirty young women of the propaganda circles who had escaped from the White troops . . . Wounded. More and more of them are arriving. They say the army is very near. And that there are many killed. . . ."

"And half the wounded will die. . . . Suffering can have meaning only when it does not lead to death, and that's where it almost always leads."

May pondered:

"Yes," she said at last. "And yet that's perhaps a man's idea. For me, for a woman, suffering—it's strange—makes me think of life rather than of death. . . . Because of child-birth, perhaps. . . ."

She reflected again:

"The more wounded there are, the nearer the insurrection is, the more people go to bed together."

"Yes, it's natural."

"I have something to tell you which is perhaps going to annoy you a little. . . ."

Leaning on his elbow, he gave her a questioning look. She was intelligent and brave, but often clumsy.

"I finally yielded to Langlen and went to bed with him, this afternoon."

He shrugged his shoulder, as if to say: "That's your affair." But his gesture, the tense expression of his face, contrasted sharply with this indifference. She was watching him, haggard, her cheek-bones emphasized by the vertical light. He too was watching her eyes, expressionless in the shadow, and said nothing. He was wondering if the expression of sensuality in her face was not due to the fact that the obliterated eyes and the slight swelling of her lips, in contrast to her features, violently accentuated her femininity. . . . She sat down on the bed, took his hand. He nearly withdrew it, but yielded it. She felt the impulse however:

"Are you hurt?"

45

"I have told you you were free. . . . Don't ask too much," he added bitterly.

The dog jumped up on the bed. He withdrew his hand, to caress it perhaps.

"You are free," he repeated. "The rest doesn't matter."

"Anyway, I *had* to tell you. For my own sake."

"Yes."

Neither of them questioned the necessity of her telling him. He suddenly wanted to get up: lying thus, with her sitting on his bed, like a sick man being nursed by her. . . . But why should he? Everything was so futile. . . . He continued nevertheless to look at her, to discover that she could make him suffer. For months, whether he looked at her or not, he had ceased to see her; certain expressions, at times. . . . Their love, so often hurt, uniting them like a sick child, the common meaning of their life and their death, the carnal understanding between them, nothing of all that existed before the fatality which discolors the forms with which our eyes are saturated. "Do I love her less than I think I do?" he thought. No. Even at this moment he was sure that if she were to die he would no longer serve his cause with hope, but with despair, as though he himself were dead. Nothing, however, prevailed against the discoloration of that face buried in the depth of their common life as in mist, as in the earth. He remembered a friend who had had to watch the disintegration of the mind of the woman he loved, paralyzed for months; it seemed to him that he was watching May die thus, watching the form of his happiness absurdly disappear like a cloud absorbed by the gray sky. As though she had died twice —from the effect of time, and from what she was telling him.

She got up, went to the window. She walked briskly in spite of her fatigue. Choosing, through mingled fear and sentimental delicacy, to say nothing more of what she had just told him, since he would not talk, and wishing to escape this conversation from which she felt none the less they would not escape, she tried to express her tenderness by saying whatever came into her mind, and appealed instinctively to an animism of which he was fond: in front of the window, one of the trees of Mars had opened out during the night; the light from the room fell on its leaves that were still curled, a delicate green against the dark background:

"It has hidden its leaves in its trunk during the day," she said, "and is bringing them out tonight while no one sees it."

She seemed to be talking to herself, but how could Kyo have mistaken the tone of her voice?

"You might have picked another day," he said none the less between his teeth.

He saw himself in the mirror, also, leaning on his elbow—his face so Japanese between the white sheets. "If I were not a half-breed . . ." He was making an intense effort to push back the hateful or base thoughts all too ready to justify and feed his anger. And he gazed at her—gazed at her as though her face should have recovered, by the suffering it was inflicting, all the life it had lost.

"But, Kyo, it's precisely today that it had no importance . . . and . . ."

She was going to add: "he wanted it so badly." In the face of death it mattered so little. . . . But she said merely:

". . . I also may die tomorrow. . . ."

So much the better. Kyo was suffering from the most

47

humiliating pain: that which one despises oneself for feeling. In reality she was free to sleep with whom she pleased. Why, then, this suffering to which he claimed no right, but which so insistently claimed a right to him?

"When you realized that I . . . was fond of you, Kyo, you asked me one day, not seriously—just a trifle perhaps—if I thought I would be willing to go to prison with you, and I answered you that I didn't know—that the difficult thing no doubt was to stay there. . . . You thought I would, none the less, since you were fond of me too. Why not think so now?"

"It's always the same ones who go to prison. Katov would go, even if he did not love deeply. He would go for the idea he has of life, of himself. . . . It's not for someone else that one goes to prison."

"Kyo, what masculine ideas . . ."

He was thinking.

"And yet," he said, "to love those who are capable of doing just that, to be loved by them perhaps, what more can one ask of love? What madness to ask them for accounts besides? . . . Even if they do it for their . . . morality. . . ."

"It's not for morality," she said slowly. "For morality, I would surely be incapable of it."

"But" (he was speaking slowly too) "this love did not prevent you from going to bed with that fellow, at the same time that you were thinking—you just said so—it would . . . annoy me?"

"Kyo, I'm going to tell you something strange, and which is true just the same . . . up until five minutes ago I thought it wouldn't matter to you. Perhaps it suited me to think so. . . . There are urges, especially when one is so near death (it's the death of others that

I'm used to, Kyo . . .), that have nothing to do with love. . . ."

Yet jealousy persisted, all the more obscure because the sexual desire she aroused in him rested on affection. His eyes shut, still leaning on his elbow, he was trying—wretchedly—to understand. He heard only May's oppressed breathing and the scratching of the dog's paws. His wound was caused, first of all (there would, alas! be other reasons: he felt them lying in wait inside him like his comrades behind those doors that were still closed) by his feeling that the man who had just had intercourse with her (after all, I can't call him her lover!) must despise her. He was an old chum of May's, Kyo scarcely knew him. But he knew the fundamental misogyny of almost all men. "The idea that having had intercourse with her, because he has had intercourse with her, he can say of her: 'That little bitch' makes me want to knock him down. Can it be that one is never jealous except because of what one supposes the other supposes? Wretched humanity. . . ." For May, sexual intercourse did not in any sense signify an emotional surrender. That fellow would have to learn it. If he went to bed with her, that was that, but he must not imagine that he possessed her. "I'm getting maudlin. . . ." But he could not help himself, and that was not the essential, he knew. The essential, what agonized him, was that he was suddenly separated from her, not by hatred—although there was hatred in him—not by jealousy (or was jealousy precisely this?) but by a feeling that had no name, as destructive as time or death: he could not find her again. He opened his eyes; this familiar athletic body, with its averted profile: an elongated eye, starting at the temple, sunk between the exposed forehead and the cheek-bone—a human being. . . . Who was she? A woman who had just had intercourse with a man? But was she not also the one who tolerated his weaknesses, his afflictions, his outbursts of irritation, the one who had helped him nurse his wounded comrades, watched with him over his dead friends? . . . The sweetness of her voice, which lingered in the air. . . . One does not forget what one wishes. And now this body was being invested with the poignant mystery of a familiar person suddenly transformed—the mystery one feels before a mute, blind, or mad being. And she was a woman. Not a kind of man. Something else. . . .

She was getting away from him completely. And, because of that perhaps, the fierce craving for an intense contact with her blinded him, for a contact, no matter what kind—even one that might lead to fright, screams, blows. He got up, went over to her. He knew he was in a state of crisis, that tomorrow perhaps he would no longer understand anything of what he was feeling now, but he was before her as before a death-bed; and as towards a death-bed, instinct threw him towards her: to touch, to feel, to hold back those who are leaving you, to cling to them. . . . She was looking at him with an intense anxiety; he had stopped two paces from her. The revelation of what he wanted finally flashed upon him; to lie with her, to find refuge in her body against this frenzy in which he was losing her entirely; they did not have to know each other when they were using all their strength to hold each other in a tight embrace.

She suddenly turned round: someone had rung. Too soon for Katov. Was the insurrection discovered? What they had said, felt, loved, hated, was brutally submerged. The bell rang again. He took his revolver from under his pillow, crossed the garden, went to open in his pajamas:

it was not Katov, it was Clappique, still in his dinner-jacket. They stood in the garden.

"Well?"

"First of all let me give you back your document: here it is. Everything is fine. The ship has left. It's going to anchor up-stream off the French Consulate. Almost on the other side of the river."

"Any difficulties?"

"Not a word. The old confidence: if not, I wonder how we would manage. In these matters, young man, confidence is all the greater the less there is to justify it. . . ."

An allusion?

Clappique lit a cigarette. Kyo could see only the spot of square black silk on the indistinct face. He went to get his wallet—May was waiting—came back, paid the commission agreed upon. The Baron put the bills in his pocket, in a roll, without counting them.

"Generosity brings good luck," he said. "My good fellow, the story of my night's adventure is a re-mar-ka-ble moral tale: it began with charity and ends in wealth. Not a word!"

Raising his forefinger, he leaned over towards Kyo's ear:

"Fantômas [1] salutes you!" then turned and left.

As though he were afraid to return into the house, he watched him disappear, his dinner jacket bobbing up and down against the white wall. "Rather like Fantômas, as a matter of fact, in that outfit. Did he guess, or suppose, or . . ." Enough of the picturesque: Kyo heard a cough and recognized it all the more quickly as he was

[1] A popular character in French detective fiction who plays the rôle of an elusive and clever criminal.

expecting it: Katov. Everyone was hurrying tonight.

In order to be less visible, perhaps, he was walking in the middle of the street. Kyo guessed his blouse rather than saw it; somewhere, above it, in the dark, a nose in the wind. . . . Especially he sensed the swinging of his hands. He walked towards him.

"Well?" he asked, as he had asked Clappique.

"All's well. And the ship?"

"Opposite the French Consulate. Far from the wharf. In half an hour."

"The launch and the men are four hundred meters from there. Let's go."

"And the uniforms?"

"Don't worry. The fellows are absolutely ready."

He went into the house, dressed in a moment: trousers, a sweater, rope-soled shoes (he might have to do some climbing). He was ready. May offered her lips. Kyo's spirit wanted to kiss her; his mouth, not—as though it bore an independent grudge. He finally kissed her, awkwardly. She looked at him with sadness, her eyelids lowered; her eyes, in deep shadow, became intensely expressive whenever the expression came from the muscles. He left.

He was walking by Katov's side once more. Yet he could not free himself from her. "A while ago she seemed to me like a mad or a blind woman. I don't know her. I know her only to the extent that I love, in the sense in which I love her. One possesses of another person only what one changes in him, says my father. . . . And then what?" He withdrew into himself as he advanced into the increasingly dark alley, in which even the telegraph insulators no longer gleamed against the sky. His torment returned, and he remembered the records: "We hear the voices of others with our ears, our own voices with our throats." Yes. One hears his own life, too, with his throat, and those of others? . . . First of all there was solitude, the inescapable aloneness behind the living multitude like the great primitive night behind the dense, low night under which this city of deserted streets was expectantly waiting, full of hope and hatred. "But I, to myself, to my throat, what am I? A kind of absolute, the affirmation of an idiot: an intensity greater than that of all the rest. To others, I am what I have done." To May alone, he was not what he had done; to him alone, she was something altogether different from her biography. The embrace by which love holds beings together against solitude did not bring its relief to man; it brought relief only to the madman, to the incomparable monster, dear above all things, that every being is to himself and that he cherishes in his heart. Since his mother had died, May was the only being for whom he was not Kyo Gisors, but an intimate partner. "A partnership consented, conquered, chosen," he thought, extraordinarily in harmony with the night, as if his thoughts were no longer made for light. "Men are not my kind, they are those who look at me and judge me; my kind are those who love me and do not look at me, who love me in spite of everything, degradation, baseness, treason—*me* and not what I have done or shall do—who would love me as long as I would love myself—even to suicide. . . . With her alone I have this love in common, injured or not, as others have children who are ill and in danger of dying. . . ." It was not happiness, certainly. It was something primitive which was at one with the darkness and caused a warmth to rise in him, resolving itself into a motionless embrace, as of cheek against cheek—the only thing in him that was as strong as death.

On the roofs there were already shadows at their posts.

Four o'clock in the morning

Old Gisors crumpled the badly torn scrap of paper on which Ch'en had written his name in pencil, and put it in his pocket. He was impatient to see his former pupil again. His eyes fell once more upon the man he was conversing with, a very old Chinaman with the head of a mandarin of the India Company, wearing the robe; he was moving towards the door, with little steps, his forefinger raised, and was speaking English: "It is well that the absolute submission of woman, concubinage and the institution of courtesans exist. I shall continue to publish my articles. It is because our ancestors thought thus that those beautiful paintings exist (he indicated the blue phœnix with his eyes, without moving his face, as though he were ogling it)—you are proud of them, and I too. Woman is subject to man as man is subject to the State; and it is less hard to serve man than to serve the State. Do we live for ourselves? We are nothing. We live for the State in the present, for the order of the dead through the centuries. . . ."

Was he ever going to leave? This man clutching to his past, even today (didn't the sirens of the battleships suffice to fill the night? . . .) in the face of China corroded by blood like its sacrificial bronzes, was invested with a certain poetic quality, like some lunatics. Order! Crowds of skeletons in embroidered robes, lost in the depth of time in motionless assemblies: facing them, Ch'en, the two hundred thousand workers of the spinning mills without embroideries, the crushing horde of the coolies. The submission of women? Every evening May brought back accounts of suicides of fiancées. . . . The old man left, his forefinger raised: "Order, Mr. Gisors! . . ." after a last bouncing nod of his head and shoulders.

As soon as he had heard the door shut, Gisors called Ch'en and returned with him to the room with the phœnixes.

Ch'en began to pace back and forth. Each time he passed before him, at a slight angle, Gisors seated on one of the divans was reminded of an Egyptian bronze hawk of which Kyo had kept a photograph through fondness for Ch'en, "because of the resemblance." It was true, in spite of the kindliness which the thick lips seemed to express. "In short, a hawk converted by Saint Francis of Assisi," he thought.

Ch'en stopped in front of him:

"It's I who killed Tang Yen Ta," he said.

He had seen in Gisors' look something almost affectionate. He despised affection, and was afraid of it. His head which was sunk between his shoulders and pushed forward when he walked, and the curved ridge of his nose, accentuated the resemblance to the hawk, in spite of his squat figure; and even his narrow eyes, almost without lashes, made one think of a bird.

"Is that what you wanted to talk to me about?"

"Yes."

"Does Kyo know?"

"Yes."

Gisors pondered. Since he would not respond with prejudices, he could only approve. He had nevertheless some difficulty in doing so. "I'm getting old," he thought.

Ch'en gave up walking.

"I'm terribly alone," he said, looking straight at Gisors at last.

The latter was upset. That Ch'en fastened himself to him did not astonish him: for years he had been his teacher in the Chinese sense of the word—a little less than his father, more than his mother; since they had both died, Gisors was without doubt the only man Ch'en needed. What he did not understand was that Ch'en, who had undoubtedly met some terrorists again that night, since he had just seen Kyo, seemed so remote from them.

"But the others?" he asked.

Ch'en saw them again, in the back-shop of the record-dealer, plunging into the shadow or emerging from it with the swinging of the lamp, while the cricket chirped.

"They don't know."

"That you did it?"

"They know that: no importance."

He again fell into silence. Gisors avoided questioning him. Ch'en finally went on:

". . . That it's the first time."

Gisors suddenly had the impression that he understood; Ch'en felt this:

"No. You don't understand."

He spoke French with a guttural accentuation of one-syllable words, which combined startlingly with certain idioms he had picked up from Kyo. He was instinctively holding his arm close to his side: once more he felt the stabbed body which the spring-mattress had caused to rebound against the knife. That meant nothing. He would do it again. In the meantime, however, he yearned for a refuge. But it was only for Kyo that Gisors could feel that deep affection which needs no explanation. Ch'en knew it. How should he express himself?

"You have never killed a man before, have you?"

"You know I haven't."

That seemed obvious to Ch'en, but today he had begun to distrust such impressions. Yet it seemed to him suddenly that Gisors lacked something. He raised his eyes. The latter was looking up at him, his white hair seeming longer because of the backward toss of his head. Gisors was puzzled by his lack of gestures. This was due to his wound which Ch'en had not mentioned; not that he was suffering from it (a chum of his, an orderly, had disinfected and bound it) but it hampered him. As always when he was reflecting, Gisors was rolling an invisible cigarette between his fingers:

"Perhaps. . . ."

He stopped, his bright eyes steady. Ch'en waited. Gisors went on, almost brutally:

"I don't think the memory of a murder is enough to upset you so."

"It's clear that he doesn't know what he's talking about," Ch'en tried to tell himself; but Gisors had hit the mark. Ch'en sat down, looked at his feet:

"No," he said, "I don't think the memory is enough, either. There's something else, the essential. I'd like to know what."

Was that why he had come?

"The first woman you ever slept with was a prostitute, of course?" asked Gisors.

"I'm a Chinaman," answered Ch'en with rancor.

No, thought Gisors. Except, perhaps, for his sexuality, Ch'en was not Chinese. The emigrants from all countries with which Shanghai overflowed had shown Gisors to what extent a man becomes separated from his nation in a national way, but Ch'en no longer belonged to

57

China, not even in the way he had left it: a complete liberty gave him over completely to his mind.

"What did you feel, afterwards?" asked Gisors.

Ch'en clenched his fists.

"Pride."

"At being a man?"

"At not being a woman."

His voice no longer expressed rancor, but a complex contempt.

"I think you mean," he went on, "that I must have felt myself . . . apart?"

Gisors avoided an answer.

". . . Yes. Terribly. And you are right to speak of women. Perhaps one thoroughly despises the man one kills. But less than the others."

"Than the ones who don't kill?"

"Than the ones who don't kill: the weaklings."

He was pacing again. The two last words had fallen like a load that one drops, and the silence spread around them; Gisors was beginning to feel, not without melancholy, the isolation that Ch'en was speaking of. He suddenly remembered that Ch'en had told him he had a horror of hunting.

"Didn't you feel horror at the blood?"

"Yes. But not *only* horror."

He had spoken these words while pacing away from Gisors. He turned round on a sudden and, considering the phœnix, but as directly as though he were looking Gisors straight in the eyes, he asked:

"So what? I know what one does with women when they want to continue to possess you: one lives with them. What about death?"

Even more bitterly, but without taking his eyes off the phœnix:

"Live with it?"

The bent of Gisors' mind made him inclined always to help out those who came to him; and he felt affection for Ch'en. But he was beginning to see the thing clearly: action in the shock groups was no longer enough for the young man, terrorism was beginning to fascinate him. Still rolling his imaginary cigarette, his head bent forward as though he were studying the carpet, a white shock of hair beating against his slender nose, he said, trying to give his voice a tone of detachment:

"You think you won't get away from it. . . ."

But his nerves getting the better of him, he spluttered in conclusion:

". . . and it's against that . . . torment that you've come to . . . me for help."

Silence.

"A torment? No." Ch'en finally said, between his teeth, "A fatality?"

Again silence. Gisors felt that no gesture was possible, that he could not take his hand, as he used to. In his turn he made a decision, and said with weariness, as though he had suddenly acquired the habit of anguish:

"Then, you must think it through, and carry it to the extreme. And if you want to live with it. . . ."

"I shall soon be killed."

Isn't that what he wants above all? Gisors wondered. He aspires to no glory, to no happiness. Capable of winning, but not of living in his victory, what can he appeal to if not to death? No doubt he wants to give it the meaning that others give to life. To die on the highest possible plane. An ambitious soul, sufficiently lucid, sufficiently separated from men or sufficiently afflicted to despise all the objects of his ambition, and his ambition itself?

59

"If you want to live with this . . . fatality, there is only one recourse: to pass it on."

"Who would be worthy of it?" asked Ch'en, still between his teeth.

The air was becoming more and more weighted, as if everything murderous that these words called forth were present there. Gisors could say nothing more: words would have sounded false, frivolous, stupid.

"Thank you," said Ch'en. He bowed before him, with his whole upper body, Chinese fashion (which he never did) as though he preferred not to touch him, and left.

Gisors went back and sat down, began again to roll his cigarette. For the first time he found himself face to face, not with fighting, but with blood. And as always, he thought of Kyo. Kyo would have found the universe in which Ch'en moved unbreathable. . . . Was he really sure of this? Ch'en also detested hunting, Ch'en also had a horror of blood—before. How well did he know his son at this depth? Whenever his love played no rôle, whenever he could not refer to many memories, he fully realized that he did not know Kyo. He was seized with an intense desire to see him again—the desire one has to see one's dead a last time. He knew he had gone.

Where? Ch'en's presence still animated the room. *He* had thrown himself into the world of murder, from which he would never emerge: with his passion, he was entering upon the life of a terrorist as into a prison. Before ten years he would be caught—tortured or killed; until then he would live like a man willfully obsessed, in a world of decision and death. He had lived by his ideas; now they would kill him.

And it was indeed this that made Gisors suffer. If Kyo went in for killing, that was his rôle. And if not, it didn't matter: what Kyo did was well done. But he was appalled by this sudden sensation, this certainty of the fatality of murder, an intoxication as terrible as his own was innocent. He felt how inadequately he had brought to Ch'en the relief which he sought, how solitary murder is—how great a distance was growing, by virtue of this torment, between himself and Kyo. For the first time, the phrase he had so often repeated, "There is no knowledge of beings," attached itself in his mind to the face of his son.

As for Ch'en, did he really know him? He did not at all believe that memories enable one to understand men. There was Ch'en's early education, which had been religious; when he had begun to be interested in the adolescent orphan—his parents had been killed in the pillage of Kalgan—Ch'en, insolent and taciturn, had just come from the Lutheran college. He had been the pupil of a consumptive intellectual who had reached pastorship late in life, and who was struggling patiently at the age of fifty to overcome, by charity, an intense religious anxiety. Obsessed by the shame of the body which tormented Saint Augustine, of the degraded body in which one must live with Christ—through horror of the ritual civilization of China which surrounded him and made the appeal of the true religious life even more imperious —this pastor had worked out in his anguished mind his own image of Luther, on which he would occasionally hold forth to Gisors: "There is life only in God; but man, through sin, is degraded to such a point, so irremediably sullied, that to attain God is a kind of sacrilege. Whence Christ, whence his eternal crucifixion." Which left grace, that is to say limitless love or terror, according to the strength or weakness of hope; and this terror was a new sin. Which also left charity; but charity does not always suffice to dispel anguish.

The pastor had become attached to Ch'en. He had no suspicion that the uncle in charge of Ch'en had sent him to the missionaries only in order that he might learn English and French, and had put him on his guard against their teaching, especially against the idea of hell which the Confucian mistrusted. The child, who learned to know Christ, and not Satan or God—the pastor's experience had taught him that men never become converted except to mediators—gave himself over to love with the wholeheartedness which he brought to everything he did. But the respect of the schoolboy for his master was sufficiently strong—the only thing which China had deeply instilled in him—for the pastor's anguish to be communicated to him, in spite of the love he had been taught; and a hell was disclosed to him, more terrible and more convincing than the one he had been supposedly forewarned against.

The uncle returned. Appalled when he found what his nephew had become, he manifested a delicate satisfaction, sent little jade and crystal trees to the director, to the pastor, to several others; a week later he sent for Ch'en to come home and, the following week, sent him to the University of Peking.

Gisors, still rolling his imaginary cigarette, his half-open mouth expressing the bewilderment of one deep in thought, made an effort to recall the adolescent as he had been at that time. But how could one separate him, isolate him from the person he had become? "I think of his religious spirit because Kyo has never had any, and at this moment every profound difference between them reassures me. . . . Why do I have the impression of knowing him better than my son?" It was because he saw more clearly the way in which he had modified him; this essential modification—*his* work—was precise, with well-defined limits, and there was nothing about men that he knew better than what he had given to them.

No sooner had he observed Ch'en than he had understood that this adolescent was incapable of living by an ideology which did not immediately become transformed into action. As he was devoid of charity, a religious calling could lead him only to contemplation or the inner life; but he hated contemplation, and would only have dreamt of an apostleship, for which precisely his absence of charity disqualified him. In order to live he therefore needed first of all to escape from his Christianity. (From half-confidences, it seemed that the acquaintance of prostitutes and students had made him overcome the only sin that had always been stronger than Ch'en's will-power, masturbation; and with it, a constantly recurring feeling of anxiety and degradation.) When his new master had opposed Christianity, not with arguments, but with other forms of greatness, faith had sifted through Ch'en's fingers, imperceptibly, without crisis, like sand. His faith had detached him from China, accustomed him to isolate himself from the world instead of submitting to it; and he had understood through Gisors that everything had happened as if this period of his life had been merely an initiation in the sense of heroism: what good is a soul, if there is neither God nor Christ?

At this point Gisors' train of thought brought him back to his son, who had never been exposed to Christianity but whose Japanese education (Kyo had lived in Japan from his eighth to his seventeenth year) had also imposed the conviction that ideas were not to be thought, but lived. Kyo had chosen action, in a grave and premeditated way, as others choose a military career, or the sea: he left his father, lived in Canton, in Tientsin, the life of day-laborers and coolies, in order to organize the syndicates. Ch'en—his uncle, taken as hostage at the capture of Swatow, and unable to pay his ransom, had been executed—had found himself without money, provided only with worthless diplomas, with his twenty-four years and with China before him. He was a truck-driver when the Northern routes were dangerous, then an assistant chemist, then nothing. Everything had pushed him into political activity: the hope of a different world, the possibility of eating, though wretchedly (he was naturally austere, perhaps through pride), the gratification of his hatreds, his mind, his character. This activity gave a meaning to his solitude.

But with Kyo everything was simpler. The heroic sense had given him a kind of discipline, not a kind of justification of life. He was not restless. His life had a meaning, and he knew what it was: to give to each of these men whom famine, at this very moment, was killing off like a slow plague, the sense of his own dignity. He belonged with them: they had the same enemies. A half-breed, an outcast, despised by the white men and even more by the white women, Kyo had not tried to win them: he had sought and had found his own kind. "There is no possible dignity, no real life for a man who works twelve hours a day without knowing why he works." That work would have to take on a meaning, become a faith. Individual problems existed for Kyo only in his private life.

All this Gisors knew. "And yet, if Kyo were to enter and tell me, like Ch'en a while ago: 'It is I who killed Tang Yen Ta,' I would think, 'I knew it.' All the possibilities within him echo in me with such force that, whatever he might tell me, I would think, 'I knew it . . .'" Through the window he looked out at the motionless and indifferent night. "But if I really knew it, and not in this uncertain and appalling fashion, I would save him." A painful affirmation, of which he did not believe a word. What confidence did he have in his own mind?

Since Kyo's departure his mind had served only to justify his son's activity, an activity which at that time was obscurely beginning somewhere in Central China or in the Southern provinces (often, for three months on end, he did not even know where). If the restless students felt his intelligence ready to help them, reaching out to them with so much warmth and insight, it was not, as the idiots of Peking then believed, because he found amusement in living vicariously in lives from which his age separated him: it was because in all those dramas that were so much alike he recognized that of his son. When he showed his students, almost all of them petty bourgeois, that they must ally themselves either with the military chiefs or with the proletariat, when he told those who had chosen: "Marxism is not a doctrine, it is a *will*. For the proletariat and those who belong with them—you—it is the will to know themselves, to feel themselves as proletarians, and to conquer as such; you must be Marxists not in order to be right, but in order to conquer without betraying yourselves,"—when he told them this he was talking to Kyo, he was defending him. And, if he knew that it was not Kyo's incisive mind answering him when, after those lectures, he found his room filled with white flowers from the students, according to the Chinese custom, at least he knew that these hands that were preparing to kill by bringing him camelias would tomorrow press those of his son, who would need them. That was why strength of character attracted him so much, why he had become attached to Ch'en. But, at the time when he had become attached to him, had he foreseen this rainy night when the young man, speaking of blood that had hardly coagulated, would come to him and say: "It's not only horror that I feel . . ."?

He got up, opened the drawer of the low table where he kept his opium tray, above a collection of small cactuses. Under the tray, a photograph: Kyo. He pulled it out, looked at it without any precise thoughts, sank bitterly into the certainty that, at the point he had reached, no one knew anyone—and that even the presence of Kyo, which he had so longed for just now, would have changed nothing, would only have rendered their separation more desperate, like that of friends whom one embraces in a dream and who have been dead for years. He kept the photograph between his fingers: it was as warm as a hand. He let it drop back into the drawer, took out the tray, turned out the electric light and lit the lamp.

Two pipes. Formerly, as soon as his craving began to be quenched, he would contemplate men with benevolence, and the world as an infinite of possibilities. Now, in his innermost being, the possibilities found no place: he was sixty, and his memories were full of tombs. His exquisitely pure sense of Chinese art, of those bluish paintings on which his lamp cast only a dim light, of the whole civilization of suggestion which China spread around him, which, thirty years earlier, he had been able to put to such delicate uses—his sense of happiness—was now nothing more than a thin cover beneath which anguish and the obsession of death were awakening, like restless dogs stirring at the end of their sleep.

Yet his mind hovered over the world, over mankind with a burning passion that age had not extinguished.

It had long been his conviction that there is a paranoiac in every man, in himself first of all. He had thought once—ages ago—that he imagined himself a hero. No. This force, this furious subterranean imagination which was in him (were I to go mad, he had thought, this part of me alone would remain . . .) was ready to assume every form, like light. Like Kyo, and almost for the same reasons, he thought of the records of which the latter had spoken to him; and almost in the same fashion, for Kyo's modes of thought were born of his own. Just as Kyo had not recognized his own voice because he had heard it with his throat, so he—Gisors—probably could not reduce his consciousness of himself to that which he could have of another person, because it was not acquired by the same means. It owed nothing to the senses. He felt himself penetrating into a domain which belonged to him more than any other. With his intruding consciousness he was anxiously treading a forbidden solitude where no one would ever join him. For a second he had the sensation that it was *that* which must escape death. . . . His hands, which were preparing a new pellet, were slightly trembling. Even his love for Kyo did not free him from this total solitude. But if he could not escape from himself into another being, he knew how to find relief: there was opium.

Five pellets. For years he had limited himself to that, not without difficulty, not without pain sometimes. He scratched the bowl of his pipe; the shadow of his hand slipped from the wall to the ceiling. He pushed back the lamp a fraction of an inch; the contours of the shadow became lost. The objects also were vanishing: without changing their form they ceased to be distinct from himself, joined him in the depth of a familiar world where a benign indifference mingled all things—a world more true than the other because more constant, more like himself; sure as a friendship, always indulgent and always accessible: forms, memories, ideas, all plunged slowly towards a liberated universe. He remembered a September afternoon when the solid gray of the sky made a lake's surface appear milky, in the meshes of vast fields of water-lilies; from the moldy gables of an abandoned pavilion to the magnificent and desolate horizon he saw only a world suffused with a solemn melancholy. Near his idle bell, a Buddhist priest leaned on the balustrade of the pavilion, abandoning his sanctuary to the dust, to the fragrance of burning aromatic woods; peasants gathering water-lily seeds passed by in a boat without the slightest sound; at the edge of the farthest flowers two long waves grew from the rudder, melted listlessly in the gray water. They were vanishing now in himself, gathering in their fan all the oppressiveness of the world, but an oppressiveness without bitterness, brought by opium to an ultimate purity. His eyes shut, carried by great motionless wings, Gisors contemplated his solitude: a desolation that joined the divine, while at the same time the wave of serenity that gently covered the depths of death widened to infinity.

Half past four in the morning

Already dressed as government soldiers with waterproofs, the men were going down one by one into the big launch rocked by the eddies of the river.

"Two of the sailors are members of the Party. We'll have to question them: they must know where the firearms are," said Kyo to Katov. Except for the boots, the uniform did not greatly modify the latter's appearance.

His military blouse was as badly buttoned as the other. But the brand-new cap solemnly sitting on his head, which was usually bare, made him look foolish. "Astonishing combination, a Chinese officer's cap and such a nose!" thought Kyo. It was pitch dark. . . .

"Slip on the hood of your waterproof," he said nevertheless.

The launch eased off from the wharf and sped into the night. It soon disappeared behind a junk. Cruisers—the shafts of light from the projectors, crossed like sabers, swung in a flash from the sky to the chaotic port.

In the bow, Katov kept his eyes glued to the *Shantung*, which seemed gradually to be approaching. While the smell of stagnant water, fish and smoke from the port, which was gradually replacing the coal smell of the dock, seemed to go through him, his mind was obsessed by the memory which the approach of every battle called forth in him. On the Lithuanian front his battalion had been taken by the White forces. The disarmed men were standing in line on the barely visible expanse of snow against the greenish dawn. "Communists, leave the ranks!" Death, they knew. Two-thirds of the battalion had advanced. "Take off your coats." "Dig the pit." They had dug. Slowly, for the ground was frozen. The White Guards, a revolver in each hand (the shovels might become weapons), uneasy and impatient, were waiting, to right and left—the center empty because of the machine-guns leveled at the prisoners. The silence was limitless, vast as the snow that stretched out as far as the eye could reach. Only the clods of earth fell with a brittle sound, more and more hurried. In spite of death, the men were hurrying to get warm. Several had begun to sneeze. "That's good now. Halt!" They turned round. Behind them, beyond their comrades, women, children

69

and old men from the village were herded, scarcely clad, wrapped in blankets, mobilized to witness the example. Many were turning their heads, as though they were trying not to look, but they were fascinated by horror. "Take off your trousers!" For uniforms were scarce. Many hesitated, because of the women. "Take off your trousers!" The wounds appeared, one by one, bandaged with rags: the machine-guns had fired low and almost all were wounded in the legs. Many folded their trousers, although they had thrown their cloaks. They formed a line again, on the edge of the pit this time, facing the machine-guns, pale on the snow: flesh and shirts. Bitten by the cold, they were now sneezing uncontrollably, one after the other, and those sneezes were so intensely human, in that dawn of execution, that the machine-gunners, instead of firing, waited—waited for life to become less indiscreet. At last they decided to fire. The following evening the Reds recaptured the village: seventeen of the victims who were still alive—among them Katov—were saved. Those pale shadows on the greenish snow at dawn, transparent, shaken by convulsive sneezes in the face of the machine-guns, were here in this rain, in this Chinese night, before the shadow of the *Shantung*.

The launch plowed ahead. The swell was heavy enough to make the low and shadowy outline of the vessel seem to rock slowly on the river; scarcely lighted, it could be made out only as a darker mass against the cloud-covered sky. The *Shantung* was undoubtedly guarded. A cruiser's search-light struck the launch, held it a moment, left it. It described a broad curve and came on the steamer from the stern, veering slightly to starboard, as though it were about to be headed towards the neighboring ship. All the men wore sailors' waterproofs, with the hoods thrown back. By order of the port commission the gangways of all the ships were down; Katov looked at the one on the *Shantung* through his spy-glass hidden by his waterproof: it swung four feet from the water, barely lighted by three electric bulbs. If the captain were to ask for the money, which they did not have, before authorizing them to go aboard, the men were to jump from the launch one by one; it would be difficult to hold it fast under the gangway. Everything would therefore depend on that little oblique bridge. If they tried to raise it, from the ship, he could fire on those who worked the ropes: there was nothing to give protection under the tackles. But the men on board would prepare to defend themselves. The launch veered ninety degrees, made for the *Shantung*. The current, which was strong at this hour, caught it on the beam; the steamer, very tall now (they were directly beneath it), seemed to move off at full speed in the night, like a phantom ship. The engineer put the launch at full speed: the *Shantung* seemed to slow down, become motionless, recede. They were approaching the gangway. Katov took hold of it as they passed; jerking himself up, he found himself on the steps.

"The document?" asked the man at the cargo-port.

Katov presented it. The man passed it on, remained at his post, revolver in hand. This meant that the captain would have to recognize his own document; it was probable that he would, since he had done so when Clappique had presented it. Still . . . Below the cargo-port the dark launch rose and fell.

The messenger returned: "You may come up." Katov did not move; one of his men, who wore lieutenant's stripes (the only one who spoke English), left the launch, went up and followed the sailor acting as messenger, who led him to the captain.

The latter, a crop-haired Norwegian with blotched cheeks, was waiting for him in his cabin, behind his desk. The messenger went out.

"We've come to take delivery of the arms," said the lieutenant in English.

The captain looked at him without answering, stupefied. The generals had always paid for the arms; up to the time Tang Yen Ta, the go-between, had been sent, the sales had been negotiated secretly by the attaché of the consulate. If the generals no longer kept their agreements with the clandestine importers, who would supply them? But, since he had to deal only with the Shanghai government, he could try to save his firearms.

"Well! Here is the key."

He fumbled in the inside pocket of his coat, calmly, then with a quick move pulled out his revolver—at a level with the lieutenant's chest, from whom he was separated only by the table. At the same moment, he heard behind him: "Hands up!" Katov, through the porthole opening on the upper deck, had him covered. The captain was now completely bewildered, for this fellow was a white man: but for the moment it was no use insisting. The cases of arms were not worth his life. "A trip to be checked up to profit and loss." He would see what he could attempt with his crew. He put down his revolver, which the lieutenant seized.

Katov entered and searched him: he had no other weapon.

"Abs'lutely no use having so many revolvers on board and only carrying one on you," he said in English. Six of his men entered behind him, one by one, in silence. Katov's heavy gait, robust air, upturned nose, his light blond hair were those of a Russian. Scotch? But that accent. . . .

"You're not from the government, are you?"

"Mind y'r business."

The second officer was being brought in, duly tied hand and foot, caught in his sleep. The men bound the captain. Two of them stayed to guard him. The others went below with Katov. The men of the crew belonging to the Party showed them where the arms were hidden; the sole precaution of the Macao importers had been to write *"Unmounted Pieces"* on the cases. The unloading began. The gangway having been lowered, this was easy, for the cases were small. When the last case was in the launch, Katov went out and destroyed the wireless apparatus, then went back into the captain's cabin.

"If you're in too much of a hurry to land I warn you you'll be abs'lutely shot down at the first turn of the street. Good evening."

Sheer bravado, but the ropes digging into the arms of the prisoners gave it some force.

The revolutionaries, accompanied by the two men of the crew who had guided them, returned to the launch: it fell away from the gangway and sped straight towards the wharf. Tossed about by the swell the men, triumphant but anxious, changed costumes: until they reached shore, nothing was certain.

There a stake truck was waiting for them, Kyo sitting beside the driver.

"Well?"

"Nothing. An affair for b'ginners."

The cases were transferred, and the truck drove off, carrying Kyo, Katov and four men, one of whom had kept his uniform. The others dispersed.

73

It rolled through the streets of the Chinese city with a rumble that was drowned at each bump by a rattle of tin: the stakes were lined with gasoline cans. They stopped at every important *ch'on:* shop, cellar, apartment. A case was taken down; stuck on the side, a ciphered note made by Kyo indicated the distribution of the arms, some of which were to be passed on to the secondary combat organizations. The truck would stop barely five minutes at each post for it had to call at more than twenty posts.

They had only treason to fear: the noisy truck, driven by a man in governmental uniform, aroused no suspicion. They met a patrol. "I've become the milk-man making his round," thought Kyo.

Day was dawning.

Part Two

Eleven o'clock in the morning

"THINGS are going badly," thought Ferral.

His car—the only *Voisin* in Shanghai, for the President of the French Chamber of Commerce could not use an American model—was speeding along the quay. To the right, under the vertical banners covered with characters: "*A twelve-hour working day*," "*No more employment of children under eight*," thousands of spinning-mill workers were standing, squatting, lying on the sidewalk in tense disorder. The car passed a group of women who were rallied round a banner—"*Right to sit down for women-workers*." The arsenal itself was empty: the metal workers were on strike. To the left, thousands of sailors in blue rags, without banners, crouched along the stream, waiting. On the quay-side, the crowd of demonstrators filled the side-streets as far as the eye could reach; on the river-side they clung to the landing-stages, concealing the edge of the water.

The car left the quay, swung into the Avenue of the Two Republics. And now it could advance only with difficulty, caught in the seething movement of the Chinese crowd which was bursting from all the streets towards the refuge of the French concession. As one racehorse outdistances another, head, neck, shoulders, the crowd was "closing in" on the car, slowly, steadily. Wheelbarrows with babies' heads sticking out between bowls, Peking carts, rickshaws, small hairy horses, hand-

75

carts, trucks loaded with sixty-odd people, monstrous mattresses piled with a whole household of furniture, bristling with table-legs, giants with cages of blackbirds dangling from the end of their arms which were stretched out to protect tiny women with a litter of children on their backs. . . . The chauffeur was at last able to turn, to get into streets that were still obstructed but where the din of the horn sent the crowd scurrying a few meters ahead of the car. It arrived at the vast headquarters of the French police.

Ferral climbed the stairs almost at a run.

In spite of his slicked-back hair, his informal tweed suit, and his gray silk shirt, his face preserved something of 1900, of his youth. He smiled at people "who disguise themselves as captains of industry," which permitted him to disguise himself as a diplomat: he had relinquished only the monocle. His drooping, almost gray mustache, which seemed to prolong the sagging line of his mouth, gave his profile an expression of refined brutality; its strength was in the combination of his aquiline nose and his jutting chin, badly shaved this morning: the water-service employees were on strike, and the limy water brought by the coolies gave the soap a poor lather. He disappeared in the midst of the bows that greeted him.

At the far end of the office of Martial, the chief of police, a Chinese secret agent—a paternal-looking Hercules—was asking:

"Is that all, Chief?"

"Also, get busy disorganizing the syndicates," answered Martial, whose back was turned. "And what's more, you'll have to snap into it. The work's been rotten. You deserve to be fired: half your men can't be trusted out of sight! I'm not paying you to hire quarter-revolutionaries who don't dare to come out in the open and say what they are: the police is not a factory for furnishing alibis. Fire all agents who traffic with the Kuomintang, and don't let me have to tell you again. And try to understand, instead of looking at me like an idiot! A nice mess it would be if I didn't know my men better than you know yours!"

"Sir . . ."

"That's that. Settled. Classified. Get the hell out of here. How do you do, Monsieur Ferral?"

He turned round: a military face: large, regular and impersonal features, less revealing than his shoulders.

"Hello, Martial. Well?"

"To keep the railroad the government is obliged to take away thousands of men from other duties. You can't hold out against a whole country, unless you have a police like ours at your disposal. The only thing the government can count on is the armored train, with its White officers. That's serious."

"A minority still implies a majority of imbeciles. Well, anyway . . ."

"Everything depends on the front. Here they're going to try to revolt. It's going to be hot for them, maybe, for they're scarcely armed."

Ferral could only listen and wait, which he thoroughly detested. The parleys held by the chiefs of the Anglo-Saxon and Japanese groups, himself, certain consulates, with the go-betweens who filled all the big hotels of the concessions to overflowing, still remained fruitless. This afternoon, perhaps . . .

Once Shanghai was in the hands of the revolutionary army, the Kuomintang would at last have to choose between democracy and Communism. Democracies are always good customers. And a company can make profits without depending on treaties. On the other hand, if the

city became sovietized, the Franco-Asiatic Consortium—
and with it all the French trade in Shanghai—would
crumble away; Ferral was of the opinion that the powers
would abandon their nationals, as England had done at
Hankow. His immediate objective was to prevent the
taking of the city before the arrival of the army, to make
it impossible for the Communists to do anything alone.

"How many troops, Martial, in addition to the armored train?"

"Two thousand police and a brigade of infantry,
Monsieur Ferral."

"And how many revolutionaries who can do something besides talk?"

"A few hundred at the most, who are armed. . . . As
for the others, they're not worth considering. As there's
no military service here, they don't know how to use a
gun, don't forget. In February there were two or three
thousand of those fellows, if you count the Communists. . . . They're no doubt a little more numerous
now."

But in February the government army had not been
destroyed.

"How many will follow them?" Martial went on.
"But you see, Monsieur Ferral, all that doesn't get us
very far. One would have to know the psychology of
the chiefs. . . . I know that of the men pretty well.
The Chinaman, you see . . ."

Ferral was looking at him with an expression he had
seen before—on rare occasions—and which was enough
to silence him: an expression less of contempt, of irritation, than of appraisal. Ferral did not say, in his cutting
and somewhat mechanical voice: "Is this going to last
much longer?" But he expressed it. He could not bear to

have Martial pass off information obtained from his agents as the fruit of his own perspicacity.

If Martial had dared he would have answered: "What difference does it make to you?" He was dominated by Ferral; and his relations with him had been established through orders to which he could only submit. Even as a man he felt him to be superior to himself; but he could not endure his insolent indifference, his way of reducing him to the status of a mechanism, of ignoring him whenever he wanted to speak as an individual and not merely as a transmitter of information. Members of Parliament on missions had told him about Ferral's effectiveness at the Chamber Committees, before his fall. In the sessions he made such use of the qualities that gave his speeches their clearness and their force that his colleagues detested him more and more every year: he had a unique talent for ignoring their existence. Whereas a Jaurès, a Briand, conferred upon them a personal life which, to be sure, they often did not possess, giving the illusion of appealing to each one individually, of wishing to convince them, of involving them in a complicity in which a common experience of life and men united them—Ferral, on the contrary, erected a structure of impersonal facts, and would conclude with: "In view of these conditions, gentlemen, it would thus *obviously* be absurd. . . ." He got his way by force or by money. He had not changed, Martial observed.

"And what about Hankow?" asked Ferral.

"We had reports last night. There are 220,000 unemployed there, enough to make a new Red army. . . ."

For weeks goods from three of the companies controlled by Ferral had been rotting on the sumptuous quays: the coolies refused to transport anything.

79

"What news of the relations between the Communists and Chiang Kai-shek?"

"Here's his last speech," answered Martial. "For my part, you know, I don't believe much in speeches. . . ."

"I believe in them. In these at least. It doesn't matter."

The telephone bell. Martial took the receiver.

"It's for you, Monsieur Ferral."

Ferral sat down on the table.

"Hello? Yes."

". . ."

"He's holding out a club to hit you with. He is hostile to intervention, that's obvious. It's only a question of deciding whether it's better to attack him as a pederast or accuse him of being bought. That's all."

". . ."

"It being perfectly understood that he is neither. Moreover, I don't like to have one of my collaborators believe me capable of attacking a man for a sexual deviation which he might really have. Do you take me for a moralist? Good-by."

Martial did not dare to question him. That Ferral did not keep him posted on his plans, did not tell him what he expected about his secret conferences with the most active members of the International Chamber of Commerce, with the heads of the great associations of Chinese merchants, appeared to him both insulting and short-sighted. On the other hand, if it is annoying for a Chief of Police not to know what he is doing, it is even more annoying to lose his post. Now Ferral, born in the Republic as in the bosom of a family, his memory full of kindly faces of old gentlemen—Renan, Berthelot, Victor Hugo—the son of a great counselor-at-law, an *agrégé* in history at twenty-seven, at twenty-nine the editor of the first collective history of France, a deputy at a very early age (favored by the epoch that had made Poincaré and Barthou ministers before forty), and now President of the Franco-Asiatic Consortium—Ferral, in spite of his political downfall, possessed in Shanghai a power and a prestige at least equal to those of the French Consul-General with whom, moreover, he was on friendly terms. The Chief was therefore respectfully cordial. He handed him the speech:

"I have spent eighteen million dollars in all, and taken six provinces, in five months. Let the malcontents look for another general-in-chief, if they wish, who spends as little and accomplishes as much as I. . . ."

"Obviously the money question would be settled by the taking of Shanghai," said Ferral. "The customs would give him seven million dollars a month, just about what is needed to make up the army deficit. . . ."

"Yes. But they say that Moscow has given the political commissars orders to have their own troops beaten before Shanghai. In that case the insurrection here might end badly. . . ."

"Why those orders?"

"So that Chiang Kai-shek would be beaten, to destroy his prestige, and to replace him by a Communist general to whom the honor of taking Shanghai would then go. It's almost certain that the campaign against Shanghai has been undertaken without the assent of the Central Committee of Hankow. The same informers claim that the Red staff is protesting against this policy. . . ."

Ferral was interested, though skeptical. He continued to read the speech:

"Deserted by a considerable number of its members, the Central Executive Committee of Hankow nevertheless is determined to remain the supreme authority of the Kuomintang Party. . . . I know that Sun Yat-sen ad-

81

mitted the Communists as auxiliaries of the Party. I have done nothing against them, and I have often admired their energy. But now, instead of being content to remain auxiliaries, they set themselves up as masters and violently and insolently aspire to govern the Party. I warn them that I shall oppose these excessive pretensions, which go beyond what was stipulated at the time of their admission. . . ."

It was becoming possible to employ Chiang Kai-shek. The present government *signified* nothing, except by its strength (which it lost by the defeat of its army) and by the fear which the Communists of the revolutionary army inspired in the bourgeoisie. Very few people had any interest in its maintenance. Behind Chiang there was a victorious army, and the whole Chinese petty bourgeoisie.

"Nothing else?" he asked aloud.

"Nothing, Monsieur Ferral."

"Thank you."

He went down the stairs, met half-way down an auburn-haired Minerva in a tailored sport-suit, with superb immobile features. She was a Russian from the Caucasus who was reputed to be Martial's occasional mistress. "I'd like to see the expression on your face when you're making love," he thought.

"Pardon me, Madam."

He passed her with a bow, climbed into his car which began to be swallowed up in the crowd, against the current this time. The horn shrieked in vain, powerless against the force of the exodus, against the seething thousands which invasions stir before them. Petty merchants with their two trays dangling like scales from beams that caught and swung wildly, carts, barrows worthy of the T'ang emperors, invalids, cages. . . . Ferral was advancing in the opposite direction to all those eyes which fear caused to look inward: if his checkered life was to be destroyed, let it be in this uproar, amid this frantic despair that came beating against the windows of his car! Just as he would have meditated upon the meaning of his life had he been wounded, so now that his enterprises were menaced he was meditating upon them. He realized, moreover, where he was vulnerable. He had had too little choice in this combat; he had been obliged to undertake his Chinese affairs to give new outlets to his production in Indo-China. He was playing a waiting game here: he was aiming at France. And he could not wait much longer.

His greatest weakness lay in the absence of a State. The development of such vast affairs was inseparable from governments. Since his youth he had always worked for them: while still in Parliament he had been president of the Society of Electrical Energy and Appliances, which manufactured the electrical equipment of the French State; he had next organized the reconstruction of the port of Buenos Ayres. Possessing the kind of arrogant integrity which refuses commissions and accepts orders, he had looked to the French possessions in Asia for the money he needed after his fall: for he did not intend to play the same game again; he was going to change the rules. In a position to utilize his brother's personal standing, which was superior to his office as director of the *Mouvement Général des Fonds*,[1] Ferral—who had remained at the head of one of the powerful French financial groups—succeeded in getting the General Government of Indo-China to undertake a pro-

[1] A department in the Ministry of Finance charged with the distribution of State funds.

gram of public works involving an expenditure of four hundred million francs. (Even his enemies were not averse to furnishing him means of getting out of France.) The Republic could not refuse the brother of one of her highest officials the management of this civilizing program; it was a great success, and caused surprise in this country in which even big financial ventures are carried on haphazardly.

Ferral knew how to act. A good deed is never lost: the group passed on to the industrialization of Indo-China. Little by little there appeared: two credit establishments (land securities and agricultural loans); four agricultural development associations—rubber, cotton, and sugar plantations and tropical cultures—controlling the immediate conversion of these raw materials into manufactured products; three mining associations: coal, phosphates, gold, and a subsidiary salt-mining enterprise; five industrial firms: light and energy, electricity, glass, paper, printing; three transport companies: barges, tugboats, street cars. At the center, the Public Works Corporation—queen of this vast organization of effort, hatred and paper, mother or midwife of almost all the sister societies engaged in living by profitable incests—was able to obtain the contract for the construction of the Central Annam railroad, whose tracks (who would have thought it?) passed through the greater part of the concessions of the Ferral group. "Things aren't going so badly," the vice-president of the administration council would say to Ferral, who said nothing, busy piling up his millions in steps on which he could climb to a position that would put Paris within his reach.

Even with the project for a new Chinese Company in each pocket, he thought only of Paris. It was his dream to return to France rich enough to buy the *agence*

Havas [1] or to negotiate with it; to get back into the political game and, having cautiously reached the cabinet, to pit the combined forces of the cabinet and a bought public opinion against the Parliament. There lay the power. But today his dreams were out of the question: the rapid growth of his Indo-Chinese enterprises had involved the entire Ferral group in the commercial penetration of the Yangtze basin, Chiang Kai-shek was marching on Shanghai with the revolutionary army, the crowd, more and more dense, was pressing against his doors. There was not a single company owned or controlled in China by the Franco-Asiatic Consortium which was not affected: those for naval constructions, at Hong Kong, by the insecurity of navigation; all the others—public works, constructions, electricity, insurance, banks—by war and the Communist menace. What they imported remained in their warehouses in Hong Kong or Shanghai; what they exported, in their Hankow warehouses, sometimes on the wharves.

The car stopped. The silence—Chinese crowds are usually among the noisiest—seemed to forbode the end of the world. A cannon-shot. The revolutionary army, so near? No: it was the noon-day cannon. The crowd scattered: the car did not move. Ferral seized the speaking-tube. No answer: the chauffeur, the valet were gone.

He remained motionless—stupefied—in the motionless car which the crowd circled clumsily. The nearest shopkeeper came out, carrying on his shoulder an enormous shutter; he turned round, nearly smashed one of the glass panes of the car: he was closing his shop. To the right, to the left, ahead of him, other shopkeepers, other artisans came out, with shutters covered with characters on their shoulders. The general strike was beginning.

[1] The leading French news-gathering and publicity syndicate.

This time it was not the Hong Kong strike, slowly set under way, epic, dismal: it was an army maneuver. As far as his eye could reach there was not a shop remaining open. He must leave as quickly as possible; he got out, called a rickshaw. The coolie did not answer him: he was running at top speed for shelter, almost alone on the street, now, with the abandoned car: the crowd had just surged back towards the sidewalks. "They're afraid of the machine-guns," thought Ferral. The children, no longer playing, were scurrying between legs, through the swarming agitation of the sidewalks. A silence full of lives at once remote and very near, like that of a forest saturated with insects; the siren of a cruiser rose, then became lost. Ferral walked towards his house as fast as he could, hands in pockets, shoulders and chin thrust forward. Two sirens took up in unison, an octave higher, the cry of the one that had just died down, as if some enormous creature, enveloped in this silence, were thus announcing its coming. The entire city was on guard.

One o'clock in the afternoon

"Five minutes to," said Ch'en.

The men of his group were waiting. They were all spinning-mill workers, clad in blue denim; he wore their garb. All of them shaved, all lean, all vigorous: before Ch'en, death had made its selection. Two were holding rifles under one arm, the barrels towards the ground. Seven carried revolvers from the *Shantung*; one, a grenade; a few others had some hidden in their pockets. About thirty held knives, clubs, bayonets; eight or ten, without weapons, were crouched beside piles of rags, kerosene cans, rolls of wire. An adolescent was examin-

86

ing large broad-headed tacks which he pulled out of a sack as though they were seeds: "Surely longer than horse-shoes. . . ." A Court of Miracles,[1] but composed of men united by a bond of hatred and decision.

He was not one of them. In spite of the murder, in spite of his presence. If he were to die today, he would die alone. For them everything was simple: they were going forth to conquer their bread and their dignity. For him . . . he did not even know how to speak to them, except of their pain and of their common battle At least he knew that the strongest of bonds is battle. And the battle was here.

They got up, sacks on their backs, cans in their hands, wire under their arms. It was not yet raining; the gloom of this empty street which a dog crossed in two leaps, as if some instinct had warned him of what was impending, was as deep as the silence. Five shots went off in a nearby street: three together, another, still another. "It's starting," said Ch'en. The silence returned, but it no longer seemed to be the same. Suddenly it was filled by the clatter of horses' hoofs, hurried, coming nearer and nearer. And, like the vertical laceration of lightning after a prolonged thunder, while they still saw nothing, a tumult suddenly filled the street, composed of mingled cries, shots, furious whinnyings, the falling of bodies; then, as the subsiding clamor was heavily choking under the indestructible silence, there rose a cry as of a dog howling lugubriously, cut short: a man with his throat slashed.

At a run they quickly reached a more important street. All the shops were closed. On the ground, three

[1] A quarter of old Paris, between the rue Réaumur and rue du Caire; it served as a retreat for beggars, vagabonds and outlaws who filled the capital in the Middle Ages.

bodies; above, streaked with telegraph wires, the restless sky darkened by clouds of black smoke; at the end of the street, some twenty horsemen (there was very little cavalry at Shanghai) were turning hesitantly, not seeing the insurgents clinging to the wall with their instruments, their glance fixed on the hesitant movements of the horses. Ch'en could not think of attacking them: his men were too poorly armed. The insurgents turned to the right, finally reached a police station: the sentinels, without a word, followed Ch'en in.

The policemen were playing cards. Their guns and Mausers were in the rack. The non-commissioned officer in command opened a window, shouted into a dark court:

"All you who hear me are witness to the violence which is being done us. You see that we are obliged to yield to force!"

He was going to shut the window again; Ch'en held it open, looked: no one in the court. But appearances had been saved, and the theatrical gesture had been made at the right moment. Ch'en knew his compatriots: since this fellow was "playing the part," he would not act. He distributed the arms among his men. The rioters left, all armed this time: useless to occupy the small disarmed police-stations. The policemen hesitated. Three got up and wanted to follow them. (Perhaps there would be plunder . . .) Ch'en had difficulty in getting rid of them. The others picked up the cards and went on playing.

"If they win," said one, "perhaps we'll get paid this month?"

"Perhaps," answered the non-commissioned officer. He dealt the cards.

"But if they're beaten, perhaps we'll be accused of treason."

"What could we have done? We yielded to force. We are all witnesses that we did not betray."

They were reflecting, their necks drawn in—cormorants crushed by thought.

"We are not responsible," said one.

All approved. They got up nevertheless and went to continue their game in a neighboring shop, the proprietor not daring to put them out. Only a pile of uniforms remained in the center of the station.

Elated and wary, Ch'en, followed by his men, was walking towards one of the central posts: "All is well," he was thinking, "but those men are almost as poor as we . . ." The White Russians and the soldiers of the armored train would certainly fight. The officers too. Distant explosions, muffled as though the low sky had weakened them, were beating the air near the center of the city.

At a street-crossing, the troop—all the men armed now, even those carrying the cans—hesitated a moment, looked about. From the cruisers and the steamships unable to discharge their cargoes rose the oblique masses of smoke which the heavy wind scattered in the direction of the insurgents' path, as if the sky were participating in the insurrection. The next station was an old red brick building, two stories high; there were two sentinels, one on each side of the door, bayonets fixed to their rifles. Ch'en knew that the special police had been on the alert for three days, and that their men were worn out by the uninterrupted vigil. There were officers here, some fifty Mauserists of the police—well paid—and ten soldiers. To live, to live at least through

89

the next week! Ch'en had stopped at the corner of the street. The arms were no doubt in the racks on the ground-floor, in the right-hand room, the guard-room, which led to the office of an officer; Ch'en and two of his men had gone in there several times during the week. He chose ten men without guns, made them hide the revolvers in their blouses, and advanced with them. Once beyond the corner, the sentinels watched them approach. As they were suspicious of everyone, they had ceased to be suspicious of anyone in particular; workers' delegations often came to parley with the officer, usually to bring him tips, an operation which required many guarantees and persons.

"To see Lieutenant Sui T'un," said Ch'en.

While eight men were passing, the two last, as if pushed in the slight shuffle, slipped between the sentinels and the wall. By the time the first ones were in the hall, the sentinels felt the muzzles of revolvers in their sides. They let themselves be disarmed: they were better paid than their wretched fellow-policemen, but not sufficiently to risk their lives. Four of Ch'en's men who had not joined the first group and who seemed to be passing in the street, led them away along the wall. Nothing had been visible from the windows.

From the hall Ch'en could see the racks filled with rifles. In the guard-room there were only six policemen armed with automatics, and those weapons were on their belts, in closed holsters. He threw himself in front of the racks, revolver held out.

If the police had been resolute, the attack would have failed. In spite of his detailed acquaintance with the places where he was to operate, Ch'en had not had time to designate to each of his men the one he was to cover with his gun; one or two of the police could have fired.

But all put up their hands. They were immediately disarmed. A new group of Ch'en's men entered. A new distribution of arms began.

"At this moment," Ch'en was thinking, "two hundred groups in the city are doing what we are doing. If they all have as good luck . . ." Hardly had he taken the third gun when he heard the sound of a headlong dash coming from the stairway: someone was running up the stairs. He went out. The moment he passed the doorway a shot was fired from the floor above. Nothing more at the head of the stairs. One of the officers, upon coming down, had seen the insurgents, fired, and immediately regained the second story.

The fighting was about to begin.

A door, in the center of the second-story landing, commanded the stairway. Send a spokesman, Asiatic-fashion? Ch'en hated all the Chinese good sense which he recognized in himself. Attempt to take the stairs by force?—as well commit suicide: the police no doubt had a supply of hand-grenades. The instructions of the military committee, transmitted by Kyo to all the groups, were to set fire in case of partial failure, to take position in the adjoining buildings, and to call the special squads for help. There was nothing else to do.

"Set fire!"

The men with the cans tried to pour out the oil in splashes like water out of a bucket, but the narrow openings only squirted derisive little jets. They were obliged to pour it slowly, on the furniture, along the walls. Ch'en looked through the window: opposite, closed shops, narrow windows commanding the exit from the station; above, the rotten curled-up roofs of Chinese houses, and the infinite calm of the gray sky now no longer streaked with smoke, of the intimate low sky on the empty street.

All fighting was absurd, nothing existed in the face of life; he caught himself just in time to see panes and window-frames tumble down, in a crystalline crash mingled with the sound of a volley of gunfire: they were being fired on from outside.

A second volley. They were now—in the room saturated with oil—between the police, who were on the alert and masters of the upper story, and the new assailants whom they could not see. All Ch'en's men were flat on their bellies, the prisoners bound in one corner. If a grenade exploded they would be consumed in flames. One of the prostrate men grunted, pointing with his finger: a skirmisher on a roof; and to the extreme left of the window, gliding into the field of vision, other irregulars were cautiously advancing, one shoulder held back. They were insurgents, their own men.

The idiots fire before sending out scouts, thought Ch'en. He had the blue flag of the Kuomintang in his pocket. He pulled it out, rushed out into the hall. The moment he was crossing the threshold he received a violent muffled blow in the back, while at the same time a formidable crash seemed to go right through him. He threw back his arms wildly, to get his balance, and found himself on the floor, half stunned. Not a sound; then, a metal object fell, and at the same time loud groans followed the smoke into the hall. He got up again: he was not wounded. He half shut the door opened by the incomprehensible explosion, held out his flag, with his left hand, through the open space. A bullet in his hand would not have surprised him. But no: there were shouts of joy. The smoke which was slowly pouring through the window prevented him from seeing the insurgents on the left; but those on the right were calling to him.

A second explosion almost knocked him down again.

From the windows of the second story the besieged policemen were throwing hand-grenades. (How could they open the windows without being fired on from the street?) The first, the one that had thrown him down, had exploded in front of the house, and the fragments had flown in through the open doorway and the shattered window, as if it had exploded in the guard-room itself; terrified by the explosion, those of his men who had not been killed had jumped out, inadequately shielded by the smoke. Under the fire of the policemen at the windows, two had fallen in the middle of the street, their knees doubled against their chests, like hunched-up rabbits; another, with his face in a pool of blood, seemed to be bleeding from the nose. The irregulars had recognized their own men; but the gesture of those who were calling Ch'en had been a signal to the officers that someone was coming out, and they had thrown their second grenade. It had exploded in the street, to Ch'en's left: the wall had protected him.

From the hall, he examined the guard-room. The smoke was slowly curling down again from the ceiling. There were bodies on the floor. Moans filled the room. In the corner, one of the prisoners, a leg torn off, was shrieking: "Stop firing!" His panting cries seemed to pierce holes in the smoke which continued its indifferent curve above the suffering, like a visible fatality. That man who was shrieking, with his leg torn off, could not remain with his hands tied behind his back. Yet wouldn't another grenade explode, at any moment? "It's none of my business," thought Ch'en, "he's an enemy." But with a hole of flesh at the end of his thigh instead of a leg, with his hands tightly bound, the feeling he experienced was much stronger than pity: he himself was that man bound hand and foot. "If the grenade explodes outside,

I'll throw myself on the ground; if it rolls here, I'll have to toss it outside right away. One chance out of twenty of getting away. What in hell am I doing here? What in hell am I doing here?" To be killed—that didn't matter much. What agonized him was the thought of being wounded in the stomach; yet this fear was less intolerable than the sight of that bound and tortured creature, of human powerlessness in suffering. Unable to do otherwise, he went towards the man, his knife in his hand, to cut his cords. The prisoner thought he was coming to kill him; he wanted to shriek still louder: his voice weakened, became a wheeze. Saturated with horror, Ch'en touched him with his left hand which stuck to the clothes drenched with sticky blood, unable however to take his eyes off the shattered window through which the grenade might fall. At last he felt the cords, slipped the knife underneath, cut them. The man no longer screamed: he had died or fainted. Ch'en, his eyes still fixed on the jagged window, returned to the hall. The change of smell surprised him; as though he had just begun to hear, he realized that the groans of the wounded had become shrieks: in the room, the débris saturated with oil, set on fire by the grenades, was beginning to burn.

No water. Before the insurgents could take the station the wounded (now the prisoners no longer counted: he could only think of his own) would be burned to ashes. . . . Out, out! First of all, think, and thereafter make the fewest possible moves. Although he was trembling, his mind fascinated by the idea of escape was not without lucidity: he had to go to the left, where a covered porch would protect him. He opened the door with his right hand, the left raised in a signal of silence. The enemy above could not see him; the attitude of the insurgents alone could have warned them. He felt the eyes of all his men centered on this open door, on his squat figure, blue against the dark background of the hall. He began to sidle to the left, his back brushing the wall, arms crossed, his revolver in his right hand. Advancing step by step, he kept looking at the windows above him: one was protected by an iron plate placed as a screen. In vain the insurgents fired on the windows. The grenades were being thrown over the screen. "When they start throwing again I'll see the grenade and I'll surely see the arm," thought Ch'en, still advancing. "If I see it, I must catch it like a package, and throw it again as far as possible. . . ." He did not cease his crab-like walk. "I won't be able to throw it far enough: if I'm not protected I'll get a handful of shot in the stomach. . . ." He was still advancing. The strong burnt smell, and the sudden absence of support behind him (he did not turn round) told him he was in front of the window of the ground floor. "If I catch the grenade, I'll throw it into the guard-room before it explodes. With the thickness of the wall, by getting beyond the window, I'm saved." What did it matter that the guard-room was not empty, that the very man whose cords he had cut was there— and his own wounded? He did not see the insurgents, not even through the clearings in the smoke, for he could not take his eyes from the screen; but he could still feel the eyes trying to see *him:* in spite of the firing directed at the windows, which handicapped the officers, he was amazed that they did not understand that something was going on. It suddenly occurred to him that they had only a small supply of grenades and that they looked before throwing them; immediately, as though the idea were born of some shadow, a head appeared under the screen—hidden to the insurgents, but not to him. Frantically, abandoning his tight-rope walker's posture, he fired with an instantaneous aim, bounded ahead, reached the porch. A volley went off from the windows, a grenade exploded at the spot he had just left: the officer, whom he had missed when he fired, had hesitated before passing his hand holding the grenade under the screen, fearing a second shot. Ch'en had received a blow in the left arm: nothing but air-pressure from one of the explosions. But the wound he had inflicted on himself with the dagger, before killing Tang Yen Ta, was sensitive and was bleeding again, though it did not hurt. Making the bandage tighter with a handkerchief, he joined the insurgents by way of the courts.

Those who were directing the attack were assembled in a dark passage.

"You couldn't send scouts, could you!"

The leader of the *ch'on*, a tall shaved Chinaman, whose sleeves were too short, watched his approaching shadow, slowly raised his eyelids, resigned:

"I had someone telephone," was all he said. Then added: "Now we're waiting for an armored truck."

"How are the other sections getting along?"

"We've taken half the stations."

"Not more?"

"That's pretty good for a start."

All that distant gunfiring came from their men who were converging towards the North Station.

Ch'en was panting, as though he had just come out of the water into a strong wind. He leaned against the wall, the angle of which protected them all, getting back his wind by degrees, thinking of the prisoner whose ropes he had cut. "I should have left the fellow alone. Why did I go and cut the rope? It couldn't make any difference." But he knew that he could not have done otherwise, that even now he would not react differently to that man with his leg cut off, helplessly struggling. Because of his wound, he thought of Tang Yen Ta. What a fool he had been all last night, all this morning! Nothing was easier than to kill.

In the station, the débris was still burning, the wounded were still shrieking before the approaching flames; their repeated, constant clamor reverberated in this low passage, rendered extraordinarily near by the remoteness of the detonations, of the sirens, of all the sounds of war lost in the dismal air. A distant metallic rumble became audible, drew nearer, submerged those other sounds: the truck was arriving. It had been converted into an armored truck overnight, very hastily: the plates were inadequately joined. The brakes were applied, the clatter ceased, and the cries could be heard again.

Ch'en, who was the only one to have entered the station, explained the situation to the chief of the rescue squad. He was a former Whampoa cadet; Ch'en would have preferred one of Katov's groups to this squad of young bourgeois. If it was true that he did not succeed in feeling an absolute bond between himself and his men, even before those dead comrades huddled up in the middle of the street, he knew that at all times he hated the Chinese bourgeoisie; the proletariat was at least the form of his hope.

The officer knew his business. "The truck's no use," he said, "it hasn't even a top. All they have to do is throw a grenade inside to blow up the whole business; but I've brought some grenades too." Those of Ch'en's men who carried them were in the guard-room—dead?—and the second group had not been able to get hold of any.

"Let's try from above."

"Agreed," said Ch'en.

97

The officer looked at him with irritation: he had not asked for his opinion; but he said nothing. Both of them —he, a soldier, in spite of his civilian clothes, with his bristling hair, his close-trimmed mustache, his blouse gathered under his revolver-belt; and Ch'en, squat and blue—examined the station. To the right of the door the smoke from the flames which were crawling ever closer to the bodies of their wounded comrades issued forth with a mechanical regularity, like their cries, whose constancy would have seemed childish but for their agonizing tone. To the left, nothing. The windows of the second story were veiled in smoke. From time to time an assailant still fired at one of the windows, and bits of wreckage sprinkled down to increase the dusty pile of plaster, splinters, sticks, in which pieces of glass glistened in spite of the dull light. Now the station was firing only when one of the insurgents left his hiding-place.

"How are the other sections doing?" Ch'en asked again.

"Almost all the stations have been taken. The main station, by surprise, at one-thirty. We seized eight hundred guns there. We can already send reënforcements against those who resist: you're the third squad we have helped. They are not getting any more reënforcements; we have already blocked the barracks, the South Station, the arsenal. But we have to get through here: we need all the men we have for the attack. And there will still be the armored train."

The idea of the two hundred groups engaged in the same activity as his own both exalted and disturbed Ch'en. In spite of the gunfiring which the listless wind brought from the entire city, violence gave him the sensation of solitary activity.

A man pulled a bicycle from inside the truck, and left.

Ch'en recognized him as he was getting on: Ma, one of the principal agitators. He was going to make a report of the situation to the Military Committee. A typographer, who had devoted his whole life, since the age of twelve, to creating Unions of printshop workers everywhere, with the hope of organizing all Chinese typographers; tried, condemned to death, a fugitive, still organizing. Shouts of joy: the men had recognized him at the same moment as Ch'en, and were acclaiming him. He looked at them. The world they were preparing condemned him—Ch'en—as much as did that of their enemies. What would he do in the factory of the future that lay hidden behind their blue blouses?

The officer distributed grenades, and ten men went up along the roofs to take position on the station-roof. They were going to give the police a dose of their own medicine, throw the explosives in through the windows: these commanded the street but not the roof, and only one was protected by a screen. The insurgents advanced from roof to roof, elongated silhouettes against the sky. The station kept up a steady fire. As if the dying alone had divined this approach, their cries suddenly changed, became moans. Now they could hardly be heard; they were the stifled cries of half-mutes. The silhouettes reached the ridge of the steep station-roof, slowly crawled down; it was harder for Ch'en to make them out now that they no longer stood out against the sky. A guttural shriek, like that of a woman in the agony of childbirth, cut across the groans, which continued like an echo, and then died away.

Despite the general commotion the sudden cessation of cries gave the impression of a sinister silence: had the flames reached the wounded? Ch'en and the officer looked at each other, shut their eyes in order to hear better. Each, upon reopening his eyes, met the silent look of the other.

One of the men, clinging to an ornament of the cornice, raised his free arm over the street, threw his grenade towards the window of the second story just below him. Too low: it exploded on the sidewalk. He threw a second one: it landed in the room where the wounded were. Yells burst from the window that had been hit; no longer the same cries, but the piercing shrieks of men in the convulsions of death, the outbursts of inexhaustible suffering. The man threw his third grenade and again missed the window.

He was one of the men who had come in the truck. He had deftly thrown himself back, through fear of the explosion. He was bending over again, his lifted arm holding a fourth grenade. Behind him one of Ch'en's men was crawling down. The arm was never lowered: he was suddenly swept off the roof, and a moment later a violent explosion resounded on the sidewalk; through the smoke, a splash of blood a yard wide appeared on the wall. The smoke lifted: the wall was spattered with blood and shreds of flesh. The second insurgent, losing his hold and sliding down the roof with his full weight, had knocked the first man off. Both had fallen on their own grenades, from which they had pulled the pins.

From the other side of the roof, at the left, men of the two groups—Kuomintang bourgeois and Communist workers—were cautiously approaching. When the fall occurred they had halted: now they were beginning again to crawl down. The February repression had been attended by too many tortures to allow the insurrection to fail through lack of resolute men. From the right, other men were approaching. "Make a chain!" Ch'en shouted from below. Insurgents close to the station repeated the order. The men held one another by the hand, the top one taking a strong hold with his left arm on a solid roof-ornament. The throwing of the grenades was resumed. The besieged could not fire back.

Within five minutes, three grenades entered through two of the windows aimed at; another blew up the iron-plate screen. Only the center one had not been hit. "Now to the center one!" shouted the cadet. Ch'en looked at him. For him commanding was a sport, and he gave himself over to it with a joyous enthusiasm. He scarcely protected himself. He was brave, beyond a doubt, but he was not attached to his men. Ch'en was attached to his, but not enough.

Not enough.

He left the cadet, crossed the street beyond the range of the police fire. He climbed up on the roof. The man who was holding on to the ridge was weakening: Ch'en took his place. Even there, with his wounded arm locked round the cement and plaster ornament, his right hand holding the hand of the first man on the chain, he did not escape his solitude. The weight of three sliding men was suspended from his arm; it passed through his chest like an iron bar. The grenades were bursting inside the station, which had ceased firing. "We are protected by the attic," he thought to himself, "but not for long. The roof will blow up." In spite of the intimacy of death, in spite of that fraternal weight which was pulling him apart, he was not one of them. "Is even blood futile?"

The cadet, down there, was looking at him without understanding. One of the men who had come up behind Ch'en offered to take his place.

"All right. I'll throw the grenades myself."

He passed him the chain of bodies. In his stretched muscles rose a limitless despair. His hawk-like face with its narrow eyes was tense, absolutely motionless; with stupefaction he felt a tear roll down his nose. "Nervousness," he thought. He pulled a grenade from his pocket, began to descend by hooking himself to the arms of the men forming the chain. But the chain was suspended from one of the ornaments which capped the roof at either end. From there it was almost impossible to reach the center window. Reaching the edge of the roof, Ch'en let go the arm of the grenade-thrower, clung to his leg, then to the eaves, swung over the edge and down by means of a drain-pipe: though he was too far from the window to reach it, he was near enough to throw. His comrades no longer stirred. Above the ground-floor a projection gave him footing. He was astonished that his wound hurt him so little. With his left hand holding on to one of the clamps which secured the drain-pipe, he gauged the weight of his first grenade: "If it falls in the street, under me, I'm as good as dead." He hurled it with as much force as his position permitted: it entered, exploded in the interior.

Below, the shooting began again.

Through the station doorway which had remained open, the policemen, driven from the last room, rushed out in a blind stampede, firing at random. From the roofs, from the porches, from the windows, the insurgents were shooting them down. The bodies fell one after another, numerous near the doorway, then more and more scattered.

The firing ceased. Ch'en climbed down, still clinging to his drain-pipe: he could not see his feet, and landed on a body.

The cadet was entering the station. He followed him, pulling from his pocket the grenade which he had not thrown. At each step he became more acutely conscious that the wails of the wounded had ceased. In the guard-room, nothing but corpses. The wounded were charred. On the second story, more dead, a few wounded.

"And now, to the South Station," said the officer. "Let's take all the guns: other groups will need them."

The arms were carried to the truck; when they had all been collected, the men hoisted themselves up on the machine, stood tightly packed, sat on the hood, clustered on the running-boards, clung to the rear. Those who were unable to ride started off by way of the alley at a rapid pace. The great abandoned splotch of blood on the wall seemed inexplicable in the deserted street; at the corner the truck, bristling with men, with its accompaniment of rattling iron, vanished towards the South Station and the barracks.

It was soon forced to stop: the street was blocked by four dead horses, and three corpses, already disarmed. They were those of the cavalry men Ch'en had seen at the beginning of the day: the first armored car had arrived in time. On the ground, broken window-glass, but nothing living except an old Chinaman with a beard like a paint-brush, who was moaning. He spoke distinctly as soon as Ch'en approached:

"It is a very unjust thing and very sad! Four! Four! Alas!"

"Only three," said Ch'en.

"Four, alas!"

Ch'en looked again: there were only three corpses—one on its side as though casually thrown there, two on their bellies—between the two rows of houses, dead too, under the heavy sky.

"I'm talking about the horses," said the old man, with contempt and fear: Ch'en was holding his revolver.

"I was talking of the men. One of the horses belonged to you?"

No doubt they had been requisitioned that morning.

"No. But I used to be a coachman. I know animals. Four killed! And for nothing!"

The driver of the truck stepped up:

"For nothing?"

"Let's not waste time," said Ch'en.

With the help of two men he dragged the horses to one side. The truck went on. At the end of the street Ch'en, seated on one of the running-boards, looked back: the old coachman was still among the corpses, moaning, no doubt, a black figure in the gray street.

Five o'clock in the afternoon

"The South Station has fallen."

Ferral hung up the receiver. While he was keeping appointments (the International Chamber of Commerce was hostile to all intervention, but he controlled the greatest newspaper in Shanghai) the progress of the insurrection was striking him blow after blow. He had wanted to be alone at the telephone. He came back into his studio, where Martial, who had just arrived, was arguing with Chiang Kai-shek's envoy: the latter had been unwilling to meet the Chief of Police either at police headquarters or at his home. Even before opening the door, Ferral overheard, in spite of the gun-fire:

"Now what do *I* represent here?—French interests . . ."

"But what support can I promise?" answered the Chinaman in a tone of nonchalant insistence. "The Consul-General himself tells me to await de-tails from you.

Because you know our country, and its people, very well."

The studio telephone rang.

"*The Municipal Council has fallen,*" said Martial.

And, changing his tone:

"I'm not saying that I don't have a certain psychological understanding of this country, and of men in general. Psychology and action, that's my job; and on the basis . . ."

"But if persons who are as dangerous to your country as they are to ours, dangerous to the peace of civilizati-on, seek refuge, as they always do, in the concession? The internati-onal police . . ."

"That's what he's after," thought Ferral, who was entering. "He wants to know if Martial, in case of a breaking-off of relations, would allow the Communist leaders to find refuge with us."

". . . have promised us their unqualified goodwill. . . . What will the French police do?"

"We'll take care of it. But watch out for this: no monkey-business with white women, except Russian ones. I have strict orders about that. But, as I told you: nothing official. Nothing official."

In the modern studio—on the walls, Picassos of the rose period, and an erotic Fragonard sketch—the two men were standing on either side of a very large Kuan Yin in black stone of the T'ang dynasty, bought on Clappique's advice and which Gisors believed to be false. The Chinaman, a young colonel with a curved nose, in civilian clothes, buttoned up to the neck, was looking at Martial and smiling, his head bent back.

"I thank you in the name of my party. . . . The Communists are very treacherous—they are betray-ing us, their faithful allies. It was understood that we would collaborate together, and that the soci-al questi-on would be put forward only when China was united. And already they are putting it forward. They do not respect our contract. They do not want to build up China, but the Soviets. The army's dead did not die for the Soviets, but for China. The Communists are capable of anything. And that is why I must ask you, Monsieur le Directeur, if the French police would have any objecti-on to thinking of the personal safety of the General."

It was clear that he had asked the same service of the international police.

"Gladly," answered Martial. "Send the chief of your police to me. Is it still König?"

"Still. Tell me, Monsieur le Directeur: have you studied Roman history?"

"Naturally."

"At night-school," thought Ferral.

The telephone again. Martial took the receiver.

"*The bridges have been taken,*" he said as he put it back. "In a quarter of an hour the insurrection will be occupying the city."

"My opinion," the Chinaman went on as if he had not heard, "is that the Roman Empire was destroyed through moral corrupti-on. Don't you believe that a technical organizati-on of prostituti-on, an occidental organizati-on, like that of the police, would make it possible to get the better of the Hankow chiefs, who are not comparable to those of the Roman Empire?"

"It's an idea . . . but I don't think it's practical. It requires a good deal of thought. . . ."

"Europeans never understand anything of China that does not resemble themselves."

A silence. Ferral was amused. The Chinaman intrigued him: that head thrown back, almost disdainful, and at

106

the same time, that embarrassment. . . . "Hankow flooded by streams of prostitutes . . ." he thought. "And he knows the Communists. And the possibility that he may have some knowledge of political economy is not excluded. Astonishing!" While soviets were perhaps being organized in the city, this fellow was dreaming of the artful precepts of the Roman Empire. "Gisors is right, they're always trying to find tricks."

Again the telephone:

"*The barracks are surrounded*," said Martial. "The reenforcements from the government have stopped coming."

"The North Station?" asked Ferral.

"Not yet taken."

"Then the government can recall troops from the front?"

"Perhaps, sir," said the Chinaman; "its troops and tanks are falling back on Nanking. It may send some here. The armored train can still give serious battle."

"Yes, it will hold its own in the vicinity of the train and the station," Martial went on. "Everything they have taken is immediately organized; the insurrection surely has Russian or European cadres; the revolutionary employees of each administration guide the insurgents. There is a military committee directing the whole thing. The entire police is disarmed now. The Reds have rallying points, from which the troops are directed against the barracks."

"The Chinese have a great sense of organization," said the officer.

"How is Chiang Kai-shek protected?"

"His car is always preceded by that of his personal guard. And we have our secret agents."

Ferral at last understood the reason for the disdainful

angle of the Chinaman's head, which was beginning to annoy him (at first it had seemed to him that the officer was continually looking over Martial's head at his erotic sketch): a white spot on his right eye obliged the officer to look downward.

"Not enough," answered Martial. "Have to do something about that. The sooner the better. Now, I have to run along: there's the matter of electing the Executive Committee which will take the government in hand. I may be able to do something there. Also the matter of the election of the prefect, which is not to be overlooked. . . ."

Ferral and the officer remained alone.

"So, Monsieur," said the Chinaman, his head back, "from now on we can count on you?"

"Liu Ti Yu is waiting," he answered.

Chief of the Shanghai Bankers' Association, honorary president of the Chinese Chamber of Commerce, linked with all the guild-masters, this man was in a position to act in the Chinese city, which the insurgent sections were no doubt beginning to occupy—to act even more effectively than Ferral in the concessions. The officer bowed and took his leave. Ferral went up to the second story. In one corner of a modern office everywhere adorned with sculptures of the best periods of Chinese art, Liu Ti Yu was waiting. He wore a white linen suit over a collarless sweater that was as white as his bristling hair. His hands seemed glued to the nickeled tubes of his armchair. His face was all mouth and jaw—an energetic old frog.

Ferral did not sit down.

"You are determined to have done with the Communists." He was not asking, he was affirming. "We too, obviously." He began to walk back and forth, shoulders thrust forward. "Chiang Kai-shek is ready for the break."

Ferral had never encountered suspicion on the face of a Chinaman. Did this fellow believe him? He handed him a box of cigarettes. This box, since he had decided to give up smoking, was always open on his desk, as if the constant sight of it affirmed the strength of his character, confirming him in his decision.

"We have to help Chiang Kai-shek. For you it's a matter of life or death. We cannot allow the present situation to continue. Behind the army, in the rural districts, the Communists are beginning to organize the peasant Unions. The first decree of the Unions will be the expropriation of the creditors. (Ferral did not use the word usurers.) An enormous proportion of your capital is invested in the country, the best part of your bank deposits is guaranteed by land. The peasant soviets . . ."

"The Communists won't dare to form soviets in China."

"Let's not play on words, Mr. Liu. Whether you call them unions or soviets, the Communist organizations are going to nationalize the land, and declare credits illegal. Those two measures wipe out the essential part of the guarantees on the basis of which you have obtained foreign credits. More than a billion dollars, counting my Japanese and American friends. It's out of the question to offer a paralyzed commerce as a guarantee for this sum. And without even mentioning our credits, those decrees alone are enough to break every bank in China. Obviously."

"The Kuomintang won't allow it."

"There is no Kuomintang. There are the Blues and the Reds. They have gotten along so far—though badly— because Chiang Kai-shek had no money. Once Shanghai is taken—tomorrow—Chiang Kai-shek can almost pay his army with the customs. Not quite. He counts on us. Everywhere the Communists have preached the seizure of lands. It is said that they are trying to put it off: too late. The peasants have heard their speeches, and they are not members of their party. They'll do as they please."

"Nothing can stop the peasants, except force. I have already said so to the Consul-General of Great Britain."

Recognizing almost the tone of his own voice in that of his listener, Ferral had the impression that he was winning him over.

"They have already tried to seize lands. Chiang-Kai-shek is determined not to let them. He has given the order that none of the lands belonging to officers or to relatives of officers must be touched. We must . . ."

"We are all relatives of officers." Liu smiled. "Is there a single piece of land in China whose owner is not the relative of an officer? . . ."

Ferral knew the Chinese family relationships.

Again the telephone.

"*The arsenal is surrounded*," said Ferral. "All the governmental cantonments have been taken. The revolutionary army will be in Shanghai tomorrow. The matter has to be settled *now*. Mark my word. As a result of the Communist propaganda, numerous lands have been taken away from their proprietors; Chiang Kai-shek must either accept this fact or give orders to put to death those who have taken them. The Red government of Hankow cannot accept such orders."

"He will temporize."

"You know what happened to the stocks of the English companies after the taking of the English concession of Hankow. You know what your situation will be when lands, no matter what they are, have been legally torn from their owners. Chiang Kai-shek knows, and says he is obliged to break *now*. Will you help him, yes or no?"

Liu spat, his head sunk into his shoulders. He shut his eyes, opened them again, looked at Ferral with the sly eyes of an old usurer:

"How much?"

"Fifty million dollars."

He spat again.

"Just from us?"

"Yes."

He shut his eyes once more. Above the splitting noise of the firing, shots from the armored train could be heard at minute intervals.

If Liu's friends made up their minds to help Chiang, it would still be necessary to fight; if they did not decide, Communism would no doubt triumph in China. "This is one of the moments when the world's destiny hangs in the balance . . ." thought Ferral, with a pride in which there was both exaltation and indifference. His eyes did not leave his interlocutor. The old man, his eyes shut, seemed to be asleep; but on the backs of his hands the blue, corded veins quivered like nerves. "A personal argument might be necessary," thought Ferral.

"Chiang Kai-shek," he said, "cannot let his officers be despoiled. And the Communists are determined to assassinate him. He knows it."

It had been rumored for several days, but Ferral doubted it.

"How much time have we?" asked Liu. And immediately, with one eye shut, the other open, cunning on the right, shamefaced on the left:

"Are you sure he won't take the money without executing his promises?"

"There is also *our* money, and there is no question of promises. He *cannot do otherwise*. And mark my word: it's not because you pay him that he is going to destroy the Communists: it's because he is going to destroy the Communists that you pay him."

"I shall call my friends together."

Ferral knew the Chinese custom, and the influence of the one who speaks.

"What will be your advice?"

"Chiang Kai-shek may be beaten by the people of Hankow. There are two hundred thousand unemployed there."

"If we don't help him he will surely be beaten."

"Fifty million. . . . It is . . . a great deal. . . ."

He finally looked straight at Ferral.

"Less than you will be obliged to give a Communist government."

The telephone.

"*The armored train has been cut off*," Ferral went on. "Even if the government wants to recall troops from the front, it is now powerless."

He held out his hand.

Liu shook it, left the room. From the vast window full of shreds of clouds Ferral watched the car disappear, the roar of the motor drowning out the volleys for a moment. Even if he were victor, the state of his enterprises would perhaps oblige him to ask for help from the French government which so often refused it, which had just refused it to the Industrial Bank of China; but to-day he was among those through whom the fate of Shanghai was being decided. All the economic forces, almost all the consulates were playing the same game as he: Liu would pay. The armored train was still firing. Yes, for the first time, there was an organization on the other side. He would like to know the men who were directing it. To have them shot, too.

The evening of war was vanishing into the night. Below, lights were appearing, and the invisible river was drawing to itself, as always, what little life remained in the city. It came from Hankow, that river. Liu was right, and Ferral knew it: there lay the danger. There the Red army was being formed. There the Communists dominated. Since the revolutionaries, like a snow-plow, had thrown off the Northerners, all the Left dreamed of that promised land: the home of the Revolution was in the greenish shadow of those foundries, of those arsenals, even before it had taken them; now it possessed them and those wretched marchers who were disappearing out of sight in the slimy mist where the lanterns became more and more numerous were all advancing in the same direction as the river, as if they too had all come from Hankow with their ravaged faces—omens driven towards him by the menacing night.

Eleven o'clock. Since Liu's departure, before and after dinner, conferences with guild-master, bankers, directors of insurance companies and river transports, importers, heads of spinning mills. All of them depended in some measure upon the Ferral group or upon one of the foreign groups that had linked their policy to that of the Franco-Asiatic Consortium: Ferral was not counting on Liu alone. Shanghai, the living heart of China, pulsated with the passage of everything that made it live; from the remotest countrysides—most of the farm-lands depended upon the banks—blood-vessels flowed like the canals towards the capital where the destiny of China was being decided. The firing continued. Nothing to do now but wait.

In the next room Valérie was lying in bed. Although she had been his mistress for a week, he had made no pretense of loving her: she would have smiled with an insolent knowing air. Nor had she revealed herself to him—perhaps for the same reason. The difficulties which beset his present life drove him into eroticism, not into love. He realized he was no longer young, and tried to convince himself that his legend made up for it. He was Ferral, and he knew women. So well, in fact, that he did not believe a word of what he told himself. He remembered Valérie saying, one day when he had spoken to her of one of his friends, an intelligent invalid, some of whose mistresses had aroused his envy: "There is nothing more appealing in a man than a combination of strength and weakness." No one can be adequately explained by his life, he firmly believed, and he remembered these words better than all the things she had confided to him about hers.

This wealthy woman, who ran a large dressmaking establishment, was not mercenary (not yet at least). She claimed that many women achieved their sexual excitement by appearing naked before a man of their choice, and that this was fully effective only once. Was she thinking of herself? Yet it was the third time she went to bed with him. He sensed in her a pride akin to his own. "Men have travels, women have lovers," she had said the day before. Did he please her, as he did so many women, by the contrast between his hardness and his attentiveness to her? He was not unaware that in this game he was involving what was most essential to him in life—his pride. This was not without danger with a partner who could say: "No man can speak of women, dear, because no man understands that every new make-up, every new dress, every new lover brings forth a new soul . . ."—with the appropriate smile.

He entered the room. She smiled at him from the bed, her waved hair falling in a thick mass over the round arm on which her head rested.

Smiles gave her that animation, both intense and abandoned, which pleasure gives. Valérie's relaxed expression was softly melancholy, and Ferral recalled that the first time he had seen her he had said she had a blurred face—a face which matched the softness of her gray eyes. But whenever coquetry came into play the smile which half opened her curved mouth, at the corners more than at the center, harmonizing in an unexpected way with her waved masses of short hair and her eyes which at such moments grew less tender, gave her in spite of the fine regularity of her features a puzzling expression, like that of a cat wanting to be petted. Ferral was fond of animals, like all those whose pride is too great to adjust itself to men; cats especially.

He took her in his arms. She offered her mouth. Through sensuality or through horror of sentimentality he wondered, while he was undressing in the bathroom. The light-bulb was broken, and the toilet articles looked reddish, lighted by the conflagrations. He looked out through the window: in the avenue, a crowd in motion, like millions of fish under the quivering surface of a black sea; it seemed to him suddenly that the soul of this mob had left it, like the mind of a sleeper in a dream, and that it was burning with a joyous energy in those harsh flames that lighted up the outlines of the buildings.

When he came back she was dreaming and no longer smiled. Although he was used to this change of expression it gave him once again the sensation of emerging from a spell of madness. Did he want merely to be loved

115

by the smiling woman from whom this unsmiling woman separated him like a stranger? The armored train was firing at minute intervals, as for a triumph: it was still in the hands of the governmental forces, as were the barracks, the arsenal and the Russian church.

"Have you seen M. de Clappique again, dear?" she asked.

The whole French colony of Shanghai knew Clappique. Valérie had met him at a dinner two days before; his whimsicality delighted her.

"Yes. I commissioned him to buy me some of Kama's wash-drawings."

"Can you get them at antique-dealers?"

"Not a chance. But Kama is just returning from Europe; he'll pass through here in a fortnight. Clappique was tired, he only told two good stories: one about a Chinese burglar who was acquitted because he had wriggled through a lyre-shaped hole into the pawn-shop he was robbing; and this one: Eminent-Virtue had been raising rabbits for twenty years. His house stood on one side of the internal revenues office, his hutches on the other. On one occasion the customs-inspectors forgot to tell the other shift about his daily trip. He arrives, his basket full of grass under his arm. 'Hey, there! Show your basket.' Under the grass there were watches, chains, flashlights, cameras. 'Is that what you feed your rabbits?' 'Yes, Sir. And (assuming a menacing attitude toward the rabbits) and if they don't like it, they won't get anything else to eat today. . . .' "

"Oh!" she said, "it's a scientific story; now I understand. The bell-rabbits, the drum-rabbits, you know, all those charming little creatures who fare so well in the moon and places like that, and so badly in children's rooms, that's where they come from. . . . The sad story

116

of Eminent-Virtue is another heart-rending injustice. And the revolutionary papers are going to make a great protest, I imagine: for you may be sure that the rabbits ate those things."

"Have you read *Alice in Wonderland*, darling?"

He despised women—though he could not do without them—sufficiently to call them darling.

"What a question! I know it by heart."

"Your smile makes me think of the ghost of the cat which never materialized. All one could see was a ravishing cat-smile floating in the air. Oh! why does a woman's intelligence always insist on choosing some other field than its own?"

"Which is its own, dear?"

"Charm and understanding, obviously."

She reflected:

"What men mean by that is a submissive mind. You recognize in a woman only the kind of intelligence which gives you its approval. It's so—so restful. . . ."

"To give herself, for a woman, to possess, for a man, are the only two means that human beings have of understanding anything whatsoever. . . ."

"Hasn't it occurred to you, dear, that women never give themselves (or hardly ever) and that men possess nothing? It's a game: 'I think I possess her, therefore she thinks she is possessed. . . .' Yes? Really? Listen, I'm going to say something very wicked—but don't you think it's the story all over again of the cork which considered itself so much more important than the bottle?"

Moral license in a woman excited Ferral, but intellectual license only irritated him. He felt an urgent need to arouse the only feeling which gave him a certain power over a woman: Christian shame, together with gratitude for the shame endured. If she did not guess this, she

117

guessed that he was slipping away from her, and as she was responsive, after all, to the physical desire which she could see growing, amused at the idea that she could catch him and bring him back at will, she looked at him with her mouth half-open (since he liked her smile . . .), expressing with her eyes the offer of herself, assured that he, like almost all men, would take her desire to seduce him for a surrender.

He joined her in bed. Caresses gave Valérie a sealed expression which he was eager to see transformed. He summoned her other expression with too much passion not to hope that the pleasure of the senses would imprint it upon Valérie's face. He believed that he was thus destroying a mask, and that what was deepest, most secret in her was necessarily what he preferred. He had never had intercourse with her except in the dark. But hardly had he gently drawn her legs apart with his hand, than she turned out the light. He turned it on again.

He had fumbled for the switch, and she thought the light had gone on by accident; she turned it off again. He immediately turned it on once more. Highly strung, she felt herself on the verge both of laughter and anger; but she met his look. He had pushed the switch out of reach, and she realized that he expected his chief pleasure from the sensual transformation of her features. She knew that she was really dominated by her sexual feelings only at the beginning of an affair, or when she was taken by surprise: when she felt she could not find the switch, a familiar warmth seized her, mounted along her body to the tips of her breasts, to her lips, which she guessed by Ferral's look were imperceptibly swelling. She gave herself up to this warmth and, pressing him against her with her thighs and her arms, plunged with long pulsations far from a shore upon which she knew she would presently be thrown back, but bringing with her the resolve not to forgive him.

Valérie was sleeping. Her regular breathing and the relaxation of sleep gently swelled her lips, and the wanton expression which pleasure gave to her features lingered like an afterglow. "A human being," thought Ferral, "an individual life, unique, isolated, like mine. . . ." He imagined himself as her, inhabiting her body, feeling in her place that enjoyment which he could experience only as a humiliation; he imagined himself—himself— humiliated by this passive voluptuousness, by this woman's sex. "It's idiotic: she feels herself in terms of her sex as I do in terms of mine, neither more nor less. She feels herself as a knot of desires, sadness, pride, as a destiny. . . . Obviously." But not at this moment: sleep and her lips gave her over to a perfect sensuality, as though she had agreed to be no longer a free and living being, but only the expression of gratitude for a physical conquest. The great silence of the Chinese night, with its smell of camphor and leaves, it too asleep far out into the Pacific, covered her over, beyond the realm of time: not a ship called; not a gun fired. She did not trail with her in her sleep memories and hopes which he would never possess: she was nothing but the other pole of his own pleasure. Never had she lived: never had she been a little girl.

The cannon, once more: the armored train was again beginning to fire.

The next day, four o'clock in the afternoon

From a clock-maker's shop which had been transformed into a post, Kyo observed the armored train.

119

Two hundred yards ahead of it and behind it the revolutionaries had blown up the rails, torn up the level crossing. Of the train which barred the street, motionless, dead, Kyo could see only two carriages, the one closed like a cattle-wagon, the other seemingly flattened out beneath its turret, from which a small-caliber gun projected. No men: neither the besieged hidden behind their blocked loop-holes nor the assailants, distributed in the houses overlooking the tracks. Behind Kyo, in the direction of the Russian church and the Commercial Printing House, the volleys did not let up. The soldiers who were ready to give up their arms were out of the fight; the rest would die. All the insurgent sections were now armed; the governmental troops, their front smashed, were fleeing in the rain-drenched wind towards Nanking by the sabotaged trains and the roads pitted with mud-holes. The army of the Kuomintang would reach Shanghai in a few hours: couriers were arriving every moment.

Ch'en entered, still dressed as a worker, sat down beside Kyo, looked at the train. His men were on guard behind a barricade, a hundred yards from there, but were not to attack.

The cannon on the train, at a right angle to where they were, moved. Like very low clouds, wisps of smoke from an extinguished fire trailed before it.

"I don't think they have much ammunition left," said Ch'en.

The cannon was emerging from the turret like a telescope from an observatory, and was moving cautiously; in spite of the steel-plates the hesitancy of its motion made it appear fragile.

"As soon as our own cannons are there . . ." said Kyo.

The one they were watching came to position, fired. In response a volley beat a tattoo against the steel-plates. A clear spot appeared in the gray and white sky, just above the train. A courier brought Kyo some documents.

"We are not in the majority on the committee," said the latter.

The assembly of delegates secretly united by the Kuomintang party, before the insurrection, had elected a central committee of twenty-six members, of whom fifteen were Communists; but this committee in its turn had just elected the Executive Committee which was going to organize the municipal government. There lay the power; there, the Communists were no longer in the majority.

A second courier, in uniform, entered, stopped in the doorway.

"The arsenal has been taken."

"The tanks?" asked Kyo.

"Off for Nanking."

"Do you come from the army?"

He was a soldier of the First Division, the one which contained the greatest number of Communists. Kyo questioned him. The man was bitter: they were wondering what the International was good for. Everything was given to the bourgeoisie of the Kuomintang; the families of the soldiers, almost all peasants, were forced to make heavy contributions to the war fund, whereas the bourgeoisie was only moderately taxed. If they wanted to seize the lands, superior orders forbade it. The taking of Shanghai would change all that, the Communist soldiers believed; he, the messenger, wasn't so sure. With his one-sided information he produced bad arguments, but it was easy to draw better ones from it. The Red Guard, Kyo told him, workers' militias, would be created in Shanghai; there were more than two hundred thousand unemployed in Hankow. Every minute or two they both stopped, listened.

"Hankow," said the man, "I know. . . . There is Hankow. . . ."

Their deadened voices seemed to stick close to them, held back by the quivering air which seemed also to be awaiting the cannon. Both thought of Hankow, "the most industrialized city in all China." There a new Red army was being organized; at this very hour the workers' sections there were learning to handle the guns. . . .

Legs apart, fists on his knees, mouth open, Ch'en watched the couriers and said nothing.

"Everything is going to depend on the Shanghai Prefect," answered Kyo. "If he's one of us, the majority doesn't matter much. If he is on the Right . . ."

Ch'en looked at the time. In this clock-maker's shop at least thirty clocks, wound up or run down, pointed to different hours. A tattoo of volleys gathered into an avalanche. Ch'en hesitated to look outside; he could not detach his eyes from that universe of clock-movements, impassive in the midst of the Revolution. The bustle of the couriers who were leaving aroused him: he decided at last to look at his own watch.

"Four o'clock. We can find out. . . ."

He operated the long-distance telephone, put back the receiver in a fury, turned to Kyo:

"The Prefect is of the Right."

"First extend the Revolution, and then deepen it . . ." answered Kyo, more as a question than as an answer. "The line of the International seems to be to leave the power here to the bourgeoisie. Provisionally. . . . We shall be robbed. I have seen couriers from the front: all workers' movements are prohibited behind the lines.

122

Chiang Kai-shek has had strikers fired on—after taking a few precautions. . . ."

A ray of sunlight entered. The blue patch of sky grew larger. The street filled with sun. In spite of the volleys, the armored train seemed deserted in this light. It fired again. Kyo and Ch'en observed it less attentively now: perhaps the enemy was nearer to them. Greatly worried, Kyo was looking vaguely at the sidewalk, which was sparkling under the provisional sunlight. A great shadow fell upon it. He raised his head: Katov.

"Before a fortnight," he went on, "the Kuomintang will prohibit our assault sections. I have just seen some Blue officers, sent from the front to feel us out; they slyly insinuate that the firearms would be better off with them than with us. They want to disarm the workers' guard: they will have the police, the Committee, the Prefect, the army and the arms. And we shall have made the insurrection for that. We must leave the Kuomintang, isolate the Communist Party, and if possible give it the power. In this whole matter it's not a question of playing chess, but of thinking seriously of the proletariat. What do we advise them to do?"

Ch'en was looking at his well-shaped dirty feet, naked in his clogs:

"The workers are right to strike. We order them to stop the strike. The peasants want to take the lands. They are right. We forbid them to."

"Our slogans are those of the Blues," said Kyo, "with a few more promises. But the Blues give the bourgeois what they promise them, whereas we do not give the workers what we promise them."

"Enough," said Ch'en without even raising his eyes. "First of all, Chiang Kai-shek must be killed."

Katov listened in silence.

"That's in the fut're," he said finally. "At present they're killing our comrades. Yes. And yet, Kyo, I'm not sure I agree with you, you know. At the b'ginning of the Rev'lution, when I was still a socialist-rev'lutionary, we were all against Lenin's tactics in Ukraine. Antonov, the comm'ssar down there, had arrested the mine-owners and had given them ten years of hard labor for sab'tage. Without trial. On his own authority as Comm'ssar of the Cheka Lenin congrat'lated him; we all pr'tested. They were real exploiters, y'know, the owners, and several of us had gone into the mines as convicts; that's why we thought we should be p'rticularly fair with them, to give the example. However, if we had let them go, the prol'tariat would not have understood. Lenin was right. Justice was on our side, but Lenin was right. And we were also against the extr'ordinary powers of the Cheka. We've got to think carefully. The present slogan is good: extend the Rev'lution, and afterwards deepen it. Lenin didn't say right away: 'The whole power to the Soviets.' "

"But he never said: Power to the mensheviks. No situation can force us to surrender our arms to the Blues. None. Because then that means that the Revolution is lost, and we have only to . . ."

An officer of the Kuomintang entered, small, stiff, almost Japanese. Bows.

"The army will be here in half an hour," he said. "We're short of arms. How many can you let us have?"

Ch'en was walking back and forth. Katov was waiting.

"The workers' militias must remain armed," said Kyo.

"My request is made in agreement with the Hankow government," the officer answered.

Kyo and Ch'en smiled.

124

"I beg you to find out for yourselves," he went on.

Kyo worked the telephone.

"Even if the order . . ." Ch'en began, in a rage.

"I've got them," Kyo exclaimed.

He was listening. Katov seized the second receiver. They hung up.

"Very well," said Kyo. "But the men are still on the firing-line."

"The artillery will be here shortly," said the officer. "We'll clean up these things . . ."

He pointed to the armored train, grounded in the sunlight.

". . . ourselves. Can you hand over arms to the troops tomorrow evening? We need them urgently. We are continuing to march on Nanking."

"I doubt if it will be possible to recover more than half the arms."

"Why?"

"All the Communists won't be willing to give them up."

"Even on orders from Hankow?"

"Even on orders from Moscow. At least, not immediately."

They felt the officer's exasperation, although he did not show it.

"See what you can do," he said. "I shall send someone about seven."

He went out.

"Are you willing that we should give up the arms?" Kyo asked Katov.

"I'm trying to understand. Before anything else, we must go to Hankow, you see. What does the Int'rnational want? First of all, use the army of the Kuomintang to unify China. After that d'velop the Rev'lution by prop'-ganda and the rest. It must change of its own accord from a dem'cratic Rev'lution into a socialist Rev'lution."

"Chiang Kai-shek must be killed," said Ch'en.

"Chiang Kai-shek will no longer allow us to go as far as that," answered Kyo, ignoring Ch'en's remark. "He cannot. He can maintain himself here only by drawing on the customs and the contributions of the bourgeoisie, and the bourgeoisie won't pay for nothing: he will have to pay them back with the corpses of Communists."

"All that," said Ch'en, "means nothing."

"Leave us alone," said Katov. "You don't think you're going to try to kill Chiang Kai-shek without the consent of the Central Committee, or at least the delegate of the Int'rnational?"

A distant rumble gradually filled the silence.

"You're going to Hankow?" Ch'en asked Kyo.

"Naturally."

Ch'en was pacing back and forth in the room, beneath all the pendulums and balance-wheels of the various time-pieces which went on ticking their measure.

"What I have said is very simple," he said at last. "The essential. The only thing to do. Let them know."

"Will you wait?"

Kyo knew that if Ch'en hesitated instead of answering, it was not because Katov had convinced him. It was because none of the present orders of the International satisfied the profound passion which had made him a revolutionary; if he accepted them, through discipline, he would no longer be able to act. Kyo watched that hostile figure beneath the clocks: he had made the sacrifice of himself and of others to the Revolution, and now the Revolution would perhaps throw him back into

126

his solitude with his memories of assassinations. At once with him and against him, Kyo could no longer either join him nor break with him. Beneath the brotherhood of arms, at the very moment when he was looking at that armored train which they would perhaps attack together, he felt the possibility of a break as he would have felt the threat of an attack in a friend who was epileptic or insane, at the moment of his greatest lucidity.

Ch'en had resumed his pacing; he shook his head as in protest, said finally: "Good," shrugging his shoulders as though he were saying this to gratify a childish whim of Kyo's.

The rumble became audible again, louder, but so confused that they had to strain their ears in order to make out what it was. It seemed to rise from the earth.

"No," said Kyo, "they are shouts."

They drew nearer, and became more distinct.

"Could they be taking the Russian church? . . ." asked Katov.

Many governmentals were entrenched there. But the cries were approaching, seeming to come from the outskirts towards the center. Louder and louder. Impossible to make out any words. Katov threw a glance towards the armored train.

"Could they be getting reënforcements?"

The shouts, still indistinguishable, were coming closer and closer, as though some capital news were being passed on from crowd to crowd. Vying with them, another sound was making itself heard, and finally became distinct: the rhythmic beating of footsteps on the ground.

"The army," said Katov. "They're our men."

Without a doubt. The shouts were acclamations. Difficult still to distinguish from yells of fear; Kyo had heard similar shouts from a mob fleeing before a flood. The hammering of footsteps changed into a ripple, then continued: the soldiers had stopped and were starting off in another direction.

"They've been told that the armored train is here," said Kyo.

Those in the train no doubt did not hear the shouts so well as they, but they could not help hearing the beating of the footsteps, transmitted by the resonance of the steel-plates.

A tremendous uproar took all three of them by surprise: with every piece, every machine-gun, every rifle, the train was firing. Katov had been in one of the Siberian armored trains; his imagination, getting the better of him, made him participate in the last moments of this one. The officers had given the command to fire at will. What could they do in their turrets, a telephone in one hand, a revolver in the other? Each soldier guessed no doubt what that hammering of footsteps meant. Were they preparing to die together, or to throw themselves upon one another, in that enormous submarine which would never rise again?

The train was working itself into a frenzy. Still firing from every gun, shaken by its very panic, it seemed to want to tear itself from its rails, as if the desperate rage of the men it sheltered had passed into the imprisoned armor, which was also struggling. What fascinated Katov in this unbridled outburst was not the mortal intoxication into which the men of the train were sinking; it was the quivering of the rails which resisted all those roars: he made a forward movement with his arm, to prove to himself that *he* was not paralyzed. Thirty seconds, and the uproar ceased. Above the dull reverberation of the footsteps and the tictac of all the clocks in the shop, a rumble of heavy iron became dominant: the artillery of the revolutionary army.

Behind each steel-plate a man on the train heard that noise as the voice of death itself.

Part Three
March 27

Hankow was close by: the to and fro movement of sampans almost covered the river. The chimneys of the arsenal became detached from the hill behind it little by little, almost invisible under their enormous smoke; through the bluish light of the spring evening the city with all its colonnaded bank buildings appeared at last through the sharp black framework of the foreground —the battleships of the Western nations. For six days Kyo had been ascending the river, without news from Shanghai.

A foreign launch whistled against the ship's side. Kyo's papers were in order, and he was accustomed to clandestine action. He merely took the precaution to move to the forward part of the ship.

"What do they want?" he asked a mechanic.

"They want to know if we have rice or coal on board. We're not allowed to bring in any."

"In the name of what?"

"A pretext. If we bring coal they say nothing, but they arrange somehow to have the ship laid up in port. No way of bringing provisions to the city."

Over there were chimneys, cranes, reservoirs—the allies of the Revolution. But Shanghai had taught Kyo what an active port was like. The one he saw before him was full of nothing but junks and torpedo-boats. He took his field-glasses: a freight-steamer, two, three.

. . . A few more. . . . His was docking on the Wu-chang side. He would have to take the ferry to get to Hankow.

He went ashore. On the dock an officer on duty was watching the passengers land.

"Why so few ships?" asked Kyo.

"The Companies have got everything out of sight: they're afraid of the requisition."

Everyone in Shanghai thought the requisition had been put into effect long before.

"When does the ferry leave?"

"Every half-hour."

He had twenty minutes to wait. He walked about at random. The kerosene lamps were being lit inside the shops; here and there silhouettes of trees and the curved-up roof-ridges rose against the Western sky, where a light without source lingered, seeming to emanate from the softness of the sky itself and to blend far, far up with the serenity of the night. In the black holes of shops—notwithstanding the soldiers and the Workers' Unions—doctors with toad-signs, dealers in herbs and monsters, public writers, casters of spells, astrologers, and fortune-tellers continued their timeless trades by the dim light which blotted out the blood-stains. The shadows melted rather than stretched on the ground, bathed in a bluish phosphorescence; the last flash of the superb evening that was being staged far away, some-where in the infinity of worlds, of which only a reflection suffused the earth, was glowing faintly through an enormous archway surmounted by a pagoda eaten away with blackened ivy. Beyond the din of bells and phonographs and the myriad dots and patches of light, a battalion was disappearing into the darkness which had gathered in the mist over the river. Kyo went down to a yard filled with enormous stone blocks: those of the walls, leveled to the ground in sign of the liberation of China. The ferry was close by.

Another fifteen minutes on the river, watching the city rise into the evening sky. At last, Hankow.

Rickshaws were waiting on the quay, but Kyo's anxiety was too great to allow him to remain idle. He preferred to walk. The British concession which England had abandoned in January, the great world banks shut down, but not occupied. . . . "Anguish—a strange sensation: you feel by your heart-beats that you're not breathing easily, as if you were breathing with your heart. . . ." It was becoming stronger than lucidity. At the corner of a street, in the clearing of a large garden full of trees in bloom, gray in the evening mist, the chimneys of the Western manufactures appeared. No smoke. Of all the chimneys he saw, only the ones of the Arsenal were operating. Was it possible that Hankow, the city to which the Communists of the entire world were looking to save China, was on strike? The Arsenal was working; could they at least count on the Red army? He no longer dared to run. If Hankow was not what everyone believed it was, all his people were already condemned to death. May too. And himself.

At last, the building of the International Delegation.

The entire villa was lighted up. Kyo knew that Borodin was working on the top story; on the ground-floor the printing-press was running at full speed, with the clatter of an enormous ventilator in bad condition.

A guard in a rough-neck sweater examined Kyo. Taking him for a Japanese he was already pointing out to him the orderly in charge of directing strangers, when his eye fell upon the papers Kyo was handing him; he immediately led him through the crowded entrance to the section of the International in charge of Shanghai. Of the secretary who received him Kyo only knew that he had organized the first insurrections in Finland; a comrade, his hand held out across his desk, while he gave his name: Vologin. He had the plumpness of a ripe woman rather than of a man; was this impression due to the delicacy of his features, both full and ruddy, slightly Levantine in spite of his fair complexion, or to the long strands of hair, turning gray, cut to be brushed back but which fell over his cheeks like stiff bands?

"Things look very bad in Shanghai," said Kyo abruptly. "We're headed in the wrong direction."

His own words surprised him: his thoughts were running ahead of him. Yet his words said what he would have wanted to say: if Hankow could not bring the help that the sections were expecting from it, to give up their arms would be suicide.

Vologin, ensconced in his armchair, drew his hands up into the khaki sleeves of his uniform and bent his head a little forward.

"Still! . . ." he muttered.

"First of all, what's going on here?"

"Go on: in what respect are we pursuing the wrong policy in Shanghai?"

"But why, why aren't the manufactures running?"

"Wait a minute. Who are the comrades who're protesting?"

"Those of the combat groups. The terrorists too."

"To hell with the terrorists. The others . . ."

He looked at Kyo.

"What do they want?"

"To leave the Kuomintang. Organize an independent Communist Party. Give the power to the Unions. And above all, not surrender their arms. Above all."

133

"Always the same thing."

Vologin got up, looked through the window towards the river and the hills. His face was expressionless except for a fixed intensity like that of a somnambulist, which alone gave it life. He was short, and his plump back, almost as round as his stomach, made him appear hunchbacked.

"I'll tell you. Suppose we leave the Kuomintang. What will we do then?"

"To begin with, a militia for every workers' union, for every syndicate."

"With what firearms? Here the Arsenal is in the hands of the generals. Chiang Kai-shek now holds the one in Shanghai. And we're cut off from Mongolia: consequently, no Russian arms."

"In Shanghai it was we who took the arsenal."

"With the revolutionary army behind you. Not in front of you. Whom can we arm here? Ten thousand workers, perhaps. In addition to the Communist nucleus of the 'Iron Army'; another ten thousand. Ten bullets per man! Against them, more than seventy-five thousand men here alone. Without mentioning, of course—Chiang Kai-shek, or the others. All too eager to make an alliance against us, upon our first really Communist move. And with what would we provision our troops?"

"What about the foundries, the manufactures?"

"Raw materials have stopped coming."

Standing motionless by the window, against the deepening night, Vologin continued—his face turned away:

"Hankow is not the capital of the workers, it's the capital of the unemployed. There are no arms; that's all the better perhaps. There are moments when I think: if we armed them they would fire on us. And yet, there are all those who work fifteen hours a day without presenting any claims, because 'our revolution is menaced'. . . ."

Kyo was sinking, as one plunges in a dream, lower and ever lower.

"We don't have the power," Vologin continued; "it's in the hands of the generals of the 'Left Kuomintang,' as they call it. They would no more accept the soviets than Chiang Kai-shek does. That's sure. We can use them, that's all. By being very careful."

If Hankow was only a blood-stained setting. . . . Kyo dared think no further. "I must see Possoz on my way out," he said to himself. He was the only comrade in Hankow in whom he had confidence. "I must see Possoz. . . ."

". . . Don't hold your mouth open with that—er— stupid expression," said Vologin. "The world thinks Hankow is Communist—so much the better. That does credit to our propaganda. It's no reason for it to be true."

"What are the instructions right now?"

"To reënforce the Communist nucleus of the Iron Army. We can weight one tray of the scale against the other. We are not a force by ourselves. The generals who are fighting with us here hate the soviets and Communism as much as Chiang Kai-shek does. I know it, I see it, in fact . . . every day. Every Communist slogan will bring them down on us. And no doubt will lead them into an alliance with Chiang. The only thing we can do is to destroy Chiang by using them. Then Fêng Yü Hsiang in the same way, if necessary. As in fact we have destroyed the generals we have fought up to now by using Chiang. Because our propaganda brings us as many men as victory brings to them. We rise with them. That's why it's essential to gain time. The Revolution cannot maintain itself, in short, under its democratic

135

form. By its very nature it must become socialist. We must let it find its own way. Our job is to safeguard its birth. And not to abort it."

"Yes. But in Marxism there is the sense of a fatality, and also the exaltation of a will. Every time fatality comes before will I'm suspicious."

"A purely Communist slogan, today, would bring about the immediate coalition of all the generals against us: two hundred thousand against twenty thousand. That's why you must arrange to get along with Chiang Kai-shek in Shanghai. If there is no way, give up the arms."

"According to that, it was a mistake to start the Revolution of October: how many Bolsheviks were there?"

"The slogan 'Peace' gave us the masses."

"There are other slogans."

"Premature ones. What would they be?"

"Complete, immediate cancellation of farm-rents and credits. The peasant revolution, without conditions or restrictions."

The six days he had spent coming up the river had confirmed Kyo in his idea: in those clay cities that had squatted on the river-junctions for thousands of years the poor would be as ready to follow the peasant as to follow the worker.

"The peasant always follows," said Vologin. "Either the worker or the bourgeois. But he follows."

"No. A peasant movement *lasts* only by attaching itself to the cities, and the peasantry by itself can only produce a Jacquerie,[1] that's understood. But there is no question of separating it from the proletariat: the suppression of credits is a fighting slogan, the only one which can mobilize the peasants."

[1] A spontaneous, unorganized peasant uprising.

"In short, the parceling of lands," said Vologin.

"More concretely: many very poor peasants are land-owners, but work for the usurer. They all know it. Moreover, in Shanghai we must train the guards of the Workers' Unions as quickly as possible. Allow them to disarm under no pretext. Make of them *our force*, against Chiang Kai-shek."

"As soon as that slogan is known, we shall be crushed."

"Then we shall be crushed in any case. The Communist slogans are making headway, even when we give them up. Speeches are enough to make the peasants want the land, speeches won't be enough to make them stop wanting it. Either we must be willing to participate in the repression with the troops of Chiang Kai-shek—does that suit you?—to compromise ourselves *irrevocably*, or they will have to crush us, whether they want to or not."

"Everyone in Moscow is agreed that it will be necessary—in short, to make the break. But not so soon."

"Then, if it's above all a matter of being crafty, don't give up the arms. Giving them up means sacrificing the comrades."

"If they follow instructions, Chiang won't make a move."

"Whether they follow them or not will make no difference. The Committee, Katov, myself, have organized the Workers' Guard. If you try to dissolve it the whole proletariat in Shanghai will cry treason."

"Let them be disarmed, then."

"The Workers' Unions are organizing of their own accord in all the poor quarters. Are you going to prohibit the syndicates in the name of the International?"

Vologin had returned to the window. He dropped his head to his chest, his double chin forming a cushion between them. Night was coming on, full of pale stars.

"To break means certain defeat. Moscow will not tolerate our leaving the Kuomintang at this time. And the Chinese Communist Party is even more favorable to an understanding with Chiang than Moscow."

"The men at the top only: below, the comrades will not give up all their arms even if you order it. You will sacrifice us, without giving Chiang Kai-shek tranquillity. Borodin can tell that to Moscow."

"Moscow knows it: the order to give up the arms was given the day before yesterday."

Stupefied, Kyo did not answer immediately.

"And the sections have given them up?"

"Half of them—barely. . . ."

Just two days ago, while he was meditating or sleeping, on the boat. . . . *He* knew, too, that Moscow would maintain its line. His realization of the situation suddenly invested Ch'en's plan with an obscure value:

"Something else—perhaps the same thing: Ch'en Ta Erh, of Shanghai, wants to execute Chiang."

"Oh! It's for that!"

"What?"

"He sent word, to ask to see me when you were here."

He picked up a message from the table. Kyo had not yet noticed his ecclesiastical hands. "Why didn't he have him come up right away?" he wondered.

"*A very serious matter* . . . (Vologin was reading the message.) They all say 'a very serious matter' . . ."

"Is he here?"

"Wasn't he supposed to come? They're all the same: They almost always change their minds. He's been here for—in fact—two or three hours: your boat was delayed considerably."

He telephoned the order to have Ch'en sent up. He didn't like interviews with terrorists, whom he considered narrow, arrogant and lacking in political sense.

"Matters were even worse in Leningrad," he said, "when Yudenich was before the city, and we managed to pull through just the same. . . ."

Ch'en entered, also wearing a sweater, passed before Kyo, sat down facing Vologin. The noise of the printing-press alone filled the silence. In the large window at a right angle to the desk the darkness, now complete, separated the profiles of the two men. Ch'en, his elbows on the desk, his chin in his hands—stubborn, tense—did not move. "Man's complete impenetrability takes on something inhuman," thought Kyo as he looked at him. "Is it because we easily feel a sense of contact through our weaknesses? . . ." Once he had got past his surprise he judged it inevitable that Ch'en should be here, that he should have come to affirm his decision himself (for he did not imagine that he would argue). On the other side of the rectangle of starry night stood Vologin, strands of his forelock falling over his face, his fat hands crossed on his chest, also waiting.

"Did he tell you?" asked Ch'en, indicating Kyo with a motion of his head.

"You know what the International thinks of terrorist acts," Vologin answered. "I'm not going to make you—in short, a speech on that subject."

"The present case is special. Chiang Kai-shek *alone* is sufficiently popular and sufficiently strong to hold the bourgeoisie united against us. Do you oppose this execution, yes or no?"

He remained motionless, leaning on the desk with his elbows, his chin in his hands. Kyo knew the argument had no essential validity for Ch'en, even though he had come here. Destruction alone could put him in accord with himself.

"It's not up to the International to approve your plan." Vologin spoke in a matter of fact tone. "Moreover, even from your point of view . . ." Ch'en still did not move ". . . is the moment, in short, well chosen?"

"You prefer to wait until Chiang has had our people murdered?"

"He will make decrees and nothing more. His son is in Moscow, don't forget. And there's also this: a number of Galen's Russian officers have not been able to leave Chiang's staff. They will be tortured if he is killed. Neither Galen nor the Russian staff will countenance it. . . ."

The question has apparently been discussed right here, thought Kyo. There was something indescribably futile and hollow in this discussion, which made him uneasy: he found Vologin singularly more determined when he ordered the arms to be given up than when he spoke of the murder of Chiang Kai-shek.

"If the Russian officers are tortured," said Ch'en, "it can't be helped. I also will be tortured. Of no interest. The millions of Chinese are surely worth fifteen Russian officers. Good. And Chiang will abandon his son."

"What do you know about it?"

"And you? You undoubtedly won't even dare to kill him."

"Undoubtedly he loves his son less than himself," said Kyo. "And if he does not try to crush us he is lost. If he does not stop peasant activity his own officers will leave him. So I'm afraid he'll abandon the boy, after obtaining a few promises from the European consuls or some other such farce. And the whole petty bourgeoisie which you want to rally, Vologin, will follow him the day he disarms us: it will be on the side of force. I know them."

"Remains to be proved. And there isn't only Shanghai."

"You say you're dying of starvation. Once Shanghai has been lost, where will you get provisions? Fêng Yü Hsiang separates you from Mongolia, and he will betray you if we are crushed. Therefore, nothing by the Yangtze, nothing from Russia. Do you think the peasants to whom you've promised the program of the Kuomintang (twenty-five per cent reduction in farm-rents, no joking— Oh, but really, no joking!) will die of hunger in order to feed the Red army? You'll put yourself in the power of the Kuomintang even more completely than you are now. To undertake to fight against Chiang now, with real revolutionary slogans, with the backing of the peasants and the Shanghai proletariat, is risky but not impossible: the First Division is almost entirely Communist, from the general down, and will fight with us. And you say we've kept half the arms. Not to try is simply to wait placidly to have our throats cut."

"The Kuomintang is there. We haven't made it. It's there. And stronger than we are, for the time being. We can destroy it from below by introducing into it all the Communist elements we have at our disposal. An immense majority of its members are extremists."

"You know as well as I do that numbers are nothing in a democracy against the ruling apparatus."

"We are demonstrating that the Kuomintang can be used by using it. Not by argument. For two years we have used it unceasingly. Every month, every day."

"As long as you have accepted its aims; not once when it was a question of its accepting yours. You have led it to accept gifts which it was dying to get: officers, volunteers, money, propaganda. The soldiers' soviets, the peasant unions—that's another matter."

141

"What about the exclusion of the anti-Communist elements?"

"Chiang Kai-shek didn't yet have Shanghai in his power."

"Before a month is up we'll have him outlawed by the Central Committee of the Kuomintang."

"After he has crushed us. What difference can it make to those generals of the Central Committee whether the Communist militants are killed or not? They'll be just that much ahead! Don't you think—really—that the obsession with economic fatality is preventing the Chinese Communist Party, and perhaps Moscow, from seeing the elementary necessity which is under our very noses?"

"That is opportunism."

"Very well! According to you Lenin shouldn't have used the parceling of lands as a slogan (for that matter it was featured much more prominently in the program of the socialist-revolutionaries, who didn't have the remotest idea of how to apply it, than in the program of the bolsheviks). The parceling of lands was the establishment of petty property; therefore he should have advocated, not parceling, but immediate collectivization—the sovkhozes. Since he was successful you can see that it was a question of tactics. For us also it's only a question of tactics! You're losing control of the masses. . . ."

"Do you imagine Lenin kept it from February to October?"

"He lost it *at moments*. But he was always *with* them, moving in the same direction. As for you, your slogans go against the current. It's not a matter of a mere side-step, but of directions which will become more and more divergent. To act on the masses as you expect to do, you would have to be in power. That doesn't happen to be the case."

"All this is beside the point," said Ch'en.

"You won't stop the activity of the peasants," Kyo answered. "At the present moment we Communists are issuing to the masses orders which they can consider only as betrayals. Do you think they will understand your waiting slogans?"

"Even if I were a coolie in the Shanghai port I would think that obedience to the Party is the only logical attitude—in short—of a militant Communist. And that all the arms must be given up."

Ch'en got up:

"It's not through obedience that men go out of their way to get killed—nor through obedience that they kill. . . . Except cowards."

Vologin shrugged his shoulders.

"We mustn't consider assassination—after all—as the chief path to political truth."

Ch'en was leaving.

"At the first meeting of the Central Committee I shall propose the immediate parceling of lands," said Kyo, holding out his hand to Vologin, "the cancellation of credits."

"The Committee won't vote them," answered Vologin, smiling for the first time.

Ch'en, a squat shadow on the sidewalk, was waiting. Kyo joined him after having obtained the address of his friend Possoz: he was in charge of the harbor commission.

"Listen . . ." said Ch'en.

The vibration of the printing-presses, transmitted by the ground, controlled and regular like that of a ship's engine, went right through them: in the sleeping city the delegation building was awake with all its lighted windows, across which black figures moved back and forth. They walked, their two similar shadows before them: the same figures, the same effect of their sweater-necks. The straw-huts glimpsed through the perspective of the streets, with their purgatory silhouettes, disappeared in the depth of the calm and almost solemn night, in the smell of fish and burnt grease; Kyo could not free himself from that reverberation of machines transmitted by the soil to his muscles—as if those machines for manufacturing truth were encountering, within himself, Vologin's hesitations and affirmations. During his journey up the river he had constantly felt how poorly informed he really was, how difficult it was for him to get a solid basis for his activity if he no longer consented purely and simply to obey the instructions of the International. But the International was wrong. It was no longer possible to gain time. The Communist propaganda had reached the masses like a flood, because it was what they wanted, because it was their own. However cautious Moscow might be, this propaganda could no longer be stopped; Chiang knew it and was henceforth committed to crushing the Communists. There lay the only certainty. Perhaps the Revolution could have been conducted in some other way; but it was too late. The Communist peasants would take over the lands, the Communist workers would demand a different labor system, the Communist soldiers would no longer fight unless they knew why they were fighting—whether Moscow wanted it or not.

Moscow and the enemy capitals of the West could organize their opposing passions over there in the night and attempt to mold them into a world. The Revolution, so long in parturition, had reached the moment of its delivery: now it would have to give birth or die. At the same time that the fellowship of the night brought Ch'en closer to him, Kyo was seized by a feeling of dependence, the anguish of being nothing more than a man, than himself; there came back to him the memory of Chinese Mohammedans he had seen, on nights just like this, prostrate on the plains covered with sun-scorched lavender, howling those songs that for thousands of years have torn the man who suffers and who knows he is to die. Why had he come to Hankow? To inform the International of the situation in Shanghai. The International was as determined as he had become. What he had heard, much more distinctly than the arguments of Vologin, was the silence of the factories, the distress of the dying city, bedecked with revolutionary glory, but dying none the less. They might as well bequeath this cadaver to the next insurrectional wave, instead of letting it dissolve in crafty schemes. No doubt they were all condemned: the essential was that it should not be in vain. It was certain that Ch'en also felt bound to him by a prisoner's friendship:

"It's not knowing . . . " said the latter. "If it's a question of killing Chiang Kai-shek, I know. As for this fellow Vologin, it's all the same to him I guess; but for him, instead of murder, it's obedience. For people who live as we do there must be a certainty. For him, carrying out orders is sure, I suppose, as killing is for me. Something *must* be sure. Must be."

He was silent.

"Do you dream much?" he went on.

"No. Or at least I don't remember my dreams much."

"I dream almost every night. There is also distraction—day-dreaming. When I let myself go, I sometimes see the shadow of a cat, on the ground: more terrible than anything real. But there is nothing worse than dreams."

"Than what kind of real thing?"

"I'm not the sort to feel remorse. In the business of murder the difficult thing isn't to kill—the thing is not to go to pieces: to be stronger than . . . what happens inside one at that moment."

Bitterness? Impossible to judge by the tone of voice, and Kyo could not see his face. In the solitude of the street the muffled hum of a distant car died away with the wind, which left the fragrance of orchards trailing among the camphor odors of the night.

". . . If it were only that. . . . No. It's worse. Creatures."

Ch'en repeated:

"Creatures. . . . Octopuses especially. And I always remember."

In spite of the vast reaches of the night, Kyo felt near to him as in a closed room.

"Has this lasted long?"

"Very. As long as I can remember. For some time it's been less frequent. And I only remember . . . those things. I hate memories, as a rule. And I seldom have any: my life is not in the past, it's before me."

Silence.

". . . The only thing I'm afraid of—afraid—is going to sleep. And I go to sleep every day."

A clock struck ten. Some people were quarreling, in short Chinese yelps, deep in the night.

". . . or going mad. Those octopuses, night and day, a whole life-time. . . . And one never kills oneself, it appears, when one is mad. . . . Never."

"Does killing change your dreams?"

146

"I don't think so. I'll tell you after . . . Chiang."

Kyo had once and for all accepted the fact that his life was menaced, and that he was living among men who knew that theirs was daily menaced: courage did not astonish him. But it was the first time that he encountered the fascination of death, in this friend whom he could scarcely see, who spoke in an absent-minded voice—as if his words were brought forth by the same nocturnal power as his own anguish, by the all-powerful intimacy of anxiety, silence and fatigue. . . . However, his voice had just changed.

"Do you think of it with . . . with anxiety?"

"No. . . . With . . ."

He hesitated:

"I'm looking for a word stronger than joy. There is no word. Even in Chinese. A . . . complete peace. A kind of . . . how do you say it? of . . . I don't know. There is only one thing that is even deeper. Farther from man, nearer . . . Do you know opium?"

"Scarcely."

"Then it's hard to explain. Nearer what you call . . . ecstasy. Yes. But thick. Deep. Not light. An ecstasy towards . . . downward."

"And it's an idea that gives you that?"

"Yes: my own death."

Still that distracted voice. "He will kill himself," thought Kyo. He had listened to his father enough to know that he who seeks the absolute with such uncompromising zeal can find it only in sensation. A craving for the absolute, a craving for immortality—hence a fear of death: Ch'en should have been a coward; but he felt, like every mystic, that his absolute could be seized only in the moment. Whence no doubt his disdain for everything that did not lead to the moment that would

147

join him to himself in a dizzy embrace. From this human form which Kyo could not even see emanated a blind force which dominated it—the formless matter of which fatality is made. There was something mad about this silent comrade meditating upon his familiar visions of horror, but also something sacred—as there always is about the presence of the inhuman. Perhaps he would kill Chiang only to kill himself. As Kyo tried to make out through the darkness that angular face with its kindly lips, he felt in himself the shudder of the primordial anguish, the same as that which threw Ch'en into the arms of the octopuses of sleep and into those of death.

"My father believes," said Kyo slowly, "that the essence of man is anguish, the consciousness of his own fatality, from which all fears are born, even the fear of death . . . but that opium frees you from it: therein lies its virtue."

"One can always find terror in himself. One only needs to look deep enough: fortunately one can act; if Moscow gives me its approval, it's all the same to me; if Moscow disapproves, the simplest thing is to know nothing about it. I'm leaving. Do you want to stay?"

"I want to see Possoz before anything else. And you won't be able to leave: you have no visa."

"I'm leaving. Certainly."

"How?"

"I don't know. But I'm leaving. I am sure of it. It was *necessary* that I kill Tang Yen Ta, and it is *necessary* that I leave. Certainly I shall leave."

Indeed, Kyo felt that Ch'en's will in the matter played a very small rôle. If destiny lived somewhere, it was there tonight, by his side.

148

"You find it important that it should be *you* who carry out the plot against Chiang?"

"No. . . . And yet I wouldn't want to leave it to another."

"Because you wouldn't trust anyone else?"

"Because I don't like the women I love to be kissed by others."

The words opened the flood-gates to all the suffering Kyo had forgotten: he suddenly felt himself separated from Ch'en. They had reached the river. Ch'en cut the rope of one of the skiffs moored to the wharf, and pushed off. Already he was out of sight, but Kyo could hear the splashing of the oars at regular intervals above the lapping of water against the banks. He knew some terrorists. They asked no questions. They composed a group: murderous insects, they lived by their bond of union in a tragic narrow group. But Ch'en . . .

Pursuing his thoughts without changing his pace Kyo was heading towards the Harbor Commission. "His boat will be stopped at the very start. . . ." He reached some large buildings guarded by army soldiers, almost empty compared to those of the International. In the hallways soldiers were sleeping or playing "thirty-six." He found his friend without any trouble. A kindly apple-round face—the ruddy cheeks of a vine-grower, the gray drooping mustache of a Gaul warrior—khaki civilian garb. Possoz had been an anarchist-syndicalist worker in Switzerland, had gone to Russia after the war and become a Bolshevik. Kyo had known him in Peking and had confidence in him. They shook hands quietly: in Hankow any ghost was a normal visitor.

"The stevedores are there," said a soldier.

"Have them come in."

The soldier went out. Possoz turned to Kyo:

149

"You observe that I'm not doing a damn thing, old fellow. When I was given the supervision of the port we estimated three hundred ships on an average: there aren't ten. . . ."

The port slept beneath the open windows: no sirens, nothing but the steady lapping of water against the banks and the piles. A great ghastly light passed across the walls of the room: the searchlights of the distant gunboats were sweeping the river. A sound of footsteps.

Possoz drew his revolver from its holster, placed it on his desk.

"They've attacked the Red Guard with iron bars," he said to Kyo.

"The Red Guard is armed."

"The danger wasn't that they would knock down the guards, old fellow, it was that the guards would pass over to their side."

The beams from the searchlights returned, cast their enormous shadows upon the white inside wall, returned to the night at the very moment the stevedores were entering: four, five, six, seven. In working-blues, one of them naked to the waist. Handcuffs. A variety of faces, hard to make out in the shadow; but, in common, a glow of hatred. With them two Chinese guards, Nagan pistols at their sides. The stevedores remained as if glued to one another. Hatred, but also fear.

"The Red Guards are workers," said Possoz in Chinese.

Silence.

"If they are guards, it's for the Revolution, not for themselves."

"And to eat," said one of the stevedores.

"It's right that the rations should go to those who

fight. What do you want to do with them? Gamble for them at 'thirty-six'?"

"Give them to everyone."

"Already there isn't enough for a few. The government is determined to use the greatest leniency towards the proletarians, even when they are mistaken. If the Red Guard were everywhere killed off, the generals and foreigners would seize the power again as before—come, now, you know that perfectly well. Well, then? Is that what you want?"

"Before, we used to eat."

"No," said Kyo to the workers: "before, we didn't eat. I know—I've been a docker. And to die just for the sake of dying—well, it might as well be in order to become men."

The whites of all those eyes which caught the feeble light grew imperceptibly larger; they tried to get a better look at this fellow in the sweater who had a Japanese air, who spoke with the accent of the Northern provinces, and who claimed to have been a coolie.

"Promises," answered one of them in a muffled voice.

"Yes," said another. "We have especially the right to go on strike and to die of starvation. My brother is in the army. Why did they kick out of his division all those who demanded the formation of soldiers' Unions?"

He was raising his voice.

"Do you think the Russian Revolution was accomplished in a day?" asked Possoz.

"The Russians did what they wanted."

Useless to argue: all they could do was to try to determine the depth of the revolt.

"The attack on the Red Guard is a counter-revolutionary act, punishable by death. You know it."

A pause.

"If we put you at liberty, what would you do?"

They looked at each other; the darkness made it impossible to see the expressions on their faces. In spite of the revolvers and the handcuffs Kyo sensed the atmosphere preparing for one of those Chinese bargainings which he had so often encountered in the Revolution.

"If we get work?" asked one of the prisoners.

"When there is any."

"Then, *in the meantime,* if the Red Guard prevents us from eating, we shall attack the Red Guard. I hadn't eaten for three days. Nothing at all."

"Is it true that they eat in prison?"

"You'll see for yourselves."

Possoz rang without saying anything further, and the soldiers led the prisoners away.

"That's the worst part of it," he went on, in French this time: "they're beginning to think that they're fed in prison like roosters who are being fattened."

"Why didn't you try harder to convince them, since you had them brought up?"

Possoz shrugged his shoulders in utter discouragement.

"My dear chap, I had them brought up because I always hope they will tell me something else. And yet there are the others, the chaps who work fifteen, sixteen hours a day without coming forward with a single demand, and who'll keep right on until we're quiet, come what may. . . ."

He had just used a Swiss expression, which surprised Kyo. Possoz smiled and his teeth, like the eyes of the stevedores a minute before, glistened in the dim light, under the obscure streak of his mustache.

"You're lucky to have kept your teeth like that, with the life one leads in the country."

"No, my dear chap, not at all: it's a set I got in Changsha. Dentists don't seem to have been affected by the Revolution. And you? You're a delegate? What in the world are you doing here?"

Kyo explained to him, without speaking of Ch'en. Possoz was listening to him, more and more uneasy.

"All that, my dear chap, is very possible, and all the more pity. Listen—I have worked with watches for fifteen years: I know what gears are, the way they depend on one another. If you don't have confidence in the International, mustn't belong to the Party."

"Half the International believes we should create the soviets."

"There is a general line that directs us—must follow it."

"And give up our arms! A line that leads us to fire on the proletariat is necessarily bad. When the peasants take the lands, the generals now arrange to involve a few Communist troops in the repression. Would you be willing to fire on the peasants, yes or no?"

"My dear chap, one isn't perfect. I'd fire in the air, and that's probably what the fellows are doing. I'd prefer it not to happen. But that's not the main thing."

"Try to understand, old man: it's as if I saw a fellow aiming at you, there, and we should be discussing the danger of revolver bullets. . . . Chiang Kai-shek cannot do otherwise than massacre us. And afterwards it'll be the same thing with the generals out here, our 'allies'! And they will be logical. We'll all be massacred, without even maintaining the dignity of the Party, which we lead every day to the whorehouse with a gang of generals, as if it were the place where it belonged. . . ."

"If each one is going to act according to his taste, it's

153

all up with us. If the International succeeds everyone will shout: Hurrah! and at that we won't be wrong. But if we fire at its legs it will certainly fail, and the essential is that it should succeed. . . . I know they say Communists have been made to fire on peasants; but are you sure of it, what I call sure? You haven't seen it yourself, and after all—I know of course you don't do it on purpose, but just the same—it suits your theory to believe it. . . ."

"The mere fact that it's being said among us would be enough. It's not the moment to undertake a six months' investigation."

Why argue? It wasn't Possoz that Kyo wanted to convince, but those in Shanghai; and no doubt they were already convinced now, just as he had been confirmed in his decision by Hankow itself, by the scene he had just witnessed. He now had only one desire: to leave.

A Chinese non-commissioned officer entered, all his features elongated and his body slightly stooped, like one of those ivory figures carved into the concave buttresses of battlements.

"We've just caught a man in a boat who was secretly trying to get away."

Kyo held his breath.

"He claims to have received authorization from you to leave Hankow. He's a merchant."

Kyo recovered his breath.

"Have given no authorization," said Possoz. "Doesn't concern me. Send to the police."

The rich who were arrested would claim a relation to some official: they sometimes managed to see him alone, and would offer him money. It was wiser than to let oneself be shot without trying to do something.

"Wait!"

Possoz drew out a list from his folder, muttered some names.

"All right. The fellow's even on here. We were looking for him. Let the police take care of him!"

The officer went out. The list, a sheet from a notebook, remained on the blotter. Kyo was still thinking of Ch'en.

"It's the list of people we're looking for," said Possoz, who saw that Kyo's eyes remained fixed on the paper. "We get descriptions of the last ones by phone, before the ships leave—when ships *do* leave. . . ."

"May I see it?"

Possoz handed it to him: fourteen names. Ch'en's was not on it. It was impossible that Vologin should not have understood that he would attempt to leave Hankow as soon as possible. And, even on a chance, to have him watched in case he tried to leave would have been no more than common precaution. "The International does not want to take the responsibility for Chiang Kai-shek's death," thought Kyo; "but perhaps it would accept such a misfortune without despair. . . . Is that why Vologin's answers were so vague? . . ." He gave back the list.

"I'm going to leave," Ch'en had said. It was easy to explain that departure; but the explanation was not sufficient. Ch'en's unexpected arrival, Vologin's reticences, the list, Kyo understood all that; but each of Ch'en's gestures brought him nearer again to murder, and things themselves seemed to be pulled along by his destiny. Moths fluttered about the little lamp. "Perhaps Ch'en is a moth who secretes his own light—in which he will destroy himself. . . . Perhaps man himself . . ." Is it only the fatality of others that one sees, never one's own? Was it not like a moth that he himself now wanted

155

to leave for Shanghai as soon as possible, to maintain the sections at any price? The officer came back, which gave him an opportunity to leave.

The peace of the night once more. Not a siren, nothing but the lapping of the water. Along the banks, near the street-lamps crackling with insects, coolies lay sleeping in postures of people afflicted with the plague. Here and there, little round red posters; on them was figured a single character: HUNGER. He felt, as he had a while ago with Ch'en, that on this very night, in all China, and throughout the West, including half of Europe, men were hesitating as he was, torn by the same torment between their discipline and the massacre of their own kind. Those stevedores who were protesting did not understand. But, even when one understood, how choose the sacrifice, here, in this city to which the West looked for the destiny of four hundred million men and perhaps its own, and which was sleeping on the edge of the river in the uneasy sleep of the famished—in impotence, in wretchedness, in hatred?

Part Four
April 11

ALMOST alone in the bar-room of the little Grosvenor Hotel—polished walnut, bottles, nickel, flags—Clappique was revolving an ash-tray on his out-stretched forefinger. Count Shpilevski, for whom he was waiting, entered. Clappique crumpled a piece of paper on which he had just been making an imaginary gift to each of his friends.

"Does this l-little sun-bathed village behold your affairs prospering, my good man?"

"Hardly. But they'll be all right at the end of the month. I'm taking orders for foodstuffs. Only from Europeans, of course."

Shpilevski's curved slender nose, his bald forehead, his brushed-back gray hair and his cheek-bones all created the odd impression that he habitually disguised himself as an eagle. This in spite of his very simple white clothes. A monocle accentuated the caricature.

"The question, you see, my dear friend, would naturally be to find some twenty thousand francs. With this sum one can make a very honorable place for himself in the food business."

"Into my arms, my good fellow! You want a l-little, no, an *honorable* place in the food business? Bravo! . . ."

"I didn't know you had so many . . . whatd'you-call'ems . . . prejudices."

Clappique regarded the eagle out of the corner of his

157

eye: a former saber-champion in Cracow, officers' section.

"Me? I'm full of them, riddled with them! I burst with them! Just imagine—if I had that money, I would use it to imitate a Dutch high official in Sumatra who every year, on his way home to caress his tulips in Holland, used to pass along the coast of Arabia; my dear fellow, he got it into his head (I must tell you that this happened in about 1860) to go and loot the treasures of Mecca. It appears that they are considerable, and all gold, in great black cellars where the pilgrims have thrown them since the beginning of time. Well, it's in that cellar that I would like to live. . . . Anyway, my tulip-fancier gets an inheritance and goes to the Antilles to gather a crew of freebooters, to take Mecca by surprise, with a lot of modern arms—double-barreled guns, detachable bayonets, and what not. Embarks these fellows—not a word!—takes them there. . . ."

He put his forefinger to his lips, enjoying the Pole's curiosity, which resembled a participation in the conspiracy.

"Good! They mutiny, meticulously murder him, and with the ship they go in for an unimaginative piracy, in any kind of an ocean. It's a true story—a moral one, what's more. But, as I was saying, if you count on me to find the twenty thousand francs—madness . . . madness, I tell you! Do you want me to go around and see people, or something of that kind? I'll do that. Besides, since I have to pay your confounded police for every deal I make, I'd rather it should be you than someone else. But while the houses are going up in flames these fellows are about as interested in opium and cocaine as *that!*"

He began once more to revolve the ash-tray.

"I am speaking about it to you," said Shpilevski, "because if I expect to succeed I naturally have to speak to everyone. I should have, at least . . . waited. But . . ." changing his manner ". . . I just wanted to render you a service when I begged you to come and offer me this alcohol (it's synthetic). Listen: leave Shanghai tomorrow."

"Ah! Ah! Ah!" said Clappique, in a rising scale. An automobile horn outside sounded an arpeggio like an echo. "Because?"

"Because. My police, as you say, have their virtues. Get out."

Clappique knew he could not insist. For a second he wondered if perhaps there was not in this a hidden maneuver to obtain the twenty thousand francs? O folly!

"And I would have to get out tomorrow?"

He looked at the bar, its shakers, its nickeled rail, as at old friendly objects.

"At the latest. But you won't leave. I see it. At least I have warned you."

A hesitant gratitude (counteracted less by suspicion than by the nature of the advice which was being given him, by his ignorance of what threatened him) slowly worked its way into Clappique's consciousness.

"What? Better luck than I had expected?" the Pole went on, noticing the change; he took his arm: "Leave! There's some story about a ship. . . ."

"But I had nothing to do with it!"

"Leave."

"Can you tell me if Old Gisors is implicated?"

"I don't think so. Young Gisors, more likely."

The Pole was obviously well informed. Clappique placed his hand on the one before him on the table.

"I'm terribly sorry not to have that money to pay for

your groceries, my good fellow: perhaps you're saving my life. . . . But I still have a few odds and ends—two or three statues: take them."

"No. . . ."

"Why not?"

"No."

"Ah! . . . Not a word? So be it. Just the same I'd like to know why you won't take my statues."

Shpilevski looked at him.

"When one has lived as I have, how could one be in this—whatd'youcallit—profession, if one did not . . . compensate once in a while?"

"I doubt that there are many professions which don't oblige one to compensate. . . ."

"Yes. For instance, you have no idea how poorly guarded the shops are. . . ."

What connection? Clappique was on the point of asking. But he knew from experience that such apparently disconnected speeches are always interesting. And he was really anxious to render this man a service, if only by letting him talk. He was none the less embarrassed to the point of discomfort:

"You watch the shops?"

For him the police were an organization of swindlers and blackmailers, a body charged with raising clandestine taxes on opium and gambling houses. The members of the police whom he had to deal with (and particularly Shpilevski) were always adversaries who were half accomplices. On the other hand he loathed and dreaded informers. But Shpilevski answered:

"Watch? No, not exactly. Whatd'youcallit? . . . The opposite."

"Really! Individual reprisals?"

"It's only for toys, you understand. I no longer have

enough money to buy toys for my little boy. It's very painful. All the more as I'm only fond of the kid when I make him—whatd'youcallit—happy. And I don't know how to make him happy in any other way. It's difficult."

"But look here—do take my statues. You don't need to take everything, if you don't want to."

"I beg you, I beg you. . . . So I go into the shops, and I say . . . (He threw back his head, contracting the muscles of his forehead and his left cheek around his monocle, in all seriousness.) 'I am an inventor. An inventor and manufacturer, naturally. I've come to see your models.' They let me look. I take one of them, never more. Sometimes they watch me, but it's rare."

"And if you were found out?"

He pulled out his pocket-book and opened it in front of Clappique, showing his policeman's card. He shut it again, and his hand described a curiously vague gesture:

"I occasionally have the money. . . . I could also lose my job. . . . But anything may happen. . . ."

Highly astonished, Clappique suddenly discovered himself to be a man of seriousness and weight. As he had never regarded himself as responsible for his own actions, he was surprised.

"I must warn young Gisors," he thought to himself.

One o'clock in the afternoon

Ch'en, who was ahead of time, walked along the quay, a brief-case under one arm. He encountered many Europeans whom he knew by sight: at this hour almost all of them were going to the bars of the Shanghai Club or of one of the neighboring hotels for a drink and a chat. A hand fell gently on his shoulder, from behind. He started, put his hand to his inside pocket where his revolver was hidden.

"It's been a long time since we've met, Ch'en. . . . Do you want to . . ."

He turned round; it was the pastor Smithson, his first teacher. He immediately recognized the handsome—now badly ravaged—face of the American, which betrayed a strain of Sioux blood.

". . . to walk along with me?"

Ch'en preferred to walk in the company of a white man. It was safer, and it was ironic: he had a bomb in his brief-case. The correct coat he was wearing gave him the feeling that his very mind was under constraint; the presence of a companion completed the disguise—and, through an obscure superstition, he did not want to hurt the pastor's feelings. He had counted the vehicles for a minute, a little while before, to find out (odd or even) whether he would succeed: the answer was favorable. He was exasperated with himself. He might as well chat with Smithson, free himself in this way from his irritation.

This irritation did not escape the pastor, but he misinterpreted it:

"Are you suffering, Ch'en?"

"No."

He still kept his affection for his former master, but not without rancor.

The old man took Ch'en's arm in his own.

"I pray for you every day, Ch'en. What have you found in place of the faith you have abandoned?"

He was looking at him with a deep affection, which however was in no way paternal. Ch'en hesitated:

162

"I am not of those whom happiness has any concern with. . . ."

"Happiness is not the only thing, Ch'en—there is peace."

"No. Not for me."

"For all. . . ."

The pastor shut his eyes, and Ch'en had the impression of leading a blind man by the arm.

"I'm not looking for peace. I'm looking for . . . the opposite."

Smithson looked at him:

"Beware of pride."

"Who tells you that I have not found my faith?"

"What political faith can account for the world's suffering?"

"I am more anxious to diminish it than to account for it. The tone of your voice is full of . . . of humaneness. I don't like a humaneness which comes from the contemplation of suffering."

"Are you sure there is any other, Ch'en?"

"Wait—difficult to explain. . . . There is another, at least, which is not composed *only* of that. . . ."

"What political faith will destroy death. . . ."

The pastor's tone was not one of interrogation, but rather of sadness. Ch'en remembered his conversation with Gisors, whom he had not seen since the night of the murder. Gisors used his intelligence in his own service, not in God's.

"I've told you that I wasn't looking for peace."

"Peace. . . ."

The pastor was silent. They continued walking.

"My poor little fellow," he went on at last, "each of us knows only his own unhappiness." His arm pressed

Ch'en's. "Do you think every really religious life is not a daily conversion? . . ."

They were both looking at the sidewalk, and seemed to have contact only through their interlocked arms. ". . . a daily conversion . . ." the pastor repeated with a weary emphasis, as though those words were merely the echo of an obsession. Ch'en did not answer. This man was speaking of himself and he was telling the truth. Like Ch'en, this man *lived* his idea: he was something more than a restless bundle of flesh. Under his left arm, the brief-case and the bomb; under his right arm, that arm tightly pressing his: ". . . a daily conversion. . . ." This confidence spoken in a tone of secrecy made the pastor suddenly appear in a pathetic light. So near to murder, Ch'en was attuned to every kind of suffering.

"Each night, Ch'en, I shall pray God to deliver you from pride. (I pray especially at night: it is favorable to prayer.) If He grant you humility, you will be saved. Now at last I can read in your eyes and understand, as I could not a while ago. . . ."

It was with his suffering, and not with his words, that Ch'en had entered into communion. Those last words, those words of a fisherman who thinks he feels the pull of a fish, stirred in him an anger which rose painfully, without altogether banishing a furtive pity. He was completely baffled by his own feelings.

"Listen," he said. "Listen to this. In two hours I shall kill a man."

He looked straight into the eyes of his companion, this time. Without reason, he raised a trembling hand to his face, crumpled the lapel of his coat:

"Can you still read in my eyes?"

No. He was alone. Still alone. His hand released his

coat, attached itself to the pastor's coat-lapel as though he were going to shake him; the latter placed his hand on Ch'en's. They remained thus, in the middle of the sidewalk, motionless, as if ready to struggle; a passer-by stopped. He was a white man, and he thought they were quarreling.

"It's a horrible lie," said the pastor in a muffled voice.

Ch'en's arm fell to his side. He could not even laugh. "A lie!" he shouted to the passer-by. The latter shrugged his shoulders and went off. Ch'en made a sudden about-face and left almost at a run.

He finally found his two companions, more than a kilometer away. "All dolled up," with their creased hats, their business-suits, which had been picked out to avoid attracting attention to the brief-cases, one containing a bomb, and the other some grenades. Suan—a redskin type of Chinaman, with an aquiline nose—was musing, looking into space; Pei . . . Ch'en had never noticed before how extremely adolescent his face seemed. The round shell-rimmed glasses perhaps accentuated his youth. They started off, reached the Avenue of the Two Republics; with all its shops open, it was returning to every-day life.

Chiang Kai-shek's car would reach the avenue by a narrow street that came into it at a right angle. It would slow down to make the turn. They would have to see it come, and throw the bomb as it slowed down. The general passed every day between one and one-fifteen on his way to lunch. The one who was watching the little street would have to signal to the other two as soon as he saw the car. An antique-dealer's shop just across the street was a good vantage-point; if only the man did not belong to the police. Ch'en himself would be the look-out. He stationed Pei in the avenue, close to the spot where the car would end its turn before picking up speed; Suan, a little farther on. Ch'en would give the signal and throw the first bomb. If the car did not stop, whether it was hit or not, the other two would throw their bombs in their turn. If it stopped, they would run towards it: the street was too narrow for it to turn. There lay the possibility of failure. If he missed them, the guards on the running-boards would open fire to prevent anyone from approaching.

Ch'en and his companions now had to separate. There were surely plain-clothes men in the crowd, along the whole way traveled by the car. From a small Chinese bar Pei was going to watch for Ch'en's signal; farther off, Suan would wait for Pei to come out. At least one of them would probably be killed, Ch'en no doubt. They were afraid to speak—afraid of the finality of words. They separated without even shaking hands.

Ch'en entered the shop of the antique-dealer and asked to see one of those small bronzes found in excavations. The dealer pulled a stack of purple satin boxes from a drawer. They tumbled in a pile on the counter, and he began to spread them out. He was not from Shanghai, but from the North or from Turkestan; his sparse, soft mustache and beard, the narrow slits of his eyes, were those of a low-class Mohammedan, as was also his obsequious mouth; but not his ridgeless face, which resembled that of a flat-nosed goat. Anyone who denounced a man found on the general's path carrying a bomb would receive a fat sum of money and great esteem among his people. And this wealthy bourgeois was perhaps a sincere partisan of Chiang Kai-shek.

"Have you been in Shanghai long?" he asked Ch'en. What sort of fellow was this strange customer? His embarrassment, his constraint, his lack of curiosity in the objects displayed, made the dealer uneasy. The young man was perhaps not used to wearing European clothes. Ch'en's thick lips, in spite of his sharp profile, gave him a good-natured look. The son of some rich peasant from the interior? But the big farmers did not collect ancient bronzes. Was he buying for a European? He was neither a houseboy nor an agent—and if he was a collector himself, he was looking at the objects he was being shown with very little love: he seemed to be thinking of something else.

For Ch'en was already watching the street. From the shop he could see to a distance of two hundred meters. How long would he be able to see the car? But what chance had he to calculate while confronted with this fool's curiosity? First of all he had to answer. To remain silent was stupid:

"I used to live in the interior," he said. "The war forced me to leave."

The other was going to question him again. Ch'en felt that he was making him uneasy. The dealer was now wondering if he was not a burglar who had come to look over his shop to plunder it the next time disorders broke out; however, the young man did not ask to look at the finest pieces. Only bronzes or fox-heads, and of moderate price. The Japanese like foxes, but this customer was not Japanese. He would have to try to draw him out with other questions.

"No doubt you live in Hupei? Life has become very hard, they say, in the central provinces."

Ch'en was wondering if he could not pretend to be partly deaf. He did not dare, afraid of seeming even stranger.

"I don't live there any more," was all he answered. His tone, the structure of his sentences, had something abrupt about them even in Chinese: he expressed himself directly, without using the customary circumlocutions. But it occurred to him to start bargaining.

"How much?" he asked, pointing to a clasp with a fox's head such as are found in great number in tombs.

"Fifteen dollars."

"I should think eight would be a good price. . . ."

"For such a piece? How can you think . . . Consider that I paid ten for it. . . . Put my profit on it yourself."

Instead of answering, Ch'en was looking at Pei seated at a little table in the open bar, his eye-glasses reflecting the light; the latter probably could not see him because of the window-pane of the antique-shop. But he would see him come out.

"I can't pay more than nine," he said finally, as if expressing the result of careful reflection. "At that I can't really afford it."

The formulas, in this realm, were traditional and they came readily to his lips.

"It's my first deal today," answered the antique-dealer. "Perhaps I'll make this little sacrifice of a dollar. If you make a sale with your first customer it's a good omen. . . ."

The deserted street. A rickshaw, in the distance, crossed it. Another. Two men appeared. A dog. A bicycle. The men turned to the right; the rickshaw had crossed. The street once more deserted; only the dog. . . .

"Just the same, couldn't you make it nine and a half? . . ."

"All right, to show my good-will."

Another porcelain fox. More bargaining. Ch'en, since his purchase, inspired greater confidence. He had earned the right to reflect: he was deciding what price he would offer, the one which would subtly correspond to the quality of the object; his worthy meditation must not be disturbed. "In this street the car travels at forty kilometers—more than a kilometer in two minutes. I'll be able to see it a little less than a minute. Not very much. Pei must keep his eye right on this door. . . ." No car was passing in this street. A few bicycles. . . . He bargained over a jade belt buckle, did not accept the dealer's price, said he would discuss it later. One of the clerks brought tea. Ch'en bought a small crystal foxhead, for which the dealer asked only three dollars. The shopkeeper's suspicion, however, had not completely disappeared.

"I have some other very fine pieces, very authentic, with some very pretty foxes. But they are pieces of great value, and I don't keep them in the shop. We could arrange a meeting. . . ."

Ch'en said nothing.

". . . I might even send one of my clerks for them. . . ."

"I'm not interested in the very valuable pieces. Unfortunately I'm not rich enough."

Apparently he was not a thief; he did not even ask to see them. The antiquarian went back to the jade belt buckle, displaying it with the delicacy of one who specializes in handling mummies; but in spite of the words which passed one by one between his gelatinous lips, in spite of his concupiscent eyes, his customer remained indifferent, distant. . . . Yet it was he who had picked out this buckle. Bargaining is a collaboration, like love; the dealer was making love to a board. Why in the world did this man buy? Suddenly he guessed: he was one of those poor young men who let themselves become childishly infatuated with the Japanese prostitutes

169

of Chapei. They have a passion for foxes. His customer was buying these for some waitress or cheap geisha; if he was not interested in them it was because he was not buying them for himself. (Ch'en did not cease thinking about the arrival of the car, the speed with which he would have to open his brief-case, pull out the bomb, throw it.) But geishas don't like objects from excavations. . . . Perhaps they make an exception in the case of little foxes? The young man had also bought a crystal object and one in porcelain. . . .

The tiny boxes, open or closed, were spread out on the counter. The two clerks were looking on, leaning on their elbows. One of them, very young, had put one elbow on Ch'en's brief-case. Each time he shifted his weight from one leg to the other he pushed it a little closer to the edge of the counter. The bomb was on the right side, three centimeters from the edge.

Ch'en could not move. Finally he put out his arm, pulled the brief-case towards him, without the slightest difficulty. None of these men had had the sensation of death, nor of the failure of his plot; nothing—a brief-case which a clerk has pushed towards the edge of the counter and which its owner pulls back. . . . And suddenly everything seemed extraordinarily easy to Ch'en. Things, even actions, did not exist; they were dreams, nothing but dreams which take possession of us because we give them force, but which we can just as easily deny. . . . At this moment he heard the horn of a car: Chiang Kai-shek.

He seized his brief-case like a weapon, paid, threw the two little packages into his pocket, went out.

The dealer was pursuing him, holding in his hand the belt buckle which Ch'en had refused to buy:

"These are pieces of jade which the Japanese ladies are particularly fond of!"

Would he ever get rid of this fool?

"I'll be back."

What merchant does not know the formula? The car was approaching, much faster than usual, it seemed to Ch'en, preceded by the Ford of the bodyguard.

"Go to hell!"

The car, speeding towards them over the uneven gutter-stones, was violently shaking the two detectives on the running-boards. The Ford passed. Ch'en stopped, opened his brief-case, and took hold of the bomb wrapped in a newspaper. With a smile the dealer slipped the belt buckle into the empty pocket of the brief-case. In doing so he was barring Ch'en's two hands:

"Pay me what you like."

"Go to hell!"

Dumbfounded by this outburst, the antiquarian did not budge, merely gaped at Ch'en whose mouth was also open.

"Aren't you a little ill?" Ch'en could no longer see anything, limp as if he were going to faint: the car was passing.

He had not been able to free himself in time from the antiquarian's gesture. "This customer is going to be ill," the latter was thinking. He made a movement to support him. With one blow, Ch'en knocked aside the two arms held up to him and started off. The blow left the dealer stunned for a moment. Ch'en was half running.

"My buckle!" shouted the merchant. "My buckle!"

It was still in the brief-case. Ch'en was at a loss. His every muscle, his every nerve was expecting a detonation which would fill the street. Nothing. The car had turned, had even passed beyond Suan no doubt. And this fool remained there. There was no danger, since everything had failed. What had the others been doing? Ch'en began to run. "Stop, thief!" shouted the antiquarian. Other dealers appeared in the doorways. Ch'en understood. In sheer rage he wanted to run away with the accursed buckle, throw it somewhere. But more onlookers were approaching. He threw it in the antiquarian's face, and only then noticed that he had not shut his brief-case. Since the passing of the car it had stayed open, right before the eyes of that imbecile and of the passers-by, the bomb visible, not even protected by the newspaper which had slipped aside. He finally closed the brief-case with caution (he was on the point of banging the flap down; he was struggling with all his might against his nerves). The dealer was hurrying back to his shop. Ch'en walked on.

"Well?" he said to Pei as soon as he joined him.

"What about you?"

They looked at each other breathlessly, each wanting the other to speak first. They stood there, outlined in profile against the blurred background of the buildings—hovering on the verge of speech, seeming to be stuck to the pavement, in postures full of hesitations. The light of the early afternoon sun, very strong despite the clouds, set off Ch'en's hawklike profile and Pei's roundish head. Among the bustling and anxious passers-by, those two figures with trembling hands, planted on their fore-shortened shadows, seemed completely isolated. All three were still carrying their brief-cases. It would not be wise to remain there too long. The restaurants were not safe. And they had already met and separated too many times in this street. Why? Nothing had happened. . . .

"To Hemmelrich's," said Ch'en finally.

They started off, picking their way through back-streets.

"What happened?" asked Suan.

Ch'en explained. As for Pei, he had been uneasy when he saw that Ch'en did not leave the antiquarian's shop alone. He had betaken himself to the spot where he was to throw his bomb, a few meters from the corner. The cars in Shanghai drive on the left side of the street; ordinarily they make a short turn, and Pei had taken his post on the left sidewalk, in order to throw his bomb at close range. As it happened, the car was going fast; there were no carriages in the Avenue of the Two Republics. The chauffeur had made a wide turn, thus skirting the opposite sidewalk, and Pei had found himself separated from it by a rickshaw.

"So much the worse for the rickshaw," said Ch'en. "There are thousands of other coolies who can live only by Chiang Kai-shek's death."

"I would have missed my aim."

Suan had not thrown his grenades because neither of the bombs had gone off—he had supposed that something was wrong, that perhaps the general was not in the car.

They were advancing in silence between walls turned to a sickly pale shade by the yellowish sky, in a wretched solitude littered with rubbish and telegraph wires.

"The bombs are intact," said Ch'en in a muffled voice. "We'll try again in a little while."

But his two companions were crushed; those who have failed in an attempted suicide rarely try it again. As they went on, their bewilderment gave way to despair.

"It's my fault," said Suan.

Pei repeated:

"It's my fault."

"Enough," said Ch'en, exasperated. He was reflecting, as they pursued their wretched walk. It wouldn't do to start all over again in the same way. The plan was bad, but it was difficult to imagine another. He had thought that. . . . They reached Hemmelrich's.

From the back of his shop Hemmelrich heard a voice speaking in Chinese, and two others which were answering. Their pitch, their excited rhythm, had attracted his attention. "Just yesterday," he thought to himself, "I saw two chaps walking by, whose faces were enough to give you chronic hemorrhoids, and who certainly weren't there for their pleasure. . . ." It was difficult for him to hear distinctly: upstairs the child was wailing incessantly. But the voices died away and short shadows on the sidewalk showed that three figures were standing there. The police? . . . Hemmelrich got up and walked towards the door. There was nothing about his looks, he reflected—conscious, as always, of his flattened nose and his sunken chest—that could inspire fear in an aggressor. But he recognized Ch'en even before his hand reached his pocket; he held it out to him instead of drawing his revolver.

"Let's go into the back room," said Ch'en.

All three passed in front of Hemmelrich. He was examining them. Each with a brief-case, not held carelessly, but squeezed tightly under his arm.

"Listen," said Ch'en as soon as the door was closed: "can you give us hospitality for a few hours? To us and to what we have in our brief-cases?"

"Bombs?"

"Yes."

"No."

174

The child, upstairs, was still crying. His most painful cries had become sobs, with occasional little clucking sounds, as though he were weeping for fun—which made them all the more poignant. The records, the chairs, the cricket were so exactly the same as when Ch'en had come there after the murder of Tang Yen Ta that Hemmelrich and he both remembered that night. He said nothing, but Hemmelrich guessed:

"The bombs," he said, ". . . I can't at this moment. If they find bombs here they'll kill my wife and the kid."

"Good. Let's go to Shia's." He was the lamp-dealer whom Kyo had visited on the eve of the insurrection. "At this hour there's only the boy."

"Understand me, Ch'en: the kid is very sick, and the mother isn't in too good shape . . ."

He was looking at Ch'en, his hands trembling . . .

"You don't know, Ch'en, you can't know how lucky you are to be free! . . ."

"Yes, I know."

The three Chinamen went out.

"God damn! . . . God damn!" Hemmelrich said to himself, "won't I ever be in his place?" He was swearing to himself, calmly, ponderously. And he was slowly climbing the stairs to the room. His Chinese wife was sitting, her eyes fixed on the bed. She did not turn round.

"The lady was nice today," said the child, "she didn't hurt me hardly at all. . . ."

The lady was May. Hemmelrich remembered: "Mastoid. . . . My poor fellow, we'll have to break the bone. . . ." Hardly more than a baby. . . . All he knew of life so far was suffering. Hemmelrich would have to "explain to him." Explain what? That it was advantageous to have the bones in his head broken so that he wouldn't die, so that he would be rewarded by a life as precious and delicate as that of his father? "Oh, the horror of youth!" he had said for twenty years. How long before he would say, "Oh, the horror of age!" and pass on to his wretched offspring those two perfect expressions of life? A month before, the cat had dislocated its paw, and they had had to hold it while the Chinese veterinary set the bone back into place, and the creature shrieked and struggled; it didn't understand; he felt that it believed it was being tortured. And the cat was not a child, did not say: "He hardly hurt me. . . ." He went downstairs again. The smell of the corpses, on which the dogs were no doubt ravenously feeding close by in the back-alleys, drifted in with the diffused sunlight. "It's not suffering that is lacking," he thought to himself.

He could not forgive himself for having refused. Like a tortured man who has yielded secrets, he knew that he would do it again, but he could not forgive himself. He had betrayed his youth, his desires and his dreams. How could he help betraying them? Some people wanted only what they could have. But all the things he wanted were things he could not have. He wanted to give shelter to Ch'en and go with him. Go. Offset by violence—any kind of violence—by bombs, this atrocious life that had poisoned him since he was born, that would poison his children in the same way. Especially his children. He could accept his own suffering: he had acquired the habit. . . . But not that of the children. "He has become very intelligent since he has been ill," May had said. As if by chance. . . .

Go out with Ch'en, take one of the bombs hidden in the brief-cases, throw it. That was good sense. In fact the only thing that had a sense, in his present life. Thirty-seven years. Another thirty years to live, perhaps. To live how? The sale of these records, whose wretched profit he shared with Lu Yu Hsüan, by which neither of them was able to live—and, when he was old . . . Thirty-seven years. As far as memory goes back, people say; his memory didn't have to go back: from beginning to end, it was only wretchedness.

A bad pupil at school: absent one day out of every two—his mother made him do her work so she could get drunk in peace. The factory: a laborer. A bad character; during his military service, always behind bars. And the war. Gassed. For whom, for what? For France? He was not French, he was wretched. But in the war one could eat. Then, sent to Indo-China, demobilized there. "The climate here makes manual labor impossible. . . ." But it allowed you to die of dysentery, especially those who were known as bad characters. He had failed in Shanghai. Bombs, for God's sake, bombs!

There was his wife: life had given him nothing else. She had been sold for twelve dollars. Abandoned by the buyer whom she had ceased to please, she had come to him in terror, to eat, to sleep; but in the beginning she had not been able to sleep, expecting every moment a display of the European wickedness and cruelty that she had always been told about. He had been good to her. Emerging little by little from the depth of her fright, she had cared for him when he was ill, had worked for him, endured his outbursts of impotent hatred. She had clung to him with the love of a blind and persecuted dog, suspecting that he too was a blind and persecuted dog. And now there was the kid. What could he do for him? Scarcely feed him. He had strength left only for the pain that he could inflict; there existed more pain in the world than stars in the sky, but the worst of all

177

was the pain he could inflict upon this woman: to abandon her by dying. Like that starving Russian, down the street, who had become a laborer and then, one day when his misery was too great, had committed suicide; his crazed wife, in a blind rage, had beaten the corpse that was abandoning her, with four youngsters in the corners of the room, one of them asking: "Why do you fight?" . . . He kept his wife, his kid, from dying. That was nothing. Less than nothing. If he had had money, if he could have left it to them, he would have been free to go and get killed. As if the universe had not treated him all his life with kicks in the belly, it now despoiled him of the only dignity he could ever possess—his death. The smell of corpses was blown in upon the motionless sunbeams by every gust of wind. He saturated himself in it with a sense of gratified horror, obsessed by Ch'en as by a friend in the throes of death, and seeking—as though it were of any consequence—whether the feeling uppermost in him was shame, fraternity or an atrocious craving.

Once more Ch'en and his companions had left the avenue. The courts and the side-streets were not closely watched, as the general's car did not pass through them. "We must get a new plan," Ch'en was thinking as he walked with bowed head, looking down at his smug shoes as they advanced one after the other. Run into Chiang Kai-shek's car with another car driven in the opposite direction? But every car might be requisitioned by the army. To try to use the fanion of a legation to protect the car—in case they were able to get one—was risky, for the police knew the chauffeurs of the foreign ministers. Bar the way with a cart? Chiang Kai-shek was always preceded by the Ford with his bodyguard. Before a suspicious obstruction both guards and the police on the running-boards would open fire on whoever attempted to approach. Ch'en listened: his companions had begun to talk.

"Many generals will abandon Chiang Kai-shek if they know he's in danger of being assassinated," said Pei. "There is faith only among us."

"Yes," said Suan, "the sons of torture-victims make good terrorists."

They both were.

"And as for the generals who remain," added Pei, "even if they build up a China that is opposed to us, they will make a great nation, because they will have built it with their blood."

"No!" said Ch'en and Suan, both at once. Neither of them ignored how great the number of nationalists among the Communists had grown, especially among the intellectuals.

Pei wrote, for periodicals that were quickly suppressed, stories that revealed a painfully self-satisfied bitterness, and articles—the last of which began in this fashion: "Imperialism being sorely pressed, China plans to solicit its benevolence once more and ask it to substitute a nickel ring for the gold ring that it has fastened to her nose. . . ." He was also preparing an ideology of terrorism. For him Communism was merely the one true way to bring about the revival of China.

"I don't want to create China," said Suan, "I want to create my people, with or without her. The poor. It's for them that I'm willing to die, to kill. For them only. . . ."

It was Ch'en who answered:

"As long as we try to throw the bomb we'll have bad

luck. Too many chances of failure. And we must get it over with today."

"There's no other way that's any easier," said Pei.

"There is a way."

The low, heavy clouds were advancing in the same direction as they, with the uncertain yet lordly movement of destinies. Ch'en had shut his eyes to meditate, but continued to walk, close to the walls as usual; his comrades were waiting for him to speak, watching his curved profile.

"There is a way. And I believe there is only one: we must not throw the bomb; we must throw ourselves under the car with it."

Lost in thought, they continued their walk through the torn-up courts where children no longer played.

They arrived. The clerk led them into the back room of the shop. They remained standing amid the lamps, their brief-cases under their arms; finally they put them down, cautiously. Suan and Pei squatted on the floor, Chinese fashion.

"Why are you laughing, Ch'en?" asked Pei, with anxiety.

He was not laughing, he was smiling, worlds removed from irony. To his amazement, he found himself possessed by a radiant exaltation. Everything became simple. His anguish had vanished. He knew the uneasiness to which his comrades were prey, in spite of their courage: throwing bombs, even in the most dangerous way, was adventure; the resolution to die was something else —the opposite, perhaps. He began to pace back and forth. In the back room there was only the light which came through the shop—now livid, as before a storm. In the diffused half-light the bellies of the storm lamps glowed with a curious effect—rows of inverted question-marks. Ch'en's shadow, too indistinct to be a silhouette, was moving above the anxious eyes of the other two.

"Kyo is right: what we lack most is the sense of hara-kiri. But the Japanese who kills himself risks becoming a god, and that's the beginning of filth and corruption. No: the blood must fall back upon men—and remain." Whenever Ch'en expressed a passionate conviction in Chinese, his voice took on an extraordinary intensity.

"I would rather try to succeed," said Suan, "—to succeed—in several attempts than to make up my mind to die in one attempt."

Yet Suan felt beneath Ch'en's words a current towards which he was being drawn. Where it led he did not know. He was sitting in rapt attention, vibrating to the sound of Ch'en's words rather than to their meaning.

"I must throw myself under the car," answered Ch'en.

They followed him with their eyes, as he came and went, without turning their necks; he no longer looked at them. He stumbled on one of the lamps standing on the floor, caught his balance by putting his hands out to the wall. The lamp fell and broke with a tinkle. But there was no room for laughter. His righted shadow stood out indistinctly against the last rows of lamps. Suan was beginning to understand what Ch'en expected of him. Nevertheless, either through mistrust of himself or to put off what he foresaw, he said:

"What do you want?"

Ch'en suddenly realized that he did not know. He felt himself struggling, not against Suan, but against his idea, which was escaping him. At last:

"That this should not be lost."

"You want Pei and me to make a pledge to imitate you? Is that it?"

"It's not a promise that I expect. I expect you to feel —a need."

The reflections on the lamps were disappearing. It was growing darker in the windowless room—no doubt the clouds were piling up outside. Ch'en remembered Gisors: "Close to death, such a passion aspires to be passed on. . . ." Suddenly he understood. Suan also was beginning to understand:

"You want to make a kind of religion of terrorism?"

Ch'en's exaltation was growing. All words were hollow, absurd, too feeble to express what he wanted of them.

"Not a religion. The meaning of life. The . . ."

His hand made the convulsive gesture of molding something, and his idea seemed to pulsate.

". . . the complete possession of oneself. Total. Absolute. To know. Not to be looking, looking, always, for ideas, for duties. In the last hour I have felt nothing of what used to weigh on me. Do you hear? Nothing."

He was so completely carried away by his exaltation that he was no longer trying to convince them otherwise than by speaking about himself:

"I possess myself. But I don't feel a menace, an anguish, as always before. Possessed, held tight, tight, as this hand holds the other . . . (he was pressing it with all his might) . . . it's not enough—like . . ."

He picked up one of the pieces of glass from the broken lamp. A large triangular fragment full of reflections. With one stroke he drove it into his thigh. His tense voice was charged with a savage certainty, but he seemed much more to possess his exaltation than to be possessed by it. Not at all mad. Now the other two could barely see him, and yet he filled the room. Suan began to be afraid:

"I am less intelligent than you, Ch'en, but for me . . . for me, no. I saw my father hung by his hands, beaten on the belly with a rattan-stick to make him tell where his master had hidden the money which he didn't have. It's for those to whom we belong that I'm fighting, not for myself."

"For them, you can't do better than to make up your mind to die. No other man can be so effective as the man who has chosen that. If we had made up our minds to it, we should not have missed Chiang Kai-shek a while back. You know it."

"You—perhaps you need that. I don't know. . . ." He was struggling with himself. "If I agreed, you see, it would seem to me that I was not dying for all the others, but . . ."

"But?"

Almost completely obliterated, the feeble afternoon light lingered without completely disappearing.

"For you."

A strong smell of kerosene recalled to Ch'en the oil cans for the burning of the station, the first day of the insurrection. But everything was plunging into the past, even Suan, since he would not follow him. Yet the only thing which his present state of mind did not transform into nothingness was the idea of creating those doomed Executioners, that race of avengers. This birth was taking place in him, like all births, with agony and exaltation—he was not master of it. He could no longer endure any presence. He got up.

"You who write," he said to Pei, "you will explain."

They picked up their brief-cases. Pei was wiping his glasses. Ch'en pulled up his trouser-leg, bandaged his thigh without washing the wound—what was the use? It would not have time to get infected—before going out.

"One always does the same thing," he said to himself, disturbed, thinking of the knife he had driven into his arm.

"I shall go alone," he said, "and I shall manage alone, tonight."

"I'll organize something, just the same," Suan answered.

"It will be too late."

In front of the shop, Ch'en took a step to the left. Pei was following him. Suan remained motionless. A second step. Pei still followed him. Ch'en noticed that the youth, his glasses in his hand—so much more human, that youngster's face, without glasses over his eyes—was weeping in silence.

"Where are you going?"

"I'm coming."

Ch'en stopped. He had always believed him to be of Suan's opinion; he pointed to the latter.

"I shall go with you," Pei persisted.

He avoided speaking any more than was necessary, his voice broken, his Adam's apple shaken by silent sobs.

"Pledge yourself."

He clutched Pei's arm.

"Pledge yourself," he repeated.

He turned away. Pei remained on the sidewalk, his mouth open, still wiping his glasses, comical. Never had Ch'en thought one could be so alone.

Three o'clock in the afternoon

Clappique had expected to find Kyo at home. But he was still out. In the large room strewn with sketches which a disciple in a kimono was picking up, Gisors was conversing with his brother-in-law, the painter Kama.

"Hello, old dear! Into my arms!"

He sat down quietly.

"Too bad your son isn't here."

"Do you want to wait for him?"

"Let's try. I need to see him like the devil. What is that new little c-cactus, under the opium-table? The collection is becoming worthy of respect. Ravishing, my dear friend, r-ravish-ing! I must buy one. Where did you find it?"

"It's a gift. It was sent me a little before one o'clock."

Clappique was reading the Chinese characters traced on the flat stake supporting the plant; a large one: Fidelity; three small ones, a signature: Ch'en Ta Erh.

"Ch'en Ta Erh. . . . Ch'en. . . . Don't know him. Too bad. He's a fellow who knows cactuses."

He remembered that the next day he would have to be gone. He must find money to leave, and not to buy cactuses. Impossible to sell objects of art in a hurry with the city under military occupation. His friends were hard up. And you couldn't touch Ferral for money on any pretext. He had commissioned him to buy some of Kama's wash-drawings when the Japanese painter arrived. Thirty or forty dollars in commissions. . . .

"Kyo should be here," said Gisors. "He had many engagements today, didn't he? . . ."

"He'd do better to miss them, perhaps," Clappique grunted.

He did not dare to add anything. He had no idea how much Gisors knew about Kyo's activity. But the absence of any question humiliated him:

"You know, it's very serious."

"Everything that has to do with Kyo is serious for me."

"You haven't any bright idea about how to earn or find four or five hundred dollars immediately?"

Gisors smiled sadly. Clappique knew he was poor: and his works of art, even if he were to consent to sell them . . .

"Well, let's earn our few cents," the Baron thought to himself. He came closer, looked at the wash-drawings scattered on the divan. Although he was sufficiently discriminating not to judge the traditional Japanese art in terms of its relation to Cézanne or Picasso, he detested it today: the taste for serenity is weak in hunted men. Dim lights over a mountain, village streets dissolved by rain, flights of wading-birds across the snow—that whole world in which melancholy prepared one for happiness. . . . Clappique imagined without difficulty, alas, the paradises at whose gates he should remain, but was irritated by their existence.

"The most beautiful woman in the world," he said, "naked, aroused, but with a chastity belt. For Ferral, not for me."

He chose four, dictated the address to the disciple.

"Because you're thinking of our art," said Gisors; "this does not serve the same purpose."

"Why do you paint, Kama-San?"

The old master was looking at Clappique with curiosity, the light emphasizing his bald head. He too was wearing a kimono. (As Gisors was still in his dressing-gown, Clappique was the only one in trousers.)

The disciple left the sketch, translated, answered:

"The master says: first, for my wife, because I love her. . . ."

"I don't say for whom, but for what?"

"The master says it is difficult to explain to you. He says: 'When I went to Europe, I saw the museums. The more your painters paint apples, and even lines which do not represent objects, the more they talk about themselves. For me it is the world that counts.' "

Kama spoke another phrase; an expression of gentleness, barely perceptible, flitted across his face, which resembled an indulgent old lady's.

"The master says: 'With us, painting is what charity would be with you.' "

A second disciple, a cook, brought bowls of sake, and immediately withdrew. Kama spoke again.

"The master says that if he were no longer to paint, it would seem to him that he had become blind. And more than blind: alone."

"Wait a minute!" said the Baron, one eye open, the other shut, his forefinger pointed. "If a doctor were to say to you: 'You have an incurable illness, and you will die in three months,' would you still paint?"

"The master says that if he knew he was going to die, he thinks he would paint better, but not differently."

"Why better?" asked Gisors.

He did not cease thinking of Kyo. What Clappique had said upon coming in was sufficient to worry him: today serenity was almost an insult.

Kama answered. Gisors himself translated:

"He says: 'There are two smiles—my wife's and my daughter's—which I should then know I would never see again, and I should be even more inclined to melancholy. The world is like the characters of our writing. What the symbol is to the flower, the flower itself—this one (he pointed to one of the drawings)—is to something. Everything is a symbol. To go from the symbol to the thing symbolized is to explore the depth and meaning of the world, it is to seek God.' He thinks that the approach of death . . . Wait. . . ."

187

He questioned Kama again, resumed his translation:

"Yes, that's it. He thinks that the approach of death would perhaps permit him to put into all things sufficient fervor and melancholy, so that all the forms he would paint would become comprehensible symbols, so that what they symbolize—what they hide, also—would be revealed."

Clappique experienced the atrocious sensation of suffering in the presence of a creature who denied suffering. He was listening with attention, without taking his eyes from Kama's face, while Gisors was translating. With his absorbed look, his elbows against his sides, his hands joined, Clappique resembled a forlorn monkey.

"Perhaps you're not asking the question in the right way," said Gisors.

He spoke a very short phrase in Japanese. Up to this point Kama had answered almost immediately. He pondered.

"What question did you just ask him?" Clappique asked in a low voice.

"What he would do if the doctor condemned his wife."

"The master says he would not believe the doctor."

The cook-disciple came back and took away the bowls on a tray. His European garb, his smile, his deference, and his gestures which betrayed an extravagant gayety—everything about him seemed strange, even to Gisors. Kama said something under his breath which the other disciple did not translate.

"In Japan these young men never drink wine," said Gisors. "He feels hurt because this disciple is drunk."

His eyes looked away into space: the outside door opened. A sound of steps. But it was not Kyo. His look once more became precise, and met Kama's firmly:

"And if she were dead?"

Would he have pursued this conversation with a European? But the old painter belonged to another universe. Before answering he smiled a long, sad smile, not with his lips but with his eyelids:

"One can communicate even with death. . . . It's most difficult, but perhaps that is the meaning of life. . . ."

He was taking his leave, was returning to his room, followed by his disciple. Clappique sat down.

"Not a word! . . . Remarkable, my dear, r-remarkable! He left like a well-bred phantom. Do you know that young phantoms are very ill-bred and that the old ones have the greatest trouble teaching them to make people afraid—the young ones don't know any language, and all they can say is: Zip-zip. . . . Which . . ."

He stopped: the knocker, again. In the silence, guitar-notes began to strum; soon they became ordered into a slow fall that spread outward in its descent, down to the gravest notes, held in suspense and lost at length in a solemn serenity.

"What does it mean, but what *does* it mean?"

"He plays the samisen. Always, when something has upset him: away from Japan, it's his defense. . . . He told me, when he came back from Europe: 'I know now that I can find my inner silence no matter where I am. . . .'"

"A bluff?"

Clappique had asked the question absent-mindedly: he was listening. At this hour when his life was perhaps in danger (although it was rare that he was sufficiently interested in himself to feel himself really in danger) those exquisitely pure notes, bringing back to him upon their current, along with the love of music which had

189

filled his youth, that youth itself and all its vanished happiness, upset him too.

Once more the sound of a foot-step: already Kyo was in the doorway.

He led Clappique into his room. A divan, a desk, a chair, blank walls: a deliberate austerity. It was hot in there; Kyo threw his coat on the divan.

"Listen," said Clappique. "I've just been given a l-little tip—you'll be making a big mistake if you don't take it seriously: if we don't clear out of here by tomorrow night, we're as good as dead."

"What's the source of this tip? The police?"

"Bravo. Useless to tell you that I can't say anything more about it. But it's serious. The affair of the ship is known. Lay low, and get out within forty-eight hours."

Kyo was about to say: it's no longer an offense since we have triumphed. He said nothing. He was too well prepared for the repression of the workers' movement to be surprised. This meant that the break had come, which Clappique could not guess; and if the latter was being prosecuted it was because, the *Shantung* having been taken by the Communists, he was believed to be allied with them.

"What do you expect to do?" Clappique went on.

"To think, first of all."

"Profound idea! And have you the cash to get out?"

Kyo shrugged his shoulders with a smile.

"I have no intention of getting out. . . . Your information is none the less of the greatest importance to me," he continued after a moment.

"No intention of getting out! You prefer to be killed?"

"Perhaps. But you want to leave, don't you?"

"Why should I stay?"

"How much do you need?"

"Three hundred, four hundred. . . ."

"Perhaps I can give you part of it. I should like to help you. Don't imagine I think I'm repaying you in this way for the service you're doing me. . . ."

Clappique smiled sadly. He was not taken in by Kyo's delicacy, but he appreciated it.

"Where will you be tonight?" Kyo continued.

"Where you like."

"No."

"Let's say at the *Black Cat*, then. I must find my few p-pennies in various ways."

"Agreed: the dive is on the territory of the concessions, so there'll be no Chinese police. Less danger of kidnaping than here, even: too many people. . . . I'll be there between eleven and eleven-thirty. But not later. I have an appointment after that. . . ."

Clappique turned his eyes away.

"Which I don't want to miss. You're sure the *Cat* won't be closed?"

"Preposterous! It will be full of Chiang Kai-shek's officers; their glorious uniforms will be intertwined in dance with the bodies of fallen ladies. In gracious garlands, I tell you! So I shall be waiting for you, while attentively contemplating this necessary spectacle until around eleven-thirty."

"Do you think you could get more information by tonight?"

"I'll try."

"You might be doing me a great service. Greater than you can imagine. Am I designated by name?"

"Yes."

"And my father?"

"No. I would have warned him. He was not involved in the *Shantung* affair."

Kyo knew that it wasn't the *Shantung* that had to be thought about, but the repression. May? Her rôle was too unimportant to make it necessary to question Clappique. As for his companions, if he was menaced, so were they all.

"Thanks."

They returned together to the phœnix-room. May was saying to Gisors:

"It's very difficult: if the Women's Union grants divorce to mistreated women, the husbands will leave the revolutionary Union; and if we don't grant it to them, they will lose all confidence in us. I don't blame them. . . ."

"I'm afraid," said Kyo, "it's either too early or too late to organize."

Clappique was leaving, without listening.

"Be munificent as usual," he said to Gisors: "Give me your cac-tuss."

"I have a great affection for the lad who sent it to me. . . . Any other, gladly. . . ."

It was a small hairy cactus.

"Oh, well, never mind."

"So long."

"So. . . . No. Perhaps. Good-by, my dear. The only man in Shanghai who does not exist—not a word: who absolutely does not exist!—salutes you."

He went out.

May and Gisors were looking at Kyo with dismay; he immediately explained:

"He has just learned from the police that I'm on their black list; he advises me not to stir from here, except to get out within two days. Moreover, the repression is imminent. And the last troops of the First Division have left the city."

It was the only division on which the Communists could count. Chiang Kai-shek knew it: he had ordered its general to join the front with his troops. The latter had proposed to the Communist Central Committee the arrest of Chiang Kai-shek. He had been advised to temporize, to pretend illness; he had quickly found himself faced with an ultimatum. And, not daring to fight without the consent of the Party, he had left the city, trying only to leave a few troops there. They in their turn had just left.

"They're not yet far off," Kyo continued; "and the division may even return if we hold the city long enough."

The door opened again, a nose was stuck in, and a cavernous voice said: "Baron de Clappique does not exist."

The door shut.

"Nothing from Hankow?" asked Kyo.

"Nothing."

Since his return he had secretly been organizing combat groups against Chiang Kai-shek, like the ones he had organized against the Northerners. The International had rejected all the slogans of opposition, but accepted the maintenance of the Communist shock groups; Kyo wanted to make the new groups of militants the organizers of the masses which were now every day joining the Unions; but the official speeches of the Chinese Communist Party, the whole propaganda of union with the Kuomintang, were paralyzing him. The Military Committee alone had joined him; all the arms had not been given up, but Chiang Kai-shek was demanding this very day that the Communists surrender those still in their possession. A last appeal from Kyo and the Military Committee had been telegraphed to Hankow.

Old Gisors—fully informed this time—was worried. He was too much inclined to see in Marxism a kind of fatality to regard questions of tactics without suspicion. Like Kyo, he was sure that Chiang Kai-shek would attempt to crush the Communists; like Kyo he believed that the murder of the general would have struck the reaction at the point where it was most vulnerable. But he detested the plot-like character of their present activity. The death of Chiang Kai-shek, even the seizure of the Shanghai government, led only to adventure. Together with some of the members of the International, he favored the return to Canton of the Iron Army and the Communist fraction of the Kuomintang: there, backed by a revolutionary city, by an active and well-supplied arsenal, the Reds could entrench themselves and await the moment that would be propitious to a new Northern campaign, which the imminent reaction would prepare from below. The generals of Hankow, eager for lands to conquer, were less eager to venture into the south of China where the Unions, faithful to those who represented the memory of Sun Yat-sen, would have driven them to a constant and rather fruitless guerilla warfare. Instead of having to fight the Northerners, and then Chiang Kai-shek, the Red army would thus be leaving the latter the task of fighting the former. Whichever enemy the Red army would then encounter at Canton would be greatly weakened. "The donkeys are too much fascinated by their carrot," said Gisors of the generals, "to bite us at this moment if we don't place ourselves between it and them. . . ." But the majority of the Chinese Communist Party, and perhaps Moscow, judged this point of view "liquidational."

194

Kyo, like his father, thought that the best policy was that of a return to Canton. He would have liked, moreover, to prepare the mass emigration of the workers, by an intensive propaganda, from Shanghai to Canton—they possessed nothing. It would be very difficult, but not impossible: the outlets for the Southern provinces being assured, the working masses would have brought a rapid industrialization to Canton. A dangerous policy for Shanghai: spinning-mill workers are more or less skilled, and to train new workers would mean forming new revolutionaries, unless the wages were raised—"an hypothesis which is excluded," Ferral would have said, "by reason of the present state of Chinese industries." To empty Shanghai for Canton's benefit, like Hong Kong in 1925 . . . Hong Kong is five hours from Canton, and Shanghai five days: a difficult enterprise, more difficult perhaps than to let themselves be killed, but less stupid.

Since his return from Hankow he was convinced that the reaction was under way; even if Clappique had not warned him, he would have considered the situation, in the case of an attack on the Communists by the army of Chiang Kai-shek, so desperate that any incident, even the assassination of the general (whatever its consequences) would be a favorable one. The Unions, if they were armed, could conceivably attempt to give battle to a disorganized army.

The bell again. Kyo ran to the door: at last, the mail which brought the answer from Hankow. His father and May watched him return, without saying anything.

"Orders to bury the firearms," he said.

The message, torn up, had become a ball in the hollow of his hand. He took the pieces of paper, spread them out on the opium table, pieced them together, shrugged his shoulders at his childishness: it was indeed the order to hide or to bury the arms.

"I have to go over there right away."

"Over there," was the Central Committee. This meant that he had to leave the concessions. Gisors knew that he could say nothing. Perhaps his son was going to his death; it was not the first time: it was the justification of his life. He had only to suffer and be silent. He took the information given by Clappique very seriously: the latter had saved König's life—the German who was now directing the police of Chiang Kai-shek—by warning him that the corps of cadets in Peking to which he belonged, was to be massacred. Gisors did not know Shpilevski. As Kyo's glance met his he tried to smile; Kyo also, and they did not turn their eyes away: both knew they were lying, and that this lie was perhaps their most affectionate communion.

Kyo returned to his room, where he had left his jacket. May was putting on her coat.

"Where are you going?"

"With you, Kyo."

"What for?"

She did not answer.

"It is easier to recognize us together," he said.

"I don't see why. If you're spotted, it doesn't matter. . . ."

"You'll do no good."

"What good will I do here, during that time? Men don't know what it is to wait. . . ."

He took a few steps, stopped, turned towards her:

"Listen, May: when your freedom was in question, I granted it."

She understood what he alluded to and was afraid: she had forgotten it. Indeed, he added in a duller tone:

". . . And you managed to take advantage of it. Now it's mine that is involved."

"But, Kyo, what's the connection?"

"To recognize the freedom of another is to acknowledge his right to it, even at the cost of suffering, as I know from experience."

"Am I 'another,' Kyo?"

He was silent once more. Yes, at this moment she was another. Something between them had been changed.

"Then," she continued, "because . . . anyway, because of that, we can no longer be in danger together? . . . Consider, Kyo: it almost looks as though you were taking revenge. . . ."

"To be able to no longer, and to try when it's useless amounts to the same thing."

"But if you held it against me as much as that, all you had to do was to take a mistress. . . . But after all, no! why do I say that? It isn't true—I didn't take a lover, I went to bed with a man. It's not the same thing, and you know very well you can have anyone you like. . . ."

"You satisfy me," he answered bitterly.

His look astonished May: it showed a mingling of many emotions. And—most disquieting of all—on his face the fearful expression of a lust which he himself was unaware of.

"At this moment, as well as two weeks ago," he went on, "I'm not looking for someone to go to bed with. I don't say you are wrong; I say that I want to go alone. The freedom you allow me is your freedom. The freedom to do what pleases *you*. Freedom is not an exchange —it is freedom."

"It's a desertion."

Silence.

"Why do people who love each other face death, Kyo, if not to risk it together?"

She guessed that he was going to leave without further discussion, and placed herself in front of the door.

"You should not have given me this freedom," she said, "if it is going to separate us now."

"You did not ask for it."

"You had already recognized it."

You should not have believed me, he thought. It was true, he had always recognized it. But that she should at this moment be discussing a question of rights separated her from him all the more.

"There are rights that one gives," she said bitterly, "only so that they shall not be used."

"If I had given them only in order that you could hang on to them at this moment, it wouldn't be so bad. . . ."

This instant separated them more than death: eyelids, mouth, temples, the place of every caress is visible on the face of a dead woman, and those high cheek-bones and those elongated eyelids now belonged to a foreign world. The wounds of the deepest love suffice to create a rather substantial hatred. Was she withdrawing, so near to death, from the threshold of that world of hostility which she was glimpsing? She said:

"I'm hanging on to nothing, Kyo. Let's say I'm wrong, that I have been wrong, anything you like. But now, at this moment, right away, I want to go with you. I ask it of you."

He said nothing.

"If you did not love me," she went on, "it would be all the same to you to let me go with you. . . . Well, then? Why make us both suffer? . . . As if this were the time for it," she added with weariness.

Kyo felt some familiar demons stirring within him, which rather thoroughly disgusted him. He had an urge to strike her, to strike directly at her love. She was right: if he had not loved her, what would it matter to him that she should die? Perhaps it was the fact that she was forcing this realization upon him at this moment that he resented most.

Did she feel like crying? She had shut her eyes, and the constant, silent trembling of her shoulders, in contrast with her motionless features, seemed the complete expression of human distress. It was no longer his will alone which separated them, but grief. And, since the sight of grief brings together as much as grief itself separates, he was thrown towards her once more by the expression of her face, in which the eyelids were slowly lifting—as when she was struck with surprise. . . . Above her closed eyes, the movement of her brow ended, and that tense face in which the eyelids remained lowered became suddenly a dead woman's face.

Many of May's expressions had no effect on him: he knew them, he always had the feeling that she was copying herself. But he had never seen this death mask—pain, and not sleep, on closed eyes—and death was so near that this illusion acquired the force of a sinister prefiguration. She opened her eyes without looking at him: her glance remained lost on the blank wall of the room; without a single muscle moving, a tear rolled down her nose, remained suspended at the corner of her mouth, betraying by its inexpressive animation, poignant as pain in animals, a mask which was as inhuman, as dead as it had been a moment ago.

"Open your eyes."

She looked at him.

"They are open."

"I had the impression you were dead."

"Well?"

She shrugged her shoulders and went on, in a voice of weary sadness:

"If *I* am to die, I am willing to have you die. . . ."

Now he understood the real feeling that urged him: he wanted to console her. But he could console her only by agreeing to let her go with him. She had shut her eyes again. He took her in his arms, kissed her on the eyelids. When they separated:

"Are we going?" she asked.

"No."

Too honest to hide her impulses, she returned to her desires with a cat's stubbornness, which often exasperated Kyo. She had moved away from the door, but he perceived that he had been anxious to pass only as long as he had been sure he wouldn't pass.

"May, are we going to part on a misunderstanding?"

"Have I lived like a woman who needs protection? . . ."

They stood there facing each other, not knowing what else to say and not accepting silence, both knowing that that moment, one of the gravest of their lives, was ruined by the time which was passing: Kyo's place was not here, but at the Committee, and impatience lurked under his every thought.

She indicated the door with a motion of her head.

He looked at her, took her head between his two hands, pressed it gently without kissing her, as though he were putting into that caress the mingled tenderness and violence of which all the virile gestures of love are capable. At last he withdrew his hands.

The two doors closed behind him. May continued to listen, as though she were waiting for a third door—

which did not exist—to close in its turn. With her mouth open and quivering, drunk with grief, she was becoming aware that, if she had given him the sign to leave alone, it was because she thought she was making in this way the last, the only move which might have made him decide to take her along.

Kyo had scarcely taken a hundred steps, when he met Katov.

"Isn't Ch'en there?"

He pointed to Kyo's house.

"No."

"You abs'lutely don't know where he is?"

"No. Why?"

Katov was calm, but his face was contracted and pale as though he were suffering from a violent headache. . . .

"There are several cars like Chiang Kai-shek's. Ch'en doesn't know it. Either the police have been tipped off, or they're s'spicious. If he isn't warned he's going to get caught and throw his bombs for nothing. I've been chasing him for a long time, you see. The bombs were to have been thrown at one o'clock. Nothing has happened —we would have known."

"He was to do it near the Avenue of the Two Republics. The best thing to do would be to go to Hemmelrich's."

Katov started off immediately.

"You have your cyanide?" Kyo asked him as he turned to go.

"Yes."

Both of them, and several other revolutionary leaders, carried cyanide in the flat buckle of their belts, which opened like a box.

The separation had not freed Kyo from his torment. On the contrary: in this deserted street May was even stronger—having yielded—than right before him, opposing him. He entered the Chinese city, not without being aware of it, but with indifference. "Have I lived like a woman who needs protection? . . ." By what right did he exercise his pitiful protection on the woman who had even consented to his going? In the name of what was he leaving her? Was he sure that there was in his attitude no element of revenge? No doubt May was still sitting on the bed, crushed by a despair that was beyond words and thought. . . .

He retraced his steps on the run.

The phœnix-room was empty: his father had gone out, May was still in the bed-room. Before opening he stopped, overwhelmed by the brotherhood of death, discovering how derisive the flesh appeared before this communion, in spite of its urgent appeal. He understood now that the willingness to lead the being one loves to death itself is perhaps the complete expression of love, that which cannot be surpassed.

He opened the door.

She hurriedly threw her coat over her shoulders, and followed him without a word.

Quarter past three in the afternoon

For a long time Hemmelrich had been looking at his records. No customers. Someone knocked according to the signal agreed upon.

He opened. It was Katov.

"Have you seen Ch'en?"

"Walking remorse!" Hemmelrich grumbled.

"What?"

"Nothing. Yes, I've seen him. About one or two o'clock. Does it concern you?"

"I abs'lutely must see him. What did he say?"

From another room one of the child's cries reached them, followed by the indistinguishable words of the mother trying to calm him.

"He came with two chums. One of them was Suan. Don't know the other one. A fellow with glasses, looked like anybody else. A noble air. Brief-cases under their arms: you understand?"

"That's why I've got to find him, you see."

"He asked me to stay here for three hours."

"Oh! Good! Where is he?"

"Shut up! Listen to what I'm telling you. He told me to stay here. I haven't stirred. Do you hear?"

Silence.

"I told you I haven't stirred."

"Where can he have gone?"

"He didn't say. Like you. Silence is spreading to-day. . . ."

Hemmelrich was standing in the middle of the room, hunched over, with a look almost of hatred. Katov said calmly, without looking at him:

"You're damning yourself too much. That way you're trying to get me to accuse you so you can defend yourself."

"What do you know about it? And what damn business is it of yours anyway? Don't stand there looking at me with that lock of hair like a cockscomb and your hands open, like Jesus Christ, waiting for someone to drive nails through them. . . ."

Without closing his hand, Katov placed it on Hemmelrich's shoulder.

"Things still bad, upstairs?"

"Not quite so bad. But bad enough. Poor kid! . . . With his skinny body and his big head, he looks like a skinned rabbit. . . . Leave me. . . ."

The Belgian freed himself savagely, stopped, then walked to the other end of the room with a curiously childish movement, as if he were sulking.

"And that's not the worst of it," he said. "No, don't act like a fellow who's got flea-bites and stands squirming and looking embarrassed: I haven't tipped off the police about Ch'en. It's all right. Not yet, at least. . . ."

Katov shrugged his shoulders gloomily.

"You'd better tell me all about it."

"I wanted to go with him."

"With Ch'en?"

Katov was sure, now, that he would no longer be able to find him. He spoke with the calm, weary voice of someone who has been beaten. Chiang Kai-shek would not return before night-fall, and Ch'en could attempt nothing until then.

Hemmelrich pointed with his thumb, over his shoulder, in the direction from which the child's cry had come:

"And there you are. There you are. What do you expect me to do?"

"Wait. . . ."

"Because the kid will die, I suppose? Listen: half the day I wish for it. And if it happens, I shall wish him to remain, *not to die*, even sick, even an invalid. . . ."

"I know. . . ."

"What?" said Hemmelrich, as if he were being robbed. "What do you know about it? You're not even married!"

"I've been married."

"I'd like to have seen that. With your looks. . . . No,

204

they're not for us, all those cute little strutting cunts we see passing in the street. . . ."

He felt that Katov was thinking of the woman who was watching the child, upstairs.

"Devotion, yes. And everything she can. The rest—what she hasn't got—is all for the rich. When I see people who look as if they're in love, I feel like smashing them in the face."

"D'votion is a lot. . . . The main thing is not to be alone."

"And that's why you're staying here, isn't it? To help me?"

"Yes."

"Through pity?"

"Not through pity. Through . . ."

But Katov could not find the word. And perhaps it did not exist. He tried to say what he meant indirectly.

"I've felt it—or almost. And also your kind of . . . rage. How do you expect anyone to understand things, except through mem'ries? . . . That's why you don't irritate me."

He had drawn near and was speaking, his head between his shoulders, with his voice that swallowed the syllables, looking at him out of the corner of his eye; both of them, their heads lowered, looked as though they were getting ready to fight, right there among the records. But Katov knew he was the stronger, although he did not know in what way. Perhaps it was his voice, his calm, his friendship even, that were telling.

"A man who's reached the point where he doesn't give a damn about anything, if he really comes across d'votion, sacrifice, anything of that sort, he's done for."

"No fooling! Then what does he do?"

"Becomes a sadist," answered Katov, looking at him quietly.

"Sadism with pins," he went on, "is rare; with words, far from rare. But if the woman is abs'lutely submissive, if she can survive it . . . I knew a fellow who took and gambled the money which his woman had saved up for years to go to the san'torium. A matter of life or death. He lost it. (In such cases you always lose.) He came home all in pieces, abs'lutely broken up like you now. She watched him come over to her bed. She understood right away, you see. And then, what? She tried to console him. . . ."

"Easier," said Hemmelrich slowly, "to console others than to console yourself. . . ." And, suddenly raising his eyes:

"Were you the fellow?"

"That'll do!" Katov banged the counter with his fist. "If it was me, I'd say so." But his anger fell immediately. "I haven't gone that far, and it isn't necess'ry to go that far. . . . If you believe in nothing, *especially* because you believe in nothing, you're forced to believe in the virtues of the heart when you come across them, no doubt about it. And that's what you're doing. If it hadn't been for the woman and the kid you would have gone, I know you would. Well, then?"

"And as we live only for those virtues of the heart, they get the better of you. Well, if you've always got to be licked, it might as well be them. . . . But all that's absurd. It's not a matter of being right. I can't stand the idea of having put Ch'en out, and I couldn't have stood to have kept him."

"We can only ask the comrades to do what they can. I want comrades, and not saints. No confidence in saints. . . ."

"Is it true that you voluntarily went with the fellows to the lead-mines?"

"I was in the camp," said Katov, embarrassed: "the mines or the camp, it's all the same thing. . . ."

"All the same thing! That's not true."

"What do you know about it?"

"It's not true! And you would have kept Ch'en."

"I have no children. . . ."

"I have a feeling it would be less . . . hard for me, even the idea that they'll kill him, if he wasn't sick. . . . I . . . I'm dumb. It's true I'm dumb. And I guess I'm not much of a worker either. I feel like a lamp-post that everything free in the world comes and pisses on."

He pointed once again to the floor above with a movement of his flat face, for the child was crying again. Katov did not dare to say: "Death will free you." It was death that had freed *him*. Since Hemmelrich had begun to speak, the memory of his wife stood between them. Having returned from Siberia without hope, beaten, his medical studies shattered, and having become a factory worker, convinced that he would die before seeing the Revolution, he had sadly proved to himself that he still possessed a remnant of life by treating a little working-girl who loved him with deliberate brutality. But hardly had she become resigned to the pains he inflicted on her than he had been suddenly struck by the overwhelming quality of the tenderness of a creature who could share his suffering in spite of his brutality. From that moment he had lived only for her, continuing his revolutionary activity through habit, but carrying into it the obsession of the limitless tenderness hidden in the heart of that slightly feeble-minded girl: for hours he would caress her hair, and they would lie in bed together for days on end. She had died, and since then . . . That, in any case, stood between Hemmelrich and himself. Not enough.

Through words, he could do almost nothing; but beyond words there were the things which gestures, looks, mere presence were capable of expressing. He knew from experience that the worst suffering is in the solitude which accompanies it. To express it also gives relief; but few words come less readily to men's tongues than those of their deep griefs. To express himself badly, or to lie, would give Hemmelrich a fresh impulse to despise himself: he suffered above all from himself. Katov looked at him without focusing his eyes on him, sadly—it struck him once more how few and awkward the expressions of manly affection are :

"You must understand without my saying anything," he said. "There is nothing to say."

Hemmelrich raised his hand, let it fall again heavily, as though he had to choose only between the distress and the absurdity of his life. But he remained standing before Katov, deeply moved.

"Soon I shall be able to leave and continue looking for Ch'en," Katov was thinking.

Six o'clock in the evening

"The money was delivered yesterday," said Ferral to the colonel, who this time was wearing a uniform. "How do we stand?"

"The Military Governor has sent a lengthy note to General Chiang Kai-shek to ask what he should do in the eventuality of an uprising."

"He wants to be covered?"

The colonel looked at Ferral over the white spot in

his eye, answered merely: "Here is the translati-on."

Ferral read the document.

"I even have the answer," said the colonel.

He handed him a photograph: above Chiang Kai-shek's signature, two characters.

"Which means?"

"The firing-squad."

Ferral looked up at the map of Shanghai on the wall, with large red patches which designated the masses of workers and wretches—the same ones. "Three thousand men of the syndical guards," he was thinking, "perhaps three hundred thousand back of them; but will they dare to budge? On the other side, Chiang Kai-shek and the army. . . ."

"He will begin by having the Communist chiefs shot before any uprising?"

"Certainly. There will be no uprising: the Communists are practically disarmed and Chiang Kai-shek has his troops. The First Division is at the front: it was the only dangerous one."

"Thank you. Good-by."

Ferral was going to Valérie's. A "boy" was waiting for him beside the chauffeur, with a blackbird in a gilded cage on his knees. Valérie had begged Ferral to bring her this bird. As soon as his car had started off, he pulled a letter from his pocket and reread it. What he had been fearing for a month was happening: his American credits were about to be cut off.

The orders from the General Government of Indo-China no longer sufficed to keep in operation the factories created for a market which was to have expanded from month to month and which now was shrinking from day to day: the industrial enterprises of the Consortium showed a large deficit. The stock prices, maintained in Paris by Ferral's banks and the French financial groups which were associated with them, and bolstered up by the inflation, had been steadily dropping since the stabilization of the franc. But the banks of the Consortium derived their only strength from the profits on its plantations—especially its rubber plantations. The Stevenson Plan [1] had raised the price of rubber from 16 cents to $1.12. Ferral, who by virtue of his rubber plantations in Indo-China was a producer, had benefited by the rise without having to restrict his production, since his was not a British enterprise. And the American banks, knowing from experience how much the Plan was costing the United States, the principal consumer, had been eager to open credits guaranteed by the plantations. But the native production of the Dutch Indies, the menace of American plantations in the Philippines, Brazil and Liberia were now leading to the fall of the rubber price; the American banks were thus withdrawing their credits for the same reasons that had induced them to grant them. Ferral was hit all at once by the crash of the only raw material that sustained him—he had been given credits, he had speculated, not on the value of his production but on that of the plantations themselves—by the stabilization of the franc, which brought about the devaluation of all his stocks (a major portion of which were held by his own banks bent on controlling the market) and by the cancellation of his American credits. And he was fully aware that, as soon as this cancellation became known, all the speculators in New York and Paris would take a short position on his stocks; a position that was

[1] The restriction of rubber production in the entire British Empire (the world's greatest producer), for the purpose of raising the price of rubber which at that time had sunk below production cost.

all too safe. . . . He could be saved only for moral reasons; hence, by the French government.

The threat of bankruptcy brings to financial groups an intense national consciousness. When their enterprises in distant corners of the world are suddenly threatened with disaster they remember with mingled pride and gratitude the heritage of civilization which their country has given them and which they in turn have helped to pass on to colonial peoples.

It was Ferral's experience that governments are indulgent task-masters, that they treat their favorite children, the big financial groups, with commendable leniency. But while governments are accustomed to seeing the treasury robbed, they do not like to see it robbed of all hope. A treasury that expects, with the tenacious hope of a gambler, to recoup its losses some day is a treasury half consoled. France had suffered a severe loss by refusing aid to the Industrial Bank of China. It was not likely that France, so soon after, would in turn abandon the Consortium and risk the wrath of a whole new army of investors.

But if Ferral were to ask her for help it was essential that his position should not appear hopeless; it was essential first of all that Communism should be crushed in China. Chiang Kai-shek as master of the Provinces meant the construction of the Chinese Railway; the anticipated loan amounted to three billion gold francs, which equaled many million paper francs. To be sure, he would not be the only one to receive orders for materials, any more than he was alone today in defending Chiang Kai-shek; but he would be in on the game. Moreover, the American banks feared the triumph of Communism in China; its fall would modify their policy. As a Frenchman, Ferral enjoyed privileges in China; "it was an accepted fact that the Consortium would participate in the construction of the railroad." To maintain himself he was justified in asking the government for a loan which it would prefer to a new crash; while his credits were American, his deposits and his stocks were French. All his cards could not win during a period of acute crisis in China; but, just as the Stevenson Plan had in its time assured the life of the Consortium, so the victory of the Kuomintang was to assure it today. The stabilization of the franc had worked against him; the fall of Communism would work for him. . . .

Would he, all his life, never be able to do more than wait, in order to take advantage of them, for the passage of those great tidal sweeps of world economy that began like offerings and ended like blows below the belt? Tonight, in case of either resistance, victory or defeat, he felt himself dependent upon all the forces of the world. But there was this woman upon whom he did not depend, who would presently depend on him; the avowal of submission on her face at the moment of possession, like a hand plastered over his eyes, would conceal from him the network of constraints on which his life rested. He had seen her again in several drawing-rooms (she had just returned from Kyoto three days before), and each time he had been thwarted and irritated by her refusal of all submissiveness, whereby she stimulated his desire, though she had consented to go to bed with him tonight.

In his limitless craving to be preferred—one admires more easily, more completely, from one sex to the other —he called upon eroticism to revive a wavering admiration. That was why he had looked at Valérie while he was lying with her: there is a great deal of certainty in lips swollen with pleasure. He detested the coquettishness without which she would not even have existed in his eyes: that in her which resisted him was what most irritated his sensuality. All this was very obscure, for it was from his need to imagine himself in her place as soon as he began to touch her body that he derived his acute feeling of possession. But a conquered body, to begin with, had more appeal for him than an offered body— more appeal than any other body.

He left his car and entered the *Astor*, followed by the "boy" who was carrying his cage in his hand with an air of dignity. There were millions of shadows on earth: the women whose love did not interest him—and one living adversary: the woman by whom he wanted to be loved. The idea of complete possession had become fixed in him, and his pride called for a hostile pride, as a passionate player calls for another player to oppose him, and not for peace. At least things were well started tonight, since they would begin by going to bed.

The moment he reached the lobby a European employee came up to him.

"Madame Serge left a message to tell Monsieur Ferral that she will not be in tonight, but that this gentleman will explain."

Ferral, dumbfounded, looked at "this gentleman"— seated, with his back turned, next to a screen. The man turned round: the director of one of the English banks, who had been paying court to Valérie for the last month. Beside him, behind the screen, a "boy," with no less dignity than Ferral's, was holding a blackbird in a cage. The Englishman got up, bewildered, shook Ferral's hand, while saying:

"You were to explain to me, Mr. . . ."

They both realized at once that they were being made fools of. They looked at each other, in the midst of the sly smiles of the "boys" and the gravity, too great to be natural, of the white employees. It was the cocktail hour, and all Shanghai was there. Ferral felt himself to be the more ridiculous: the Englishman was almost a youth.

A contempt as intense as the anger which inspired him immediately compensated for the humiliation which was being imposed on him. He felt himself surrounded by the very essence of human stupidity, that which sticks like glue, which weighs on one's shoulders: the creatures who were looking at him were the most despicable fools on earth. Nevertheless, having no idea how much they knew, he imagined that they knew everything and felt himself stricken, in the presence of their sly amusement, by a paralysis shot through with hatred.

"Is it for a bird show?" his "boy" asked the other.

"Don't know."

"Mine is a male."

"Yes. Mine is a female."

"It must be for that."

The Englishman bowed before Ferral, went up to the porter. The latter handed him a letter. He read it, took out a visiting card from his pocketbook, attached it to the cage, said to the porter: "For Madame Serge," and went out.

Ferral tried to bring himself to think, to defend himself. She had struck him at his most sensitive point, as though she had put his eyes out during his sleep: she denied him. What he might think, do, want, did not exist. This ridiculous scene *was*, nothing could prevent its having happened. He alone existed in a world of phantoms, and it was he, precisely he, who was being outraged. And to make matters worse—for he did not think of it as a consequence, but as one more blow in a succession of defeats, as if rage had made him a masochist—to make matters worse, he would not even be going to bed with her. More and more intent on avenging himself on that ironic body, he stood there alone, facing those nincompoops and the expressionless "boys" with their cages dangling from their arms. Those birds were a constant insult. But he must by all means remain. He ordered a cocktail and lighted a cigarette, then remained motionless, busy breaking up a match between his fingers in his coat-pocket. A couple attracted his eye. The man had the charm which gray hair gives to a youngish face; the woman—sweet, but a little flashy—was looking at him with an amorous gratitude born of tenderness or sensuality. "She loves him," thought Ferral enviously. "And he's undoubtedly some obscure fool who perhaps is dependent on one of my enterprises. . . ." He sent for the porter.

"You have a letter for me. Give it to me."

The porter, astonished but maintaining his seriousness, handed him the letter.

"Do you know, dear, that Persian women beat their husbands with their nailed slippers when they are angry? They are irresponsible. And then, of course, they afterwards return to everyday life, the life in which to weep with a man does not commit you, but in which to go to bed with him makes you a slave, the life in which one 'has' women. I am not a woman to be had, a stupid body in which you may find your pleasure by telling lies as to children and invalids. You know a good many things, dear, but you will probably die without its ever having occurred to you that a woman is also a human being. I have always met (perhaps I shall never meet any who are different, but so much the worse—you can't know how thoroughly I mean 'so much the worse!') men who have credited me with a certain amount of charm, who

215

have gone to touching lengths to set off my follies, but who have never failed to go straight to their men-friends whenever it was a question of something really human (except of course to be consoled). I must have my whims, not only to please you, but even to make you listen when I speak; I want you to know what my charming folly is worth: it resembles your affection. If any unhappiness could have resulted from the hold you wanted to have on me, you would not even have noticed it. . . .

"I have met enough men to know how to regard a passing affair: nothing is without importance to a man the moment it involves his pride, and pleasure allows him to gratify it most quickly and most often. I refuse to be regarded as a body, just as you refuse to be regarded as a check-book. You act with me as the prostitutes do with you: 'Talk, but pay. . . .' I am also that body which you want me to be wholly; I know it. It is not always easy for me to protect myself from the idea people have of me. Your presence brings me close to my body with disgust, as springtime brings me close to it with joy. Speaking of spring, have a good time with the birds. And, by the way, the next time do leave the electric switches alone.

"V."

He told himself that he had built roads, transformed a country, torn from their straw-huts the thousands of peasants now housed in the cabins of corrugated iron-sheets around his factories—like a feudal lord, like a delegate of empire; in its cage, the blackbird seemed to be making fun of him. Ferral's energy, his lucidity, the audacity which had transformed Indo-China and whose crushing weight he had just felt upon reading the letter from America, led to nothing but this ridiculous bird—

ridiculous as the universe—which was undeniably making fun of him. "So much importance given to a woman." The woman had nothing to do with it. She was nothing but a bandage torn away from his eyes: he had thrown himself with all his might against the boundaries of his will. His thwarted sexual excitement fed his anger, threw him into the choking state of hypnosis in which ridicule calls for blood. One can get quick revenge only on bodies. Clappique had told him a gruesome story about an Afghan chief whose wife, after having been violated by a neighboring chief, had returned with a letter, saying: "I am returning your woman, she is not so good as she is said to be"; and who, having caught the offender, had tied him in front of the naked woman to tear out his eyes, saying: "You have seen her and despised her, but you can swear that you will never see her again." He imagined himself in Valérie's room, with her tied to the bed, screaming till her exhausted cries became choking sobs, so close to cries of pleasure, bound with cords, writhing under the possession of suffering, since it was not under that of sex. . . . The porter was waiting. "I must remain unmoved, like this idiot—I'd like to box his ears, just the same." The idiot did not betray the slightest smile. He was saving it up for later on. Ferral said: "I'll return shortly," did not pay for his cocktail, left his hat and went out.

"To the biggest bird-dealer," he said to the chauffeur. It was near by. But the shop was closed.

"In Chinese city," said the chauffeur, "street of bird-dealers."

"Go ahead."

As the car drove along there ran through Ferral's mind the confession, which he had read in some medical book, of a woman seized with an uncontrollable desire to be flagellated, making an assignation by letter with an unknown man and discovering with terror that she wanted to run away at the very moment when she was lying on the hotel-bed and the man armed with the whip was completely paralyzing her arms under her lifted skirt. The face was invisible, but it was Valérie's. Stop at the first Chinese brothel? No: no flesh would give him relief from the outraged sexual pride which tormented him.

The car was forced to stop before the barbed-wires. Ahead, the Chinese city, very black, unsafe. So much the worse. Ferral left the car, slipped his revolver into his coat-pocket, hoping for some assault: one kills what one can.

The street of the pet-shops was asleep; the "boy" quietly knocked at the first shutter, crying "Buyer": the shopkeepers were afraid of the soldiers. Five minutes later someone opened. In the magnificent russet half-light, around a lantern, a few smothered leaps of cats or monkeys and beatings of wings announced the awakening of the animals. In shadows beyond the radius of the light, were long splotches of dull red: macaws chained to perches.

"How much for all those birds?"

"Just the birds? Eight hundred dollars."

He was a small dealer, and he had no rare birds. Ferral pulled out his check-book, hesitated: the dealer would want cash. The "boy" understood. "He is Monsieur Ferral," he said; "his car is over there." The dealer went out, saw the headlights of the car, scratched by the barbed wires.

"That's all right."

This confidence, a proof of his authority, exasperated Ferral; his power, obvious to the point that his name was known to this shopkeeper, was absurd since he could not use it. Pride, however, helped by the activity in which he was engaged and by the cold night-air, came to his rescue: sadistic anger and imaginings were breaking up into disgust, even though he knew he had not done with them.

"I also have a kangaroo," said the dealer.

Ferral shrugged his shoulders. But already a youngster, who had also been awakened, was approaching with the kangaroo in his arms. It was a small, furry creature, and it looked at Ferral with the frightened eyes of a deer.

"Fine."

Another check.

Ferral returned slowly to the car. It was necessary above all that, if Valérie told the story of the cages—she would not fail to—he would only have to tell the end in order to escape ridicule. The dealer, the youngster and the "boy" were bringing the small cages, arranging them in the car, and returning to fetch more; finally, the last ones, the kangaroo and the parrots, brought in large round cages. Beyond the Chinese city, a few shots. Very good: the more they fought the better it would be. The car started off again, before the bewildered eyes of the post.

At the *Astor* Ferral sent for the manager.

"Will you please come upstairs with me to Madame Serge's room. She is away and I want to give her a surprise."

The manager concealed his astonishment, and even more his disapproval: the *Astor* was dependent on the Consortium. The mere presence of a white man to whom he could talk detached Ferral from his universe of humiliation, helped him to return among "the others"; the Chinese dealer and the night had left him in his obsession; he was not entirely freed from it yet, but at least it no longer dominated him wholly.

Five minutes later he was having the cages arranged in the room. All the precious objects were put away in the closets, one of which was left open. He picked up a pair of pajamas that lay spread out on the bed, but the moment he touched the warm silk it seemed to him that this warmth became communicated through his arm to his whole body and that the material he was grasping had exactly covered one of her breasts: the dresses, the pajamas hanging in the half-open closet, held within them something more sensual, perhaps, than Valérie's body itself. He had an impulse to bury his face in those pajamas, to press or tear, as though he were penetrating them, those garments still saturated with her presence. He would have taken the pajamas with him, if he had been able. He threw them into the closet, and the "boy" closed the door upon them. As the pajamas left his hand, the legend of Hercules and Omphale brusquely seized his imagination—Hercules dressed as a woman in soft, flimsy garments like these, humiliated and content in his humiliation. In vain he tried to summon the sadistic scenes that had insistently come before him awhile ago: the man worsted by Omphale and Dejanira weighed upon his whole mind, drowned it in a humiliating satisfaction. A sound of steps approached. He put his hand to his revolver in his pocket: if she had entered at that moment he would undoubtedly have killed her. The steps passed by the door and grew fainter. Ferral's hand changed pockets and he nervously pulled out his handkerchief. He had to act, do something, escape from this state of mind: he had the parrots and cockatoos unchained, but the timid birds took refuge in the corners and in the curtains. The kangaroo had jumped on the bed and remained there. Ferral turned out the center light, left only the night-lamp: pink and white, with the magnificent curved flashes of their ornate wings, reminding him of the phœnixes of the East India Company, the cockatoos began to stir about with a clumsy and restless flutter.

Those boxes full of excited little birds, scattered about on all the furniture, on the floor, in the fireplace, bothered him. He tried to discover why, could not imagine. Went out. Came in again, immediately understood: the room seemed devastated. Would he escape idiocy tonight? In spite of himself he had left here the blatant image of his anger.

"Open the cages," he said to the "boy."

"The room will get dirty, Monsieur Ferral," said the manager.

"Madame Serge will change her room. Don't worry, it won't be tonight. You'll send me the bill."

"Flowers, Monsieur Ferral?"

"Nothing but the birds. And let no one come in here, not even the servants."

The window was protected from mosquitoes by a screen. The birds would not fly away. The manager opened the casement to prevent the room from smelling foul.

And now, on the furniture and the curtains, in the corners of the ceiling, the island birds were wildly fluttering, their colors dull in this feeble light, like those of Chinese frescoes. Through hatred he would have offered Valérie his handsomest gift. . . . He turned out the light, turned it on again, turned it out, then on. He was using the bed-side switch; he remembered the last night he had spent with Valérie in his apartment. He had an impulse to tear off the switch so that she would never be able to use it—with anyone. But he wanted to leave no trace of anger here.

"Take away the empty cages," he said to the "boy." "Have them burned."

"If Madame Serge should ask who sent the birds," said the manager, looking at Ferral with admiration, "is she to be told?"

"Won't ask. It's signed."

He went out. He must have a woman tonight. However, he had no desire to go to the Chinese restaurant immediately. It was enough—for the time being—that he was sure there were bodies at his disposal. Often, when he was awakened with a start from a nightmare, he would feel the desire to continue his sleep in spite of the nightmare which would seize him again, and at the same time, the desire to escape it by becoming completely awake; sleep was the nightmare, but it was *himself;* awakening was peace, but the world. Tonight lust was the nightmare. He finally made up his mind to awaken from it, and had himself driven to the French Club: to talk, to enter into relation again with a human being, if only through conversation, was the surest awakening.

The bar was crowded: troubled times. Close to the half-open window, a beige cape of rough wool over his shoulders, alone and almost isolated, Gisors was seated with a sweet cocktail before him; Kyo had telephoned him that all was well and his father had come to the bar to pick up the rumors of the day, often absurd but at times significant: they were not so tonight. Ferral went up to him amid the greetings. He knew the nature of his lectures, but attached no importance to them; and he did not know that Kyo was in Shanghai at the present time. He considered it beneath his dignity to question Martial about persons, and Kyo's rôle did not have a public character.

All those idiots who were looking at him with timid disapproval believed the bond between him and the old man was opium. They were wrong. Ferral pretended to smoke—one, two pipes, always less than would have been necessary for him to feel the effect of the opium—because he found in the atmosphere of smoke-sessions, in the pipe that passed from mouth to mouth, a means of making advances to women. Having a horror of courtship, of the exchange in which he paid by attributing importance to a woman for what she gave him in the way of pleasure, he eagerly seized everything that enabled him to dispense with it.

It was a more complex impulse which, not so long ago, in Peking, had occasionally made him come and stretch out on old Gisors' couch. The pleasure of scandalizing, to begin with. And then, he did not want to be merely the President of the Consortium, he wanted to be distinct from his activity—a way of considering himself superior to it. His almost aggressive love of art, of thought, of the cynicism which he called lucidity, was a defense: Ferral had the backing neither of the "families" of the great credit establishments, nor of the Ministry of Finance. The Ferral dynasty was too closely linked to the history of the Republic to make it possible to consider him as a mere upstart; but he remained an amateur, no matter how great his authority. Too clever to attempt to fill the ditch that surrounded him, he widened it. Gisors' great culture, his intelligence which was always at the service of anyone who sought him out, his disdain of conventions, his almost always singular "points of view," which Ferral did not hesitate to pass off as his own when he had left him, brought them together more than all the rest separated them; with Ferral, Gisors talked politics only on the philosophical level. Ferral said he needed intelligence, and, when it was not the kind that offended him, this was true.

He looked around: at the very moment he sat down, almost all eyes turned away. Tonight he would gladly have married his cook, for no other reason than to force this crowd to accept her. It exasperated him to have all those idiots pass judgment on what he was doing; the less he saw them, the better: he suggested to Gisors that they go out for a drink on the terrace overlooking the garden. In spite of the coolness the "boys" had brought out a few tables.

"Do you think it is possible to know—really *know—* a human being?" he asked Gisors. They sat down near a small lamp. Its halo of light was absorbed by the darkness which was gradually filling with mist.

Gisors looked at him. "He would have no taste for psychology if he could impose his will."

"A woman?" he asked.

"What difference does it make?"

"There is something erotic about a mind which applies itself to elucidating a woman. . . . To want to know a woman, it seems to me, is always a way of possessing her or of taking revenge on her. . . ."

A little tart at the next table was saying to another: "They can't fool me that easy. I'll tell you: the woman is jealous of my style."

"I think," Gisors went on, "that recourse to the mind is an attempt to compensate for this: the knowledge of a person is a negative feeling: the positive feeling, the reality, is the torment of being always a stranger to what one loves."

"Does one ever love?"

"Time occasionally causes this anguish to disappear, time alone. One never knows a human being, but one occasionally ceases to feel that one does not know him. (I am thinking of my son, of course, and also of . . . another lad.) To know with one's intelligence is the futile attempt to dispense with time. . . ."

"The function of intelligence is not to dispense with things."

Gisors looked at him:

"What do you mean by 'intelligence'?"

"In general?"

"Yes."

Ferral reflected:

"The possession of the means of coercing things or men."

Gisors smiled imperceptibly. Each time he asked this question the other person, no matter who he was, would answer by producing the image of his desire. But Ferral suddenly became more intense.

"Do you know what was the torture inflicted on women for infidelity to their masters in this country during the first empires?" he asked.

"Well, there were several, weren't there? The most common one, apparently, consisted in tying them to a raft, their hands cut off at the wrists, eyes gouged, and in . . ."

While he was speaking, Gisors noticed the growing attention and, it seemed, the satisfaction with which Ferral listened.

". . . letting them drift down those endless rivers, till they died of hunger or exhaustion, their lover bound beside them on the same raft. . . ."

"Their lover?"

How was it possible to reconcile such a slip with his

concentrated attention, with his look? Gisors could not guess that, in Ferral's mind, there was no lover; but the latter had already caught himself.

"The most curious thing about it," Gisors went on, "is that those brutal codes seem to have been drawn up, until the fourth century, by men who were wise, humane and gentle, from all we know of the private lives. . . ."

"Yes, they were undoubtedly wise."

Gisors looked at his sharp face. The eyes were closed; the little lamp cast its light upon him from below, little gleams catching in his mustache. Shots in the distance. How many lives were being destroyed out there in the night mist? He was looking at Ferral's countenance, tense with bitterness over some humiliation that rose from the depth of his being, defending itself with the derisive force of human rancor; the hatred of the sexes hovered over his humiliation, as though the oldest hatreds were being reborn from the blood that continued to flow upon the already gorged earth.

New shots, very near this time, caused the glasses on the table to tremble.

Gisors had grown used to those shots that came daily from the Chinese city. In spite of Kyo's telephone call these, suddenly, made him anxious. He did not know the extent of the political rôle played by Ferral, but he knew this rôle could be used only in the service of Chiang Kai-shek. He considered it natural to be sitting next to him—he never found himself "compromised," even in his own eyes—but he no longer wished to be of help to him. New shots, farther away.

"What's going on?" he asked.

"I don't know. The Blue and the Red leaders have

made a great proclamation of union. Things seem to be straightening out."

"He lies," thought Gisors: "he is at least as well informed as I am."

"Red or Blue," said Ferral, "the coolies will continue to be coolies just the same; unless they have been killed off. Don't you consider it a stupidity characteristic of the human race that a man who has only one life should be willing to lose it for an idea?"

"It is very rare for a man to be able to endure—how shall I say it?—his condition, his fate as a man. . . ."

He thought of one of Kyo's ideas: all that men are willing to die for, beyond self-interest, tends more or less obscurely to justify that fate by giving it a foundation in dignity: Christianity for the slave, the nation for the citizen, Communism for the worker. But he had no desire to discuss Kyo's ideas with Ferral. He came back to the latter:

"There is always a need for intoxication: this country has opium, Islam has hashish, the West has woman. . . . Perhaps love is above all the means which the Occidental uses to free himself from man's fate. . . ."

Under his words flowed an obscure and hidden counter-current of figures: Ch'en and murder, Clappique and his madness, Katov and the Revolution, May and love, himself and opium. . . . Kyo alone, in his eyes, resisted these categories.

"Far fewer women would indulge in copulation," answered Ferral, "if they could obtain in the vertical posture the words of admiration which they need and which demand a bed."

"And how many men?"

"But man can and must deny woman: action, action

227

alone justifies life and satisfies the white man. What would we think if we were told of a painter who makes no paintings? A man is the sum of his actions, of what he has *done*, of what he can do. Nothing else. I am not what such and such an encounter with a man or woman may have done to shape my life; I am my roads, my . . ."

"The roads had to be built."

Since the last shots, Gisors had resolved to play the justifier no longer.

"If not by you, then by someone else. It's as if a general were to say: 'with my soldiers I can shoot the town.' But if he were capable of shooting it, he would not be a general. . . . For that matter, men are perhaps indifferent to power. . . . What fascinates them in this idea, you see, is not real power, it's the illusion of being able to do exactly as they please. The king's power is the power to govern, isn't it? But man has no urge to govern: he has an urge to compel, as you said. To be more than a man, in a world of men. To escape man's fate, I was saying. Not powerful: all-powerful. The visionary disease, of which the will to power is only the intellectual justification, is the will to god-head: every man dreams of being god."

What Gisors was saying disturbed Ferral, but his mind was not prepared to welcome it. If the old man did not justify him, he ceased to free him from his obsession:

"In your opinion, why do the gods possess mortal women only in human or bestial forms?"

As if he had seen it, Gisors felt a shadow settling next to them; Ferral had got up.

"You need to involve what is most essential in yourself in order to feel its existence more violently," said Gisors without looking at him.

Ferral did not guess that Gisors' penetration had its source in the fact that he recognized elements of his own personality in those he spoke to, and that one could have made the most subtle portrait of him by piecing together his examples of perspicacity.

"A god can possess," the old man went on with a knowing smile, "but he cannot conquer. The ideal of a god, I believe, is to become a man while knowing that he can recover his power; and the dream of man, to become god without losing his personality. . . ."

Ferral absolutely had to have a woman. He left.

"A curious case of elaborate self-deception," Gisors was thinking: "It's as if he were looking at himself through the eyes of a romantic petty bourgeois." When, shortly after the war, Gisors had come into contact with the economic powers of Shanghai, he had been not a little astonished to discover that the idea he had always had of a capitalist corresponded to nothing. Almost all those whom he met at that time had regulated their love-life according to one pattern or another—and almost always the pattern was marriage: the obsession which makes the great business-man, unless he is just another heir, can rarely adjust itself to the dispersion of irregular sexual experiences. "Modern capitalism," he would explain to his students, "is much more a will to organization than to power. . . ."

Ferral, in the car, was thinking that his relations with women were always the same, and always absurd. Perhaps he had loved, once. Once. What dead-drunk psychologist had had the idea of giving the name of love to the feeling which now poisoned his life? Love is an exalted obsession; his women obsessed him, yes—like a desire of vengeance. He went to women to be judged, he who countenanced no judgment. The woman who would have admired him in the giving of herself, whom he would not have had to fight, would not have existed in his eyes. Condemned to coquettes or to whores. There were their bodies. Fortunately. Otherwise . . . "You will die, dear, without having suspected that a woman is a human being. . . ." To her, perhaps; not to him. A woman, a human being! She is relaxation, a voyage, an enemy. . . .

He picked up a courtesan on the way in one of the houses on Nanking Road: a girl with a gentle, pleasing face. Beside him in the car, with her hands resting modestly on her zither, she looked like a T'ang statuette. They arrived at his place at last. He strode up the steps ahead of her, his usual long step now falling heavily. "Let's go and sleep," he was thinking. . . . Sleep was peace. He had lived, fought, created; beneath all those appearances, deep down, he found this to be the only reality, the joy of abandoning himself, of leaving upon the shore, like the body of a drowned companion, that creature, himself, whose life it was necessary each day to invent anew. "To sleep is the only thing I have always really wanted, for so many years. . . ."

What better could he expect than a soporific from the young woman whose slippers resounded sharply at each step behind him on the stairway? They entered the smoking-room: a small room with divans covered with Mongolian rugs, more suggestive of sensuality than of revery. On the walls, a great wash-drawing of Kama's first period, a Thibetan banner. The woman placed her zither on a divan. On the tray, the ancient instruments with jade handles, ornamental and impractical, were clearly not in use. She put out her hand towards them:

he stopped her with a gesture. A distant shot shook the needles on the tray.

"Do you want me to sing?"

"Not now."

He looked at her body, both suggested and hidden by the sheath of mauve silk. He knew she was stupefied: it is not the custom to embrace a courtesan before she has sung, chatted, served food, or prepared pipes. Otherwise, why not choose a prostitute?

"Don't you want to smoke either?"

"No. Get undressed."

He denied her dignity, and he knew it. He had an urge to demand that she take off all her clothes, to make her stand completely naked, but she would have refused. He had left only the night-lamp turned on. "Lust," he thought, "is the humiliation of oneself or of the other person, perhaps of both. An idea, obviously. . . ." She was, for that matter, more exciting as she was, with her clinging Chinese chemise; but he was barely aroused, or perhaps he was aroused only by the submission of this body that was awaiting him, while he did not move. He derived his pleasure from putting himself in the place of the other, that was clear: of the other, compelled; compelled by him. In reality he never went to bed with anyone but himself, but he could do this only if he were not alone. He understood now what Gisors had only suspected: yes, his will to power never achieved its object, lived only by renewing it; but if he had never in his life possessed a single woman, he had possessed, he would possess through this Chinese woman who was awaiting him, the only thing he was eager for: himself. He needed the eyes of others to see himself, the senses of another to feel himself. He looked at the Thibetan painting, placed there without his quite knowing why: on a discolored world over which travelers were wandering, two exactly similar skeletons were embracing each other in a trance.

He went toward the woman.

Half past ten at night

"If only the car doesn't delay much longer," thought Ch'en. In the complete darkness he would not be so sure of his act, and the last street-lights would soon go out. The desolate night of the China of rice-fields and marshes had reached the almost deserted avenue. Dim in the mist, the lights that passed between the slits of the partly open shutters, went out one by one; the last reflections clung to the wet rails, to the telegraph insulators; they gradually grew fainter; soon Ch'en could see them only on the vertical sign-boards covered with gilt characters. This misty night was his last night, and he was satisfied. He would blow up with the machine, in a blinding flash that would illuminate this hideous avenue for a second and cover a wall with a sheaf of blood. The oldest Chinese legend came to his mind: men are the vermin of the earth. It was necessary that terrorism become a mystic cult. Solitude, first of all: let the terrorist decide alone, execute alone; the police derive their whole strength from informers; the murderer who operates alone does not risk giving himself away. The ultimate solitude, for it is difficult for one who lives isolated from the everyday world not to seek others like himself.

Ch'en knew the objections that are made to terrorism: police repression of the workers, the appeal to fascism. But the repression could not be more violent than it was already, nor fascism more obvious. And perhaps Kyo and he were not thinking of the same men. The problem was not to maintain the best elements among the oppressed masses in their class in order to liberate it, but to give a meaning to their very oppression: let each one assume a responsibility and appoint himself the judge of an oppressor's life. Give an immediate meaning to the individual without hope and multiply the attempts, not by an organization, but by an idea: revive the martyrs. Pei, writing, would be listened to because he, Ch'en, was going to die: he knew how much weight an idea acquires through the blood that is shed in its name.

Everything that was not identified with his resolute gesture was decomposing in the night in which the car that would soon arrive remained hidden. The mist, fed by the smoke from the ships, was gradually obliterating the streets at the end of the avenue: bustling passers-by were walking one behind the other, rarely passing each other, as if war had imposed an all-powerful order upon the city. The prevailing silence made their movements almost fantastic. They did not carry parcels or baskets, did not push carts; tonight it seemed as if their activity had no purpose. Ch'en looked at all those shadows flowing noiselessly towards the river, with an inexplicable and constant movement; was not Destiny itself the force that was pushing them towards the end of the avenue where the archway on the edge of the shadowy river, illuminated by indistinguishable signs, was like the very gates of death? The enormous characters disappeared in confused perspective, into that blurred and tragic world as if into the centuries; and, as if it, too, were coming, not from general headquarters but from a remote past, the military horn of Chiang Kai-shek's car began to sound faintly at the end of the almost deserted street.

Ch'en gratefully pressed the bomb under his arm. The headlights alone emerged from the mist. And almost immediately, preceded by the Ford of the guard, the entire car pierced through; again it seemed to Ch'en that it was coming extraordinarily fast. Three rickshaws suddenly obstructed the street, and the two cars slowed down. He tried to regain control of his breathing. Already the way was clear. The Ford passed, the car was coming: a huge American automobile, flanked by the two body-guards on the running-boards; it gave such an impression of force that Ch'en felt that if he did not advance, if he waited, he would jump aside in spite of himself. He took his bomb by the neck, like a milk-bottle. The general's car was five meters away, enormous. He ran towards it with an ecstatic joy, threw himself upon it, with his eyes shut.

He came to a few seconds later: he had neither felt nor heard the cracking of bones that he expected: he had sunk into a dazzling globe. No more coat. With his right hand he was holding a piece of the car-hood full of mud or blood. A few meters away a pile of red wreckage, a surface of shattered glass on which shone a last reflection of light, some . . . already he was unable to make out anything further: he was becoming aware of pain, which in less than a second went beyond consciousness. He could no longer see clearly. He felt nevertheless that the square was still deserted. Did the police fear a second bomb? He was suffering with all his flesh, from a pain that could not even be localized: nothing was left in him but suffering. Someone was approaching. He remembered that he was to seize his revolver. He felt for his trouser-pocket. No more pocket, no more trousers, no more leg. . . . Hacked flesh. The other revolver, in his shirt-pocket. The button had come off. He seized the weapon by the barrel, turned it round without knowing how, instinctively pulled the trigger with his thumb. He opened his eyes at last. Everything was turning, slowly and inevitably, along a great circle—and yet nothing existed but pain. A policeman was near by. Ch'en wanted to ask if Chiang Kai-shek was dead, but he wanted to know this in another world; in this world, that death itself was unimportant to him.

With a violent kick in the ribs, the policeman turned him over. Ch'en shrieked, fired straight ahead, at random, and the rebound rendered the pain, which he believed limitless, even more intense. He was going to faint or die. He made the most terrific effort of his life, managed to get the barrel of the revolver into his mouth. Expecting the new rebound, even more painful than the preceding one, he no longer moved. A furious kick from another officer caused all his muscles to contract: he fired without being aware of it.

Part Five

PLOWING through the mist, the car entered the long sandy driveway that led to a gambling-house. "I have time to go up," Clappique thought, "before going to the *Black Cat*." He was determined not to miss Kyo, because of the money he expected from him and because this time, perhaps, he would not only warn him, but save his life. He had had no trouble obtaining the information Kyo had asked him for: the spies knew that a movement of Chiang Kai-shek's special troops was planned for eleven o'clock, and that all the Communist Committees would be surrounded. It was too late now to say: "The reaction is imminent." The order must be: "Don't go to any of the Committees tonight." He had not forgotten that Kyo was to leave at eleven-thirty. Some Communist meeting, then, was planned for tonight, which Chiang Kai-shek intended to crush. What the police knew was occasionally inaccurate, but the coincidence was too obvious. If Kyo were warned he could put off the meeting, or, if it was too late, not go there.

"If he gives me one hundred dollars, I will perhaps have enough money: a hundred, and the hundred and seventeen I collected this afternoon in congenial and uniformly illegal ways, two hundred and seventeen. . . . But perhaps he won't have anything. This time there aren't any firearms to turn the trick. Let's first try to manage by ourselves." The car stopped. Clappique, who

236

was wearing his dinner-jacket, gave two dollars. The driver, bare-headed, thanked him with a broad smile: the fare was one dollar.

"The purpose of this liberality is to permit you to buy a l-little Derby hat."

He raised his forefinger, a symbol of truth:

"I say: *Derby*."

The driver was driving off.

"For from the plastic point of view, which is that of all worthy minds," continued Clappique, standing in the middle of the gravel driveway, "that fellow requires a Derby."

The car was out of sight. He was addressing only the night; and, as though it were answering him, the fragrance of the wet boxwood and spindle-trees rose from the garden. That bitter fragrance was Europe. The Baron put his hand to his right pocket, and instead of his wallet, felt his revolver: the wallet was in the left pocket. He looked at the dark windows, which could barely be made out. "Let's think. . . ." He knew he was merely trying to prolong the moment when the game was not yet begun, when flight was still possible. "The day after tomorrow, if it has rained in the meantime, this same fragrance will be here; and I shall perhaps be dead. . . . Dead? What am I talking about? Madness! Not a word; I am immortal." He went in, climbed the stairs to the second floor. The sound of counters and the voice of the croupier seemed to rise and fall with the layers of smoke. The boys were sleeping; but the Russian detectives of the private police, their hands in the pockets of their coats (the right clasped round a Colt), leaning against the door-cases or walking about perfunctorily, were wide awake. Clappique went into the large hall: in a haze of tobacco-smoke through which the scroll-orna-

237

ments on the walls shone dimly, alternate splotches—black dinner-jackets, bare white shoulders—were leaning over the green table.

"Hello, Toto!" several voices shouted.

The Baron was often called Toto, in Shanghai. Yet he had come to this place only a few times, to accompany friends: he was not a gambler. Opening his arms, assuming the air of a fond-father-who-joyfully-finds-his-lost-children, he shouted:

"Bravo! It moves me deeply to be able to join this l-little family-party. . . ."

But the croupier was starting the ball; the attention left Clappique. He lost his value, here; these people did not need distraction. Their eyes were all magnetized by that ball, in an absolute discipline.

He had a hundred and seventeen dollars. To play straight on the numbers would have been too dangerous. He had decided, beforehand, to play odd or even.

"A few congenial l-little counters," he said to the man who was distributing these.

"At how much?"

"Twenty dollars."

He decided to play one counter each time; always even. He had to win at least three hundred dollars.

He placed his counter. Number 5 came up. Lost. Neither important nor interesting. He placed again, still even. The 2. Won. Again. The 7: lost. Then, the 9: lost. The 4: won. The 3: lost. The 7, the 1: lost. He had lost eighty dollars. He had only one more counter.

His last chance.

He tossed it with his right hand; he no longer moved the left one, as if the motionlessness of the ball were somehow holding it tied. And yet this hand seemed to be drawing him. He suddenly remembered: it was not

238

his hand that was disturbing him, it was the watch he was wearing on his wrist. Eleven twenty-five. He had five minutes to reach Kyo.

The time before the last he had been sure of winning: even if he was to lose, he could not lose so fast. He had been foolish to attach no importance to his first loss; it was certainly a bad omen. But one almost always wins on the last stake; and the last three times the number had come out odd. Since his arrival, however, there had been more odds than evens, since he was losing. . . . Should he change, play odds? But something was now urging him to remain passive, to submit: it seemed to him that he had come just for this. Any gesture would have been a sacrilege. He left the stake on an even number.

The croupier started the ball. It began to go round, slowly as always, seemed to hesitate. Since the beginning, Clappique had seen neither red nor black come out. Those points now had the best chance. The ball continued its course. Why had he not played red? The ball slowed down. It stopped on the 2. Won.

He must put the forty dollars on the 7, and play the number. It was obvious: henceforth he must play his own game. He placed his two counters, and won. When the croupier pushed fourteen counters in his direction, he discovered with stupefaction that he *could* win: it was not something he was imagining, a fantastic lottery with unknown winners. It seemed to him suddenly that the bank owed him money, not because he had staked on the winning number, not because he had lost in the beginning; but from the beginning of time, because of the capriciousness and freedom of his mind—it seemed to him that this ball was placing chance in his service to pay all fate's debts. However, if he played a number again, he would lose. He staked two hundred dollars on odd—and lost.

Outraged, he left the table a moment and went over to the window.

Outside, night. Under the trees, the red tail-lights of the cars. In spite of the window-panes he could hear a great babble of voices, laughter, and suddenly, without being able to make out the words, something said in a tone of anger. Passions. . . . All those creatures who were passing in the haze, what weak, stupid lives did they lead? Not even shadows: voices in the night. It was in this hall that blood flowed fast into life. Those who did not gamble were not men. Was not his whole past but one long folly? He returned to the table.

He staked sixty dollars on even, once more. That ball which was slowing down was a destiny—*his* destiny. He was not struggling with a creature, but with a kind of god; and this god, at the same time, was himself. The ball started off again.

He immediately recovered the passive turmoil he was seeking: again he had the feeling of seizing his life, of holding it suspended to the whim of that absurd ball. Thanks to it he was able for the first time to gratify at once the two Clappiques that composed him, the one who wanted to live and the one who wanted to be destroyed. Why look at the watch? He threw Kyo back into a world of dreams; it seemed to him that he was sustaining that ball, no longer with counters, but with his own life—by not meeting Kyo he lost all chance of getting any more money—and with the life of another; and the fact that the other was wholly unaware of it gave to the ball, which was again slowing down, the living reality of conjunctions of planets, of chronic diseases, of everything by which men believe their destinies to be governed. What did that ball, hesitating on the edges of the compartments like a dog's muzzle, have to do with money? Through its agency he was embracing his own destiny—the only means he had ever found of possessing himself! To win, no longer in order to take flight, but to remain, to risk more, so that the stake of his conquered liberty would render the gesture even more absurd! Leaning on his forearm, no longer even looking at the ball which continued to roll, more and more slowly, the muscles of his calves and shoulders trembling, he was discovering the very meaning of gambling, the frenzy of losing.

5.

Almost everyone was losing; smoke filled the room together with a dismal relaxation of nerves and the shuffle of counters gathered by the rake. Clappique knew he was not through. Why keep his seventeen dollars? He pulled out the ten-dollar bill and staked it again on even.

He was so sure he would lose that he had not played everything—as if to prolong the sensation of losing. As soon as the ball began to hesitate, his right hand followed it, but the left one remained attached to the table. He understood now the intense aliveness of gambling instruments: that ball was not a ball like any other—like those that are not used for gambling; the very hesitancy of its movement lived: that movement, both inevitable and passive, wavered thus because lives were linked to it. While the ball turned none of the players puffed at his lighted cigarette. The ball entered a red compartment, left it, strayed again, entered that of the 9. With his left hand resting on the table, Clappique made an imperceptible gesture of pulling it away. Once more he had lost.

241

Five dollars on even: the last counter again.

The ball was describing wide circles, not yet alive. The watch, however, distracted Clappique's eyes from it. He did not wear it on top of his wrist, but underneath, where the pulse is taken. He placed his hand flat on the table and managed to concentrate on the ball. He was discovering that gambling is a suicide without death: all he had to do was to place his money there, to look at the ball and wait, as he would have waited after having swallowed poison; a poison endlessly renewed, together with the pride of taking it. The ball stopped on the 4. Won.

Winning hardly mattered. Yet, if he had lost . . . He won once more, lost once. Again he had forty dollars left, but he wanted to recover the sensation of turmoil of the last play. The stakes were piling up on the red which had not come out in a long time. This compartment, on which almost all eyes were converging, fascinated him too; but to quit the even numbers would be like giving up the battle. He stuck to even, staked the forty dollars. No stake would ever be worth this one: Kyo had perhaps not yet left: in ten minutes he would surely no longer be able to catch him; but now perhaps he could. Now, now he was playing his last cent, his life and that of another, especially that of another. He knew he was sacrificing Kyo; it was Kyo who was chained to that ball, to that table, and it was he, Clappique, who was that ball, which was master of everyone and of himself—of himself who was nevertheless looking at it, living as he had never lived, outside of himself, held spellbound and breathless by an overpowering shame.

He went out at one o'clock: the "club" was closing. He had twenty-four dollars left. The outside air soothed him like that of a forest. The mist was much lighter than at eleven. Perhaps it had rained: everything was wet. Although he could see neither the boxwood nor the spindle-trees in the darkness, he guessed their dark foliage by their bitter fragrance. "It is r-remarkable," he thought, "how people can say that the player's sensation is caused by his hope of winning! It's as if they said that men fight duels to become fencing champions. . . ." But the serenity of the night seemed to have put to flight, together with the fog, all the anxieties, all the griefs of men. And yet . . . volleys in the distance. "They've begun firing again. . . ."

He left the garden, making an effort not to think of Kyo, began to walk. Already there were fewer trees. Suddenly, through what was left of the mist, a lusterless moonlight appeared upon the surface of things. Clappique raised his eyes. The moon had just emerged from a tattered bank of dead clouds and was slowly drifting into an immense, dark and transparent hole like a lake with its depths full of stars. Its light, growing more intense, gave to all those sealed houses, to the complete desertion of the city, an extra-terrestrial life as if the moon's atmosphere had come and settled in the great sudden silence together with its light. Yet behind that scene of a dead planet there were men. Almost all were asleep, and the disquieting life of sleep was in harmony with the desolation of a buried city, as if this life too had belonged to another planet.

"In the *Arabian Nights* there are l-little cities full of sleepers, abandoned for centuries with their mosques under the moon, sleeping-cities-of-the-desert. . . . Which doesn't alter the fact I'm perhaps going to die." Death, even his own death, was not very real in this atmosphere, so inhuman that he felt himself an intruder. And those who were not sleeping? "There are those who read. Those who are gnawed by their conscience. (Lovely phrase!) Those who make love." The life of the future trembled behind all that silence. Mad humanity, which nothing could free from itself! The smell of corpses from the Chinese city was borne on the wind which was again rising. Clappique had to struggle for his breath: anguish was returning. He could endure the idea of death more easily than its smell. The latter, little by little, was taking possession of the scene which concealed the madness of the world beneath the appeasement of serenity; the wind still blowing without the slightest murmur, the moon reached the opposite bank, and all fell back into darkness. "Is it a dream?" But the terrific odor threw him back to life, to the anxious night in which the street-lights, just now blurred by mist, formed large tremulous circles on the sidewalks where the rain had blotted out the footprints.

Where now? He hesitated. He would be unable to forget Kyo if he tried to sleep. He was now passing through a street of small bars, tiny brothels with signs written in the languages of all the maritime nations. He entered the first one.

He sat down near the window. The three girls on duty—one half-breed, two white women—were sitting with clients, one of whom was getting ready to leave. Clappique waited, looked outside: nothing, not even a sailor. In the distance, rifle-shots. He started, on purpose: a squarely-built blond girl, disengaged, had just sat down beside him. "A Rubens," he thought, "but not perfect: she must be by Jordaens. Not a word. . . ." He twirled his hat on his forefinger, rapidly, threw it up in the air, caught it dexterously by the brim and placed it on the knees of the woman.

"Take good care of this l-little hat, my dear girl. It's the only one in Shanghai. What's more, it's tame. . . ."

The woman's face broadened into a smile: he was a funny guy. And gayety gave a sudden animation to her face, stolid up to this moment.

"Shall we have a drink, or go upstairs?" she asked.

"Both."

She brought some Schiedam. "It's a specialty of the house."

"No fooling?" said Clappique.

She shrugged her shoulders.

"Do you suppose I give a God damn?"

"Are you in trouble?"

She looked at him. With the funny guys you had to be on your guard. However, he was alone, he wasn't trying to show off; and he really didn't seem to be making fun of her.

"What else can you expect, in this sort of life?"

"Do you smoke?"

"Opium is too high. You can use the needle, of course, but I'm afraid: with their dirty needles you get abscesses, and if you've got boils they throw you out of the house. There are ten women for every job. And besides . . ."

Flemish, he thought. . . . He cut her short:

"You can get opium pretty cheap. I pay two dollars and seventy for this."

"Are you from the North too?"

He gave her a box without answering. She was grateful to him—for being a compatriot, and for the gift.

"Even so it's too much for me. . . . But this one won't have cost me much. I'll chew some tonight."

"You don't like to smoke?"

"You think I've got a pipe? How do you get that way?"

She smiled bitterly, still pleased however. But the habitual suspicion returned:

"Why do you give me this?"

"Never mind. . . . I enjoy it. I've been 'in the game.' " . . .

As a matter of fact, he didn't look like a man who pays for his pleasures. But he surely hadn't been "in the game" for a long time. (He occasionally felt the need of inventing whole biographies for himself, but rarely when a sexual adventure was involved.) She sidled over to him on the bench.

"Just try to be nice. It'll be the last time I have a woman."

"Why is that?"

She was slow, but not stupid. After having answered she understood: "You're going to kill yourself?"

He wasn't the first one. She took Clappique's hand between her own, and kissed him, clumsily and almost maternally.

"That's too bad. . . ."

"Do you want to go upstairs?"

She had heard that men sometimes had such an urge before death. But she didn't dare to get up first: it would be like hastening his suicide. She had kept his hand in both of hers. Slumped on the bench, legs crossed and arms held tightly to his sides like a delicate insect, nose pushed forward, he looked at her from afar, in spite of the contact of their bodies. Although he had scarcely been drinking, he was drunk with his lie, with this heat, with the fictive world he was creating. When he said he would kill himself he did not believe what he was saying; but, since she believed it, he was entering a world

246

where truth no longer existed. It was neither true nor false, but real. And since neither his past which he had just invented, nor the elementary gesture, presumably so close, upon which his relation to this woman was based—since neither of these existed, nothing existed. The world had ceased to weigh upon him. Liberated, he lived now only in the romantic universe which he had just created, strengthened by the bond which all human pity establishes before death. His intoxication was so strong that his hand trembled. The woman felt it and thought it was due to anguish:

"Isn't there a way of—fixing it?"

"No."

The hat, poised on the corner of the table, seemed to be looking at him ironically. He pushed it over on the bench so as not to see it.

"A love affair?" she went on asking.

A volley of shots burst in the distance. "As if there weren't enough who are going to die tonight," she thought.

He got up without answering. She thought her question brought up memories in him. In spite of her curiosity, she felt like begging his pardon, but did not dare. She got up, too. Slipping her hand under the bar, she pulled out a parcel (a syringe, towels) from between two glass jars. They went upstairs.

When he went out—he did not turn round, but knew she was following him with her eyes through the window—neither his mind nor his sensuality had been quenched. The mist had returned. After walking fifteen minutes (the cool night air did not calm him) he stopped before a Portuguese bar. Its windows had not lost their polish. Standing apart from the clients, a slim brunette with very large eyes, her hands on her breasts as if to protect them, was looking out into the night. Clappique looked at her without moving. "I am like a woman who doesn't know what a new lover is going to get out of her. . . . Let's go and commit suicide with this one."

Half past eleven at night

In the din of the *Black Cat*, Kyo and May had waited. The five last minutes. Already they should have left. It astonished Kyo that Clappique had not come (he had collected almost two hundred dollars for him), although he had half expected it: each time Clappique behaved in this way he was so much himself that he only half surprised those who knew him. Kyo had at first considered him a rather picturesque eccentric, but he was grateful to him for having warned him, and was beginning little by little to feel a real friendship for him. However, he was beginning to doubt the value of the information the Baron had given him, and his failure to keep his appointment made him doubt it all the more.

Although the fox-trot was not over, there was a great stir in the direction of one of Chiang Kai-shek's officers who had just come in: couples left the dance, drew near, and, although Kyo could hear nothing, he guessed that some important event had occurred. Already May was moving in the direction of the group: at the *Black Cat* a woman was suspected of everything, and therefore of nothing. She returned very quickly.

"A bomb has been thrown at Chiang Kai-shek's car," she told him in a low voice. "He was not in the car."

"And the murderer?" asked Kyo.

She returned towards the group, came back followed by a fellow who insisted on her dancing with him, but who left her as soon as he saw she was not alone.

"Escaped," she said.

"Let's hope so. . . ."

Kyo knew how inaccurate such information usually was. But it was scarcely probable that Chiang Kai-shek had been killed. The importance of such a death would be so great that the officer would not have ignored it. "We will find out at the Military Committee," said Kyo. "Let's go there right away."

He was too hopeful of Ch'en's escape to doubt it entirely. Whether Chiang Kai-shek was still in Shanghai or had already left for Nanking, the unsuccessful attempt at his life gave a capital importance to the meeting of the Military Committee. And yet, what was to be expected of it? He had transmitted Clappique's statement, in the afternoon, to a Central Committee that was skeptical and made a point of being so: the repression confirmed Kyo's thesis too directly not to make his confirmation of it lose some of its validity. Besides, the Committee was agitating for union with the Kuomintang, not for struggle: a few days earlier the political chief of the Reds and one of the Blue chiefs had made some touching speeches in Shanghai. And the failure of the attempt to seize the Japanese concession, at Hankow, was beginning to show that the Reds were paralyzed in Central China itself; the Manchurian troops were marching on Hankow, which would have to fight them before fighting those of Chiang Kai-shek. . . . Kyo was advancing through the fog, May at his side, without speaking. If the Communists had to fight tonight, they would scarcely be able to defend themselves. Whether they had given up their last firearms or not, how would they fight, one against ten, in disagreement with the instructions of the Chinese Communist Party, against an army that would oppose them with its corps of bourgeois volunteers armed with European weapons and having the advantage of attack?

Last month the whole city was for the united revolutionary army; the dictator had represented the foreigner, and the city hated foreigners; the immense petty bourgeoisie was democratic, but not Communist; this time the army was there, menacing, not in flight towards Nanking; Chiang Kai-shek was not the executioner of February, but a national hero, except among Communists. All against the police last month; the Communists against the army today. The city would be neutral, rather favorable to the general. Scarcely would they be able to defend the workers' quarters; Chapei perhaps? And then? . . . If Clappique had been misinformed, if the reaction delayed a month, the Military Committee, Kyo, Katov would organize two hundred thousand men. The new shock groups, composed of thoroughgoing Communists, were taking the Unions in hand; but at least a month would be necessary to create an organization sufficiently strong to maneuver the masses.

And the problem of firearms remained unsolved. What he wanted to know was not whether the two or three thousand guns they possessed ought to be surrendered, but how the masses were to be armed in case of an attack by Chiang Kai-shek. As long as discussions continued, the men would be disarmed. And if the Military Committee, on the one hand, insisted on being given arms, no matter what happened, the Central Committee, knowing that the Trotskyist theses were attacking the union with the Kuomintang, was terrified by any attitude which might, rightly or wrongly, seem to be linked to that of the Russian Opposition.

Now Kyo could just make out the dim lights of the Military Committee headquarters, through the fog that had not yet lifted, and that obliged him to walk on the sidewalk to avoid the passing cars. Opaque mist and night: he had to light his cigarette-lighter to see his watch. He was a few minutes late. Deciding to hurry, he slipped his arm into May's; she pressed gently against him. After a few steps, he felt in May's body a jerk and a sudden limpness: she was falling, slipping in front of him. "May!" He stumbled, fell on all fours, and, the moment he was starting to get up, received a violent blow from a bludgeon in the nape of the neck. He fell forward on top of her, full length.

Three policemen stepped out from a building and joined the one who had struck the blow. An empty car stood parked a short distance away. They bundled Kyo into it and drove off, binding him only after they were under way.

When May came to (the jerk that Kyo had felt had been caused by a blow below the ribs) a picket of Chiang Kai-shek's soldiers was guarding the entrance to the Military Committee headquarters; because of the mist, she perceived them only when she was almost up to them. She continued to walk in the same direction (she was breathing with difficulty, and was suffering from the blow), and hurried back to Gisors' house.

Midnight

As soon as he had learned that a bomb had been thrown at Chiang Kai-shek, Hemmelrich had run to get news. He had been told that the general was killed and that the murderer had gotten away; but, before the overturned car, the torn-off hood, he had seen Ch'en's corpse on the sidewalk—small and bloody, already drenched by the fog—guarded by a soldier seated nearby; and had learned that the general was not in the car. Absurdly, it seemed to him that his having refused to give Ch'en shelter was one of the causes of his death; he had run to the Communist post of his quarter, in despair, and had spent an hour there vainly discussing the attempt upon Chiang Kai-shek's life. A comrade had entered.

"The Union of the spinning-mill workers at Chapei has just been closed by Chiang Kai-shek's soldiers."

"Didn't the comrades resist?"

"All who protested were immediately shot. At Chapei the militants are also being shot or their homes are burned down. . . . The Municipal Government has just been dispersed. All the Unions are being closed."

No orders from the Central Committee. The married comrades had immediately run home, to save their wives and children through flight.

The moment Hemmelrich stepped outside, he heard volleys of gun-fire; he risked being recognized, but he must at all costs get the child and the woman off to safety. Before him, through the fog, passed two armored cars and trucks loaded with Chiang Kai-shek's soldiers. In the distance the volleys continued; and others, close by.

No soldiers in the Avenue of the Two Republics, nor in the street where he had his shop. No: *no more* soldiers. The door of the shop was open. He ran in: on the floor, heaps of smashed records scattered in large pools of blood. The shop had been "cleaned" with grenades, like a trench. The woman was slumped against the counter, almost crouching, her whole chest the color of a wound. In a corner, a child's arm; the hand, thus isolated, appeared even smaller. "If only they are dead!" thought Hemmelrich. He was especially afraid of having to stand by and watch a slow death, powerless, only able to suffer, as usual—more afraid even than of those cases riddled with grenade fragments and spattered with red spots. Through his shoe-soles he could feel the stickiness of the floor. "Their blood." He remained motionless, no longer daring to stir, looking, looking. . . . He discovered at last the body of the child, near the door which hid it. He was scarcely breathing, overwhelmed by the smell of the spilt blood. In the distance, two grenades exploded. "No question of burying them. . . ." He locked the door with a key, stood there before the shop. "If they come and recognize me, I'm done for." But he could not leave.

He knew he was suffering, but a halo of indifference surrounded his grief, the indifference which follows upon an illness or a blow in the head. No grief would have surprised him: on the whole, fate this time had dealt him a better blow than usual. Death did not astonish him: it was no worse than life. The thing that appalled him was the thought that behind this door there had been as much suffering as there was blood. This time, however, destiny had played badly: by tearing from him everything he still possessed, it freed him.

He entered the shop again, shut the door. In spite of the catastrophe, of the sensation of having the ground give way under his feet, leaving nothing but empty space, he could not banish from his mind the atrocious, weighty, profound joy of liberation. With horror and satisfaction he felt it rumble within him like a subterranean river, grow nearer; the corpses were there, his feet which were stuck to the floor were glued by their blood, nothing could be more of a mockery than these murders—especially that of the sick child: he seemed even more innocent than the dead woman;—but now, he was no longer impotent. Now, *he too could kill.* It came to him suddenly that life was not the only mode of contact between human beings, that it was not even the best; that he could know them, love them, possess them more completely in vengeance than in life. Again he became aware of his shoe-soles, stuck to the floor, and tottered: muscles were not aided by thought. But an intense exaltation was overwhelming him, the most powerful that he had ever known; he abandoned himself to this frightful intoxication with entire consent. "One can kill with love. With love, by God!" he repeated, striking the counter with his fist—against the universe, perhaps. . . . He immediately withdrew his hand, his throat tight, on the verge of sobbing: the counter was also bloody. He looked at the brown blot on his hand which was trembling, as if shaken by an attack of nerves: little flakes were falling from it. He wanted to laugh, to weep, to find relief from the awful pressure on his chest. . . . Nothing stirred, and the immense indifference of the world settled, together with the unwavering light, upon the records, the dead, the blood. The sentence: "They wrenched off the members of the victims with red-hot tongs," rose and fell in his brain; it was the first time it came back to him since he had read it at school; but he felt that it somehow meant that he must leave, that he too must tear himself away.

At last, without his knowing how, departure became possible. He was able to go out, and began to walk in a state of oppressive well-being which covered over eddies of limitless hatred. When he had gone thirty meters he stopped. "I left the door open on them." He retraced his steps. As he drew near, he felt sobs rising, becoming knotted in his chest below his throat, and remaining there. He shut his eyes, drew the door shut. The lock clicked: locked. He started off again. "It's not finished," he said hoarsely as he walked. "It's beginning. It's beginning. . . ." His shoulders thrust forward, he pushed ahead like a barge-tower towards a dim country of which he knew only that one killed there, pulling with his shoulders and with his brain the weight of all his dead who, at last! no longer prevented him from advancing.

His hands trembling, his teeth chattering, carried away by his terrible liberty, he was back at the Post in ten minutes. It was a two-story building. Behind the windows, mattresses were undoubtedly piled up: in spite of the absence of blinds, no luminous rectangles were visible through the fog, but only vertical slits. The calm of the street, hardly more than an alley, was absolute, and those slits of light took on the intensity, both tiny and sharp, of spark-plug flashes. He rang. The door opened a fraction of an inch: he was known. Behind, four militants holding Mausers watched him pass. Like a nest of insects, the vast hall was alive with an activity whose meaning was obscure but whose movement was clear—everything came from the cellar; the ground-floor was deserted. Two workers on the landing of the stairs were installing a machine-gun which commanded the hall. It did not even glisten, but it attracted attention like the tabernacle in a church. Students, workers were running. He passed in front of bundles of barbed wires (what use could they be?), mounted the stairs, circled the machine-gun, and reached the stair-head. Katov was coming out of an office, and looked at him questioningly. Without a word, Hemmelrich held out his bloody hand.

"Wounded? There are bandages downstairs. You've hidden the kid?"

Hemmelrich could not speak. He stubbornly showed his hand, with a stupid air. "It's their blood," he was thinking. But it could not be said.

"I have a knife," he said at last. "Give me a gun."

"There aren't many guns."

"Grenades."

Katov hesitated.

"Do you think I'm scared, you son of a bitch?"

"Go downstairs. There are grenades in the cases. Not many. . . . Do you know where Kyo is?"

"Haven't seen him. I saw Ch'en: he's dead."

"I know."

Hemmelrich went down. With their arms buried up to their shoulders, comrades were rummaging in an open case. So the supply was nearly exhausted. The mingled bodies were moving about in the full light of the lamps—there were no vent-holes—and the volume of those dense bodies around the case, encountered after the shadows that passed back and forth under the dimmed light-bulbs in the corridor above, surprised him as if, in the face of death, these men had acquired a sudden right to a life more intense than that of the others. He filled his pockets, went upstairs again. The others, the shadows, had finished installing the machine-gun and placed the barbed wires behind the door, back just far enough to allow it to open. Every minute or two the door-bell rang. He looked through the peep-hole: the misty street was still calm and empty. The comrades were arriving, formless in the fog like fish in stirred water, in the streak of shadow cast by the roofs. He was turning round to go and look for Katov: suddenly, two hurried rings, a shot, and the piercing gasp of someone being strangled, then the fall of a body.

"Here they are!" several of the men guarding the door shouted at once. Silence fell upon the corridor, subdued by the voices and the rattle of arms that rose from the cellar. The men were taking their fighting-posts.

Half past one in the morning

Clappique, emerging from his lie as from a fit of drunkenness, was stalking through the lobby of his Chinese hotel where the "boys," slumped on a round table under the call-board, were spitting sunflower seeds at the spittoons. He knew he would not sleep. He opened his door mechanically, threw his coat on the familiar copy of the *Tales of Hoffmann* and poured himself some whiskey: alcohol would sometimes banish the torment which seized him at moments. Something was changed in this room. He strove not to notice it: the inexplicable absence of certain objects would have been too alarming. He had managed to escape almost everything upon which men base their lives—love, family, work; but not fear. It rose in him, like an acute consciousness of his solitude; to banish it he usually ran to the nearest *Black Cat*, sought refuge in the women who open their thighs and their hearts while thinking of something else. Impossible tonight: worn out, fed up with lying and provisional intimacies. . . . He saw himself in the mirror, went up to it:

"After all, my good fellow," he said to the Clappique in the mirror, "why run away? How long is all this going to last? You've had a wife: let's forget it, oh! let's forget it! Mistresses, money; you can always think

257

of them when you need phantoms to make an ass of you. Not a word! You have gifts, as they say, a sense of humor, all the qualities needed to make a parasite: you can always be a valet at Ferral's when age has brought you to perfection. There is also the profession of gentleman-beggar, the police and suicide. A pimp? The delusion of grandeur again. Which leaves suicide, I tell you. But you don't want to die. You don't want to die, you little bastard! And yet look at yourself—a fine face to use for a dead man. . . ."

He drew still nearer, his nose almost touching the glass; he twisted his face, mouth open, into a gargoyle's grimace; and, as if the mask had answered him:

"Everyone can't be dead? Obviously: it takes a little of everything to make a world. Pshaw! When you're dead you'll go to Paradise. And what a companion God will be for a fellow of your sort. . . ."

He made a different face, mouth shut and drawn towards the chin, eyes half-opened, like a carnival samurai. And immediately, as if he had found a way of expressing directly in all its intensity the torment which words were not adequate to translate, he began to make faces, transforming himself into a monkey, an idiot, a terrified person, an apoplectic, into all the grotesques that a human face can express. This no longer sufficed: he used his fingers, drawing out the corners of his eyes, enlarging his mouth for the toad face of the man-who-laughs, flattening his nose, pulling out his ears. Each of these faces spoke to him, revealed to him a part of himself hidden by life; this debauchery of the grotesque in the solitary room, with the night mist piled against the window, was assuming the atrocious and terrifying humor of madness. He heard his own laughter—a single note, the same as his mother's; and, suddenly perceiving his face, he withdrew with horror and sat down, panting. There was a pad of paper and a pencil on the arm-chair. If he went on in this way he would really go mad. To protect himself from the frightful mirror he began writing to himself:

You would end up as a king, my old Toto. King: good and warm in a cozy insane-asylum, thanks to delirium tremens, your only friend, if you keep on drinking. But at this moment, are you drunk or sober? . . . You who imagine so many things, what are you waiting for to imagine yourself happy? Do you think . . .

Someone knocked.

He tumbled down to earth. Rescued but dumbfounded. The knocking was repeated.

"Come in."

A wool cloak, a black felt hat, a head of white hair: old Gisors.

"But I . . . I . . ." Clappique spluttered.

"Kyo has just been arrested," said Gisors. "You know König, don't you?"

"I . . . But I've got nothing to do with it. . . ."

Gisors studied him carefully. "If only he isn't too drunk," he thought.

"You know König," he repeated.

"Yes, I, I . . . know him. I have . . . done him a service. Great service."

"Can you ask him to return it?"

"Why not? But what?"

"As the chief of Chiang Kai-shek's secret police he can have Kyo released. Or, at least, prevent his being shot: you understand it's most urgent. . . ."

"Y-yes. . . . All right."

He had so little confidence in König's gratitude, however, that he had considered it useless and perhaps im-

259

prudent to go and see him, even after Shpilevski's warning. He sat down on the bed, his nose pointed straight down to the floor. He did not dare to speak. The tone of Gisors' voice convinced him that the latter did not suspect that he was responsible for Kyo's arrest: Gisors saw in him the friend who had come to warn Kyo that afternoon, not the man who was gambling at the hour of his appointment. But Clappique could not convince himself of this. He did not dare to look at him and could not calm himself. Gisors was wondering from what drama or what extravagance he was emerging, not guessing that his presence was one of the causes of his panting breath. It seemed to Clappique that Gisors was accusing him:

"You know, old man, that I'm not . . . anyway that I'm not as mad as all that; I, I . . ."

He could not stop stammering; it seemed to him at times that Gisors was the only man who understood him; and at times that he took him for a buffoon. The old man was looking at him without speaking.

"I . . . What do you think of me?"

Gisors was more inclined to take him by the shoulders and lead him to König's than to talk to him; but beneath what he took to be his intoxication he discerned such a turmoil that he did not dare to refuse to enter into the game.

"There are those who need to write, those who need to dream, those who need to talk. . . . It's all the same thing. The theater is not serious, but the bull-fight is; novels aren't serious, but mythomania is."

Clappique got up.

"Have you hurt your arm?" asked Gisors.

"A twist. Not a word. . . ."

Clappique had awkwardly turned his arm to hide his

wristwatch as if this watch which had shown him the time in the gambling-hall would have betrayed him. He perceived by Gisors' question that this was idiotic.

"When will you go and see König?"

"Tomorrow morning?"

"Why not now? The police are awake tonight," said Gisors with bitterness, "and anything might happen. . . ."

Clappique was only too glad. Not through remorse (had he been at the game again he would have stayed again), but by way of compensation.

"Let's run, old dear. . . ."

The change which he had noticed in the room upon entering again made him uneasy. He looked carefully, was stupefied at not having seen it before: one of his Taoist paintings—"to make one dream"—and his two finest statues had disappeared. On the table, a letter: Shpilevski's handwriting. He guessed. But he did not dare to read the letter. Shpilevski had warned him that Kyo was in danger: if he were to let himself go to the point of talking about him, he would be unable to avoid telling everything. He took the letter and put it in his pocket.

As soon as they were outside they encountered armored cars and trucks loaded with soldiers.

Clappique had almost recovered his calm; to hide the anxiety from which he could not yet free himself, he played the fool, as usual:

"I would like to be a wizard, to send the caliph a unicorn—a sun-colored unicorn, I tell you—which would appear in the palace, shouting: 'Know, Caliph, that the first sultana is unfaithful to you!' Not a word! I would be grand as a unicorn myself, with my nose! And of course, it wouldn't be true. Apparently nobody realizes

261

how voluptuous it is to live in another person's eyes an altogether different life from his own. Especially a woman's. . . ."

"What woman has not invented a life-history for at least one of the men who have accosted her on the street?"

"You . . . think everyone is a mythomaniac?"

Clappique's eyelids flickered nervously; he walked more slowly.

"No, listen," he said, "tell me frankly: why do you think they aren't?"

He now felt an urge, curiously foreign to himself but very strong, to ask Gisors what he thought of gambling; and yet, if he spoke of gambling he would surely confess everything. Was he going to speak? Silence would have forced *him* to; luckily Gisors answered:

"Perhaps I'm the person least capable of answering you. . . . Opium teaches only one thing, which is that aside from physical suffering, there is nothing real."

"Suffering, yes. . . . And . . . fear."

"Fear?"

"You are never afraid, with o-opium?"

"No. Why?"

"Ah. . . ."

In truth, Gisors believed that if the world was without reality, men—even those who are most opposed to the world—have an intense reality; but that Clappique, precisely, was one of the rare beings who had none. And this conviction tormented him, for it was into those unsubstantial hands that he was giving over Kyo's fate. Beneath the attitudes of every man there is a base that can be touched, and thinking of his affliction enables one to have an inkling of its nature. Clappique's affliction was independent of him, like that of a child: he was not responsible for it; it could destroy him, it could not modify him. He could cease to exist, disappear in a vice, in a monomania; he could not become a man. "A heart of gold, but hollow." Gisors perceived that at the base of Clappique there was neither affliction nor solitude, as in other men, but sensation. Gisors sometimes gauged other men by imagining their old age: Clappique could not grow old. Age did not bring him human experience, but an intoxication—lust or drugs—in which all his means of ignoring life would at last merge. "Perhaps," the Baron was thinking, "if I told him everything, he would find it quite normal. . . ." Shots were now firing everywhere in the Chinese city. Clappique begged Gisors to leave him at the boundary of the concession: König would not receive him. Gisors stopped, watched his thin, loose figure disappear in the mist.

The special section of Chiang Kai-shek's police was quartered in a plain villa built about 1920: suburban style, but with windows framed in extravagant blue and yellow Portuguese ornaments. Two sentinels and more orderlies than usual; all the men armed; that was all. On the card which a secretary handed him Clappique wrote "Toto," leaving the occasion of his visit blank, and waited. It was the first time he found himself in a lighted place since he had left his room: he drew Shpilevski's letter from his pocket:

My Dear Friend:
I have yielded to your insistence. My scruples were well founded, but I have thought it over: you enable me in this way to recover my peace of mind, and the profits which my venture promises are so great and so certain

*that I will surely be able to repay you, within a year,
with objects of the same kind, and finer. The food business, in this city . . .*

There followed four pages of explanation.

"It doesn't look very good," thought Clappique, "not
good at all. . . ." But an orderly was coming for him.

König was waiting for him, seated on his desk, facing
the door. Thick-set, dark, a crooked nose in a square
face. He came towards him, shook his hand in a brisk,
firm manner that separated rather than united them.

"How are you? Good. I knew I would see you today.
I'm glad I was able to be of use to you in my turn."

"You are for-r-midable," answered Clappique, half
playing the buffoon. "I'm only wondering if there isn't
a misunderstanding: you know I'm not interested in poli-
tics. . . ."

"There's no misunderstanding."

"His gratitude is rather condescending," thought
Clappique.

"You have two days to get out. You did me a service
once. Today I've warned you."

"Wh-what? You? . . ."

"Do you think Shpilevski would have dared? You're
dealing with the Chinese Secret Service, but the Chinese
are no longer directing it. Enough of nonsense."

Clappique was beginning to admire Shpilevski, but not
without irritation.

"Well," he went on, "since you are good enough to
remember me, allow me to ask you something else."

"What?"

Clappique no longer had much hope: each new response of König's showed him that the fellowship on
which he counted did not exist, or no longer existed.

264

If König had warned him, he no longer owed him any-thing. It was more to relieve his conscience than with any hope of success that he said:

"Couldn't something be done for young Gisors? I don't suppose you give a damn about all that. . . ."

"What is he?"

"A Communist. Important, I believe."

"First of all, why is that fellow a Communist? His father? A half-breed? No job? That a worker should be a Communist is idiotic enough, but he! Well, what?"

"It's not easy to summarize. . . ."

Clappique was reflecting:

"Because he's a half-breed, perhaps. . . . But he could have adjusted himself: his mother was Japanese. He didn't try. He says something like this: a will to dig-nity. . . ."

"Dignity!"

Clappique was stupefied: König was yelling at him. He did not expect that one word to produce such a vio-lent effect. "Have I made a blunder?" he wondered.

"First of all, what does that mean?" König asked, shaking his forefinger as though he had been talking without being understood. "Dignity," he repeated. Clap-pique could not mistake the tone of his voice: it was that of hatred. He stood a little to the right of Clappique, and his nose, which had a sharp curve at this angle, strongly accentuated his face.

"Tell me, my little Toto, do you believe in dignity?"

"In others. . . ."

"Yes?"

His tone said: "Is this going to go on much longer?"

"You know what the Reds did to the officers who were taken prisoners?"

Clappique was careful not to answer. This was getting

265

serious. And he felt that this question was a preparation—
a help which König was giving himself: he expected no
answer.

"In Siberia, I was an interpreter in a prisoner's camp.
I was able to get away by serving in the White army,
with Semenoff. Whites or Reds—they were all the same
to me: I wanted to return to Germany. I was caught by
the Reds. I was half dead of cold. They beat me with
their fists, calling me captain (I was a lieutenant), till I
fell. They lifted me up. I was not wearing Semenoff's
uniform with little skulls and cross-bones. I had a star on
each epaulette."

He stopped. "He might refuse without making so
much fuss," thought Clappique. Breathless, heavy, the
voice implied a need which he nevertheless was seeking
to understand.

"They drove a nail into each shoulder, through each
star. Long as a finger. Listen carefully, little Toto."

He took him by the arm, looking steadily into his eyes,
with the look of a man in love.

"I wept like a woman, like a calf. . . . I wept before
them. You understand, don't you? Let's leave it at that.
No one will lose anything by it."

That lustful look enlightened Clappique. The confidence was not surprising: it was not a confidence, it was
a revenge. Beyond a doubt he told this story—or told it
to himself—each time he had a chance to kill, as if this
tale could rub into the limitless humiliation which tortured him until it bled.

"Listen, little fellow, it would be better not to talk to
me too much about dignity. . . . *My* dignity is to kill
them. Do you think I give a damn about China! Yeah!
China, no fooling! I'm in the Kuomintang only to kill
them off. I live as I used to—like a man, like anybody,

like the lowest of the riff-raff that pass in front of that window—only when I'm killing them. It's like opium smokers with their pipes. A rag, that's all. You came to ask me to save his skin? Even if you had saved my life three times . . ."

He shrugged his shoulders, continued passionately:

"Do you even have an idea what it is, my poor Toto, to see one's life assume a meaning, an absolute meaning: disgust you with yourself . . . ?"

He ended the sentence between his teeth, his hands in his pockets, his hair quivering as he snapped out the words.

"There is forgetfulness . . ." said Clappique in a low voice.

"It's more than a year since I've had a woman! Is that enough for you? And . . ."

He stopped short, went on in a lower voice:

"But I say, little Toto. Young Gisors, young Gisors . . . You were speaking of a misunderstanding; you still want to know why you're wanted? I'll tell you. It's you who handled the matter of the guns on the *Shantung*, isn't it? Do you know whom the guns were for?"

"One asks no questions in that game, not a word!"

He was raising his forefinger to his lips, in accordance with his purest traditions. He was immediately embarrassed by the gesture.

"For the Communists. And as you were risking your life, you might have been told. And it was a swindle. They used you to gain time: that very night they plundered the ship. If I'm not mistaken it was your present protégé who launched you in this affair?"

Clappique was on the point of answering: "I got my commission just the same." But König's face expressed such gloating satisfaction at the revelation he had just made that Clappique had no longer any other desire than to leave. Although Kyo had kept his promises, he had made him risk his life without telling him. Would he have risked it? No. Kyo had been right to prefer his cause to him: *he* would now be right to disinterest himself in Kyo. All the more so since in truth he could do nothing. He simply shrugged his shoulder.

"So I have forty-eight hours to get out?"

"Yes. You don't insist. You are right. Good-by."

He says he hasn't had a woman in a year, thought Clappique as he went down the stairs. Impotence? Or what? I would have thought that kind of . . . experience . . . would make a man an erotomaniac. He must make such confidences, as a rule, to those who are about to die: in any case I'd better get out. He could not get over the tone in which König had said: "To live as a man, as anybody . . ." He remained dazed by that complete intoxication, which only blood could satisfy: he had seen enough wrecks from the civil wars of China and Siberia to know that a deep humiliation calls for a violent negation of the world; only drugs, neuroses, and blood insistently shed, can feed such solitudes. He understood now why König had liked his company, as he was not unaware that in his presence all reality vanished. He was walking slowly, and was startled to find Gisors waiting for him on the other side of the barbed wires. What should he tell him? . . . Too late: goaded by impatience, Gisors was advancing to meet him, was emerging from the mist two meters away. He was staring at him with a madman's haggard intensity. Clappique became frightened, stopped. Gisors was already seizing his arm:

"Nothing to be done?" he asked, in a voice that was gloomy but calm.

Clappique shook his head and said nothing.

"Well. I'll try to get another friend to do something."

Upon seeing Clappique come out of the mist, he had realized his own folly. The whole dialogue he had imagined between them on the Baron's return was absurd: Clappique was neither an interpreter nor a messenger—he was a card. The card had been played—he had lost, as Clappique's face showed. He would have to find another. Gorged with anxiety, with distress, he remained lucid beneath his desolation. He had thought of Ferral; but Ferral would not intervene in a conflict of this nature. He would try to get two friends to intercede in his behalf. . . .

König had called a secretary.

"Tomorrow.—Young Gisors—here. As soon as the councils are over."

Five o'clock in the morning

Above the short flashes of the gun-shots, yellowish in the fading night, Katov and Hemmelrich, through the windows of the second story, saw the first leaden reflections of dawn on the neighboring roofs. The outlines of the buildings were becoming distinct. Pale, with their hair disheveled, they could begin to distinguish each other's features, and each knew what the other was thinking. The last day. Hardly any ammunition left. No popular movement had come to their rescue. Volleys, in the direction of Chapei: comrades besieged like themselves. Katov had explained to Hemmelrich why there was no hope: at any moment Chiang Kai-shek's men would be bringing the small-caliber guns which the general's guard had at their disposal; as soon as one of those cannons could be set up in one of the houses facing the post, mattresses and walls would fall as at a country-fair. The Communists' machine-gun still commanded the door of that house; when it ran out of ammunition it would cease to command it. Which would be very soon.

For hours they had been firing furiously, egged on by the anticipated vengeance. They knew they were doomed, and killing was the only means of making their last hours count. But they were beginning to be weary of that too. Their adversaries, better and better sheltered, now appeared only at rare intervals. It seemed as if the battle were weakening with the night—and, absurdly, as if the dawning day, which did not reveal a single enemy shadow, were bringing their freedom, as the night had brought their imprisonment.

The reflection of dawn, on the roofs, was turning pale gray; above the suspended battle the light seemed to be inhaling large segments of the night, leaving only black rectangles in front of the buildings. The shadows grew shorter: looking at them helped to avoid thinking of the men who were about to die here. The shadows were contracting as on any other day, with their eternal movement, which today had a savage majesty because they would never see it again. Suddenly all the windows across the street were lighted up, and bullets came beating about the doorway like a volley of pebbles: one of their men had swung out a coat at the end of a stick. The enemy were satisfied to remain on the watch.

"Eleven, twelve, thirteen, fourteen . . ." said Hemmelrich. He was counting the corpses now visible in the street.

"All that's a joke," answered Katov almost in a whisper. "All they have to do is to wait. Daylight is in their favor."

There were only five wounded lying in the room: they were not groaning: two were smoking, watching daylight appear between the wall and the mattresses. Beyond, Suan and another combatant were guarding the second window. The volleys had practically ceased. Were Chiang Kai-shek's troops waiting everywhere? Victors the month before, the Communists had known their moves hour by hour; today they knew nothing, like those who had then been the vanquished.

As if to confirm what Katov had just said, the door of the enemy building opened (the two halls faced each other); immediately the crackling of a machine-gun enlightened the Communists. "They brought it by way of the roofs," thought Katov.

"Over here!"

It was his machine-gunners who were calling. Hemmelrich and he ran out, and understood: the enemy machine-gun, no doubt protected by an armor-plate, was firing steadily. There were no Communists in the corridor of the post, since it was under the fire of their own machine-gun which, from the top steps of the stairway, commanded the adversaries' entrance. But now the latter were protected by the steel plate. Nevertheless it was imperative to maintain their fire. The marksman had fallen on his side, killed, no doubt; it was the feeder who had shouted. He was both feeding and firing, but slowly. The bullets caused splinters of wood from the steps and bits of plaster from the wall to bounce out, and occasional deadened sounds, forming imperceptible gaps in the terrific uproar, indicated that a few were entering the flesh of the living or the dead. Hemmelrich and Katov rushed forward. "Not you!" bellowed the Belgian. With a blow to the chin he sent Katov rolling in the hall, and jumped to the post of the gunner. The enemy was now

271

firing a little lower. Not for long. "Are there any more cartridge-belts?" asked Hemmelrich. Instead of answering, the feeder plunged head forward, rolling limply down the whole length of the steps. And Hemmelrich discovered that he did not know how to feed a machine-gun.

He rushed up the stairs again, felt himself hit in the eye and in the calf. In the hall, above the angle of the enemy's fire, he halted: his eye had been hit merely by a piece of plaster detached by a bullet; his calf was bleeding—another bullet, which had made a surface wound. Already he was in the room where Katov, propped against a wall, was pulling a mattress towards himself with one hand (not to protect himself but to hide from the enemy), and holding in the other a bundle of grenades: the grenades alone, if they exploded right against it, could be effective against the steel plate.

They had to be thrown through the window into the enemy corridor. Katov had placed another bundle behind him; Hemmelrich seized it and threw it at the same time as Katov over the mattress. Katov found himself on the floor, mowed by bullets, as if by his own grenades: when their heads and arms had passed above the mattress, the enemy had fired on them from all the windows. Hemmelrich, who had ducked in time, was wondering if that splitting of matches, so close to him, did not come from his own legs. The bullets continued to pour in, but the two men were protected by the wall now that they had fallen: the opening of the window was three feet above the floor. In spite of the gun-shots, Hemmelrich had an impression of silence, for the two machine-guns had ceased firing. He crawled forward on his elbows towards Katov, who did not stir; he pulled him by the shoulders. Out of range of the firing, they looked at each other in silence: in spite of the mattresses and other protection which obstructed the window, broad daylight now flooded the room. Katov was fainting. On his thigh was a large red spot which was spreading on the floor as on a blotter. Hemmelrich heard Suan shout: "The cannon!" then an enormous, deafening explosion, and, just as he was raising his head, a blow at the base of his nose: in his turn he fainted.

Hemmelrich was coming to, little by little, rising from the depths towards that surface of silence which was so strange that it seemed to revive him: the cannon was no longer firing. The wall was torn away obliquely. On the floor, covered with plaster and wreckage, Katov and the others, unconscious or dead. He was very thirsty, and feverish. His wound in the calf was not serious. He crawled to the door, and in the hall got up on his feet, heavily, leaning against the wall. Except for his head, where a piece of the masonry had hit him, his pain was diffused; clutching the banister, he went down, not the street-stairway, where the enemy were undoubtedly still waiting, but that of the court. The firing had ceased. Against the walls of the entrance hall there was a row of niches, which had formerly held tables. He slipped into the first one, crouched down, and looked out upon the court.

To the right of a building which seemed deserted (but he was sure that it was not), a sheet-iron shed; in the distance a house with curved-up gables and a row of telegraph poles that extended, in diminishing perspective, towards the open country which he would not see again. The network of barbed wires in front of the door made black streaks across that dead scene and the gray daylight, like cracks in a porcelain dish. A shadow appeared outside, a kind of bear: a man facing in his direction, his back stooped; he began to climb through the barbed wires.

Hemmelrich had no more bullets. He was watching that mass passing from one wire to another. The wires stood out sharp against the light, but without perspective, so that he was unable to gauge the progress it was making. Like an enormous insect, it hung to a wire, fell back, attached itself again. Hemmelrich drew nearer, along the wall. It was clear that the man would pass; at this moment, however, he was entangled, and was trying with a strange grunting to free himself from the barbs that had caught his clothes, and it seemed to Hemmelrich that the monstrous insect might remain there forever, enormous and knotted, suspended against the gray light. But one hand reached out, black and sharp, to seize another wire, and the body resumed its movement.

This was the end. Behind, the street and the machine-gun. Up there, Katov and his men, on the floor. The deserted house, opposite, was certainly occupied, no doubt by machine-gunners who still had cartridges. If he went out, the enemy would aim at his knees, to make him a prisoner (he suddenly felt the fragility of those small bones, the knee-caps . . .). At least he would perhaps kill this one.

The monster—man, bear and spider combined—continued to disentangle itself from the wires. Alongside of the black mass a line of light marked the ridge of his large pistol. Hemmelrich felt himself at the bottom of a hole, fascinated less by the creature that was moving so slowly, approaching like death itself, than by everything that followed it, everything that was once more going to crush him, like a coffin-lid screwed down over a living person; it was everything that had choked his everyday life, which was now returning to crush him with one blow. "They have beaten me for thirty-seven years, and now they're going to kill me." It was not only his own suffering which was approaching, it was that of his wife with her belly ripped open, of his murdered child: everything mingled in a haze of thirst, of fever, and of hatred. Again, without looking at it, he felt the blood-stain on his left hand, neither as a burn nor as a discomfort: he simply knew that it was there, and that the man would finally emerge from his barbed wires. It was not for money that this man who was the first to pass was coming to kill those upstairs who were still alive, it was for an idea, for a faith; Hemmelrich hated this shadow that had now stopped before the barrage of wires—hated everything it stood for: it was not enough that the race of the fortunate should assassinate them, they also had to believe they were right. The silhouette, its body now upright, was prodigiously stretched against the gray court, against the telegraph wires that vanished into the limitless peace of the rainy spring morning. From a window came a shout, which the man answered; his response filled the corridor, enveloped Hemmelrich. The line of light on the pistol disappeared, buried in the holster and replaced by a flat bar, almost white in the dim light: the man was pulling out his bayonet. He was no longer a man, he was everything that Hemmelrich had suffered from until now. In this black corridor, with the machine-gunners lying in ambush on the other side of the door, and this enemy who was approaching, the Belgian became crazed with hatred. "They have made us starve all our lives, but this one is going to get it, he's going to get it. . . ." The man was approaching, step by step, his bayonet held out. Hemmelrich crouched, and the silhouette immediately grew larger, the torso diminishing above legs that were strong as posts.

The instant the bayonet passed over his head, he jumped up, seized the man's neck with his right hand, tightened his grip. The bayonet was knocked to the floor by the impact. The man's neck was too large for a single hand, and the fingers plunged convulsively into the flesh without greatly checking the respiration, but the other hand, furiously clutching at the panting face, was seized by an uncontrollable rage. "You'll pay for it," Hemmelrich shouted hoarsely. "You'll pay for it!" The man was staggering. Instinctively he backed up against the wall. Summoning all his strength, Hemmelrich smashed the head against that wall, then bent down a second; the Chinaman felt an enormous body entering into him, tearing his intestines: the bayonet. He opened both hands, brought them back to his belly with a piercing groan and fell, shoulders forward, between Hemmelrich's legs. He straightened out with a jerk; a drop of blood fell from the bayonet on his open hand, then another. And as if this hand that was being spattered with blood had avenged him, Hemmelrich dared at last to look at his own, and understood that the blood-stain had rubbed off hours before.

And he discovered that perhaps he was not going to die. He undressed the officer with feverish haste, seized both with love for this man who had come to bring him his freedom and with rage because the clothes did not come off the body readily enough, as though the latter were holding on to them. Finally, dressed in the China-man's uniform, he showed himself at the window, his bent-over face hidden by the visor of the cap. The enemy, across the courtyard, opened their windows with shouts of jubilation. "I must get out before they're here."

He went out on the street-side, turned to the left as the man he had killed would have done to rejoin his group.

"Any prisoners?" shouted the men at the windows.

He made a vague gesture towards those he was supposed to rejoin. That no one fired on him was both stupid and natural: there was no astonishment left in him. He again turned to the left and headed in the direction of the concessions: they were guarded, but he knew all the buildings with double entrances on the Avenue of the Two Republics.

One after the other the men of the Kuomintang were coming out.

Part Six

Ten o'clock in the morning

T EMPORARY," said the guard.

Kyo understood that he was being incarcerated in the common-law prison.

As soon as he entered the prison, even before he was able to look around, he was stunned by the frightful smell: slaughter-house, dog-kennel, excrements. The door through which he had just passed opened on a corridor similar to the one he was leaving; right and left, up to the ceiling, enormous wooden bars. Within the wooden cages, men. In the center, the warder seated before a small table, on which lay a whip: a short handle, a flat thong, broad as a hand, thick as a finger—a weapon.

"Stay there, son of a pig," he said.

The man, accustomed to the dim light, was writing out a description of the prisoner. Kyo's head still ached, and standing still made him feel faint; he leaned against the bars.

"How, how, how are you?" someone called behind him.

A disturbing voice, like that of a parrot, but a human voice. The place was too dark for Kyo to make out his face; he could see only enormous fingers clutching the bars—not very far from his neck. Behind, lying down or standing, swarmed shadows that were too elongated for human proportions: men, like worms.

"Could be better," he answered, moving away.

278

"Shut that, son of a turtle, if you don't want my fist in your face," said the warder.

Kyo had heard the word "temporary" several times; he knew therefore that he would not remain here long. He was resolved not to hear the insults, to endure everything that could be endured; the important thing was to get out of there, to resume the struggle. Yet he felt the nauseating humiliation that every man feels before someone upon whom he depends, powerless against that foul shadow with a whip—shorn of himself.

"How, how, how are you?" the voice called again.

The warder opened a door, luckily in the bars on the left: Kyo entered the stall. At the back, a low bench on which a solitary man was lying. The door shut.

"Political?" asked the man.

"Yes. And you?"

"No. Under the empire, I was a mandarin. . . ."

Kyo was getting used to the darkness. Indeed, the man was well along in years—an old white cat, almost without a nose, with a thin mustache and pointed ears.

". . . I sell women. When things are good, I give money to the police and they leave me alone. When things are bad, they think I keep the money and they throw me in prison. But as long as things are bad I prefer to be fed in prison rather than die of hunger in freedom. . . ."

"Here!"

"You know, one gets used to it. . . . Outside, it's not so good, when you're old, like me, and feeble. . . ."

"How is it that you're not with the rest?"

"I sometimes give money to the clerk at the entrance. Also, every time I come here I get the same fare as the 'temporaries.'"

The warder was bringing the food: he passed between

279

the bars two small bowls filled with a mud-colored doughy mass exuding a steam as fetid as the atmosphere. He dipped his ladle into a pot, tossed the compact porridge into a bowl with a "plop," and thereupon passed it to the prisoners in the other cage, one by one.

"No use my taking any," said a voice: "it's for to-morrow."

("His execution," said the mandarin to Kyo.)

"Me too," said another voice. "So you could very well give me a double portion, couldn't you? It makes *me* hungry?"

"Do you want my fist in your face?" asked the warder.

A soldier entered, asked him a question. He passed into the right-hand cell, kicked a limp body:

"He stirs," he said. "No doubt he's still alive. . . ."

The soldier left.

Kyo looked with concentrated attention, tried to see to which of those shadows belonged those voices so close to death—like himself, perhaps. Impossible to make out: those men would die without having been anything to him but voices.

"Aren't you eating?" asked his companion.

"No."

"In the beginning it's always that way. . . ."

He took Kyo's bowl. The warder entered, gave him a violent slap in the face and went out again carrying the bowl, without a word.

"Why didn't he touch me?" asked Kyo in a low voice.

"I was the only guilty one, but it's not that: you're a political prisoner, temporary, and you're well dressed. He's going to try to get money out of you or your friends. But that doesn't prevent . . . Wait. . . ."

Money pursues me even into this hole, thought Kyo.

So true to the legend, the warder's vileness did not seem to him altogether real; and, at the same time, it seemed to him a foul fatality, as if power were enough to change almost every man into a beast. Those obscure beings who stirred behind the bars, disturbing like the colossal insects and crustaceans in his childhood dreams, were no more human. Complete solitude and humiliation. "Look out," he thought, for already he felt himself weaker. He felt certain that, had he not been the master of his death, terror would have gotten the better of him in this place. He opened the buckle of his belt, and slipped the cyanide into his pocket.

"How, how, how are you?" called the voice again.

"Enough!" came a chorus of shouts from the prisoners in the other cell. Kyo was by now used to the darkness, and the number of the voices did not astonish him: there were more than ten bodies lying on the bench behind the bars.

"Are you going to shut up?" shouted the warder.

"How, how, how are you?"

The warder got up.

"Is it a joke, or is he pig-headed?" asked Kyo in a low voice.

"Neither," answered the mandarin: "crazy."

"But why . . ."

Kyo did not finish. His neighbor was stopping up his ears. A sharp, raucous cry, both of terror and pain, filled the whole place. While Kyo was looking at the mandarin, the warder had entered the other cage with his whip. The thong cracked, and the same cry rose again. Kyo did not dare to stop up his ears, and waited, clutching two bars, for the dreadful cry which was about to run through him again, and make his finger-nails tingle.

"Beat him up good and plenty," said a voice, "so he'll leave us in peace!"

"Put a stop to it," said four or five voices, "we want to sleep!"

The mandarin, with his hands still stopping up his ears, leaned towards Kyo:

"It's the eleventh time he has beat him in seven days, it seems. I've been here two days—it's the fourth time. And in spite of everything, you can't help hearing it a little. . . . I can't shut my eyes, you see: it seems to me that by looking at him I'm helping him, that I'm not deserting him. . . ."

Kyo was also looking, hardly able to see anything. . . . "Compassion or cruelty?" he wondered, terrified. What is base, and also what is susceptible to fascination in every man was being appealed to with the most savage vehemence, and Kyo was struggling with his whole mind against human ignominy—he remembered the effort it had always required of him to get away from tortured bodies seen by chance: he had literally had to tear himself away. That men could stand by and watch the flogging of a harmless lunatic, who, judging by his voice, was probably old, and approve such torture, called forth in him the same terror as Ch'en's confidences, the night in Hankow—"the octopuses. . . ." Katov had told him what a constraint the medical student must exercise upon himself the first time he sees an abdomen cut open and the living organs exposed. It was the same paralyzing horror, quite different from fear, an all-powerful horror even before the mind had appraised it, and all the more upsetting as Kyo was excruciatingly aware of his own helplessness. And yet his eyes, much less accustomed to the gloom than those of his companion, could make out only the flash of the leather, coming down like a hook, tearing out agonizing howls. Since the first blow he had not stirred: he stood clinging to the bars, his hands level with his face.

"Warder," he shouted.

"You want some, too, do you?"

"I want to speak to you."

"Yes?"

While the warder was furiously securing the enormous lock, the prisoners he was leaving were roaring with delight. They hated the "political" prisoners, who were not of them.

"Go to it! Go to it, warder! Let's have some fun."

The man was in front of Kyo, his figure cut vertically by a bar. His face expressed the most abject anger, that of a fool who thinks his power is being contested; but his features were not base—they were regular, anonymous. . . .

"Listen," said Kyo.

They were looking each other in the eye, the warder taller than Kyo, whose hands he saw still clutching the bars on each side of his head. Before Kyo knew what was happening, he felt his left hand paralyzed by an unbearable shot of pain. The whip, held behind the warder's back had come down with full force. He could not help crying out.

"Good work!" bellowed the prisoners on the other side. "Not always the same ones."

Both Kyo's hands had pulled back and fastened themselves to his sides, without his even being aware of what he was doing.

"You still have something to say?" asked the warder.

The whip was now between them. Kyo clenched his

teeth, and with the same effort that it would have required to lift an enormous weight, still keeping his eyes steadily on the warder, again raised his hands to the bars. While he was slowly lifting them, the man drew back imperceptibly to give himself room. The whip cracked—on the bars this time. The reflex had been too strong for Kyo: he had withdrawn his hands. But already he was raising them again, with an exhausting tension of his shoulders, and the warder understood by his look that this time he would not withdraw them. He spat in his face and slowly raised the whip.

"If you . . . stop flogging the idiot," said Kyo, "I'll give . . . you fifty dollars . . . when I get out."

The warder hesitated.

"All right," he said finally.

He turned away and Kyo felt such a release of tension that he thought he would faint. His left hand was so painful that he could not shut it. He had raised it at the same time as the other to the level of his shoulders, and it remained there, extended. New bursts of laughter.

"You want to shake hands?" asked the warder, also making fun of him.

He shook it. Kyo felt that in his whole life he would not forget this clasp, not because of the pain, but because life had never imposed upon him anything more hideous. He withdrew his hand, fell back in a sitting posture on the low bench. The warder hesitated, tossed his head, then began to scratch it with the handle of the whip. He returned to his table. The idiot was sobbing.

Hours of monotonous abjection. At last soldiers came to fetch Kyo to take him to the Special Police. No doubt he was going to his death, and yet he left with a joy whose violence surprised him. It seemed to him that he was leaving behind a loathsome part of himself.

"Come in!"

One of the Chinese guards pushed Kyo by the shoulder, but gently; whenever they had to deal with foreigners (and to a Chinaman, Kyo was Japanese or European, but certainly a foreigner) the guards were afraid of the brutality to which they considered themselves obliged. Upon a signal from König the guards remained outside. Kyo stepped forward to the desk, hiding his swollen left hand in his pocket, and looking at this man who was also looking him straight in the eye—an angular face, clean-shaved, nose awry, hair close-cropped. "A man who is no doubt about to have you put to death looks quite like any other." König extended his hand towards his revolver lying on the table: no, he was taking a box of cigarettes. He held it out to Kyo.

"Thanks. I don't smoke."

"The prison-fare is vile, as it should be. Will you have lunch with me?"

On the table, coffee, milk, two cups, slices of bread.

"Only bread. Thanks."

König smiled:

"It's the same coffee-pot for you and for me, you know. . . ."

Kyo was determined to be cautious; for that matter, König did not insist. Kyo remained standing in front of the desk (there was no seat), biting into his bread like a child. After the abjectness of the prison everything had an unreal lightness. He knew that his life was at stake, but even dying was easy for one who returned from the place where he had been. The humaneness of a chief of police inspired him with little confidence, and König remained distant, as though he were separate from his cordiality—the latter held, as it were, at arm's length before him. However, it was not impossible that this man was

285

courteous through indifference: belonging to the white race, he had perhaps come into this job by accident or through cupidity. Kyo hoped this was the case. He felt no liking for him, but he would have liked to relax, to free himself from the tension of the prison, which had completely exhausted him; he had just discovered that to be obliged to seek refuge entirely in oneself is almost unbearable.

The telephone rang.

"Hello!" said König. "Yes, Gisors, Kyoshi.[1] Perfectly. He's here with me. . . . I'm asked if you are still alive," he said to Kyo.

"Why did you send for me?"

"I think we're going to come to an understanding."

The telephone again.

"Hello! No. I was just telling him that we would surely come to an understanding. Shot? Call me back. We'll see."

Since Kyo had entered, König had not taken his eyes off him.

"What do you think of it?" he asked, hanging up the receiver.

"Nothing."

König lowered his eyes, raised them again:

"You want to live?"

"It depends how."

"One can also die in various ways."

"At least one doesn't have the choice. . . ."

"Do you think one always chooses one's way of living?"

König was thinking of himself. Kyo was determined to yield nothing essential, but he had no desire to irritate him:

[1] Kyo is an abbreviation.

"I don't know. And you?"

"I've been told that you are a Communist through dignity. Is that true?"

Kyo at first did not understand. Tense in the expectation of the phone-call, he was wondering what this strange examination meant. Finally:

"Does it really interest you?" he asked.

"More than you can imagine."

There was a menace in the tone, if not in the words themselves. Kyo answered:

"I think that Communism will make dignity possible for those with whom I am fighting. What is against it, at any rate, forces them to have none, unless they possess a wisdom as rare among them as among the others—more perhaps, for the very reason that they are poor, and that their work separates them from their lives. Why do you ask me this question, since you aren't even listening to my answer?"

"What do you call dignity? It doesn't mean anything."

The telephone rang. "My life," thought Kyo. König did not pick up the receiver.

"The opposite of humiliation," said Kyo. "When one comes from where I come, that means something."

The phone was ringing amid the silence. König put his hand on the instrument.

"Where are the arms hidden?" he asked.

"You can leave the phone alone. At last I understand. That call is merely stage-business for my benefit."

Kyo ducked his head: König had been on the point of throwing one of the two revolvers—no doubt empty—in his face; but he put it back on the table.

"I've got something better," he said. "As for the telephone, you will soon see if it was a fake, little fellow. I take it you've seen men tortured?"

In his pocket, Kyo was trying to press his swollen fingers together. The cyanide was in this left pocket, and he was afraid of dropping it if he were to lift it to his mouth.

"At least I've seen men who had been tortured: I've been in the civil war. What puzzles me is why you asked me where the arms are. You know where they are, or you will know it. So what?"

"The Communists have been crushed everywhere."

"It's possible."

"They have been. Think carefully: if you work for us, you are saved, and no one will know it. I'll help you to get away. . . ."

"That's how he should begin," thought Kyo. Nervousness gave him wit, in spite of himself. But he knew that the police did not content itself with vague promises. However, the proposal surprised him as though, by being conventional, it ceased to be true.

"Only I will know it," König went on. "That's all that's necessary. . . ."

Why, Kyo wondered, did he seem to gloat over the words: "That's all that's necessary"?

"I shall not enter your service," he said, almost absent-mindedly.

"Look out: I can lock you up with a dozen innocent men, telling them that their fate depends on you, that they will remain in prison if you don't speak and that they are free to choose their own means. . . ."

"It's simpler with executioners."

"The alternate entreaties and tortures are worse. Don't talk about what you don't know—not yet, at least."

"I have just seen a lunatic practically tortured. A lunatic. You understand?"

"Do you fully realize what you are risking?"

"I have been in the civil war, I tell you. I know. Ours also have tortured: men will need a good many pleasures to compensate for all this. . . . Enough. I shall not serve you."

König was thinking that, in spite of what Kyo was saying, he had not understood his threat. "His youth helps him," he said to himself. Two hours before he had questioned a prisoner who had been a member of the Cheka; after ten minutes he had felt a bond of brotherhood: the world in which they both lived was no longer that of men; henceforth they belonged elsewhere. If Kyo was immune to fear through lack of imagination, patience . . .

"Aren't you wondering why I haven't yet sent this revolver flying into your face?"

"I think I am very close to death: that kills curiosity. And you have already said, 'I've got something better. . . .'"

König rang.

"Perhaps I'll come tonight and ask you what you think of human dignity. . . . To the prison-yard, series A," he said to the guards who were entering.

Four o'clock in the afternoon

Clappique mingled in the stir that was pushing the crowd of the concessions towards the barbed wires: in the Avenue of the Two Republics the executioner was passing, his short saber on his shoulder, followed by his escort of Mauserists. Clappique immediately turned about, and made for the concession. Kyo arrested, the Communist defense crushed, a great number of sympathizers murdered in the European city itself. . . . König had given him until evening: he would no longer be protected after that. Gun-shots here and there on every side. Carried by the wind, it seemed to him that they were coming nearer to him, and death with them. "I don't want to die," he said between his teeth, "I don't want to die." He became aware of the fact that he was running. He reached the docks.

No passport, and not enough money left to get a ticket.

Three steamships, one of them French. Clappique stopped running. Stow away in one of the life-boats under the tarpaulin? But he would have to get aboard, and the man at the gangway would not let him pass. Anyway, the idea was idiotic. The hatches? Idiotic, idiotic, idiotic. Go and find the captain and try to bluff him? He had gotten out of scrapes in this way before; but this time the captain would take him for a Communist, and would refuse to take him on board. The ship was leaving in two hours: a bad moment to disturb the captain. If he were discovered on board once the ship was out at sea, he could manage; but the trick was to get aboard.

He could just see himself hidden in some corner, crouched in a barrel; but this time his imagination did not save him. He seemed to be offering himself, as if to the mediators of an unknown god, to those enormous, bristling steamships, charged with destinies, indifferent to the point of hatred. He had stopped before the French ship. He was thinking nothing, looking, fascinated by the gangplank, at the men who were getting on and off (none of whom was thinking of him, nor guessed his torment and whom he would have liked to kill for this), who showed their tickets as they passed the bulwarks. Make a false ticket? Absurd.

A mosquito stung him. He brushed it away, touching his cheek as he did so: he needed a shave. As though any act of attention to one's personal appearance were propitious to departures, he decided to go and get a shave, but without going far from the ship. Beyond the sheds, among the bars and curio-shops, he discovered a Chinese barbershop. The proprietor also ran a wretched café, and the two businesses were separated only by a hanging mat. While waiting for his turn, Clappique sat down near the mat and continued to watch the gangway of the ship. On the other side, people were talking:

"It's the third one," said a man's voice.

"With the baby, nobody will take us. What if we tried one of the rich hotels?"

A woman answered:

"Dressed as we are? The fellow at the door would throw us out before we even reached it."

"There they don't mind if the children make a noise. . . . Let's try some more—anywhere."

"As soon as the managers see the kid, they'll refuse. Only the Chinese hotels would take us in, but the kid would get sick from their dirty food."

"In a poor European hotel, if we could manage to get him in without their noticing it, perhaps they wouldn't dare to throw us out, once we were there. . . . In any case, we'd be gaining time. We'd have to wrap up the little fellow, so they would think it was linen."

"Linen doesn't cry."

"With the bottle in his mouth he won't cry. . . ."

"Perhaps. I could make arrangements at the desk, and

you could come in afterward. You could just pass by the clerk without stopping."

Silence. Clappique was looking at the gangway. A rustle of paper.

"You can't imagine how it hurts me to carry him like this. . . . I have the feeling that it's a bad omen for his whole life. . . . And I'm afraid it will hurt him."

Silence again. Had they left? The client was getting out of the barber's chair. The barber made a sign to Clappique, who got into it, still keeping his eye on the ship. The gangplank was deserted, but scarcely was Clappique's face covered with lather than a sailor went on board, carrying two new pails (which he had perhaps just bought) and brooms on his shoulder. Clappique's eyes followed him, step by step—he would have identified himself with a dog, if the dog were climbing the gangplank and leaving with the ship. The sailor passed in front of the man at the bulwark without a word.

Clappique paid for the shave, throwing the coins on the washstand, tore off the towels and ran out, his face full of soap. He knew where he could find some second-hand dealers. People were looking at him: after taking ten steps, he went back, washed his face, started off again.

He had no trouble in finding a blue sailor-suit at the first dealer's. He hurried back to his hotel, changed clothes. "I ought to have a few brooms, or something like that." Buy some old brooms from the "boys"? Absurd: Why would a sailor be parading about on land with his brooms? To look more handsome? Completely idiotic. If he crossed the gangway with brooms, it would be because he had just bought them on land. They must be new. . . . Let's go and buy some. . . .

He entered the shop with his usual Clappique-air. Before the disdainful look of the English salesman, he exclaimed: "Into my arms!" put the brooms on his shoulder, turned round, knocking down one of the brass lamps, and went out.

"Into my arms," in spite of his deliberate extravagance, expressed what he felt: up to that point, he had been playing an uncomfortable comedy, through an obscure prompting of his conscience and through fear, but without freeing himself from the unavowed sense that he would fail; the salesman's disdain—although Clappique, forgetting about his costume, had not assumed the manner of a sailor—proved to him that he could succeed. With the brooms on his shoulder, he was walking towards the steamer, watching all eyes as he went, to find in them the confirmation of his new status. As when he had stopped before the gangplank, he was stupefied to discover how indifferent his fate was to others—it existed only for him. The travelers, awhile ago, had gone aboard without noticing the man left standing on the quay, perhaps to be killed; the passers-by were now looking indifferently at this sailor; no one came out of the crowd to express astonishment or to recognize him; not even a curious face. . . . Not that there was anything about an assumed life to astonish him, but this time it was imposed upon him, and his real life perhaps depended on it. He was thirsty. He stopped at a Chinese bar, put down his brooms. As soon as he started to drink, he realized that he was not thirsty at all, that he had merely wanted to try himself out once more. The manner in which the man behind the counter gave him back his change was enough to enlighten him. Since he had changed his costume, the world around him had become transformed. He tried to discover how: it was the way people looked at him that had changed. The habitual single witness of his mythomania had become a crowd.

At the same time—pleasure or a defensive instinct—the general acceptance of his new civil status pervaded him, too. He had found, suddenly, by accident, the most dazzling success of his life. No, men do not exist, since a costume is enough to enable one to escape from oneself, to find another life in the eyes of others. It was the same feeling of strangeness, of happiness that had seized him the first time he had found himself in a Chinese crowd—but now the sensation had not only surface, but depth. "Now I'm living a story, not merely telling one!" Carrying his brooms like guns, he crossed the gangplank, passed the man at the bulwark (he felt his knees almost giving way), and found himself on the deck. He hurried forward among the passengers of the bridge, put his brooms on a coil of rope. He was safe, at least until they struck the first port. However, he was far from feeling at ease. One of the deck passengers, a Russian, came up to him:

"You belong to the crew?"

And, without waiting for an answer:

"Do you like the life on board ship?"

"Say, my dear fellow, you have no idea! A Frenchman likes to travel, that's a fact: not a word. The officers are sons of bitches but no worse than the owners, and you don't sleep very well (I don't like hammocks—a matter of taste) but you eat well. And you see things. When I was in South America, the missionaries had made the savages learn l-little Latin canticles by heart—taught them day and night. The bishop arrives, the missionary beats the time: silence—the savages are struck dumb with respect. But not a word! the canticle comes all by itself: the parrots of the forest, my g-good man, who have never heard anything else, sing it with reverence. . . . And just imagine, in the Sea of Celebes, ten years ago, I came across some Arabian caravels, adrift, sculptured like cocoanuts and full of corpses—victims of the plague —with their arms hanging like this over the bulwarks, under a whirling cloud of seagulls. . . . Absolutely. . . ."

"You're lucky. I've been traveling for seven years, and I've never seen anything like that."

"You must introduce the means of art into life, my g-good man, not in order to make art—God, no!—but to make more life. Not a word!"

He tapped him on the belly, and turned away prudently: a car which he recognized was stopping at the end of the gangplank—Ferral was returning to France.

A cabin-boy was beginning to pace the first-class deck, ringing the bell of departure. Each stroke resounded in Clappique's chest.

"Europe," he thought; "the feast is over. Now, Europe." It seemed to be coming towards him with the bell that was approaching, no longer as one of liberation, but as of a prison. But for the menace of death he would have gone back on land.

"Is the third-class bar open?" he asked the Russian.

"Been open for an hour. Anyone can go there till we are at sea."

Clappique took him by the arm:
"Let's go and get drunk. . . ."

Six o'clock in the evening

In the large hall—formerly a school-yard—two hundred wounded Communists were waiting to be taken out and shot. Katov, among the last ones brought in, was

295

propped up on one elbow, looking. All were stretched out on the ground. Many were moaning, in an extraordinarily regular way; some were smoking, as had done those of the Post, and the wreaths of smoke vanished upward to the ceiling, already dark in spite of the large European windows, darkened by the evening and the fog. It seemed very high, above all those prostrate men. Although daylight had not yet disappeared, the atmosphere was one of night. "Is it because of the wounds," Katov wondered, "or because we are all lying down, as in a station? It is a station. We shall leave it for nowhere, and that's all. . . ."

Four Chinese sentries were pacing back and forth among the wounded, with fixed bayonets, and their bayonets reflected the weak light strangely, sharp and straight above all those formless bodies. Outside, deep in the fog, yellowish lights—street-lamps no doubt—also seemed to be watching them. As if it had come from them (because it also came from out there in the fog) a whistle rose and submerged the murmurs and groans: that of a locomotive; they were near the Chapei station. In that vast hall there was something atrociously tense, which was not the expectation of death. Katov was enlightened by his own throat: it was thirst—and hunger. With his back against the wall, he was looking from left to right: many faces that he knew, for a great number of the wounded were fighters of the *ch'ons*. Along one of the narrower walls, a free space, three meters wide, was reserved. "Why are the wounded lying on top of each other," he asked aloud, "instead of going over there?" He was among the last brought in. Leaning against the wall, he began to raise himself up; although he suffered from his wounds, it seemed to him that he would be able to hold himself upright; but he stopped, still bent over: although not a single word had been said, he sensed around him such a startling terror that it made him motionless. In the looks? He could scarcely make them out. In the attitudes? They were, above all, the attitudes of wounded men, absorbed in their own suffering. Yet, however it was transmitted, the dread was there —not fear, but terror, that of beasts, of men who are alone before the inhuman. Katov, without ceasing to lean against the wall, straddled the body of his neighbor.

"Are you crazy?" asked a voice from the level of the floor.

"Why?"

It was both a question and a command. But no one answered. And one of the guards, five meters away, instead of knocking him down, looked at him with stupefaction.

"Why?" he asked again, more fiercely.

"He doesn't know," said another voice, also from the ground, and at the same time, another, still lower: "He'll find out. . . ."

He had uttered the second question very loudly. The hesitancy of the crowd was terrifying—both in itself and because almost all these men knew him: the menace hanging over that wall weighed upon them all, but particularly upon him.

"Lie down again," said one of the wounded.

Why did no one call him by his name? And why did the sentry not interfere? He had seen him, awhile ago, knock down one of the wounded with the butt of his gun, when he had tried to change places. . . . He approached the last one who had spoken and lay down alongside of him.

"That's where they put those who are to be tortured," said the man in a low voice.

Katov understood. They all knew, but they had not dared to say it, either because they were afraid to speak of it, or because no one dared to speak to *him* about it. A voice had said: "He'll find out. . . ."

The door opened. Soldiers entered with lanterns, surrounding stretcher-bearers who deposited several wounded, like packages, close to Katov. Night was coming on, it rose from the ground where the groans seemed to run into one another like rats, mingled with a frightful stench: most of the men could not move. The door shut.

Time passed. Nothing but the pacing of the sentries and the last gleam of the bayonets above the thousand sounds of suffering. Suddenly, as if the darkness had made the fog more dense, the locomotive whistle sounded, more muffled, as if from a great distance. One of the new arrivals, lying on his belly, tightened his hands over his ears, and screamed. The others did not cry out, but terror was there again, close to the ground.

The man raised his head, lifted himself up on his elbows.

"Scoundrels," he screamed, "murderers!"

One of the sentries stepped forward, and with a kick in the ribs turned him over. He became silent. The sentry walked away. The wounded man began to mumble. It was too dark now for Katov to make out his features, but he heard his voice, he felt that he was becoming coherent. Yes—". . . don't shoot, they throw them alive into the boiler of the locomotive," he was saying. "And now, they're whistling. . . ." The sentry was approaching again. Silence, except for the pain.

The door opened again. More bayonets, now lighted up from below by a lantern, but no wounded. A Kuomintang officer entered alone. Although he could no longer see anything but the bulk of the bodies, Katov could feel each man stiffening. The officer, over there, incorporeal, a shadow between the flickering light of the lantern and the twilight behind him, was giving orders to a sentry. The latter approached, sought Katov, found him. Without touching him, without saying a word, with respect, he simply made Katov a sign to get up. He got to his feet with difficulty, faced the door, over there, where the officer continued to give orders. The soldier, with a gun on one arm, the lantern on the other, came and stood on his left. To his right, there was only the free space and the blank wall. The soldier pointed to the space with his gun. Katov smiled bitterly, with a despairing pride. But no one saw his face, and all those of the wounded who were not in the throes of death, followed him with their eyes. His shadow grew upon the wall of those who were to be tortured.

The officer went out. The door remained open.

The sentinels presented arms: a civilian entered. "Section A," shouted a voice from without, and thereupon the door was shut. One of the sentinels led the civilian towards the wall, grumbling as he went; when he was quite close, Katov, with stupefaction, recognized Kyo. As he was not wounded, the sentinels upon seeing him arrive between two officers had taken him for one of the foreign counselors of Chiang Kai-shek; now recognizing their mistake, they were abusing him from a distance. He lay down in the shadow beside Katov.

"You know what's ahead of us?" the latter asked.

"They've been careful to advise me—I don't care: I have my cyanide. Have you yours?"

"Yes."

"Are you wounded?"

"In the legs. But I can walk."

"Have you been here long?"

"No. When were you caught?"

"Last night. Any way of getting out of here?"

"Not a chance. Almost all are badly wounded. Soldiers everywhere outside. And you saw the machineguns in front of the door?"

"Yes. Where did they get you?"

Both needed to get away from this death wake, to talk, to talk: Katov, of the taking of the Post; Kyo, of the prison, of his interview with König, of what he had learned since; even before he reached the temporary prison, he had found out that May had not been arrested.

Katov was lying on his side, right beside him, separated from him by the vast expanse of suffering—mouth half-open, lips swollen under his jovial nose, his eyes almost shut—but joined to him by that absolute friendship, without reticence, which death alone gives: a doomed life fallen next to his in the darkness full of menaces and wounds, among all those brothers in the mendicant order of the Revolution: each of these men had wildly seized as it stalked past him the only greatness that could be his.

The guards brought three Chinamen. Separated from the crowd of the wounded, but also from the men against the wall. They had been arrested before the fighting, summarily tried, and were now waiting to be shot.

"Katov!" one of them called.

It was Lu Yu Hsüan, Hemmelrich's associate.

"What?"

"Do you know if they're shooting us far from here, or near by?"

"I don't know. We can't hear it, in any case."

A voice said, a little beyond:

"Seems that the executioner, afterwards, pilfers your gold teeth."

300

And another:

"I don't give a damn. I haven't any."

The three Chinamen were smoking cigarettes, puffing away stubbornly.

"Have you several boxes of matches?" asked one of the wounded, a little farther away.

"Yes."

"Throw me one."

Lu threw his.

"I wish someone could tell my son that I died bravely," he said in a low voice. And, even a little lower: "It is not easy to die."

Katov discovered in himself a lusterless joy: no wife, no children.

The door opened.

"Send one out!" shouted the sentry.

The three men were pressing close to one another.

"Come on, now," said the guard, "make up your minds. . . ."

He did not dare to make a choice. Suddenly, one of the two unknown Chinamen took a step forward, threw down his scarcely burnt cigarette, lit another after breaking two matches and went off with a hurried step towards the door, buttoning as he went, one by one, all the buttons of his coat. The door again shut.

One of the wounded was picking up the broken matches. His neighbors had broken into small fragments those from the box Lu Yu Hsüan had given them, and were playing at drawing straws. In less than five minutes the door again opened:

"Another!"

Lu and his companion went forward together, holding each other by the arm. Lu was reciting in a loud voice, without resonance, the death of the hero in a famous play; but the old Chinese solidarity was indeed destroyed: no one was listening.

"Which one?" asked the soldier.

They did not answer.

"Well, is one of you going to come?"

With a blow of his rifle-butt he separated them. Lu was nearer to him than the other; he took him by the shoulder.

Lu freed his shoulder, stepped forward. His companion returned to his place and lay down.

Kyo felt how much more difficult it would be for this one to die than for those who had preceded him: he remained alone. As brave as Lu, since he had stood up with him. But now his manner of lying on the ground, like a hunting-dog, his arms held tight around his body, loudly proclaimed fear. In fact, when the guard touched him, he was seized with a nervous attack. Two soldiers took hold of him, one by his feet, and the other by his head, and carried him out.

Stretched out full length on his back, his arms resting on his chest, Kyo shut his eyes: it was precisely the posture of the dead. He imagined himself, stretched out, motionless, his eyes closed, his face composed in the serenity which death dispenses for a day to almost all corpses, as though the dignity of even the most wretched had to be asserted. He had seen much of death, and, helped by his Japanese education, he had always thought that it is fine to die by one's own hand, a death that resembles one's life. And to die is passivity, but to kill oneself is action. As soon as they came to fetch the first of their group, he would kill himself with full consciousness. He remembered—his heart stopped beating—the phonograph records. A time when hope still had meaning! He would not see May again, and the only grief that left him vulnerable was her grief, as if his own death were a fault. "The remorse of dying," he thought with a contracted irony. No such feeling with regard to his father, who had always given him the impression not of weakness, but of strength. For more than a year May had freed him from all solitude, if not from all bitterness. The memory of the poignant flight into the ecstasy of bodies linked for the first time burst forth, alas! as soon as he thought of her, already separated from the living. . . . "Now she must forget me. . . ." To write her this would only have heightened her grief and attached her all the more to him. "And it would be telling her to love another."

O prison, place where time ceases—time, which continues elsewhere. . . . NO! It was in this yard, separated from everyone by the machine-guns, that the Revolution, no matter what its fate or the place of its resurrection, was receiving its death-stroke; wherever men labor in pain, in absurdity, in humiliation, they were thinking of doomed men like these, as believers pray; and, in the city, they were beginning to love these dying men as though they were already dead. . . . In all of the earth that this last night covered over, this place of agony was no doubt the most weighted with virile love. He could wail with this crowd of prostrate men, join this sacrificed suffering even in its murmur of complaint. . . .

And an inaudible chorus of lamentation prolonged this whispering of pain into the depth of the night: like Hemmelrich, almost all these men had children. Yet the fatality which they had accepted rose with the murmur of these wounded men like the peace of evening, spread over Kyo—his eyes shut, his hands crossed upon his abandoned body—with the majesty of a funeral chant.

He had fought for what in his time was charged with the deepest meaning and the greatest hope; he was dying among those with whom he would have wanted to live; he was dying, like each of these men, because he had given a meaning to his life. What would have been the value of a life for which he would not have been willing to die? It is easy to die when one does not die alone. A death saturated with this brotherly quavering, an assembly of the vanquished in which multitudes would recognize their martyrs, a bloody legend of which the golden legends are made! How, already facing death, could he fail to hear this murmur of human sacrifice crying to him that the virile heart of men is for the dead as good a refuge as the mind?

He had opened the buckle of his belt and was holding the cyanide in his hand. He had often wondered if he would die easily. He knew that if he made up his mind to kill himself, he would kill himself; but knowing the savage indifference with which life unmasks us to ourselves, he had not been without anxiety about the moment when death would crush his mind with its whole weight and finality.

No, dying could be an exalted act, the supreme expression of a life which this death so much resembled; and it was an escape from those two soldiers who were approaching hesitantly. He crushed the poison between his teeth as he would have given a command, heard Katov still question him with anguish and touch him, and, at the moment when, suffocating, he wanted to cling to him, he felt his whole strength go outward, wrenched from him in an all-powerful convulsion.

The soldiers were coming to fetch two prisoners in the crowd who could not get up. No doubt being burned alive entitled one to special, although limited, honors:

transported on a single stretcher, almost on top of each other, they were laid down at Katov's left; Kyo, dead, was lying at his right. In the empty space which separated them from those who were only condemned to death, the soldiers crouched near their lantern. Little by little, heads and eyes fell back into the darkness, now emerging only rarely into this light which marked the place of the condemned.

Katov, since the death of Kyo—who had panted for at least a minute—felt himself thrown back into a solitude which was all the stronger and more painful as he was surrounded by his own people. The Chinaman whom they had had to carry out in order to kill, shaken by a nervous attack, obsessed him. And yet he felt in this complete desertion a sense of repose, as if for years he had been awaiting just this; a repose he had encountered, found again, in the worst moments of his life. Where had he read: "It was not the discoveries, but the sufferings of explorers which I envied, which attracted me. . . ."? As if in response to his thought, the distant whistle reached the hall for the third time. The two men on his left started. Very young Chinamen; one was Suan, whom he knew only through having fought by his side in the Post; the second, unknown. (It was not Pei.) Why were they not with the others?

"Organizing combat groups?" he asked.

"Attempt at Chiang Kai-shek's life," Suan answered.

"With Ch'en?"

"No. He wanted to throw his bomb alone. Chiang was not in the car. I was waiting for the car much further on. They caught me with the bomb."

The voice which answered him was so choked that Katov scrutinized the two faces: the young men were weeping, without a sob. Suan tried to move his shoulder, and his face contracted with pain—he was wounded also in the arm.

"Burned," he said. "To be burned alive. The eyes, too, the eyes, you understand . . ."

His comrade was sobbing now.

"One can be burned by accident," said Katov.

It seemed as if they were speaking, not to each other, but to some invisible third person.

"It's not the same thing."

"No: it's not so good."

"The eyes too," the young man repeated in a lower voice, "the eyes . . . each finger, and the stomach, the stomach . . ."

"Shut up!" said the other with the voice of a deaf man.

He would have liked to cry out, but could not. His hands clutched Suan close to his wounds, causing the latter's muscles to contract.

"Human dignity," Katov murmured, thinking of Kyo's interview with König. The condemned men were no longer speaking. Beyond the lantern, in the darkness that was now complete, the murmur of the wounded continued. . . . He edged still closer to Suan and his companion. One of the guards was telling the others a story: their heads close together, they were between the lantern and the condemned: the latter could no longer even see one another. In spite of the hum, in spite of all these men who had fought as he had, Katov was alone, alone between the body of his dead friend and his two terror-stricken companions, alone between this wall and that whistle far off in the night. But a man could be stronger than this solitude and even, perhaps, than that atrocious whistle: fear struggled in him against the most terrible temptation in his life. In his turn he opened the buckle of his belt. Finally:

"Hey, there," he said in a very low voice. "Suan, put your hand on my chest, and close it as soon as I touch it: I'm going to give you my cyanide. There is abs'lutely enough only for two."

He had given up everything, except saying that there was only enough for two. Lying on his side, he broke the cyanide in two. The guards masked the light, which surrounded them with a dim halo; but would they not move? Impossible to see anything; Katov was making this gift of something that was more precious than his life not even to bodies, not even to voices, but to the warm hand resting upon him. It grew taut, like an animal, immediately separated from him. He waited, his whole body tense. And suddenly, he heard one of the two voices:

"It's lost. Fell."

A voice scarcely affected by anguish, as if such a catastrophe, so decisive, so tragic, were not possible, as if things were bound to arrange themselves. For Katov also it was impossible. A limitless anger rose in him, but fell again, defeated by this impossibility. And yet! To have given *that* only to have the idiot lose it!

"When?" he asked.

"Before my body. Could not hold it when Suan passed it: I'm wounded in the hand too."

"He dropped both of them," said Suan.

They were no doubt looking for it in the space between them. They next looked between Katov and Suan, on whom the other was probably almost lying, for Katov, without being able to see anything, could feel beside him the bulk of two bodies. He was looking too, trying to control his nervousness, to place his hand flat, at regular intervals, wherever he could reach. Their hands brushed his. And suddenly one of them took his, pressed it, held it.

"Even if we don't find it . . ." said one of the voices.

Katov also pressed his hand, on the verge of tears, held by that pitiful fraternity, without a face, almost without a real voice (all whispers resemble one another), which was being offered him in this darkness in return for the greatest gift he had ever made, and which perhaps was made in vain. Although Suan continued to look, the two hands remained united. The grasp suddenly became a tight clutch:

"Here!"

O resurrection! . . . But:

"Are you sure they are not pebbles?" asked the other.

There were many bits of plaster on the ground.

"Give it to me!" said Katov.

With his fingertips, he recognized the shapes.

He gave them back—gave them back—pressed more strongly the hand which again sought his, and waited, his shoulders trembling, his teeth chattering. "If only the cyanide has not decomposed, in spite of the silver paper," he thought. The hand he was holding suddenly twisted his, and, as though he were communicating through it with the body lost in the darkness, he felt that the latter was stiffening. He envied this convulsive suffocation. Almost at the same time, the other one: a choked cry which no one heeded. Then, nothing.

Katov felt himself deserted. He turned over on his belly and waited. The trembling of his shoulders did not cease.

In the middle of the night, the officer came back. In a clatter of rifles striking against one another, six soldiers were approaching the condemned men. All the prisoners had awakened. The new lantern, also, showed only long, vague forms—tombs in the earth already turned over—and a few reflections in the eyes. Katov managed to raise himself. The one who commanded the squad took Kyo's arm, felt its stiffness, immediately seized Suan's; that one also was stiff. A rumble was spreading, from the first rows of prisoners to the last. The chief of the squad lifted the foot of one of the men, then of the other: they fell back, stiff. He called the officer. The latter went through the same motions. Among the prisoners, the rumble was growing. The officer looked at Katov:

"Dead?"

Why answer?

"Isolate the six nearest prisoners!"

"Useless," answered Katov: "I gave them the cyanide."

"And you?" he finally asked.

"There was only enough for two," answered Katov with deep joy.

("I'm going to get a rifle-butt in my face," he thought to himself.)

The rumble of the prisoners had become almost a clamor.

"Come on, let's go," said the officer merely.

Katov did not forget that he had been condemned to death before this, that he had seen the machine-guns leveled at him, had heard them fire. . . . "As soon as I'm outside, I'm going to try to strangle one of them, and to hold my hands tightened to his throat long enough so they will be forced to kill me. They will burn me, but dead." At that very moment one of the soldiers seized him by the waist, while another brought his hands behind his back and tied them. "The little fellows were lucky," he said to himself. "Well! let's suppose I died in a fire."

He began to walk. Silence fell, like a trap-door, in spite of the moans. The lantern threw Katov's shadow, now very black, across the great windows framing the night; he walked heavily, with uneven steps, hindered by his wounds; when the swinging of his body brought him closer to the lantern, the silhouette of his head vanished into the ceiling. The whole darkness of the vast hall was alive, and followed him with its eyes, step by step. The silence had become so great that the ground resounded each time his foot fell heavily upon it; all the heads, with a slight movement, followed the rhythm of his walk, with love, with dread, with resignation. All kept their heads raised: the door was being closed.

A sound of deep breathing, the same as that of sleep, began to rise from the ground: breathing through their noses, their jaws clenched with anguish, motionless now, all those who were not yet dead were waiting for the whistle.

The next day

For more than five minutes, Gisors had been looking at his pipe. Before him, the lighted lamp ("which doesn't mean that I will use it"), the little open box of opium, the clean needles. Outside, the night; in the room, the light of the small lamp and a great bright rectangle at one end—the open doorway to the next room, where they had brought Kyo's body. The yard had been cleared for new victims, and no one had objected to the removal of the bodies thrown outside. Katov's had not been found. May had brought back Kyo's, with the precautions she would have taken for one severely wounded. He lay there, stretched out, not serene as Kyo, before killing himself, had thought he would become, but convulsed by the suffocation, already something else than a man. May was combing his hair before the preparation of the body for burial, speaking with her mind to the last presence of this face with horrible maternal words that she did not dare to pronounce, afraid herself to hear them. "My love," she murmured, as she would have said, "my flesh," knowing full well that it was something of herself, not foreign, which was torn from her; "my life . . ." She perceived that it was to the dead that she was saying this. But she had long been past tears.

All grief that helps no one is absurd, Gisors was thinking, hypnotized by his lamp, finding refuge in this fascination. "Peace is here. Peace." But he did not dare to advance his hand. He believed in no survival, had no respect for the dead; but he did not dare to advance his hand.

She came towards him, her mouth distorted by grief, her eyes staring into space. . . . She placed her fingers gently on his wrist.

"Come," she said in an anxious voice, almost a whisper. "It seems to me he feels a little warmer."

He looked up into her face, so human, so grief-stricken, but betraying no delusion. She was looking at him calmly, less with hope than with the attitude of prayer. The effects of poison are always uncertain; and she was a doctor. He got up, followed her, guarding himself against a hope so strong that it seemed to him he would be unable to endure its being withdrawn. He put his hand on Kyo's bluish brow, that brow which would never be touched by wrinkles: it was cold, with the special coldness of death. He did not dare to withdraw his fingers, to meet May's eyes, and he kept his own eyes fastened upon Kyo's open hand, in which the lines had already begun to disappear. . . .

311

"No," he said, returning to his distress. He had not left it. He realized that he had not believed May.

"Oh . . ." she said merely.

She watched him return into the other room, hesitant. What was he thinking of? As long as Kyo was there, every thought belonged to him. This death demanded something of her, an answer which she did not know, but which existed none the less. Oh, the abject good fortune of others, with their prayers, their funeral flowers! An answer beyond anguish which tore from her hands the maternal caresses which no child had received from her, with the frightful urge that causes one to speak to the dead with the most affectionate gestures of life. This mouth which only yesterday had said to her: "I thought you were dead," would never speak again; it was not with the derisive remnant of life—a body—it was with death itself that she must enter into communion. She stood there, motionless, wrenching from her memories so many agonies beheld with resignation, all tense with passivity in the vain welcome that she wildly offered to nothingness.

Gisors was once more stretched out on the divan. "And presently I shall have to wake up. . . ." How much longer would each morning bring this death back to him again? The pipe was there: peace. Advance his hand, prepare the pellet: after a few minutes, think of death itself with a limitless indulgence, as of some paralytic who might wish to harm him: it would no longer be able to reach him; it would lose its hold on him and would gently dissolve into the universal serenity. Liberation was there, within his reach. No help can be given to the dead. Why continue to suffer? Is grief an offering to love, or to fear? . . . He still did not dare to touch the tray, and anguish, as well as desire and repressed tears, choked him. He picked up at random the first pamphlet which his hand fell on (he never touched Kyo's books, but he knew he would not read it). It was a copy of the *Peking Politics* which had fallen there when they had brought in the body and which contained the speech for which Gisors had been dismissed from the University. In the margin, in Kyo's handwriting: "This speech is *my father's* speech." Kyo had never even told him that he approved him. Gisors folded the pamphlet gently and looked at his dead hope.

He opened the door, threw the opium into the night and came back and sat down, his shoulders drooping, waiting for the dawn, waiting for his grief to be reduced to silence, to become exhausted in its dialogue with itself. . . . In spite of the suffering which half opened his mouth, which cast over his grave face a deforming expression of bewilderment, he did not lose all control. Tonight, his life was going to change: the power of thought is not great against the metamorphosis to which death can oblige a man. He was henceforth thrown back upon himself. The world no longer had any meaning, no longer existed: the irretrievable immobility, there, beside that body which had bound him to the universe, was like a suicide of God. He had expected of Kyo neither success, nor even happiness; but that the world should be without Kyo . . . "I am thrown outside of time"; the child was the submission to time, to the flow of things; no doubt, deep down, Gisors felt hope, as he felt anguish, hope of nothing, expectation, and his love had to be crushed in order that he should discover that. And yet! All that was destroying him found in him an avid welcome: "There is something beautiful in being dead," he thought. He felt the basic suffering trembling within him, not that which comes from creatures or from things, but that which gushes forth from man himself and from which life attempts to tear us away; he could escape it, but only by ceasing to think of it; and he plunged into it deeper and deeper, as if this terrified contemplation were the only voice that death could hear, as if this suffering of being a man which pervaded him, reaching down to the very depth of his heart, were the only prayer that the body of his dead son could hear.

Part Seven

Ferral, fanning himself with the newspaper in
which the Consortium was being most violently attacked,
was the last to arrive in the waiting-room of the Minister of Finance: in groups were waiting the vice-director
of the *Mouvement Général des Fonds*—Ferral's brother
had wisely fallen ill the week before—the representative
of the Bank of France, the representative of the principal French business-bank, and those of the credit establishments. Ferral knew them all: one son, one son-in-
law, and former officials of the *Mouvement Général des
Fonds;* the link between the State and the Establishments
was too close for the latter not to consider it in their interest to attach to themselves officials who were favor-
ably received by their former colleagues. Ferral observed
their surprise: ordinarily he would have been the first
one there; not seeing him there, they had thought he
had not been invited to be present. That he should permit himself to come last suprised them. Everything
separated them: what he thought of them, what they
thought of him, their manner of dress: almost all were
dressed with an impersonal carelessness, and Ferral was
wearing his wrinkled tweed suit and the gray silk shirt
with a soft collar from Shanghai. Two races.

They were almost immediately admitted.

Ferral knew the minister only slightly. Was that facial
expression which recalled another age due to his white

hair, thick like that of the wigs of the Regency? That delicate face with its bright eyes, that open smile—he was an old Parliamentarian—accorded with the tradition of ministerial courtesy; a tradition which ran parallel to that of his brusqueness when he was bitten by a Napoleonic fly. While everyone was taking his seat, Ferral thought of a famous anecdote: the minister—then Minister of Foreign Affairs—on one occasion upon pulling the coat-tail of the French envoy to Morocco, had caused the seam suddenly to rip up the back; he rang for the door-keeper: "Bring one of my coats for Monsieur!" then rang again just as the door-keeper was leaving: "The oldest one! He doesn't deserve another!" His face would have been very attractive but for the expression of the eyes which seemed to deny what his mouth promised: he had one glass eye.

They were all seated: the director of the *Mouvement Général* at the right of the minister, Ferral at his left; the representatives, at the other end of the office, on a couch.

"You know, gentlemen, why I have called you. You have no doubt examined the question. I leave M. Ferral to summarize it for you and to present his point of view."

The representatives patiently waited for Ferral to tell them fantastic tales, as usual.

"Gentlemen," said Ferral, "it is customary in a conference like this to present an optimistic picture. You have before you the report of the Inspection of Finance. The situation of the Consortium is, practically speaking, worse than this report would lead one to assume. I submit to you neither exaggerated items nor uncertain credits. The liabilities of the Consortium you know, obviously; I wish to call your attention to two points in the assets which no balance-sheet can indicate, and on the strength of which your aid is requested.

"The first is that the Consortium represents the only French enterprise of its kind in the Far East. Even though it showed a deficit, even though it were on the verge of bankruptcy, its structure would remain intact. Its network of agents, its trading-posts in the interior of China, the connections established between its Chinese buyers and its Indo-Chinese production companies, all that *exists* and can be maintained. I don't exaggerate in saying that, for half the merchants of the Yangtze, France means the Consortium, as Japan is the Mitsubishi Company; our organization, as you know, can be compared in its scope with the Standard Oil. Now, the Chinese Revolution will not be eternal.

"The second point: thanks to the bonds that unite the Consortium to a great part of Chinese commerce, I have participated in the most effective way in the seizure of power by General Chiang Kai-shek. It is now definitely settled that the share in the construction of the Chinese Railways promised to France by the treaties will be given to the Consortium. You know its importance. It is upon this point that I ask you to base your decision in granting to the Consortium the aid which it requests of you; it is because of its presence that it appears to me defensible to wish that the only powerful organization which represents our country in Asia should not disappear—even though it were to leave the hands of those who have founded it."

The representatives were carefully examining the balance-sheet, with which, for that matter, they were already familiar, and which could tell them nothing new: all were waiting for the minister to speak.

"It is not only to the interest of the State," said the

latter, "but also to that of the Establishments that credit should not be endangered. The fall of such important organizations as the Industrial Bank of China, as the Consortium, cannot but be a serious blow to all. . . ."

He was speaking nonchalantly, leaning back in his armchair, looking off into space, tapping the blotting paper in front of him with the tip of his pencil. The representatives were waiting for his attitude to become more precise.

"Will you allow me, Sir," said the Representative of the Bank of France, "to submit to you a somewhat different opinion. I am the only one here who does not represent a credit establishment, and I am therefore impartial. For several months the crashes have caused the deposits to diminish, it is true; but, after six months, the sums withdrawn automatically return, and precisely in the principal establishments, those which offer the most guarantees. Perhaps the fall of the Consortium, far from being prejudicial to the establishments which these gentlemen represent, would on the contrary be favorable to them. . . ."

"Except for this, that it is always dangerous to play with credits: fifteen provincial bank failures would not be profitable to the Establishments, if for no other reason than that of the political measures which they would call for."

All this means nothing, thought Ferral, if not that the Bank of France is afraid of being involved and having to pay if the establishments pay. Silence. The questioning look of the minister met that of one of the representatives: the face of a cavalry lieutenant, a piercing look ready to reprimand, a sharp voice:

"I must confess that I am a little less pessimistic than M. Ferral on the aggregate of the items in the balance-sheet which we have before us. The situation of the banks of the group is disastrous, it is true; but certain companies can be maintained, even in their present form."

"It is the whole enterprise which I am asking you to maintain," said Ferral. "If the Consortium is destroyed, its affairs lose all meaning for France."

"On the contrary," said another representative, with slender, delicate features, "M. Ferral seems to me to be optimistic, after all, as to the principal asset of the Consortium. The loan has not yet been issued."

He was looking as he spoke at the lapel of Ferral's coat; the latter, puzzled, followed his look, and understood; he alone in the room was not decorated. Purposely. The man who spoke was a Commander of the Legion of Honor, and regarded this disdainful button-hole with hostility. Ferral had never wanted consideration except for his own power.

"You know that it will be issued," he said; "issued and covered. That concerns the American banks and not their clients, who will take what they are told to take."

"Let's assume it. The loan covered, who guarantees that the railroads will be built?"

"But," said Ferral with a little astonishment (his questioner could not help knowing what he would answer), "there is no question of giving the major part of the funds to the Chinese government. They will go directly from the American banks to the enterprises engaged to manufacture the rolling-stock, obviously. Otherwise, do you think the Americans would issue the loan?"

"To be sure. But Chiang Kai-shek may be killed or beaten; if Bolshevism rises again, the loan will not be issued. For my part, I don't believe Chiang Kai-shek can

319

maintain himself in power. According to information we have received, his downfall is imminent."

"The Communists have been crushed everywhere," answered Ferral. "Borodin has just left Hankow and is returning to Moscow."

"The Communists, no doubt, but not Communism. China will never again become what she was, and, after Chiang Kai-shek's triumph, new Communist waves are to be feared. . . ."

"My opinion is that he will still be in power in ten years. But there is no business that does not involve risk."

(Only listen to your courage, he was thinking, which never tells you anything. And Turkey, when it did not reimburse you one cent and was buying war-implements with your money? You never have carried out a single great enterprise by yourselves. When you're through prostituting yourselves to the State, you take your cowardice for wisdom, and believe that to be a Venus de Milo all you need is to be armless—which is going a little far.)

"If Chiang Kai-shek maintains himself in the government," said the soft voice of a young representative with curly hair, "China will recover the autonomy of its customs. What is there to guarantee that, even granting M. Ferral all he assumes, his activity in China will not lose all its value on the day when Chinese laws will suffice to reduce it to nothing? Several answers can be made to that, I know. . . ."

"Several," said Ferral.

"None the less the fact remains," answered the representative who looked like an officer, "that this undertaking is uncertain, or, even admitting that it involves no risk, the fact remains that it involves a long-term credit,

and, in truth, a participation in the activity of an enterprise. . . . We all know that M. Germain nearly
brought about the ruin of the *Crédit Lyonnais* through
having become interested in Anilin Dyes, which was
nevertheless one of the best French ventures. Our function is not to participate in business ventures, but to lend
money on guarantees, on short terms. Anything else is
outside our field, it's a matter for business banks."

Silence, again. A long silence.

Ferral was wondering why the minister did not intervene. All of them, including himself, spoke a conventional and ornate language, like the ritual languages of
Asia: there was no doubt, for that matter, that all this
had a considerable Chinese flavor. That the guarantees
of the Consortium were insufficient was indeed obvious;
otherwise, why was he here? Since the war, the losses
suffered by the French Reserve which had subscribed
to the stocks or obligations of commercial enterprises
recommended by the Establishments and the great commercial banks, amounted to about forty billions—ap-
preciably more than the cost of the Treaty of Frankfort.
A bad venture paid a higher commission than a good
one, that was all. But a bad venture, to be accepted, had
to be submitted by *one of them*—not by an outsider.

They would not pay, unless the minister formally
intervened, because Ferral was not one of them. Not
married: stories about women that had become known.
Suspected of smoking opium. He had turned down the
Legion of Honor. Too much pride to be either a con-
formist or a hypocrite. Perhaps great individualism could
be fully developed only on a dung-heap of hypocrisy:
Borgia was not a pope by accident. . . . It was not at
the end of the eighteenth century among the French
revolutionaries, drunk with virtue, that the great in-

dividualists would be found, but in the Renaissance, in a social structure which was Christianity, obviously. . . .

"Monsieur le Ministre," said the oldest of the delegates, swallowing both his syllables and his short mustache, white like his wavy hair, "it goes without saying that we are disposed to come to the aid of the State. That's understood. You know it."

He removed his monocle, and the gestures of his hands with slightly parted fingers became the gestures of a blind man.

"But after all, we would have to know how far we were going into it! I don't say that each of us could not involve himself to the extent of, say, five million. Good."

The minister shrugged his shoulders imperceptibly.

"But that's not the question, since the Consortium must reimburse at a minimum 250,000,000 in deposits. And then, what? If the State believes a crash of this magnitude would be serious, it has its own means of obtaining funds; to save the French and Annamite depositors, the Bank of France and the General Government of Indo-China are after all the ones who should be called upon rather than we, who also have our depositors and our stockholders. Each one of us is here in the name of his Establishment. . . ."

(It being understood, Ferral was thinking, that if the minister made it clear that he wants the Consortium to be refloated, there would no longer be either depositors or stockholders.)

". . . Who among us can affirm that his stockholders would approve a loan made for no other purpose than to maintain a tottering enterprise? What these stockholders think, Sir—and not they alone—we know very well; they think that the market must be made sound, that enterprises that are not viable must blow up; that

322

to maintain them artificially is the worst service one can render to all. What becomes of the efficacy of competition, which is the very life of French commerce, if doomed enterprises are automatically maintained?"

(My friend, thought Ferral, your Establishment demanded a thirty-two per cent raise in tariffs from the State, just last month; to facilitate free competition, no doubt.)

". . . And so? Our business is to loan money on guarantees, as has very justly been observed. The guarantees which M. Ferral offers . . . You have heard M. Ferral himself. Will the State substitute for M. Ferral in this case and give us the guarantees against which we will grant the Consortium the funds it needs? In other words, is the State appealing to our loyalty without offering any compensation, or does it ask us—the State and not M. Ferral—to facilitate an operation of the Treasury, even on a long term? In the first case, of course, it can count on our loyalty, but after all we are bound to consider our stockholders' interests; in the second, what guarantees does it offer us?"

A complete ciphered language, Ferral was thinking. If we were not engaged in playing a comedy, the minister would answer: "I appreciate the comic value of the word 'devotion.' Your principal benefits come from your relations with the State. You live on commissions, which determine the importance of your establishment, and not on independent activities. The State has given you this year one hundred million, in one form or another; it is taking back twenty—bless its name, and calling it quits." But there is no danger of that.

The minister pulled out from a drawer of his desk a box of soft caramels, and passed it around. Each ate one, except Ferral. He knew now what the delegates of the

Establishments wanted: pay, since it was impossible to leave this cabinet without granting the minister something, but pay as little as possible. As for the latter . . . Ferral waited, assured that he was busy thinking: "What would Choiseul have appeared to do in my place?" Appeared: the minister did not ask the great lords of the kingdom for lessons in will, but in behavior or in irony.

"The Vice-Director of the *Mouvement Général des Fonds*," he said, tapping the table with his pencil, "will tell you as I do that I cannot give you these guarantees without a vote of Parliament. I have called you together, gentlemen, because the question we are debating concerns France's prestige; do you think that bringing this question before public opinion is a good way to defend it?"

"No dlout, no dlout, but pelmit me, monsieur le Ministle . . ."

Silence; the representatives, chewing their caramels, sought refuge from the Auvergnat accent in a meditative air. They suddenly felt that by opening their mouths they would be exposing themselves to an unseen menace. The minister looked at them without smiling, one after the other, and Ferral, who saw him in profile—the side with the glass eye—looked upon him as a great white Carolina parrot, motionless and bitter, in the midst of other birds.

"I see, then, gentlemen," the minister went on, "that we are agreed upon that point. In whatever way we look upon this problem, it is necessary that the deposits be reimbursed. The General Government of Indo-China would participate in the refloating of the Consortium to the amount of one-fifth. What share could you offer?"

Now each one sought refuge in his caramel. "Just a small pleasure," said Ferral to himself. "He wants a little distraction, but the result would have been the same without the caramels. . . ." He knew the value of the argument put forward by the minister. It was his brother who had answered those who asked the *Mouvement Général* for a conversion without vote of Parliament: "Why shouldn't I after that give two hundred millions on my own authority to my little girl-friend?"

Silence. Longer than the preceding ones. The representatives were whispering among themselves.

"Monsieur le Ministre," said Ferral, "if the healthy enterprises of the Consortium are, in one form or another, to be continued; if the deposits are, in any case, to be reimbursed, don't you think there is occasion to wish for a greater effort, from which the maintenance of the Consortium should not be excluded? Does not the existence of so extensive a French organization have in the eyes of the State an importance equal to that of a few hundred million in deposits?"

"Five million is not a serious figure, gentlemen," said the minister. "Must I appeal in a more urgent way to the devotion of which you have spoken? I know you are anxious, that your Boards of Directors are anxious to avoid the control of banks by the State. Do you think the fall of enterprises like the Consortium will not arouse public opinion to the point of demanding such control in a manner that might become imperious, and perhaps urgent?"

More and more Chinese, thought Ferral. This merely means: "Stop proposing to me five ridiculous millions." The control of the banks is an absurd threat when it is made by a government whose policy is directly opposed to such measures. And the minister has no more desire really to have recourse to it than the representative who holds the Havas Agency among his cards desires to launch a press-campaign against the minister. The State can no more play seriously against the banks than the banks against the State. They are accomplices in every way: a common personnel, common interests and psychology. A struggle between the department heads of the same firm—by which, for that matter, the firm subsists. But poorly. As at the *Astor*, not so long ago, he could save himself only by not weakening and by showing no trace of anger. But he was beaten: having made personal effectiveness his essential value, nothing could compensate for the fact that he was now facing these men, whose persons and methods he had always despised, in this humiliated position. He was weaker than they, and by that very fact, in his own system, all that he might think was of no avail.

"Monsieur le Ministre," said the oldest delegate, "we are anxious to show our good will to the State once again; but, if there are no guarantees we cannot, in view of our stockholders, consider extending to the Consortium a credit beyond the sum total of the deposits to be reimbursed, and guaranteed by the resumption of the healthy affairs of the group. God knows that we have no desire for this resumption, that we are undertaking it through respect for the superior interest of the State. . . ."

This fellow, Ferral was thinking, is really extraordinary, with his air of a retired professor transformed into a blind Œdipus. And all the numbskulls, including France, who come to his agency-directors for advice, and to whom State funds are thrown like asses' skins when it's a matter of building strategic railways in Russia, in Poland, in the North Pole! Since the war, that skewer sitting on the couch has cost the French reserve billions in State funds alone. Very well. As he used to say, ten years ago: "Any man who asks advice about investing his money from a man he does not know intimately, deserves to be ruined." Eighteen billions. Without mentioning the forty billions in commercial enterprises. Nor myself.

"Monsieur Damiral?" said the minister.

"I can only endorse, Sir, the words you have just heard. Like M. de Morelles, I cannot involve the establishment which I represent without the guarantees which he mentioned. I could not do so without violating the principles and the traditions which have made this establishment one of the most powerful in Europe, principles and traditions which have often been attacked, but which enable it to prove its devotion to the State when the latter appeals to it, as it did five months ago, as it is doing today, as it will perhaps do tomorrow. It is the frequency of these appeals, Monsieur le Ministre, and the resolution we have made to hear them, which oblige me to ask for the guarantees which these principles and traditions require that we assure to our depositors, and thanks to which—as I have allowed myself to tell you, Sir—we are at your disposal. We can no doubt dispose of twenty million."

The representatives looked at one another in consternation: the deposits would be reimbursed. Ferral now understood what the minister had wanted: to give satisfaction to his brother without committing himself; have the depositors reimbursed; make the Establishments pay, but as little as possible; be able to draw up a satisfactory report. The bargaining continued. The Consortium would be destroyed; but its annihilation mattered little if the deposits were reimbursed. The Establishments obtained the guarantee which they had demanded (they would lose, nevertheless, but very little). A few enter-

327

prises, which would be maintained, would become the affiliates of the Establishments; as for the rest . . . All that had happened in Shanghai was about to be dissolved, here, in a complete meaninglessness. He would have preferred to see himself despoiled, to see his work go on living completely out of his hands, conquered or stolen. But the minister would see only his own fear of the Chamber; he would tear no jackets today. In his place, Ferral would have begun by banishing himself from the Consortium, which would thereby have been rendered more healthy, and would then have maintained it at any price. As for the Establishments, he had always affirmed their incurable avarice. He remembered with pride a phrase of one of his adversaries: "He always wants a bank to be a gambling house."

The telephone rang, close by. One of the attachés entered:

"Monsieur le Ministre, the President of the Council on the private wire."

"Tell him matters are being satisfactorily arranged. . . . No, I'll go myself."

He went out, returned a moment later, gave the delegate of the principal commercial bank (the only one which was here represented) a questioning look. A straight mustache, parallel to his glasses, bald head, weariness. He had not yet said a word.

"The maintenance of the Consortium does not in any way interest us," he said slowly. "A share in the building of the Railways is assured to France by the treaties. If the Consortium falls, another enterprise will be formed, or will develop, and will succeed it. . . ."

"And this new corporation," said Ferral, "instead of having industrialized Indo-China, will distribute dividends. But, as it will have done nothing for Chiang Kai-shek, it will find itself in the situation in which you would be here, if you had never done anything for the State; and the treaties will be manipulated by some American or British society with a French screen, obviously. To whom you will lend, for that matter, the money which you refuse me. We have created the Consortium because the policy of the French banks of Asia maintained a policy of guarantees that would have led them to make loans to the English in order to avoid making loans to the Chinese. We have followed a policy of risk, it is . . ."

"I did not dare to say so."

". . . obvious. It is natural that we should reap the consequences. The savings will be protected (he smiled with one corner of his mouth) to the extent of a fifty-eight billion franc loss, and not fifty-eight billion and a few hundred million. Let us now examine together, gentlemen, if you wish, the manner in which the Consortium will cease to exist."

Kobe

In the full light of spring, May—too poor to hire a carriage—was walking up the hill towards Kama's house. If Gisors' baggage was heavy, they would have to borrow some money from the old painter to get back to the ship. Upon leaving Shanghai, Gisors had told her he would seek refuge with Kama; upon arriving he had sent her his address. Since then, nothing. Not even when she had informed him that he had been appointed professor in the Sun Yat-sen institute of Moscow. Fear of the Japanese police?

As she walked she was reading a letter from Pei which

had been delivered to her upon the arrival of the ship at Kobe, when she had had her passport visaed.

"... *and all those who were able to flee Shanghai are awaiting you. I have received the pamphlets. ..."*

He had published two anonymous accounts of Ch'en's death, one according to his heart: "The murder of the dictator is the duty of the individual towards himself, and must be separate from political action, which is determined by collective forces ...," the other for the traditionalists: "Even as filial duty—the faith which our ancestors have in us—enjoins us to seek what is noblest in our lives, even so it requires of each of us the murder of the usurper." The clandestine presses were already publishing these pamphlets again.

"... *I saw Hemmelrich yesterday. He thinks of you. He is a mounter in the electric plant. He said to me: 'Before, I began to live when I left the factory; now, I begin to live when I enter it. It's the first time in my life that I work and know why I work, not merely waiting patiently to die. ...' Tell Gisors that we are waiting for him. Since I have been here, I have been thinking of the lecture where he said:*

" 'A civilization becomes transformed, you see, when its most oppressed element—the humiliation of the slave, the work of the modern worker—suddenly becomes a *value*, when the oppressed ceases to attempt to escape this humiliation, and seeks his salvation in it, when the worker ceases to attempt to escape this work, and seeks in it his reason for being. The factory, which is still only a kind of church of the catacombs,

330

must become what the cathedral was, and men must see in it, instead of gods, human power struggling against the Earth. . . .' "

Yes; no doubt the value of men lay only in what they had transformed. The Revolution had just passed through a terrible malady, but it was not dead. And it was Kyo and his men, living or not, vanquished or not, who had brought it into the world.

"I am going to return to China as an agitator: I shall never be a pure Communist. Nothing is finished over there. Perhaps we shall meet; I have been told that your request has been granted. . . ."

A newspaper clipping fell from the letter; she picked it up:

> Work must become the principal weapon of the class-struggle. The vastest industrialization plan in the world is at present being studied: the aim is to transform the entire U.S.S.R. in five years to make it one of the leading industrial powers in Europe, and then to catch up with and surpass the United States. This gigantic enterprise . . .

Gisors was waiting for her, in the doorway. In a kimono. No baggage in the hallway.

"Did you receive my letter?" she asked, entering a bare room—mats and paper—whose panels were drawn aside, revealing the entire bay.

"Yes."

"Let's hurry. The ship is leaving again in two hours."

"I'm not leaving, May."

She looked at him. "Useless to question him," she

thought; "he'll explain." But it was he who questioned her.

"What are you going to do?"

"Try to serve in one of the sections of women agitators. It's practically arranged, it appears. I shall be in Vladivostok the day after tomorrow, and I shall immediately leave for Moscow. If it can't be arranged, I shall serve as a doctor in Moscow or in Siberia. I hope the first thing succeeds. . . . I am so weary of nursing. . . . To live always with sick people, when it isn't for a combat, requires a kind of special grace—and there is no grace left in me of any sort. And besides, the sight of death has become almost intolerable to me now. . . . Well, if I must . . . It is still a way of avenging Kyo."

"Revenge is no longer possible at my age. . . ."

Indeed, something in him was changed. He was distant, isolated, as if only a part of himself were there in the room with her. He lay down on the floor: there were no seats. She lay down too, beside an opium tray.

"What are you going to do with yourself?" she asked.

He shrugged his shoulder with indifference.

"Thanks to Kama, I have been made professor of Occidental art. . . . I return to my first profession, as you see. . . ."

She sought his eyes, stupefied:

"Even now," she said, "when we are politically beaten, when our hospitals have been closed down, clandestine groups are forming again in all the provinces. Our people will never forget that they suffer because of other men, and not because of their previous lives. You used to say: 'They have awakened with a start from a sleep of thirty centuries, to which they will never return.' You also used to say that those who have given a consciousness of their revolt to three hundred million wretches were not shadows like men who pass—even beaten, even tortured, even dead. . . ."

She was silent for a moment:

"They are dead, now," she said finally.

"I still think so, May. It's something else. . . . Kyo's death is not only grief, not only change—it is . . . a metamorphosis. I have never loved the world over-much: it was Kyo who attached me to men, it was through him that they existed for me. . . . I don't want to go to Moscow. I would teach wretchedly there. Marxism has ceased to live in me. In Kyo's eyes it was a will, wasn't it? But in mine, it is a fatality, and I found myself in harmony with it because my fear of death was in harmony with fatality. There is hardly any fear left in me, May; since Kyo died, I am indifferent to death. I am freed (freed! . . .) both from death and from life. What would I do over there?"

"Change anew, perhaps."

"I have no other son to lose."

He drew the opium tray towards him, prepared a pipe. Without speaking she pointed with her finger to one of the nearby hillslopes: attached by the shoulder, some hundred coolies were pulling a heavy weight which could not be seen, in the centuries-old posture of slaves.

"Yes," he said, "yes."

"And yet," he went on after a moment, "note this: these men are ready to die for Japan."

"For how much longer?"

"Longer than I shall live."

Gisors had been puffing steadily at his pipe. He opened his eyes:

"One can fool life for a long time, but in the end it always makes us what we were intended to be. Every old man is a confession, believe me, and if old age is usually so empty it is because the men were themselves empty and had managed to conceal it. But that in itself is unimportant. Men should be able to learn that there is no reality, that there are worlds of contemplation—with or without opium—where all is vain. . . ."

"Where one contemplates what?"

"Perhaps nothing other than this vanity. . . . That's a great deal."

Kyo had told May: "Opium plays a great rôle in my father's life, but I sometimes wonder if opium determines his life, or if it justifies certain forces that make him uneasy. . . ."

"If Ch'en," Gisors went on, "had lived outside of the Revolution, don't forget that he would undoubtedly have forgotten his murders. Forgotten . . ."

"The others have not forgotten them; there have been two terrorist attempts since his death. He did not like women, and I therefore scarcely knew him; but I don't think he would have lived out of the Revolution even a year. There is no dignity that is not founded on suffering."

He had barely listened to her.

"Forgotten . . ." he continued. "Since Kyo died, I have discovered music. Music alone can speak of death. I listen to Kama, now, whenever he plays. And yet, without effort on my part (he was speaking to himself as much as to May), what do I still remember? My desires and my anguish, the very weight of my destiny, my life. . . ."

(But while you are freeing yourself from your life, she was thinking, other Katovs are burning in boilers, other Kyos . . .)

Gisors' eyes, as though they were continuing his gestures of forgetfulness, looked away, became absorbed in the world outside: beyond the road, the thousand sounds of the port seemed to be setting out with the waves towards the radiant sea. Those noises matched the dazzling Japanese springtime with all the efforts of men, with the ships, the elevators, the cars, the active crowd. May was thinking of Pei's letter: it was in work pursued with warlike energy, released over the whole Russian land, in the will of a multitude for whom this work had become life, that her dead had found refuge. The sky was sparkling like the sun in the spaces between the pine-trees; the wind which gently stirred the branches glided over their reclining bodies. It seemed to Gisors that this wind was passing through him like a river, like Time itself, and for the first time the idea that the time which was bringing him closer to death was flowing through him did not isolate him from the world, but joined him to it in a serene accord. He looked down at the bristling cranes on the edge of the city, the steamships and the sailboats on the sea, the men—black specks—on the road. "All suffer," he thought, "and each one suffers because he thinks. At bottom, the mind conceives man only in the eternal, and the consciousness of life can be nothing but anguish. One must not think life with the mind, but with opium. How many of the sufferings scattered about in this light would disappear, if thought were to disappear. . . ." Liberated from everything, even from being a man, he caressed the stem of his pipe with gratitude, contemplating the bustle of all those unknown creatures who were marching towards death in the dazzling sunlight, each one nursing his deadly parasite in a secret recess of his being. "Every man is a madman," he went on thinking, "but what is a human destiny if not a life of effort to unite this madman and the universe. . . ." He saw Ferral again, lighted by the low lamp against the background of the night full of mist. "Every man dreams of being god. . . ."

Fifty sirens at once burst upon the air: today was the eve of a festival, and work was over. Before any change was visible in the port, tiny men emerged, like scouts, upon the straight road that led to the city, and soon the crowd covered it, distant and black, in a din of automobile horns: foremen and laborers were leaving work together. It was approaching, as if for an attack, with the great uneasy movement of every crowd beheld from a distance. Gisors had seen the dash of animals towards watering-holes, at night-fall: one, several, then all, thrown in the direction of the water by a force that seemed to fall from the darkness; in his memory, opium gave to their cosmic rush a savage harmony, and the men lost in the distant clatter of their wooden clogs all seemed mad, separated from the universe whose heart beating somewhere up there in the shimmering light seized them and threw them back upon solitude, like the grains of some unknown harvest. Very high up, the light clouds passed above the dark pine trees, and little by little became absorbed in the sky; and it seemed to him that one of their group, precisely the one he was looking at, expressed the men he had known or loved, and who were dead.

Humanity was dense and heavy, heavy with flesh, with blood, with suffering, eternally clinging to itself like all that dies; but even blood, even flesh, even suffering, even death was being absorbed up there in the light like music in the silent night; he thought of Kama's music, and human grief seemed to him to rise and to lose itself in the very song of earth; upon the quivering release hidden within him like his heart, the grief which he had mastered slowly closed its inhuman arms.

"Do you smoke much?" she repeated.

She had already asked this, but he had not heard her. His eyes returned to the room:

"Do you think I don't guess what you are thinking, and do you think I don't know it better than you? Do you even think it would not be easy for me to ask you by what right you judge me?"

He looked at her:

"Have you no desire to have a child?"

She did not answer: this always passionate desire now seemed to her a betrayal. But she was contemplating his serene face with terror. It was in truth returning from the deep regions of death, foreign like one of the corpses in the common ditches. In the repression that had beaten down upon exhausted China, in the anguish or hope of the masses, Kyo's activity remained incrusted like the inscriptions of the early empires in the river gorges. But even old China, which these few men had hurled irrevocably into the darkness of the past with the roar of an avalanche, was not more effaced from the world than the meaning of Kyo's life from the face of his father. He went on:

"The only thing I loved has been torn from me, you see, and you expect me to remain the same. Do you think my love was not as great as yours—you whose life has not even changed?"

"As the body of a living person who becomes a dead one does not change. . . ."

He took her hand:

"You know the phrase: 'It takes nine months to make a man, and a single day to kill him.' We both know this as well as one can know it. . . . May, listen: it does not take nine months, it takes fifty years to make a man, fifty years of sacrifice, of will, of . . . of so many things! And when this man is complete, when there is nothing left in him of childhood, nor of adolescence, when he is really a man—he is good for nothing but to die."

She looked at him, stunned: he was looking at the clouds.

"I loved Kyo as few men love their children, you know that. . . ."

He was still holding her hand; he drew it towards him, took it between his two hands:

"Listen to me: one must love the living and not the dead."

"I am not going to Moscow to love."

He looked out upon the magnificent bay, saturated with sunlight. She had withdrawn her hand.

"On the road of vengeance, little May, one finds life. . . ."

"That's not a reason for seeking it."

She got up, gave him back her hand for a good-by. But he took her face between the palms of his hands and kissed her. Kyo had kissed her in this way, the last day, exactly in this way, and never since had hands held her head.

"I hardly ever weep any more, now," she said with a bitter pride.

ANDRÉ MALRAUX was born in 1901 in Paris. Through-out his life Malraux has been actively involved in poli-tics. Between 1923 and 1927 he participated in the revolutionary movements then taking place in China. In 1936 Malraux helped to organize and then fought in the air force of the Spanish Republican Govern-ment against Franco. During World War II he was a member of the French Resistance. In 1945, Malraux became Minister of Information in Charles de Gaulle's first government. Malraux is now Minister of State in charge of cultural affairs in France.

His other works include *Man's Hope, The Voices of Silence, The Metamorphosis of the Gods*, and (available in Vintage Books) *The Temptation of the West* and *The Royal Way*

Man's Fate received the Prix Goncourt in 1933.

VINTAGE BIOGRAPHY AND AUTOBIOGRAPHY

VINTAGE FICTION, POETRY, AND PLAYS

A free catalogue of VINTAGE BOOKS *will be sent at your request. Write to* Vintage Books, 457 Madison Avenue, New York, New York 10022.